KEYS TO THE CROWN

RELLMIRA DUOLOGY
BOOK ONE

LEAH MARA

PAPER HEART
PUBLISHING

Cover Design by Moonpress, www.moonpress.co
Map by Etheric Tales
Ornamental Design by Alex B.

Ebook ISBN 978-1-965527-00-9
Paperback ISBN 978-1-965527-01-6
Hardcover ISBN 978-1-965527-02-3

For my 15-year-old self who dreamed up the first idea for this story—told you we'd see it published one day!

To all the other dreamers out there—never, ever give up!

AUTHOR NOTE

This is a high-stakes fantasy romance that contains content that might be triggering for some readers.

- Violence: death, torture/mutilation, imprisonment, request for death, intense injuries (all related to human adults, including parents—NO children or animals)
- Some graphic language
- A scene of consensual, romantic, graphic sex
- Verbal abuse

PRONUNCIATION GUIDE

- **Aiden:** ay-den
- **Kiera:** keeruh
- **Renwell:** ren-well
- **Weylin:** way-lin
- **Everett:** ev-rit
- **Delysia:** deh-liss-ee-uh
- **Korvin:** kor-vin
- **Mazkull:** maz-cuhl
- **Melaena:** muh-lay-nuh
- **Nikella:** ni-kel-luh
- **Terraum, God of Earth and Architecture:** turawm
- **Arduen, God of Fire and Desire:** ar-dew-when
- **Viridana, Goddess of Life:** veer-i-dawn-uh
- **Mynastra, Goddess of Sea and Sky:** min-ass-truh
- **Rellmira (this story's kingdom):** rell-meer-uh
- **Aquinon (the royal city of Rellmira):** ah-qwi-non

- **Calimber (the mining town north of Aquinon):** cal-im-burr
- **Lancora (name for the known world):** lan-cor-uh
- **Pravara (the southern Rellmiran province):** pruh-var-uh
- **Winspere (the northern Rellmiran province):** win-speer
- **Niviath Sea:** ni-vee-ath see

AQUI

NON

THE SILK DANCER GARYTH

SOUTH MEDRIA RIVER

ASHER

NOBLE QUARTER

CHAPTER 1
KIERA

THE WORST PART ABOUT BEING A SPY WAS THE WAITING.

Even though this was my first official mission, I already disliked the hours I'd spent crouched in a hot, fetid alley in the Noble Quarter, body immobile, eyes restless.

To pass the time, I played a silent game, guessing the intention of each person who walked by me.

The group of young noblemen was easy. They had switched their glittering jewels and silk clothes for rough cotton. But their well-groomed appearances, careless laughter, and fat purses marked them for what they were. No doubt they were headed for a bit of fun in the Docks Quarter. Eager to gamble on a game of Death and Four and drink all night with the sailors.

It was Mynastra's Tide, after all. The goddess would love the carousing.

A few servants hurried past, darting in and out of the mansions that lined the winding cobblestone streets. They were most likely preparing their lords and ladies for a more refined night of celebration. The old meeting hall was hosting a soiree, and *The Silk Dancer* had announced a performance worthy of the goddess herself.

But still, I didn't see the three people I watched for.

I rolled my neck to ease the stiffness. Gods damn this heat. Even the night air was stifling.

Mother used to laugh and say that our royal city of Aquinon didn't have seasons, only moods. Balmy, sunny skies one day and raging thunder and rain from black clouds the next, thanks to the temperamental sea that pounded our cliffs.

I glanced up at the starry sky smudged here and there with dark clouds. I had no bones to offer, but I prayed Mynastra kept her rain for the night. I couldn't afford to leave a wet trail.

"No one can see you," Renwell had said. "No one can ever know that you were there."

A burst of laughter across the busy street snagged my attention. At last, Lord Garyth and his wife stepped out of the mansion I'd been watching for hours—days, really. The lady laughed again as her husband twirled her once by the hand so that her simple white dress floated around her like dove wings.

A twinge of jealousy surprised me.

Was it their easy laughter? Or the love in their expressions as they gazed at each other?

Gods only knew. I'd experienced precious little of either since my mother's death. My whole world changed that night. The night I gave up my life as a princess for the life of a spy.

I blinked. Wait a moment. Where was their little girl? Isabel. She usually dogged her parents' steps every time they left their mansion.

I waited, my fingers dancing along the hilts of my throwing knives. But no one else followed the High Councilor and his wife as they walked up the street and out of sight.

Gods damn it, they must have left her behind. Unless she had left earlier. Or was with friends or family.

I had been watching the house since the sun had fallen, but maybe I missed something.

Or she was still in the house, a witness I couldn't risk.

But I wouldn't get another opportunity like this. The High Councilor's house, along with most of the other dwellings on these streets, was rarely empty apart from a divine holiday. I would have to wait months for another chance.

It had to be now.

I pulled the brim of my hood down and ensured my black neckcloth masked all but my eyes. My soft leather boots didn't make a sound as I darted across the street, having a care to keep to the darkness between torches.

I slipped around the back of the house and opened the servant's door without a sound. I'd tested it once already, pleased that the hinges were well oiled.

The kitchen stood empty of noise and light as I'd hoped. I eased my way across the smooth tiles, using the toes of my boots to feel around a large table and some chairs.

Dimmed lamps fixed to golden wall sconces lit a long, carpeted hallway, which probably led to all sorts of gathering rooms. But the room I needed was on the topmost floor.

I tiptoed up a wooden staircase that wound past the sleeping quarters up to the third floor. Other than a few creaks under my tentative boots, the house remained silent. A smile pulled at my stiff lips. Mynastra's luck was with me so far.

I hurried to the only door on the eastern wall and reached for my lock-picking set. Then I hesitated, staring at the shiny gold knob.

"Always check," Renwell liked to remind me in our training sessions. "Why lose essential moments over someone's carelessness?"

I clenched my gloved fingers over the knob and twisted it easily. I frowned and slipped inside, silently closing the door behind me.

Soft light from the street filtered through the large window. Shelves of books lined the study walls, and a heavy desk took up half the room. The same desk I'd watched the High Councilor hunch over every night from a rooftop perch I'd found across the street.

A small table by the still-warm fireplace held a magnificent set of Death and Four tiles. The weak light made the gold inlay shimmer in a way that made my fingers itch to snatch them up.

But I couldn't stray from my purpose.

"Garyth is hiding something," Renwell had told me. "Search his correspondence, his ledgers, any document that seems odd. Find proof."

But the High Councilor's desk was clear of everything but an inkpot, a quill, and a stack of blank writing paper. My gaze raced over the spines of the books on his shelves, and I pulled out random ones, looking for a secret compartment. Nothing.

A door closed somewhere in the house, and I froze, a bead of sweat slipping down my spine.

The girl—Isabel—was probably still here somewhere. Perhaps with a maid.

Too many people. Too little time. Too dangerous. But I

couldn't fail the first real mission Renwell had given me after two years of training.

Garyth *must* be hiding something. As the High Enforcer, Renwell was rarely wrong when it came to matters of intelligence. He'd protected my father's reign for decades. And one day, I would do the same for my brother.

If I could prove myself.

I strode to the window and checked its seams. My heart leapt when I discovered I could easily pop it open. A narrow ledge ran under the window and around the house.

An escape, if I needed it.

I took another turn around the study, fiddling with the table, the fireplace, even the large violet rug.

The blood in my veins pulsed hard and hot. Where in the deep, dark, wandering hell would a High Councilor hide sensitive documents?

My focus narrowed on the heavy wooden desk, the pride and joy of the room from the way the precious Twaryn wood shone, every delicate carving free of dust. It had no drawers, but that didn't mean it couldn't hide anything.

I carefully shifted Garyth's leather armchair away and knelt in front of the desk. Renwell had told me once that desks and tables with secret compartments were very popular in years past. He'd even shown me how to work the one in my father's study—without my father's knowledge, of course.

Dancing my fingers along the ridges and seams of the wood panels, I searched for a keyhole and found none. But— there. My forefinger snagged on an uneven piece of wood under the top of the desk. I pressed it and a panel near the foot of the desk popped open.

I grinned in triumph.

A space barely the span of my hand held a stack of papers. I gently tugged them out and held them closer to the window to read.

My heart sank. Gibberish. Pages and pages of strange symbols, letters, and numbers. A code. But why? What was he hiding?

And more importantly, was it dangerous?

My mother's deathly pale face and bloodied chest shimmered in my mind.

The papers shook in my hands, but I kept flipping through them until I reached the last one. In the top right corner of the yellowed page, someone had inked a symbol.

"No," I breathed.

But there was no mistaking the joined hands beneath Rellmira's half sun. The symbol of the People's Council.

Something creaked in the hallway. I ducked behind the desk. I hadn't locked the door behind me in case that was unusual for Garyth. Which made him a forgetful fool . . . or a trusting one. But a fool nonetheless, with treasonous documents in his possession.

I held my breath. One heartbeat. Two. Three. I counted to ten and slowly exhaled.

Time to go.

I couldn't bring the papers with me for fear of tipping off Garyth, and I didn't have time to copy them. But the symbol coupled with the strange code was damning enough. I slid the papers back into the hole and closed it.

I rose to my feet.

"What are you doing in my father's study?"

I instinctively reached for one of my knives before realizing who spoke. A young girl in a frilly white nightdress hovered by the open door.

Curses bellowed through my mind. The *one* time well-oiled hinges worked against me. Renwell would be furious.

Isabel squinted at me, her soft red curls framing her pink, freckled cheeks. Maybe seven or eight years old. Innocent, so innocent. She probably had no idea what her father was involved in.

But she'd seen me. Granted, I was little more than a faceless shadow. But—

No one can see you. No one can ever know you were there.

Renwell didn't want Garyth to know we were investigating him, and from the suspicious glint in Isabel's eyes, she might tell her father of the mysterious intruder in his study.

I released the hilt of my knife, giving her a debonair bow. "A merry Mynastra's Tide to you, my lady," I said, my voice hoarse from hours of silence.

If I couldn't fight my way out, I'd lie my way out.

She frowned. "Who are you? And why aren't you at the festival? Mother said I couldn't go because I'm sick."

I thought fast. "I'm a messenger and I desperately needed to deliver my message to your father, or I'll be in trouble."

"I get in trouble too. Mostly when I get my dress dirty, or I bring home a new pet." She smiled and leaned forward. "Do you like lizards?"

I had the insane desire to laugh, even as my mind warned me that the child's servant would be nearby and hear us talking any moment.

"I love them," I said. "Especially the little green ones with sticky toes."

Her blue eyes widened. "Yes! Me too!"

"Isabel! Child, where have you gotten to now?" a woman's voice called out.

Isabel and I stiffened.

"Oh, gods, I'm supposed to be in bed," she muttered.

"I won't tell if you don't tell anyone I was here," I whispered quickly, desperately. "I would be forever in your debt, Lady Isabel."

She grinned. "Deal. But you'd better hurry."

I delivered another bow and raced for the window as she closed the door. Popping open the window, I swung over the ledge. The narrow piece of wood bit into my fingers. The skies also chose that moment to release their rain. I gritted my teeth as fear threatened to overwhelm me.

My body dangled high above the flickering streetlamps. A strange sight if any passersby looked up. For a moment, I imagined my fingers slipping on the wet wood and my body falling.

My stomach heaved, and I shook the thought from my head. Fear could kill me faster than a fall.

I slid my fingers along the ledge, working my way around the house. The rain pattered on my hood and dripped down my chest.

Just as I reached the corner, I heard the study door open. With a smothered grunt, I swung my body to the slanting roof below. I landed on all fours with a quiet thump, out of sight of the street. I flattened myself to the slick tiles as the window swung shut with a mumbled oath.

Holy Four, that was close. Even now, I had to trust that

Isabel would keep our secret. There were much worse things than an angry nursemaid.

I crawled over to the mansion's chimney ladder and scurried down. Now that I was off the roof, the rain was a blessing. It cooled my sweaty skin as people dashed for cover with their chins dipped down and curtained carriages splashed by—none the wiser to my escapade.

I kept my eyes on my boots and the puddles forming between cobblestones as I hurried to the Royal Gate. I flashed Renwell's token at the guards, and they yanked open the gate without question.

Gritting my teeth, I stared at the vacant stone bridge spanning the roaring waterfall that split the palace from the rest of the city. This was the reason I hated heights.

Exactly ten years ago, back when Father still held public court and allowed us out of the palace, we stood here for the Bone Ceremony—the offering of fish bones to the water. A woman had leaned too far over, slipping on the stone, and fell to her death. Not the usual offering Mynastra expected, but she took it all the same, carrying the woman's body out to sea.

I shuddered and put more thought into my footsteps than I had all night.

The thundering waterfall echoed in my chest. But I ignored it. I also ignored the gods-built palace. I knew its sky-high columns and pink marble turrets too well.

It was a tomb and a prison. But it held the only people left in the world whom I loved.

I skirted around the dozens of long steps leading to the main doors and the ever-watchful palace guards to use a servant's entrance on the side. Because that was my role now—

a servant to the crown. I didn't pause through the labyrinth of halls and secret passageways that led to my small room, situated next to Renwell's room and his study.

I checked his study and found it locked, which meant he wasn't there.

Just as well. My clothes, weighed down with weapons and rain, were choking me.

Dry clothes, some hot tea, and a biscuit would be perfect. The cook still let me nab biscuits from the larder despite my decline in rank.

I reached for my key but stopped when I found my door hanging ajar. I silently unsheathed my dagger and pushed the door open, taking a tentative step inside.

Only for the sharp, cold edge of a blade to press against my throat.

CHAPTER 2
KIERA

"YOU DIDN'T CHECK THE CORNERS FIRST."

I swallowed hard, the blade moving with my throat. "And I told you to stop breaking into my room."

Renwell's breath warmed my ear. "I grew tired of waiting."

"How is that possible when your cloak is still damp with rain?"

The knife disappeared, and I spun to face him, my heart beating erratically. He stood in the shadows like he was a part of them. His dark brown hair and closely trimmed beard hid most of his pale face. His black clothing, from cloak to gloves to boots, hid the rest. He had twice my twenty-three years, yet his strength was evident in every controlled movement as he sheathed his sunstone knife.

"You noticed my wet cloak, yet I still got my knife to your throat." Renwell stepped closer, smelling of rain, leather, and smoke. "I could've been an assassin."

I glared up at him, tired of his games. "What assassin could breach these walls without your knowledge?"

His lips twisted in a smirk. "None."

None . . . if only my mother hadn't been outside the palace when an assassin came for her.

I tossed my dagger onto my tiny bed, peeled off my sopping cloak, and draped it over the cracked wooden chair in front of my washstand. As I lit a fire in the hearth, Renwell shut the door and locked it.

My skin prickled with unease, but I ignored it.

"What did you find at Garyth's?" he asked.

"You were right," I said. "He was hiding something. I found a sheaf of papers in a secret hole in his desk."

Renwell gestured impatiently. "And?"

"They were written in code. I couldn't read them." Renwell's cheeks hollowed with anger, and I rushed on. "But one of them bore a symbol. The People's Council symbol."

Something like triumph flared in Renwell's dark eyes. "You're sure?"

"Yes," I whispered. I cleared my throat and said louder, "Yes, but how can we be sure what it means if we can't translate the papers?"

"Why else would a High Councilor hide coded papers with a traitorous symbol?" Renwell snapped.

I stepped backward. "But by all accounts, he seems like a good man—"

"As did the People's Councilors before they started a rebellion against your father. Everyone has something to hide, Kiera. You can't do my job without accepting that basic truth."

My cheeks burned with anger and humiliation. As if I

KEYS TO THE CROWN · 13

needed reminding. I would *never* forget those days and how they changed our lives. The public executions at the foot of the Temple still crept into my nightmares from time to time.

"Were you seen?"

My gaze darted back to his. "Of course not."

He studied me for an agonizing moment. *Gods, please believe me.* It was rare that I could lie to Renwell and get away with it, even after many, many lessons. The few times I thought I succeeded, I couldn't be sure if that was just what he wanted me to think.

Like now.

"So be it," he said quietly. "I'll handle Garyth while you handle something else for me."

I frowned. "Handle what?"

He hesitated, and that one flicker of indecision sent a thrill of foreboding through me. Renwell never second-guessed himself. He planned for everything and was never caught off guard.

"What happened?" I demanded.

His jaw clenched. "My Wolves caught a man prowling through the Den."

My lips parted in shock.

Renwell was not only the High Enforcer, responsible for the safety and execution of justice for our kingdom of Rellmira, but also the captain of the night guards—nicknamed the Shadow-Wolves. I'd only caught glimpses of the infamous guards from afar. Their barracks—the Den—was in the Docks Quarter at the foot of the cliffs by the sea.

No one but Shadow-Wolves and Renwell himself entered that place of their own volition. I didn't know what other business he conducted from there. But he promised I'd find out one day.

I sputtered. "How . . . how did he—"

"He was wearing a Shadow-Wolf uniform and mask. He even carried a sunstone knife." Renwell gripped the hilt of his own.

Sunstone was our most precious commodity, mined out of the cliffs north of Aquinon. It could be forged into unbreakable knives that never needed sharpening. Black and glittery, the stones were pieces of the night sky, if the legend was true.

But if this man had stolen a uniform and a knife, the only way he could've was from a Wolf. A dead Wolf. Which made him a thief and a killer.

No one else was allowed to carry a sunstone knife—a rule I flouted on occasion. But I would never use it to do something as foolish as to sneak into the Den.

"What was he doing there?" I asked. "Was he alone?"

"He was alone, and he refused to tell me."

My eyebrows flew up. "*Refused?*"

"Under extreme duress."

My stomach twisted. That was a part of his job I hated thinking about. But Renwell had always seemed content to let me train for espionage while he handled the dirtier bits of the business.

Unless—

"What do you want *me* to do?"

"I want you to find out what he was doing in my gods-damned Den and if he's working with others. You'll have to go undercover, which shouldn't be too difficult for you, considering."

I scowled. Considering I'd lied about who I was many times over the years that I used to sneak out to taverns or to meet lovers. And Renwell knew about each time. Those lies were one of the reasons he agreed to take me on as his apprentice.

"And you think this prisoner will simply spill his secrets to me, a stranger, when you couldn't beat them out of him?" I asked.

Renwell's lips twitched. "I think your approach may be more effective, yes. But it may take time."

My eyes narrowed. "How much time?"

"Earn his trust. Help him escape the Den, and you could unlock all the information we desire."

My breathing turned shallow. Escape with a violent criminal? Stay by his side for days? Weeks? Make him trust me? I had never attempted such a thing. Holy Four, I'd just completed my first real mission—and that with a few mistakes.

Renwell came closer, his gaze searing into mine. I backed up another step, my boots hitting the bed post. "This is no coincidence, Kiera. If Garyth is in league with other traitors and this man managed to infiltrate the Den, something is happening. Perhaps something worse than the Pravaran rebellion. Worse than the assassination of your mother. We can't—"

"Stop," I gasped. "Stop. Just . . . give me a moment." I twisted away from him and stumbled to my only window. I pressed my forehead to the cool glass as rain pelted against it.

This window didn't open, so I was safe from the sharp cliffs and stone parapets below. But for once, the height didn't bother me as much as the thoughts swirling in my head.

There were so many ways this mission could go wrong. I

had no idea who this man was or what he was like. He might see through me as easily as these glass panes.

But isn't this what you've been training for? Since the night Mother was murdered, all you've wanted was to protect the rest of your family from further threats. To be the High Enforcer for your brother when he takes the throne. To finally have the power you didn't have as a princess.

What will happen if you don't do this? There's no one else who will.

My breath fogged the glass, blurring the dark sky and the tireless sea. I had to do this. For Mother. For my family. For myself.

"Fine," I rasped. "I'll do it. But how? I need a cover story, a way in." I turned to face Renwell, but he wasn't looking at me.

He was staring at the dagger I'd thrown on my bed. I grimaced but made no move to retrieve it.

"I thought I told you to stop carrying that around," he whispered.

I hated it when he spoke like that. Unlike my father who loved to rage and rant at the top of his voice, Renwell grew quieter the angrier he was.

"I'm sorry," I whispered back. "I feel safer with it."

"And what if someone saw it? Recognized it? Your father wanted it buried with your mother."

I bit my lip. He knew why I kept it.

The dagger was one-of-a-kind, meant for royalty. The sunstone blade was straight and longer than my hand, the edges jagged. The hilt and guard were gold and studded with bits of sunstone. I had no idea where my mother had gotten it.

I'd seen her with it a few times before an assassin used it to stab her in the heart.

And I'd kept it for myself ever since. A reminder and a promise.

Renwell drew in a deep breath and finally met my eyes. "It doesn't matter. You'll be leaving it with me."

I opened my mouth to protest but then realized I couldn't bring it with me where I was going. I nodded.

Renwell straightened, squaring his shoulders. "Good. Now, let's plan your way into that cell."

"And a way out if . . . if it goes poorly," I added.

His dark gaze turned deadly. "If the prisoner refuses to believe you or threatens to harm you, I will retrieve you come sunrise and kill him where he stands."

My heart thumped harder as heat rose up my neck. Renwell would damn the consequences for me. He would execute our only other lead to the potential threat he felt looming over my family. For me.

It was moments like this when I questioned if some hidden part of Renwell did actually care for me.

A memory flashed through my mind—of the night Renwell had first spoken to me. I was eighteen years old, and I'd stolen a few hours of freedom at a seedy tavern. After winning a few games of Death and Four, one of the defeated drunkards ambushed me in an alley.

I'd panicked and tried to shove him off, but he was twice my size. Renwell had swooped in from the shadows and slit the man's throat before I could scream.

Wiping his blade on the dead man's dirty cloak, Renwell

had stared at my blood-drenched face, his eyes burning with fury. "Never let an enemy surprise you, princess."

He was looking at me now as he had then, and I knew he would protect me as he always had. As no one else had.

"Then we'd better come up with a damn good story," I said.

Renwell smiled.

WE SPENT HOURS DISCUSSING THE DETAILS OF MY MISSION—MY cover story, our "escape," and what to do afterward.

The key was getting the prisoner to owe me, so he would feel beholden to protect me—or at least keep me with him—once we escaped.

If he was the kind of man to care about that sort of thing. He'd already committed multiple crimes—that we knew about. And codes of honor never had much of a place with criminals.

If I failed and Renwell killed him, we would have to hope that the prisoner's plans died with him.

But I wouldn't fail. Whatever this prisoner hoped to accomplish by infiltrating the Den with a stolen uniform, I would learn the truth. My mother's guards had believed no harm could come to her in the Temple, and she paid the price for their negligence.

I would not make the same mistake.

Renwell left to tell my father of our plan and to fetch me a guard's uniform. We figured that me being the personal guard of the princesses would raise less questions for the skills and scars I possessed.

He stood outside the door while I changed, my mother's dagger sheathed in his boot.

I stripped off my thin white shirt and the brown vest prickled with my favorite throwing knives. I kept on my tight black pants and black knee-high, lace-up boots. They worked well with the black button-up shirt and belted violet tunic Renwell had brought me. Rellmira's insignia—a rising sun half-covered in darkness—was stitched across the front in gold and black thread. He hadn't bothered with armor as I would've been stripped of it as a prisoner.

Then I sat down at my washstand and looked into the small, cracked mirror I'd nailed above it. My lips twisted as I studied myself. Every day I hoped I would see some bit of my mother looking back at me, but it was never the case.

My light brown eyes were nothing like her blue ones. The damp brown hair I shook out of its knot and re-tied would never shine like the sun as hers had.

But I was proud of the muscles that lined my body and of the little scars that adorned my hands. They were evidence of how hard I trained. And somewhere deep in the corner of my heart that never seemed to cease bleeding, I hoped she'd be proud of me, too.

After throwing my damp cloak around my shoulders, I glanced over my little room one more time. I doubted I would miss it much. But I would miss my knives, which I left on my bed, and the lock picks, keys, coins, and tokens I emptied from my pockets. Each one felt like a piece of armor I had to leave behind.

I would be vulnerable. And alone.

Gritting my teeth, I turned my back on them and opened

the door. Renwell's gaze swept over me, and he nodded. That slight gesture of approval still managed to send a beat of pride through my chest.

It truly dawned on me that, for the first time in two years, I would be beyond his reach. We had talked of a way to meet up after the prison escape, but gods only knew when or if that would happen.

The same thought seemed to flicker over his face as his eyebrows drew together and we stood in silence.

Renwell had been woven into the tapestry of my life since before I was born. He'd served my father from when Father was just a People's Councilor to when he became the High Advisor for King Tristan. When King Tristan died leaving no heirs, my father was named King, and Renwell rapidly rose to the elite rank of High Enforcer.

He'd always been in my family's shadow, keeping us safe.

Even when I'd considered him my enemy for several years after the Pravaran rebellion. Until he saved me that night in the alley.

And then he saved me again when he became my mentor. He gave me purpose. Something to fight for. I would have crumbled without his constant support these past few years.

"Renwell—" I started.

"Enough," he said, his voice as sharp and unyielding as the knives he carried. "The king wishes to speak with you."

My heart flinched at his dismissal, but I held my ground. "Very well. But I want a moment with Everett and Delysia first." It'd been weeks since I'd spoken with either of them, and the gods only knew when—or if—I'd get another chance.

Renwell shook his head, his nose flared in disgust. "Gods

damn your little weaknesses," he growled. "Go on then. But don't make him wait long. And do *not* tell your brother and sister what we're doing. Only the king knows."

I nodded, but he'd already stalked down the hall, torches dipping in his wake. I turned and headed in the opposite direction, deeper into the heart of the palace. My soft boots whispered against the polished marble floors. I kept my hood pulled low over my face, but even so, the halls were empty.

Less than a dozen people knew that Princess Emilia Torvaine of Rellmira had ceased to exist. After the Pravaran rebellion—so named for the province it sparked from—was decimated, my father had kept us from the public eye for fear of retribution. But five years later, my mother was assassinated on one of her rare trips to the Temple.

Heartbroken and furious that the assassin escaped, I'd decided that nothing was more important than protecting my family. Even if that meant giving up my crown, my position in line to the throne, and my name—as ordered by Father.

He'd hated the idea at first, but Renwell had convinced him it was where my talents truly thrived. Father insisted on keeping up the façade of my presence, effectively earning me the reputation of a recluse.

Which suited me fine . . . except I missed Everett and Delysia. I rarely spoke with them anymore. I wasn't even sure if they would be awake at this hour or if they'd welcome me.

But I needed to try.

I passed by the double glass doors that led to my mother's garden and stopped. When I closed my eyes, I could almost see her bright smile, her hand tugging mine out to the garden.

Come look, sweetheart, I finally managed to grow a sunset lullaby lily! It's almost as beautiful as you!

The memory faded as I stared at the dark, dead garden. Her bones lay somewhere beneath the untended soil. One of the few wishes Father had granted her—to be buried in the place she loved best.

I pressed my hand to the cold glass. "May the gods find and keep your soul, Mother. May you never wander in the Longest Night. May my soul find yours again . . . one day."

My throat tightened in the silence, but this wasn't the time to fall apart. I swallowed hard and kept walking.

I checked the library first, smiling when I found my older brother surrounded by stacks of books and scrolls, his own messily penned notes scattered like pale leaves. A few candles lit the desk where he worked.

The palace library was modest compared to the great library in the Temple. But Father forbade us from going to the Temple after Mother died. So now, Everett did his best to add to the shelves with his own knowledge and a few smuggled books.

I slipped between the dark, looming shelves until I stood right behind him—Everett as oblivious as ever when nose-deep in a book.

"Merry Mynastra's Tide, brother," I whispered.

Everett leapt out of his chair as if it'd stabbed him. "Holy Four!" He twisted to face me. "Oh, I—I didn't hear you come in."

I smiled. "Of course not. You have so many books and papers around you that it deadened the sound of my footsteps."

He gave a weary chuckle and raked a hand through his dark hair, which already stood on end. His fancy gold jacket was tossed over a chair, and his shirt was unbuttoned with a few splotches of ink on it.

"Did you come here just to frighten me?" he asked, a sad smile on his face.

Gods, I wanted to tell him about tonight. What I had done and what I was about to do. I wanted to ease my burden just a little by letting him in. To share secrets and worries as we once did. I had few friends before giving up my crown and none now.

But obeying Renwell mattered more than a fleeting comfort.

"Of course not," I said lightly. "I came here to ask you a serious question."

He leaned back against the desk and folded his arms. "Go on."

"Do we throw bones into the water because that was Mynastra's favorite thing to eat or because she honed them into weapons or—"

Everett laughed. "You know the story."

"But you tell it so well! Remind me," I pleaded, my hands clasped in front of me—just as I had when we were young, and I would beg him to read to me. Stories always seemed to come more alive in his voice.

"Fine, fine. But you get the short version." He breathed deeply. "Centuries ago, in the Age of Gods, the goddess Mynastra lived in the sea and the storms. One day, far out in the Niviath Sea, a ship carrying one hundred souls sailed into a massive storm. For days, their ship was tossed about on waves taller than palaces and chased by lightning that cracked the air like a thousand whips. The sailors begged Mynastra to save them, to calm the storm, but Mynastra was angry. She loved her storms and none of the sailors had given her a single thought before death started to take them.

"One of the sailors offered her recompense by way of the bones from his meal, saying, 'You have given sustenance and a way of life. Take the bones of what is yours and let us keep our souls.' Pleased with this, Mynastra accepted the bones and fashioned a belt from them, similar to the one she wore. She gave it back to the sailor, saying, 'Wear it always. When you cry out to me, I will see you as one of my own and look kindly on you.' Then the storm ceased, and forevermore, we offer bones to the goddess for her mercy."

I smiled and clapped softly, despite the lump in my throat. "Excellent story, Ev."

He dipped his head in acknowledgement, but the light faded from his blue eyes. "What are you really doing here, Kiera?"

I winced.

My mother and siblings had always called me Kiera—the name my mother confessed she wanted to give me, but my father overruled her with the name of his cruel mother.

"I miss you," I whispered.

The corners of his mouth turned down as they had since he was a boy whenever he was disappointed. "I miss you too. It doesn't have to be this way."

I threw up my hand. "Please don't lecture me, Everett. Can't we just talk like we used to?"

He reached out and caged my fingers in his hands. "But

things *aren't* the way they used to be. You chose to become the apprentice of a man with blood on his hands—blood he seems determined to smear on yours. Who failed to save Mother—"

"He'd heard nothing of a possible assassination, and he did everything he could to find her," I snapped, using the weak arguments Renwell had wielded like paper knives against my own accusations that night.

It was instinct that made me defend my mentor. And not a good one from the concerned look in Everett's eyes.

I drew a deep breath. "Don't you see that's why I have to train so hard? Why I want to become High Enforcer when you become king? I will succeed where he failed. I will hunt every threat to extinction. No one will ever harm my family again."

"Are we still your family, Kiera? You also chose to give us up in your quest for justice."

I yanked my hand out of his, my heart burning. "Father *forced* me to renounce any legal ties. To make sure I had no claim to the throne. To make sure I could never be used as leverage."

"To make sure your work will never bring shame to the legacy he's building," Everett finished softly. "Yes, I'm familiar with our father's tireless defense of his reputation."

"You and Delysia will always be my family," I whispered, squeezing the words around the knot in my throat.

"If I ever become king—"

"You will," I snapped.

"*If* I live to see that day, *if* Father deems it so, that will be one of the first things I do—proclaim you as my High Enforcer *and* my sister." His dark brows scrunched as he studied me. "If that is still what you wish."

The knot in my throat grew larger, blocking any words of gratitude I had. I simply nodded vigorously.

Everett's face smoothed, but the worry lingered in his eyes, much the same as our mother's had looked in the years before she died. A worry I had done little to ease until it was too late.

"Whatever you're doing," he whispered, "be careful. I can't lose you too."

I fought to keep my voice steady. "You won't. I swear it."

He straightened away from the desk, and for one hopeful moment, I thought he meant to hug me. Instead, he squeezed my shoulder. "Gods go with you then."

I laid my hand over his. "And you."

His hand slid out from under mine, and he sat in his chair, burying himself in work again. I was gone before he could watch me leave.

CHAPTER 3
KIERA

HEART WEARY, I HURRIED TO DELYSIA'S ROOM. FATHER WAS likely already angry that I'd kept him waiting this long, but I couldn't leave yet.

Just as I was about to knock, I heard heavy footsteps coming down one of the halls toward me.

I ducked into a curtained alcove as they rounded the corner and stopped in front of Delysia's room. A soft knock, the creak of her door opening. A man's deep whisper and my sister's hushed giggle.

I peered around the curtain to see the back of a tall man in a soldier's uniform stepping into Delysia's room.

I closed my eyes. Oh, Delysia, an affair with a soldier? Father would never approve. And I knew full well what he was capable of, the lengths he would go to in order to destroy a relationship. There was once a time I would've risked anything for love, for an escape, but not anymore.

But little sisters never wanted to hear that. She wouldn't

understand until she'd made the same mistakes. But gods, I wished I could change her mind before it was too late.

I supposed the least I could do for her was ensure that Father was busy for a few minutes.

"Love you, little Lys," I whispered to the door.

Sooner than I wished, I came to a stop in front of the monstrous wooden door of his study. Two of his personal guards flanked it, armed to the teeth and staring straight ahead. They wouldn't stop me.

Still, I hesitated. I couldn't ignore his summons, but I also couldn't help taking this extra moment to drain my face of expression and my heart of feeling.

Even if my efforts were always for nothing.

Gods damn your little weaknesses.

I knocked.

"Enter," he commanded from within.

I tugged the door open and slipped inside. Of the two studies I'd been in tonight, this one felt more dangerous. Thick velvet draperies the color of my tunic and stitched with glittering gold and onyx thread covered the stone walls. A massive fireplace provided heat and light, as well as a useful incinerator for sensitive correspondence.

Father's brown eyes, dreadfully like mine, fastened on me as he fed letters to the hungry flames. "Renwell never keeps me waiting. Neither should you."

He still refused to call me by a name, any name, since the day he'd stripped me of my title and, effectively, my family. I was now a servant to the crown, an apprentice to his most trusted High Councilor. Nothing else.

"Forgive me, Your Majesty," I said through stiff lips.

"Renwell told me of your mission." A hint of disgust wrinkled his thick nose. "Ridiculous to send a girl to do something Korvin could accomplish in half the time."

My shoulders twitched at the mention of his beloved torturer. "Renwell believes—"

"Yes, I know what Renwell believes," Father snapped. "There are times I question that man's judgment—usually in regard to you." He threw the last letter into the fire, the flames puncturing it into pieces. "But he has yet to fail me. A quality he needs to train into you."

Bitterness rose up my throat like bile. "I will not fail, Father—"

"Don't call me that!" he snarled.

I flinched. "Apologies, Your Majesty. I misspoke."

He turned away from the hearth, straightening his heavily embroidered coat of violet, gold, and black with one sharp tug. His beloved crown sat atop his iron-gray hair. The gold points shimmered in the firelight as the chunks of sunstone winked mockingly at me—a perfect match for Mother's dagger.

His scathing gaze raked over me. "Look at you. Playing dress-up in the shadows when I gave you the greatest life a child could ever hope to have."

My lips curled into a snarl. "That was no life. You imprisoned me, you beat me, you took away the only chance I had at love—"

"Silence!" he thundered. He stalked toward me, his ringed fingers clenching into fists at his sides.

My legs quivered from the strength it took to hold my ground.

"So ungrateful," he hissed, "when you have no idea what

it's like to grow up with nothing, to *be* nothing. To have the world look down on you and think you're as worthless as the gods-damned gutter you were born in. You have no conception of how hard I labored for *years* to educate myself, to ingratiate myself with the very people who kicked me aside as a child. I worked my way up from *nothing* to be a king—just to have a daughter who refuses to do her duty and further the royal Torvaine bloodline, to ensure *Torvaine* is the longest-lasting and most prosperous of all the Rellmiran royals."

Fury and humiliation from our old argument stabbed my chest like a hot poker. "You wanted to auction me off for breeding rights to the highest bidder, all to preserve a crown you got by chance."

His palm whipped over my cheek hard enough to make me stumble. Bursts of light flickered over my vision as my face throbbed with pain. For a moment, I wanted to scream and fight back, but instead, Renwell's voice filtered through the cacophony in my mind.

"Never show an enemy how wounded you are."

I inhaled deeply through my nose and slowly stood at attention once more, my hands clasped firmly behind my back, eyes cast downward.

He barked out a harsh laugh. "I see Renwell has managed to teach you something at least. Look at me, apprentice."

I forced myself to meet his gaze.

He studied me as if I were the papers curling to ash in his hearth. "I will let you keep your job—for now. But if you ever speak to me that way again, I will make sure you never become High Enforcer. Do you understand?"

My heart twisted. "Yes, Your Majesty."

"Dismissed."

I executed the shallowest bow I could afford and marched out of his study—where I collided with a pillar of darkness. Lurching backward, I looked up into Renwell's hooded face. His eyes tightened as they focused on my burning cheek.

Wordlessly, he jerked his head to the side, and I followed him down the hall, out of earshot of the *king* and his guards. I yanked up my hood, and we both covered our faces as we left the palace. The rain had stopped but had left silver puddles on the smooth stone of the bridge.

I spoke over the crashing waterfall beneath us. "He thinks I will fail."

"Yes," Renwell said. "He thinks you are weak and will cave under the pressures of this new life." His covered face tilted toward me. "But I disagree. You will succeed and thrive. Then you will earn his favor."

"I'm not doing this for him," I said, my mind full of my parting words with Everett.

Renwell's tone sharpened. "Careful. That is almost treasonous."

I halted, staring at him as he also stopped and faced me. "Will you betray me, Renwell?"

His gaze was steady yet unfathomable. "No."

We continued onward, and the guards let us through the gate without question. No one roamed the dark streets of the Noble Quarter. Everyone must be long abed. I couldn't help a quick glance at the lord's house I'd snuck into earlier. Gods, it seemed a lifetime ago already. What would become of my discovery?

As representatives of the provinces of Winspere and

Pravara and the royal city of Aquinon, the People's Council had been tasked with bringing the people's needs before the king. But when they had rallied behind the belligerent province of Pravara and incited rebellion in the streets of Aquinon, Father had dismantled the council, executed those he deemed traitors, and forbade any mention of the People's Council.

I'd not heard of them again until tonight. Did some of the nobility—like Lord Garyth—want to bring the council back? What would happen if they tried? Was the prisoner I was about to meet connected somehow?

My mind raced, rehearsing my cover story and trying not to panic over the many unknowns.

We approached the Noble Quarter gate, and a rush of excitement dulled my nerves. The gate separated the upper-class quarter from the rest of the city. Renwell hadn't allowed me on the other side of it in two years, since my mother's assassination.

Even if this newfound freedom came with a heavy price, I would happily pay it.

The guards here also opened the gate without question. After all, they were there to keep the rest of the city out, not keep the nobles in.

Renwell hurried me along at breakneck speed, but that didn't stop me from drinking in the sights. I'd never wandered far from the main city road as it led straight to the taverns. But I could see the Temple rising above the brown buildings of the Old Quarter like a giant pearl nestled in the sand.

Renwell took a sharp left, and we plunged into the Market Quarter. The many workshops and market stalls were quiet and hollow this time of night, but they would wake before dawn. I could already smell cinnamon bread baking. My stomach rumbled.

Gods damn it, I should've stopped by the kitchen before going to see my father. Perhaps I would've been harder to provoke with a full stomach. My cheek throbbed as if to agree.

A few minutes later, we reached the cliff road.

Most of Aquinon sat atop the cliffs, but the last quarter—the Docks Quarter—could only be reached by way of the cliff road that cut back and forth down to the docks. The high wall that ran around the whole city had a portcullis at the top of the road, to cut off the rest of the city from sea invasion if necessary.

But I'd never seen it lowered. I'd also never walked down this road.

I gritted my teeth as I followed Renwell, trying to focus on my boots so as not to look out over the dizzying height above the Docks Quarter and the harbor. My legs were trembling by the time we reached the bottom.

The docks were a wide, sprawling part of the city that spilled into the Niviath Sea. Full of bawdy taverns and dilapidated houses that leaned over and under each other like drunk sailors. Ships, large and small, bobbed in their berths. The ever-shifting breeze smelled alternatively of salt and ale.

Where most of the city had been asleep, the Docks Quarter was still alive with light, music, and laughter. Mynastra's Tide was a sailor's favorite. The singing bone-rattlers on shore leave paid us no mind as they wandered from tavern to tavern wearing their strings of bones. I thought of Everett's story and almost smiled, but my nerves strangled it.

Ignoring the revelers, Renwell stalked toward the moonlit

waterfall—the same one we'd crossed at the top. Without warning, he caught my arm in a bruising grip.

He dipped his head to mutter in my ear. "Act frightened."

I flinched, my gaze fluttering around the increasingly abandoned buildings. Were we being watched?

Renwell yanked on my arm, and I whimpered, cowering away from him. It was almost a relief to let a sliver of fear show.

He dragged me to two tall black doors. I caught my breath. This must be the entrance to the infamous Den. It was unmarked, unguarded, and clearly avoided. But the doors opened outward without a sound the moment Renwell appeared before them.

"No, no!" I sobbed, digging my heels into the broken cobblestones.

"Shut up, idiot girl," Renwell hissed as he pulled me forward hard enough for me to stumble. "Or lose your tongue."

I whimpered again, barely keeping myself upright as he hauled me through the gate. I gasped—in real fear this time—when I came face to face with a Shadow-Wolf on the other side.

He was swathed in black from head to toe, not a bit of skin to be seen. A few sunstone knives glittered in his belt. Worst of all was his dark metal mask, shaped like a snarling wolf. He looked like a drawing I'd seen in an old book on the demons from the Abyss. Waiting to snatch souls into the wandering hell.

Never interfere with my Wolves. That had been one of Renwell's rules. Seeing one, there was little chance of that.

Renwell hurried me past one then two then a dozen more Shadow-Wolves. They lined the wide, barren yard where training dummies and racks of weapons were set up. A few more trailed in and out of the dark maw of a cave.

My heart pounded louder than the waterfall that cascaded nearby. Gods, the Den was truly cut *into* the cliff most of the city resided on.

Renwell didn't hesitate as he towed me into the cave. The sound of the waterfall faded as we rushed through a maze of rocky tunnels that dripped with moisture and smelled of mildew. Several tunnels looked wide enough for a wagon while others Renwell would have to turn sideways to slip through.

What all did he do down here? Did my father or brother ever see it? I couldn't imagine either man in this sun-forsaken hole.

We came to another gate that a large, greasy man with a fistful of keys opened from the inside. He leered at me as Renwell dragged me through. Rusty doors lined the torch-lit tunnel, and the thunder of the waterfall came loudest from the other end. We must be right behind it.

Renwell flung me into the first room on the left and slammed the door behind us. I caught myself against a heavy wooden chair and immediately recoiled. It was sticky and smelled of blood. Crusted shackles lay like coiled snakes at its feet. A few torches on the walls illuminated the deep crimson stains and scorch marks that marred the wood.

This place, these smells.

Rising panic blurred my vision as I swung around wildly,

noting the many weapons strewn about the room. Whips, knives, tools for cutting and sawing.

My stomach heaved.

I bolted for the door, but Renwell snatched my wrist and swung me against one of the walls, pinning me with his entire body.

"Calm yourself, Kiera. Breathe," he growled.

"Not him," I gasped, a scream clawing from my throat. "You swore, Renwell. Not him."

"Look at me."

I did, black smudges still blotting my vision. The wavering torchlight only deepened the hardness of Renwell's eyes.

"Korvin is not here," he rasped. "I will be the one to deal with you."

Not here, not here, not here. The words ricocheted around my skull until my mind finally calmed enough to grasp them.

A few moments more, and I'd wrestled the hideous memories back into the darkest cavern of my memory where they waited like bats to swarm my sanity.

My shallow breaths deepened. "Let go of me."

Renwell's jaw clenched, but he stepped away, releasing my aching wrist.

"Where is the prisoner?" I asked hoarsely.

"You'll meet him shortly. Do you remember everything we talked about? What you need to do?"

"Yes." Even though my mind was utterly blank at the moment.

"Good. Now . . . to make your capture look convincing."

I swallowed against my dry throat. He had said as much

earlier, back in the warmth and safety of my room. But here? Those words felt much more ominous.

Renwell had struck me plenty of times before in training. But to let him felt wrong. Just as it had with my father.

His gloved hands flexed, and his eyes glittered with something like a challenge. This wouldn't be the first time he'd tested my resolve.

Drawing my chin up, I walked to the chair and sank down upon it as if it were a throne. "Try not to break anything."

I focused on Mother's sweet face, her gentle laugh, as Renwell reared back and slammed his fist into my jaw.

Grunting in pain, I clawed my nails into the arms of the chair to keep from fighting back.

He jabbed me a few times in the ribs, making me double over, gasping for air. He slammed my shoulders back against the chair. An animalistic snarl twisted his face as he gripped my shirt sleeve and tore it.

I gaped at him, but he wasn't done. His gloved fingers dug under my collar and split the seams to my shoulder. He ripped the belt from my waist and lashed my uninjured cheek with it. My hand flew to my face and came away wet with blood.

Finally, he stepped back, breathing hard. He tossed the belt atop a pile of dirty clothes in the corner.

I sat there, desperately fighting against the sting of tears, while he looked over his work.

"Final touch," he murmured, fetching a pair of chained manacles. He latched the cold, scratched metal around my wrists.

Panic nibbled at the back of my mind like a rat, but I deadened my mind to it.

This is who you are now. Believe it, and the prisoner will too.

Renwell whistled sharply, and the jailer barreled into the room. Renwell tossed him my chains. "Do you have a chain key?"

"Aye, sir." I watched carefully as the jailer produced a small iron key before tucking it back in his left pants pocket.

"Take this one to the cell at the end," Renwell commanded. Then he gave me a smirk that sent a shiver down my spine. "And no need to be gentle with her."

The jailer grinned. "As you wish, sir. Come on, you wretch." He yanked me forward. As I stumbled past him, he kicked me in the back.

I went sprawling to the dirt floor, barely catching myself with my manacled hands. Rage flooded my veins. *This* man I could fight back. I rolled over and kicked the leering jailer in the groin.

He bellowed curses and dropped to his knees. Snarling, I struggled to my feet. I paid little mind to Renwell watching me with a small smile. Instead, I swung my fists at the jailer's head, but he jerked my chains downward at the last moment. I used my momentum to ram my shoulder into his gut. He grunted, his sour pork breath filling my nostrils.

I could snatch the key now, but it had to be where the prisoner could see me do it.

Renwell's mocking voice filled the tunnel. "Is it really so difficult to deliver one chained, injured woman to her cell?"

The jailer seized my chains and flung me halfway down the tunnel. My battered body screamed in protest. Gods damn it, he was stronger than he looked. But I had to get close to him again.

He dragged me to the last cell and unlocked it. The door screeched on rusty hinges as he opened it and tried to throw me inside.

But I clung to him instead, my nails digging into his fleshy arm. "No! You can't do this! I've done nothing wrong!"

"Get off me, bitch!" he roared.

While he tried to shake me loose, my fingers slipped into his pocket and fished out the little key. Gods, I hoped the prisoner was watching. My stomach twisted in anticipation.

The jailer grabbed a fistful of my hair and yanked. Needles of fire stabbed my scalp, and I released him. Cursing profusely, he kicked me into the shadowy cell.

I rolled, using the opportunity to shove the key into my mouth.

Two large, rough hands gripped my arm and gently pulled me to the side. A hulking shadow stepped between me and the jailer.

The prisoner.

I froze, shock overpowering the pain pounding through my body.

"Leave her be, jailer."

CHAPTER 4

KIERA

THE JAILER'S HARSH LAUGH RICOCHETED AROUND THE CELL. "You think you're going to stop me, boy? Come on, then." He pulled a short, rusty club from his belt.

The prisoner crouched on bare feet, his chains scraping over the ground. The glow from the torches illuminated his shirtless body—a rippling mass of blood, sweat, and muscles. Dark hair fell like glistening crow wings to his broad shoulders.

I scowled at his back. Gods damn it, if he got himself killed, all this would be for nothing. But my scowl faded when I saw the twisted scars—and was that black ink?—etched into his back.

The jailer lunged. The prisoner twisted away, seizing the club then lashing out with it. *Crack!* The jailer howled and fell backward, clutching his nose. Blood seeped between his fingers.

The prisoner leaned over him. "Hurt her again, and I'll break more than your nose."

I couldn't see his face, but his words and his tone were enough to send a chill through my heart. Why did he bother to protect me? He didn't know me.

But then my heart dropped to my toes.

Two Shadow-Wolves appeared soundlessly in the doorway. Renwell must've called them.

They stepped over the squealing jailer. The prisoner tossed the club at their boots. Even he must know he couldn't win a fight with two Shadow-Wolves while chained.

One of the Wolves slammed him against the wall and held him there. The other one approached me.

I cringed, but he simply gathered my chains and hauled me against the opposite wall as if I weighed nothing. As he secured my chains to the iron ring anchored there, I glanced over his shoulder.

My gaze collided with a pair of hard, bright green eyes. The prisoner's bronze, angular face was marred by dirt and blood. But it was his look of fury that stole my breath away. This was the farthest thing from a man beaten into submission.

But was he angry with me or the jailer?

The Wolves finished securing us and departed without a word, dragging the jailer behind them like a bloody carcass for butchering. The door clanged shut behind them, stealing most of the light.

The only sounds were my roaring pulse and ragged breaths, the key still clenched between my teeth.

But he was there. Could he see me? Could he reach me?

I cowered against my wall, praying his chains would keep him from me.

"Are you hurt?" a deep, quiet voice asked.

I blinked. *That* was what he wanted to know first? I used my tongue to shove the key into my cheek so I could speak. "I —I'll live. Who are you?"

He hesitated. "A prisoner like yourself. I won't harm you."

I suppressed a snort. As if I would trust him so easily. Yet I still felt the ghost of his warm fingers wrapped around my arms, tugging me behind him.

I shook my head. *Focus.*

My eyes searched for him in the darkness. But it was as if I were talking to a wandering soul in the Longest Night. I shivered.

"Why are you here?" I asked.

His voice sharpened. "Why do you want to know?"

I let my voice wobble. "Are—are you a murderer or a rapist?"

"No. And I already told you I wouldn't hurt you."

"Am I to believe the word of a half-naked man chained to a Shadow-Wolf prison cell?" I demanded, unable to keep the bite from my voice.

He made a low noise—of either derision or amusement, I couldn't tell. "I suppose not. But if that's true, then I shouldn't trust a beautiful, bloodied woman in a royal guard's uniform . . . who is also chained up in a Shadow-Wolf prison cell."

I bit my lip, heat searing my cheeks. Not because he'd paid me a backhanded compliment, but that he'd twisted my words against me.

His melodic voice came again. "Are *you* going to hurt *me*?"

I took a deep breath and told the first lie. "No."

Ringing silence filled the cell as if that word had struck a bell, marking the beginning of a time we couldn't take back.

The meager torchlight that came through the barred window at the top of the cell door slowly shifted the black shadows into deep gray. His outline began to take shape—a man sitting against the opposite wall.

If I could see him, he could see me.

I quietly spat the key into my palm and clenched my hand into a fist.

"Would my name help put you at ease?" he asked suddenly.

By the Four, what difference did it make if I were at ease? Aloud, I said, "If you were intelligent, you'd only lie. If you're a fool, you won't live long enough for your name to matter, anyway."

"Allow me to play the fool, then. My name is Aiden."

I swallowed, my mouth dry and tasting of metal from the key. Was that the truth? Why would he give that so easily to me when Renwell hadn't been able to beat it out of him?

"Kiera," I whispered.

"Kiera," he repeated, as if getting a feel for the weight of my name on his tongue. "Well, Kiera, if you're planning to use that key you stole, I would do it soon."

Suddenly, everything made sense. Why he'd protected me, why he was trying to put me at ease. He'd seen me steal the key and knew I was his best shot at escaping.

A cold ribbon of disappointment snaked through my gut. Which was ridiculous. Things were progressing as planned. I'd needed him to see me stealing the key so he wouldn't be suspicious when I revealed it.

His features were like a smudged painting, but I felt his eyes on me all the same.

"I'm curious," he continued. "I assume it's the key to your chains as the door keys are much bigger. Tell me, after you unlock your chains, how do you plan to get out?"

Whatever he claimed, Aiden was no fool.

I lifted my chin. "I'll jump that grubby worm of a jailer when he comes back and knock him unconscious."

"And if it's the Wolves again, what then?"

I frowned. "I'll just hope they've come for you, not me."

Aiden hummed, undoubtedly sensing the holes in my plan. "And if you get out of this cell, where will you run? Into the arms of dozens more Shadow-Wolves?"

"No, I'll go the other way. I heard the waterfall more clearly at the other end of this passage. It could be a way out." I knew it was—Renwell had told me.

Aiden shifted closer. A weak beam of light brought one side of his face into focus. "What if it's not? What if you're trapped?"

I flapped my chained arms, wincing at the clashing metal. "Then I'll die faster! At least I will have tried. Better than waiting for my next beating like a caged animal."

His glowing green eyes narrowed. "The shackles are worse than the beatings."

I surveyed the cuts and bruises that mapped Renwell's rage on his skin. They had to be causing him pain. My own fewer ones pulsed like painful heartbeats. Then there were the scars and ink on his back. Where did this man come from? Why was he here?

I dragged my gaze back only to realize he was studying me too. "You want me to free you."

"Yes. I think an extra pair of hands would help with your . . . plan." He held out his bound hands as if presenting how capable they were.

But I'd already seen what they could do. What I needed to know was what *else* they'd done.

"You don't think I could handle the jailer if I weren't shackled?" I asked.

This time, his gaze traveled over me, taking in my torn uniform and dirty boots. "You were truly a palace guard?"

Annoyed that he hadn't answered my question, I demanded, "Does that surprise you?"

He shrugged. "Only that Weylin allowed a woman to be trained as a guard. He's the only king in Lancora who keeps women out of his guard and his army. Apart from you, apparently." He tipped his head at me, the question clear in his voice.

"I wasn't just a palace guard," I said slowly, as if reluctant to admit my role. "I was trained as the personal guard for the princesses. His Majesty believed a woman would be less conspicuous to potential assailants."

Aiden snorted. "Only to fools like Weylin, perhaps. In my experience, when women are barred from learning to fight, it's because the men in charge are afraid they'll fight back."

My eyes widened. I had always hated that my father refused to let women join the guard or the army—which were the only two ways for anyone to learn how to fight, how to use weapons. He claimed that women were naturally weaker in mind and body, and he wanted the strongest. Yet Renwell had trained me in both fighting and weapons, among other things.

But to hear this prisoner say such things kindled a fire in my chest I didn't understand. I also didn't miss the way he called my father "Weylin" as if he were a fellow criminal on the street.

Renwell was right to suspect Aiden.

"You speak treason," I breathed.

"I speak truth."

"They will kill you for it."

"Maybe." His gaze burned into me, his half-dark, half-light visage reminiscent of a vengeful god. "But I don't fear the Abyss. There are worse things in this world."

My heart pounded so hard I thought he might hear it. "I can't tell if you're a madman or a fanatic."

His voice softened. "A little of both, perhaps. Or something else entirely." His gaze fell to my mouth.

My lips tingled as if he'd reached out and touched them. Realizing I'd shifted closer to him at some point, I pressed my spine into the rocky crags of the wall.

He said nothing. Simply pursed his full lips, curiosity glittering in his eyes before he too retreated into the shadows.

I cast about for a question to ask, a comment to make— anything that would break the strange silence between us.

But then he spoke again. "I must say, you are far more effective at carving out my secrets than Renwell was with his torture. But then again, he knew you would be, didn't he?"

CHAPTER 5
KIERA

MY HEART STOPPED.

Panic turned my world into cracked glass that felt like it would shatter at any moment. And me along with it.

But I couldn't. He was guessing. Playing with me to see what I'd do.

"R-Renwell?" The stammer was unfeigned. "He's the one who—who did this to me." I gestured pathetically at my torn clothes and throbbing face.

"Convincing, very convincing," Aiden murmured. "But why?"

Inwardly, I sneered. He thought he was getting the upper hand—forcing me to reveal my identity and my crime. But it would all be a lie. I just had to sell it.

I sagged against the wall, cradling my aching ribs. "I already told you I am—*was*—the princesses' personal guard. I was rarely allowed free time, let alone friends. But . . ." I sniffed and wiped my nose on my sleeve. "But there was a boy, a young boy, named Julian." A memory of the real Julian pierced my mind. His sweet smile and deep brown eyes coaxed real tears to my eyes. It was why I'd chosen this as my story. A lie was always stronger with threads of truth.

"He worked in the kitchen," I continued. "He'd lived and worked in the palace his whole life, just as I had, and he always had a kind word for everyone. Even me, the ignored shadow in a world of light. But . . . but they caught him stealing." I swallowed a sob, but more built up in my throat. "I had no idea he was so desperate, or I would've . . . I would've done something. Anything. But they arrested him. I pled for him. But they sentenced him to death. I attacked his executioner— no thought, no plan—but they killed him anyway and sent me here," I finished in a dull voice.

I could still hear the thud of the axe, even though it was years ago. It would haunt me until the gods found my soul. I hated using Julian this way, using my real emotions to lie about what really happened to him.

But it was all I could think of to convince Aiden of my place in his cell. He was the true criminal here. But *why*?

"Well, does that satisfy you?" I asked, impatience carving through my words.

"For now."

For now. His words echoed my father's. Both men reserving judgment on me, waiting for me to make a mistake.

My hands fisted in my lap, the key digging into my palm. "What about you? Why are you here? What makes you so special that you think I was beaten up and chained here to spy on *you*?"

Another long silence. His shadow didn't budge. His head was tipped back against the wall as if he were sleeping.

I fought the urge to speak again, but he was like a tricky lock. I had to find the right pressure at the right angle. If he was using silence as a tool, so could I.

But waiting was torture. Renwell would be back at dawn. The thought of witnessing another execution soured my stomach. How much time did I have left?

"They captured me impersonating a Shadow-Wolf here in their Den," Aiden said.

I blinked, surprised he'd admitted it. Then I laughed. "You lie. No one would be stupid enough to break in here dressed like them. That's . . . that's—"

"—what a madman or a fanatic would do?" Aiden finished for me.

"Holy Four," I whispered, trying to keep the eagerness out of my voice. "Why?"

Aiden's long fingers wrapped around his chains and choked them. "A sad story, not unlike your own."

I frowned. What in the wandering hell did that mean? "Were you trying to save someone? Someone in here?" I remembered the other cells doors lining the passage.

He chuckled, warm and deep. Goosebumps prickled my skin. "I'm happy to hear I've gone from murderer to rescuer in your eyes. But no, nothing so noble."

"Then what?"

He hesitated. "Gold."

"*Gold?*" I sputtered.

"Yes, gold," he said, dropping his chains. "I need a great deal. Quickly. As I'm not foolish enough to rob the palace vault, I thought perhaps our dear High Enforcer kept a stash of it in his Den."

I rubbed the key in my palm with my thumb, back and forth, over and over. This was what Renwell had wanted to know. At least part of it. Except, why would Aiden risk so much on the frail hope he would find gold?

Unless he was lying.

"Did you find any?" I asked out of true curiosity.

"Not a single coin. Were you hoping to steal some on your way out?"

I narrowed my eyes at the mirth in his voice. "It's not a terrible idea. I'll have less than nothing if I escape." I gnawed my lip. Perhaps I could push him one answer further. "Why are you so desperate for gold?"

His tone darkened. "Now that is one secret even you can't pry out of me, Kiera."

For now, I taunted him in my mind.

But I would steal it from him, eventually. Renwell assumed I would have to escape with him to uncover all his secrets, but *how* I convinced Aiden to ally with me was up to me.

Aiden said he needed gold, but for what? He could be funding an army of rebels for all I knew. Or sending support to my father's enemies in other kingdoms. The barbaric Dags from the north were always raiding along our borders. Pirates from the Eloren Isles occasionally attacked our ships. Keldiket was the farthest away, on the other side of the treacherous Twaryn forest, but Renwell had told me it had the most skilled spies and assassins in Lancora.

Any of them would love to discover where Rellmira kept its wealth.

A flash of inspiration hit me. The perfect bait. A golden opportunity to learn Aiden's secrets, to bind us together until I'd learned what Renwell—what *I*—needed to know.

Father might truly imprison you for this.

But His Majesty wasn't here. This was my decision.

"Very well," I said, as if his refusal were of no consequence. "But why did you come here? Why not the High Treasurer's house?"

The musty air shifted between us as Aiden leaned forward. "Explain."

"I went there once three years ago, with the prince and princesses. It was one of the only times they, as well as myself, were allowed out of the palace. Asher had just taken over as High Treasurer from his father and wanted to assure the royal family he was taking good care of their additional treasures and payrolls." *Showing off was more like it.* The pompous man had waved his arms at the gleaming fortune like he'd been personally responsible for obtaining it.

I lowered my voice. "Chests of coins, piles of jewels, and even some handfuls of fireseeds and raw sunstone. It was the most treasure I'd ever seen, and it was just sitting there."

Delysia had been dazzled by the glitter and glow of it all while Everett had simply nodded in his best impression of Father. My fingers had ached to snatch a few coins to spend on a game of Death and Four at a tavern with a pile of hot, buttered biscuits next to me.

Now, that trip might end up being the perfect enticement for the silent man in front of me. His head was bowed as if he were lost in his own thoughts and didn't want me to witness them.

All I can do now—I slid the small key into the lock on one of my wrist cuffs—*is turn the key.* The lock clicked open, igniting a familiar thrill in my chest. Aiden's head slowly lifted.

"But none of that matters," I said as I worked the other cuff. "The best I can hope for is my life. I'll either escape or die trying." The second lock sprang apart.

Cool air kissed my raw skin, and a groan escaped my lips.

"Kiera."

I turned my back to his alluring voice. There was a rustle of movement as if he were rising to his feet.

Merciful Mynastra, grant me luck. I tested the key in the lock that held the ends of my two chains. It gave way, and I scrambled to catch the chains before they clattered to the ground.

A smile touched my lips as I draped the chains over my shoulders like a mantle. They would make suitable weapons if needed.

"Kiera, please."

My heart twisted at the quiet desperation in his voice. Gods damn it. I faced him, clutching the key.

He held out his shackled wrists, every muscle in his face taut.

"How can I trust you?" I whispered. *Not to hurt me, not to kill me, not to abandon me to save yourself.*

I had no doubt Renwell would keep to his word and kill Aiden if he didn't give us the information we wanted. And he'd given me some, but only a tantalizing peek at his true purpose. My gut told me to escape with Aiden even if I didn't trust him.

He'd protected me from the jailer, but I remembered something Renwell had said during a brutal fight session: "Every person has a monster caged inside, Kiera. All it takes is the right key to set it free."

What kind of monster lurked inside Aiden?

He slowly shook his head. "Only you know the answer to that," he murmured, startling me as if he'd answered my thought instead of my spoken question. "But is it worth wasting your one chance to live?"

He didn't know it was *his* life I held in my hand. That even if I freed him, if we became allies, he would still be my enemy.

Because I was meant to be his destruction. I only hoped he wouldn't be mine.

I stepped closer to him. He didn't move a muscle. His shadowed eyes tracked me as his bare chest rose and fell with deep breaths. I found myself trying to match them.

He let me come to him until I was fully within his grasp. But he did nothing. Just waited, towering over me like a statue devoid of emotions.

I lifted my chin until our gazes met. And, Holy Four, was I wrong. An inferno of emotions lived in his eyes. They consumed me, consumed what little air existed between us. Something sparked to life in my veins, burning from my heart to my toes. The most dangerous thing of all.

Tearing my gaze away, I fumbled the key into one lock then the other, being careful not to brush hands with him. The chains fell away. I retreated immediately, but there was nowhere to go now. Nowhere he couldn't reach me.

He flexed his hands, then held one out to me. "May I have the key?"

I clenched it tighter for a moment, reluctant to give it up even though it was essentially useless now.

"For the wall lock," he added. He gestured to the chains around my shoulders. "They make decent weapons, as you already know."

"So long as you don't use them on me," I said, trying to sound nonchalant, but my voice trembled. To cover it up, I dropped the key into his palm.

His fingers curled around it. "Why would I do that to the woman who set me free?" Without waiting for an answer, he turned and unleashed his chains from the wall, then slipped the key into the pocket of his black pants. My eyes lingered on his narrow hips and chiseled stomach.

I swallowed hard and wrenched my gaze away. I would fight him if I had to. He was clearly still suspicious of me and my intentions. Ingratiating myself with him was going to be like tiptoeing on the ledge of the bridge, barefoot, in a hurricane.

My palms grew clammy at the thought.

Aiden wrapped the chains around his forearms and his knuckles, a sort of armor on top of the gauntlets of muscle he already had.

We faced each other in our dim cage.

My heart fluttered wildly. The silence felt more unbearable than ever. How long would we have to wait? What would we do until then? Would he—

"Tell me your favorite food," he said, leaning against the wall as if we were in a cozy tavern settling on something to eat.

I blurted out the first thing that came to mind. "Biscuits." My cheeks heated. But it was almost a relief to say something truthful.

He smiled. "Sweet or savory?"

I twisted my mouth to one side, thinking hard. My stomach rumbled loudly as if I'd woken it up by thinking about food. "Right now? Both. But a freshly baked biscuit, slathered in butter with a touch of garlic and rosemary is my absolute favorite."

His smile deepened, and the flutter in my chest moved to my stomach. "I prefer sweet, myself, with a dash of cinnamon and warm honey."

"That's your favorite food?"

"Merely my favorite biscuit. Favorite food?" He hummed to himself. "Have you ever tasted a moonblood fruit?"

I frowned and shook my head.

"Ah," he said with a soft sigh. "They grow on the banks of the Twaryn River in the heart of the forest. They have a silvery-white peel on the outside with a crimson flesh inside. Legend says they were Viridana's favorite and taste the best picked on a full moon, but I would eat one any time. The sweetest, most refreshing treat."

I smiled. "Sounds perfect. Maybe I'll have the chance to try one someday."

"I truly hope you do."

I bit my lip. "Why did you ask me about food?"

"Perhaps I just wanted to pass the time."

"Or?"

He grunted. "Or I wanted to save myself the barrage of questions and accusations I could sense brewing in your head. You looked ready for war."

I scoffed, trying to surreptitiously release my fierce grip on my chains. "You don't know me. You don't know what I'm thinking or feeling."

"Maybe not. But now I know your favorite food," he said with a smirk.

"And I know yours. And that you've been to Twaryn. Which is more significant, so I believe I've won this little game."

He straightened and stalked toward me. I scrambled backward, my back meeting the wall the moment his hands pressed against the rock on either side of my shoulders. Yet, he still didn't touch me.

"You don't want to play games with me, Kiera," he whispered.

My breath froze in my lungs. "Because you hate to lose?"

His eyes traveled over my upturned face. "Because I would do anything to win."

I scowled, pulling myself to my full height, our noses nearly colliding. His breathing sharpened. My fingers floated toward his pants pocket while I allowed my gaze to flicker over his face, as if evaluating it.

I didn't falter once as I pinched the key between my fingertips, slipped it out of his pocket, and held it up between us. "As would I."

His eyes flared, and he pulled away from me. I grinned and clenched the key in my fist. He opened his mouth to say something, but a heavy fist beat on our door.

My heart leapt into my throat. The jailer. But why would he knock?

"Aiden?" a man's deep voice came from the other side.

Aiden heaved a sigh and strode closer to the door. "It's about time, Maz."

"Then how about I play the gods-damned lunatic next time

and *you* be the rescuer," the man named Maz grumbled, keys rattling. "Thought you were nothing but dog scraps by now when you didn't answer—"

"You tried other cells?" Aiden asked.

"You didn't hear me?"

I felt more than I saw Aiden's quick glance over his shoulder at me.

"No," he answered quietly.

The door swung open, framing a huge man. He was tall and broad, bigger than Aiden. Torchlight glimmered on short golden hair. And he was soaked. A short wooden pole and a small axe were tucked into his belt.

"Fucking Four, what did they do to you?" he growled, gesturing at Aiden with the ring full of keys I'd last seen on the jailer. "Where are your clothes and why are you unchained?"

Aiden moved to the side and nodded his head at me. "Because of Kiera."

Maz peered into the gloom. A smile warmed his handsome, bearded face. He looked to be the same age as Aiden, perhaps a few years older than me. "Ah, I see. I'm surprised at you, Aiden, but I understand. That still doesn't explain how you freed yourself."

My mouth dropped open at the insinuation, but Aiden merely rolled his eyes. "Enough, Maz. She's coming with us."

Maz nodded. I nearly melted with relief. This was it. I was truly escaping with Aiden—who, apparently, had a plan all along.

"We don't have much time," Maz said, his tone taking on the snap of a soldier. "The guards will wake soon. Ruru has a boat just outside the cave."

My eyebrows lifted. The same sea cave Renwell had told me about? The one no one was supposed to know of?

Aiden grunted. "Good." His gaze pierced me. "Leave your tunic here."

I balked. "Why?" My shirt would cover me well enough, but I disliked the order.

"Do you want everyone to know you're from the palace?" Aiden demanded.

Maz's eyebrows flew up his forehead. "The palace? Who the—"

"Later," Aiden cut him off, craning his neck to look both ways down the passage. "Kiera, it's now or never."

I gritted my teeth and threw off my chains to tug the ripped tunic over my head. I tossed it on the ground, the torchlight sparkling in the golden thread of the half sun. Hopefully, Renwell would see it and know I'd escaped, that I'd succeeded.

I'd never worn a uniform like that before, but it was strange, leaving it behind. As if I were severing the last connection between me and the palace.

I threw the chains back around my neck and faced Aiden and Maz with a mask of confidence. "Let's go."

I followed Aiden out of our cell and eased the door shut behind me.

CHAPTER 6
ΛIDEN

I COULD STILL FEEL THE COLD GRASP OF THE SHACKLES AROUND my wrists.

It was a feeling that had haunted me for years. I hadn't been lying to Kiera when I told her that the shackles were worse than the beating.

Strangely, I'd lied to her very little. I couldn't say the same for her. The corner of my mouth twitched. Little thief.

I kept her shadowy figure in the corner of my eye as I gazed down the tunnel of cells. "Hand me the keys," I told Maz.

He frowned. "Aiden . . . we can't. It would take time we don't have to hunt down the right key for each cell." He jangled the ring of dozens of keys for emphasis.

Kiera added softly, "And they could be dangerous, Aiden."

The back of my neck prickled. That was the first time she'd said my name. Another thing I probably should've lied about.

A low groan came from one of the cells as a thorny tendril of desperation snaked through my chest. Regardless of Maz and Kiera's worries, if anyone was being held captive in these particular cells, they were most likely criminals in Weylin's eyes alone. Otherwise, they would be held at the city prison.

A wet grunt jerked my attention to see the jailer in a dirty heap at the other end of the tunnel. He was stirring. My upper lip curled. Surprising that the lout was still alive after failing the way he did. The Wolves weren't known for being forgiving.

I thrust my hand out to Maz. "Keys."

Sighing, he dropped them into my palm then shoved his hand through his hair—a habit he'd picked up ever since he'd shorn his long hair. "I knocked on half the doors and they all had at least one person inside."

That somewhat soothed my suspicion about why Kiera had been dragged into *my* cell. But that meant many more fates staked to my conscience.

The jailer grunted again. I snarled in frustration. If only Maz had gotten here sooner . . . but it wasn't his fault.

I strode to the jailer. He was struggling to sit up, bracing one hand on the door of the room where Renwell had questioned me for hours. His broken nose still leaked blood. A swollen lump on his temple marked where Maz must've hit him. His blackened eyes widened when he spotted me.

I smirked and rammed my chain-covered fist into his other temple. He collapsed without a sound. But distant voices echoed down the tunnel on the other side of the gate.

Gods damn these Wolves and their relentless master.

I whipped around and nearly tripped over Kiera. She moved like a whisper. I hated that now both she and Maz had slipped past my notice.

"Please, Aiden, we have to go. If they catch us, death will be the least of what they'll do to us." The fear in her honeyed brown eyes cut through my anger like a cold knife.

Cursing Renwell and his minions to the depths of the wandering hell, I threw the key ring through the barred window of the closest cell door.

After a moment's hesitation, Kiera also flung in the little key she'd stolen twice. A spark of warmth lit my chest, but I smothered it.

We raced down the passage and followed Maz around the bend. The roar of the waterfall on the other side of the rock wall drowned out our footsteps.

"How many guards?" I asked Maz as we fumbled through the dark tunnel. Sparks of light danced at the far end, marking our destination.

"Just two, thank the gods. I only had two dreamdew darts, which was why I had the pleasure of bashing that jailer's skull." A smile lifted his voice. "Although it looked like one of you got to share that delight."

Kiera made a noise next to me, and I tensed.

When she'd arrived at my cell in a storm of violence, her bruised and bloodied face had ignited my rage like a spear of lightning. As had her torn clothes and desperate pleas. I'd acted on instinct, wanting to inflict every bit of pain he'd caused her on the jailer.

Neither of us answered Maz, and for once, he left it alone.

The tunnel spat us out into a small sea cave that Renwell had turned into a secret harbor. A handful of dinghies were tied to the short wooden dock that jutted out over the dark water. The soft creak of the boats and splash of the water echoed in the narrow cavern.

Two bodies swathed in black lay in a tangled mass at the mouth of the tunnel. Kiera pulled up short when she saw them.

Maz chuckled, patting the whistler strapped to his hip. "They can't bite when they're asleep."

"Why not kill them?" she asked.

Maz's eyebrows shot upward. "A wee bit bloodthirsty, are you? I like that in a woman. But no, we don't need to attract any more attention than we are." He gave me a significant glance.

My jaw clenched. Attention was unavoidable. But we'd evaded Renwell and his Wolves for years. We only needed to stay ahead of them for a little while longer.

"Loose the rope," I commanded, leaping into the dinghy closest to the cave entrance—a shadowy crack in the rock face.

Maz obeyed while I threaded the oars through their locks. A large, thick ring was bolted to the bottom of the boat, marking it for what the boat was usually used for—prisoner transport. I peeled off my chains and dropped them next to the ring.

Kiera watched us, a frown creasing her brow. "How did you know about this cave?" She turned to Maz, eyeing his wet clothing. "Did you *swim* in here?"

Gods, the incessant questions. Though perhaps she'd been sheltered in her life as a palace guard.

Maz puffed out his chest. "I've swum greater distances than that. And through some water that was a lot bloody colder—"

"Maz," I warned.

Kiera's gaze darted toward me. She could glare all she

wanted, but she didn't need any more details of who we were. The barb about Twaryn still needled me.

"More secrets?"

I clambered out of the dinghy to stand in front of her. "Always. But none that concerns our current escape. Now, get in." I held out my hand to help her.

Her eyes narrowed as if I'd offered her a snake. Brushing past me, she jumped into the boat. She wobbled a bit then sat down hard on one of the benches. I smirked.

But the expression faded when I caught Maz watching me with a curious glint in his eyes. I jerked my head. "I'll shove off."

He leapt into the boat, considerably more graceful than Kiera, despite his bulk. I waited until he was seated in the middle with oars in hand before I gripped the bow and gave it a gentle push.

Kiera's eyes widened at something behind me. "Aiden!" Her shout clattered around the cave like a bell.

I whirled around just as a gloved fist swung at my face. I leaned back, but the fist still glanced off my cheek and sent me spinning. The world went hazy. I blinked furiously, trying to clear it.

Maz was cursing, but I roared, "Get out of here!"

The Wolf wrapped an arm around my neck and squeezed while his other hand brought a long sunstone knife plunging to my chest.

I seized his wrist. The blade tip scraped along my skin. My worn muscles screamed. If only I'd kept the damn chains.

I was weakened. But so was he.

I gave his wrist a vicious twist, even as black specks darted over my vision. He grunted and loosened his chokehold on my neck, but didn't drop the knife. I swung his knife arm down, burying the blade in his thigh.

He screamed and released me. I kicked backward, my heel jabbing his abdomen. His body thudded to the dock.

More shouts echoed. I glanced up, my breath searing my lungs. The other Shadow-Wolf had also woken and was swimming to where Maz and Kiera floated away from the dock. Maz brandished his small axe, the boat rocking with his movement. Kiera stood shakily behind him, her chains gripped in her hands and her jaw set.

My bare feet slipped through a pool of blood to seize the sunstone knife from the Wolf's drained body. At least my aim had been true. Then I leapt into the dark water. I slipped the blade's handle between my teeth and paddled hard. The Wolf had caught up to the boat and was trying to climb in.

Maz swung for the Wolf's neck, but the Wolf blocked the axe with his sunstone blade. A screech of shattered steel and Maz's axe fell in pieces to the water. Maz bellowed and tackled the Wolf off the boat. They both splashed into the water. I spat my knife into my hand.

"Fucking Four, Maz, break!" I shouted, trying to separate the thrashing bodies.

Maz reared back, narrowly avoiding a swipe from the Wolf's knife. I lunged. My blade sank into the Wolf's shoulder. He grunted and elbowed me in the jaw, but his reactions were slow in the water wearing so much clothing.

Maz ducked another swipe and wrenched the knife from the Wolf's hand, then drove it deep into his gut.

The Wolf stiffened, gasping and choking on moldy water.

Even in the throes of death, he didn't speak a word. He was trained not to. All of them were.

My heart felt like a stone in my chest as the body slipped into the shadowy depths. Maz and I clenched our ill-gotten knives, a grim look passing between us. Renwell would be out for blood.

"That was my gods-damned favorite axe," Maz grumbled as we swam back to Kiera and the boat.

She was still standing, the chains in her hands trembling. Had she never seen death before? Ah, the boy she told me about. Julian. If what she told me were true, he had died differently than this, but death stained the mind in a way that could never be scrubbed out. The more violent the death, the darker the stain.

I had a few that rivaled the Longest Night.

Kiera stared at me as if she could see the blackened fabric of my mind. The renewed fear in her eyes churned my gut, and I looked away.

Wordlessly, we settled into the boat. Maz picked up the oars again and rowed hard for the cave mouth. The passage to the sea was so narrow, the oars scraped against the rock in some places. A few times, I braced my hands on the slimy, moss-covered walls and pushed us along. The water grew choppier, the drumbeat of the sea building.

Then we were free.

The moon had disappeared behind the cliffs, a sure sign that dawn was coming. But the sun had yet to peek through the dark, angry clouds piled on the eastern horizon. A little boat with a boy holding a lantern bobbed not far away on the raucous sea. A smile tugged at my lips. Ruru.

As Maz rowed us closer, I pulled in a deep breath fragrant with salt and rain, sending a silent prayer of thanks to the Four. I could never truly breathe in close quarters. It'd taken years to smooth the jagged edges of panic that sank into me whenever I was enclosed.

I glanced back at the cave. It was almost impossible to see, especially in the dark, as one of the many shadowy gashes in the cliff face. Maz and I had discovered it by accident.

After months of observing the Shadow-Wolf's movements, we determined they must have another way in and out. We were lucky enough to catch a glimpse of a prisoner transport coming out of the cave and being loaded onto a ship. They hadn't noticed our own small boat with the lights doused before they'd sailed away. North.

"All right?" Ruru called softly.

"All right," Maz grunted, drifting our boat as close as he could to Ruru's.

Ruru grinned when he caught sight of me. "Skelly owes me two coppers."

I raised one eyebrow. "He thought I wouldn't escape?"

"He didn't think you *or* Maz would come out alive."

"Such a hopeful ray of sunshine," Maz grumbled. He jerked his head at Kiera. "He should dish out double for a third live one."

Ruru's eyes widened, looking like the coppers he loved so much. "Who's she?"

"Kiera," she answered with the hint of a smile, "and you must be the other half of the daring rescue party. Ruru?"

His fifteen-year-old chest swelled in an unnerving imitation of Maz. "That's me! Do you need a hand?" He offered his.

She hesitated for a moment, then flung her chains to the bottom of the boat and took Ruru's open palm. She half-crawled, half-jumped into the fishing boat.

Maz looked at me. "Sink it?"

I nodded. We raised our sunstone knives high above our heads and drove them into the bottom of the boat. They cut through the wood like butter. We stabbed and sawed for a few more moments until the hole was big enough to drink in great gulps of sea water.

It would be better if the boat were completely wrecked; then perhaps Renwell would think a storm had swallowed us. But this was the best we could do.

I stared at the knife in my hand—the inky black stone and the occasional sparkle of dead stars. The representation of so much death and destruction. But so gods-damned useful in a pinch.

With a growl, I flung the knife into the sea.

Maz grimaced, clutching his knife. "Must I?"

"We're dead if we're caught with them. We have to fit in."

"Gods-damn shame," Maz muttered and whipped the black knife into the hungry sea.

Timing the swells, we leapt from the sinking boat into Ruru's.

Kiera sat in the stern wrapped in a blanket Ruru must have brought. Her eyes avoided mine, fixing on the cliffs instead, as if Renwell was going to burst out of the cave at any moment. Which he might.

I sat down at the oars, ignoring the sting and shudder of my wounds. I refused to give her my back. Maz collapsed behind me in the bow.

Ruru hooked the lantern on its metal pole. "We should hurry. The harbor is still crowded, but Skelly said Mynastra's got one more storm left in her."

As if the goddess had heard him, the sky darkened further under the weight of ominous clouds and the first raindrops landed.

Maz laughed as I started to row. "Of course she does. She can never resist when Aiden sails her seas."

Ruru frowned, tucking his tall, thin body between me and Kiera. "Why?"

"Perhaps because I was born in a storm at sea," I grunted between pulls.

"Or she just wants his pretty bones to decorate her bed," Maz joked.

Ruru laughed, but Kiera merely watched me as if she were spooling each thread she plucked from me to create her own tapestry of who I was.

The wind rose with a howl. The waves heaved, crowned with silver foam. I pulled harder, Maz calling out bearings as he kept an eye on the flickering harbor watchtowers. The heavy rain veiled us from any guards who marched the stone wall that extended from the watchtowers like two great, curving arms embracing the harbor.

We just needed to slip through the harbor opening and pray no one had alerted the watchtowers to any escaped prisoners.

I cursed as the waves drove us closer to the wall. "Ruru, get in the bow! Maz, take an oar!"

They scrambled into place. Kiera clung to her bench, her face paler than the hidden moon. Then she doubled over the side, presumably to retch. But I had little strength left for sympathy.

Maz and I fell into a steady rowing rhythm, matching strokes. Thunder crunched and crumbled like rocks through the sky. Lightning pierced the endless waves.

After what felt like hours, we rounded the first watchtower. The great fire at the top was burning steadily, and the shadowy figures of the guards were barely visible.

Our boat joined a few others racing into the harbor. Likely some sailors out celebrating Mynastra's Tide. Even through the storm's symphony, shouts of song and laughter reached us.

"Bloody fools!" Maz shouted with a grin.

I couldn't help casting a glance at Kiera. Of course, I was the fool who had chosen this night specifically for this reason. Cover and distraction.

The Docks Quarter glowed like a shimmering ember before us. We rowed toward it without incident, sliding into the berth next to Skelly's ship, *Mynastra's Wings*. Skelly was nowhere to be seen, probably drinking to our deaths in a tavern. Ruru and Maz tied us off while Kiera scrambled onto the dock like a drowning cat. I almost expected her to hiss at the boat. I pursed my lips to keep from smiling.

"Are you all right?" I asked her in a low tone. She'd tossed aside the useless blanket and her whole body shook.

She looked up at me, her wet hair clinging to her cheeks. "I never want to do that again."

"Escape a prison or sail in a storm?"

She grimaced. "Neither. But I think I'd take the former over the latter at this point."

My jaw tightened. She wouldn't like what I had planned

for her then. "We'll rest soon. Just act like a drunken reveler, and no one will notice us."

"That shouldn't be a problem," she muttered, her arms wrapped around her middle.

Now that we were on solid land, I thanked Mynastra for the storm. Dawn was surely upon us, despite the storm's darkness, which meant the Shadow-Wolves would be slinking out of the city and back into their Den. The day guards would care little for straggling revelers. Especially in the half-drowned Docks.

Kiera followed close behind me as I weaved through the haphazard streets. Maz and Ruru flanked us, singing a bawdy sea shanty. Random bone-rattlers cheered and joined the song for a moment as we passed. Maz belted out the words, slightly off-key, and nudged me to join in, but I shook my head.

"Oh, come on, Aiden!" Maz said, adding a drunken slur. He swaggered closer to Kiera. "He has the most beautiful singing voice. Go on, tell him to sing."

Kiera looked like she'd rather eat the broken bottles in the gutter.

I feel the same, little thief.

I turned a corner sharply and charged ahead to the dilapidated house I rented a room in. Chipped stone and moldy wood held it together, but it was dry inside and the owner didn't ask questions, which was all I needed.

I shoved the door open with my shoulder and ushered Kiera and Ruru inside. "Hold a moment, Maz."

He nodded. I shut the door, then walked a few feet away. We hovered under the building's eave. A steady stream of water poured between us and the street, conveniently muffling our voices from any passerby.

"What did you find?" he asked.

"Enough." Grimly, I recounted everything up until I was caught.

"Fucking Four," Maz breathed, dropping his head back on the wall. "We need more gold."

A sardonic chuckle escaped my lips. "Which is what I told Kiera I was looking for in there."

Maz's eyebrow lifted. "And she believed that?"

"Why not? It's true enough, as you said."

"Everything comes back to gold in this bloody city," Maz grumbled. "We already pay a fortune in bribes, and you keep picking up strays." He jabbed his thumb toward the door.

"She won't be staying," I said.

"Why not?"

"I don't trust her, and we have enough people who need our help. She seems like she can take care of herself, anyway."

Maz gave me a long look. "She unchained you back there."

"To help save her own skin."

"And yours, it seems. She's a good one. I feel it in my gut." He rubbed his stomach as if that was where all his wisdom resided.

I shook my head, staring into the rain. I wasn't sure what she was. But *my* gut told me Kiera wanted something from me, whether she unchained me out of pity or necessity. As such, she was a threat. A rogue spark dancing through the air, ready to start a fire wherever it landed.

"How did she get in your cell?" he asked.

"She arrived *after* my interrogation."

"Ah, that's why you don't trust the pretty one. What was her story?"

I told him what she'd told me.

Maz nodded along, frowning. "Seems likely enough. Whoever brought her in wasn't gentle."

"She claims Renwell beat her. Same as me." The man's twisted sneer and cold eyes blinked into my mind. Gods, that face always heralded death and pain.

"Damn that bastard to the deepest, darkest corner of the wandering hell," Maz snarled. "If I ever get my hands on that maniac—"

I smirked. "What, no axe for his worthless neck?"

Maz crossed his arms with a vicious smile. "You didn't let me finish. There are a great many ways to kill a man, and I have plenty of weapons to explore each one." He patted the whistler at his hip.

"His time will come," I promised. "But I told him nothing."

"I'm surprised he didn't dump you on Korvin's table."

"He still wouldn't have his answers." But my stomach twisted at the thought. I'd seen the remnants of Korvin's handi-work—barely enough to fill a bucket. I hated to think of the ones we didn't find.

Maz frowned. "Then why leave you be? What was his plan?"

"He found something else to threaten me with." The skin on my shoulder twitched involuntarily.

Maz rolled his shoulder as if his scar was twinging as well. Understanding filled his gaze. "I see. Then if we hadn't come to get you tonight—"

"I would be boarding a different boat about now."

"Gods damn it, Aiden, if we hadn't gotten to you in time, if those Wolves had gotten us . . ."

"I know," I said quietly.

He heaved a sigh. "You know I'd do anything for you, Aiden. But I told my mother and my sisters I would come home to them. That *we* would make it back. Which means no more crazy plans. We have to get through this alive, together. That was the deal."

"I know," I repeated, my voice harder. The ridges of guilt, of failure, were impossible to soften. He was here to honor an oath he made when I'd broken *him* out of a prison.

But I also had promises to keep. And I'd failed too many times already. I couldn't let anything—or anyone—steal my victory. I'd tried to impress that warning on Kiera, even though it was a silly game we played. Then she'd stolen from me with a sparkle in her eyes. That gleam of the triumph I fought so hard for.

You didn't learn your lesson, little thief. But you will.

"What would you say to one final crazy plan?" I asked Maz. "Something far more enticing than traipsing through the Den's backwater?"

"I'd say I'm not surprised, but very intrigued. As long as it doesn't involve me sacrificing my only other axe," he added morosely.

I grinned. "No. But you could certainly afford to buy another one if we pull this off . . ."

CHAPTER 7
KIERA

I'D NEVER BEEN SO WET AND MISERABLE IN MY LIFE.

The moment Aiden shut the door between us, I wanted to sink to a puddle on the floor and sleep for several days. Preferably in dry clothes, but I would take a dry blanket at this point. Something to simply cocoon myself in and forget the last few hours. Especially the worsening ache in my ribs.

Every time I drew breath, pain crackled through my torso. Vomiting what little food I had left in my stomach had nearly made me black out. Hopefully, Mynastra didn't take offense to my putrid offering.

Ruru pattered around the dark room, turning up the oil lamp hanging from the ceiling and rummaging through a crate in the corner. A couple of hammocks were strung from the wooden posts that supported the ceiling. A wise forethought as the dirt floor pooled with water here and there, sinking beneath my boots. A wash basin stood in the corner. Two shelves high on the stone wall held a few tins.

"Whose place is this?" I asked, my voice a croak. My throat was ablaze with thirst, and my tongue felt furry.

"Aiden's, I guess," Ruru answered, still digging through the crate. "We just use it when we need to catch a wink or hold our cargo. Ah, here they are." He proudly held up a brown, long-sleeved shirt and a pair of darker brown pants. "I figure some of my clothes would fit you best. Anything from Maz or Aiden would fall right off." He grinned, and I grimaced my way into a smile.

"What cargo do you ship?" I asked, wringing out my soggy hair.

I glanced up when Ruru remained quiet. A frown creased his young face. "I'm not supposed to say."

Of course, it wouldn't be that easy.

I shrug. "Then you shouldn't. And I can't take your clothes, Ruru. You're soaked through. I'll take a blanket, if you have it. Or something to dry myself with."

He shook his head, his unkempt brown hair falling into his eyes. "I really don't need these. I'm used to being out in all kinds of weather. Anyway, I have more clothes at the Old Quarter apartment."

Aiden had two hideouts? If he had two, he could have more. To store more "cargo"? I prayed Ruru wouldn't tell Aiden I'd asked about it.

Ruru's eyes narrowed at me. "They're clean, if that's what you're worried about. Sophie uses soap and everything." He gave the shirt a sniff as if to make sure he was right. "Yep. She calls it lavender. That's a flower."

I suppressed a smirk. "I've heard of it. Well, if you insist, I would be deeply grateful."

His thin shoulders straightened, and his voice deepened as if he were trying to show me the man he wanted to be one day. "I do insist."

"That's twice you've helped me then. Thank you, Ruru. For everything."

Even in the pale light, I could see the crimson blush creeping up his smooth cheeks. Such a tender heart for one trailing along with the likes of Aiden and Maz. How long before that tenderness was beaten out of him by this life? I'd only been a few years older than him when it happened to me.

As he handed me the clothes, my stomach clenched. Where his left thumb should be was a mess of puckered flesh.

He followed my gaze. "Oh, a guard chopped that off about three years ago. Caught me stealing some sticky bread. That's actually how I met Aiden." He waggled his other thumb at me, flashing a thin white scar along the knuckle. "The guard almost got this one too when Aiden barreled into him out of nowhere and told me to run."

I frowned. "And then he just took you in?"

"I *work* for him. He said I had skills he could use. Whatever errands he needs running, I do them faster and better than any kid in Aquinon. He pays the best, too." He smiled, bouncing on the balls of his feet. "Now, I can buy sticky bread whenever I want. As well as treats for the little ones at the orphanage I used to live at."

Shrewd of Aiden to use a young, indebted boy to do his bidding. But for what errands? Did they have something to do with the cargo Ruru mentioned? Aiden sounded more like a merchant in need of funding rather than a rebel seeking gold for an army. But there was still the tricky matter of him disguising himself like a Shadow-Wolf and breaking into the Den. Down-on-their-luck merchants didn't do that.

"Speaking of food," Ruru rambled on, "would you like some crackers? Or dried fruit? My stomach's flapping against my backbone. That's what Maz always says."

A weak chuckle escaped me. His cheerful chatter reminded me of Delysia. Gods, I wished I could've said good-bye. She was probably wrapped up with her lover in front of a warm fire, a platter of fresh food available at the tug of a bell cord. Or she'd already smuggled him out and was enjoying her sleep with a smile.

Be safe, little sister. May your dreams stay sweet.

"Kiera?"

I roused myself, blinking at Ruru. Gods, I needed sleep. "I'll take a few crackers. My stomach feels like it's inside out *and* wrapped around my backbone." Ruru laughed. "But I should probably change first. Do you think they'll be outside for a while?" I nodded toward the door. I couldn't hear their voices over the rain, and I didn't want to try with Ruru watching me.

"Could be. Maz probably wants to know what happened." Ruru popped open a metal tin and shoved a cracker in his mouth. "What *did* happen in there? Did you see a Wolf? Did you get tortured? Did you have to kill anyone to escape?"

I sighed. Suddenly, I was less amused by his wagging tongue.

"Does that hurt?" he asked, pointing to his own cheek. I assumed he meant where Renwell had slashed me with my belt. It'd bled more than the scratch I'd received from Father's ring.

"My face feels mostly numb now," I admitted. A mercy that wouldn't last. "I was a prisoner, like Aiden. I did see Shadow-Wolves. No, I didn't kill anyone."

But Maz and Aiden had. Between Aiden treading through a puddle of blood and him and Maz stabbing the other Wolf to death, I had more nightmares to add to my repertoire.

I wasn't sure who I'd wanted to win between Aiden and the Wolf. Perhaps Aiden's mysterious plot would've died with him. Or the Wolf would've simply pruned a branch from a flourishing tree of treason. But that thought wasn't the first one I had as I watched the Wolf's knife dive toward Aiden's chest.

Loud chewing distracted me from my thoughts. Ruru's wide eyes blinked at me like an owl's. In my exhaustion, my emotions were probably written all over my face.

"How did Aiden get caught?" I asked nonchalantly as I dumped my borrowed clothes into the nearest hammock.

"Don't know." Ruru devoured another cracker. "Maz came to get me, saying we had to help Aiden. So here I am." As if breaking a prisoner out of the Den was just another errand on his list.

What was it like to earn such loyalty? I didn't have anyone who would rescue me from a prison. Renwell would've never let me inside one I couldn't break out of. Everett and Delysia would probably send guards after me if I were in trouble. Father? He might've put me there in the first place—with no escape.

Mother . . . Mother wouldn't have crossed Father if it was his doing—something I'd hated her for in my darkest moments. But she would've never left my side, as had been her way many times before when I was in trouble.

But now I had no one.

I leaned against the post, eyeing the laces on my boots. Gods, this was going to hurt. With Renwell's blows peppering my rib cage and that damn jailer kicking me twice, my torso felt like a tree trunk someone had taken a dull axe to. The escape and retching over the side of the boat hadn't helped, either.

Taking a deep breath, I bent over, reaching for the laces. Blinding pain seared through my ribs. I gritted my teeth. My fingers trembled as they tore out the knot. Steamy sweat gathered under my damp hair. Shadows purpled my vision until I yanked off the boot with a strangled curse. I slid down the post to sit in a heap on the ground.

"Kiera! What's wrong?" Ruru rushed to crouch beside me, the cracker tin still clutched in his fist.

I tipped my head back, trying to steady my breathing. "I think that bastard hit me harder than I thought."

"Who? A Wolf?"

No, my mentor.

"I'll be fine," I muttered. "Just give me a moment. Is there any water to drink?"

Ruru hurried over to the crate and uncorked a bottle from within. "It might taste a little stale, but it's good."

I would've thrust my head into the waterfall if it meant quenching my thirst. He passed it to me, and I drank deeply, the cool water easing the fire in my throat and chest, even trickling over my ribs. After taking another gulp, I wiped my mouth with the back of my hand and offered it to Ruru. He traded me a cracker.

The dry bread with a hint of salt nearly sucked all the

water back out of my mouth, but my stomach growled in appreciation.

The door banged open, and I struggled to my feet, trying not to flinch. Aiden and Maz crowded into the small room. Maz jammed the uneven door closed as Aiden's eyes immediately fell to me.

"What were you doing on the floor?" he asked.

I opened my mouth to tell him I was merely resting, but Ruru spoke faster. "Some bastard beat her pretty good."

Aiden's dark eyebrows lowered like a storm cloud. "You said you weren't hurt."

"I said I would live," I muttered. Louder, I added, "I didn't slow you down, did I? That's what counts."

Aiden breathed heavily through his nostrils, as if he were straining to control his patience. Maz walked past him, casting a sly glance between us.

I folded my arms over my chest, trying to keep from shivering. Whether it was from my damp clothing, or the chilly gaze Aiden swept over me, I couldn't say. His eyes held fast to my discarded boot. Without a word, he knelt in front of me and beckoned. "Give me your other boot."

I blinked, not sure I heard him correctly. "Excuse me?" This was ridiculous.

His bright green eyes stared up at me, and I forgot how to breathe. Water droplets slipped from his hair, over his flexing throat, to escape down his chest.

"Unless you want to injure yourself further, give me your boot."

My leg shifted of its own accord and planted my boot heel in his palm. With gentleness I hadn't thought possible from someone who had savagely murdered two Wolves *barefoot*, Aiden pulled apart my laces and worked my boot off.

Heat trembled in my stomach. For only a moment. As soon as my toes were clear, I pulled my foot away from him. "I'm not helpless," I snarled, but the words lacked bite.

He tossed the boot aside and rose to his feet in a heartbeat. "Helpless is better than foolish."

"Good thing I'm neither."

His jaw flexed, and he walked away. Maz tossed him a dry shirt, having already plucked one out for himself. Ruru was back to scrounging through the food tins. Aiden tugged on the shirt, giving me only the smallest glimpse of the strange markings on his back.

My nose scrunched in frustration. I desperately wanted to see what they were, but the likelihood of catching him shirtless again would be slim. Hopefully.

Maz stripped off his wet shirt, and I gasped. Intricate patterns and symbols in dark ink coated his muscular body as if his skin were a canvas or a page in a book.

Maz's eyebrows lifted. "See something you like, lovely?"

I ignored his flirtatious tone. "You're a Dag."

"Have you never seen one of us before?" He did a slow turn for me under the light. The image of a mountain took up most of his back with many other symbols woven around it. A tangle of scars marked his left shoulder, similar to Aiden. Had they been scarred by the same thing or same person?

"No." I'd never stepped foot out of Aquinon. The Dags were our closest neighbors—if that was a term one could use for people who raided our border as they pleased. I wracked my brain, trying to remember if they were even allowed passage in Rellmira anymore.

"Then I'm glad to be your first," Maz said, his smile strained for the first time. "And may I say I'm an excellent representation of my people."

"All Dags have tattoos? Why?"

Maz traced a long tree tattoo on his forearm. "We believe that stitching our stories into skin helps the gods find our souls when our bodies are burned in death. The more stories you've lived, the more your soul has to show the gods."

A strangely fascinating tradition. Was that what Aiden had on his back? A story to cover the scar they shared? I glanced at him, but he busied himself by tucking his shirt into his pants.

"Is it . . . safe for you here?" I asked Maz.

His huge shoulders hunched. "As long as I keep my hair cut and my skin covered, no one much notices." He pulled on a long-sleeved shirt, then ran a hand through his blond hair. "You should see me with my grown hair and braids, like a true Dag warrior," he said wistfully.

Why not go home then? I almost asked, but decided against it, seeing the scowl on Aiden's face.

"What will your next tattoo depict?" I asked instead.

Maz's grin came back in full force. "My lost axe. A tragic sacrifice for a heroic rescue."

I winced, the explosion of metal ringing in my memory. Renwell never told me sunstone knives could do *that*.

"I want one too!" Ruru piped up. "But can I have a bolt of lightning or something?"

Maz smirked and ruffled Ruru's hair. "You'd have to come with me to Dagriel to find a stitcher first."

I glanced over to see Aiden watching me. Did he think I would run for the nearest guard and tell him all about Maz?

Lifting my chin, I announced, "I think I'd like a key."

Aiden quirked an eyebrow. "In memory of your thievery? Interesting."

"Or in memory of a moment of pity," I retorted.

His face darkened. "A regrettable moment, surely."

For him or for me? Gods damn it, what was I doing? I was supposed to be earning his favor, wheedling my way into his life and his secrets. Not antagonizing him.

"I don't regret it," I said softly, rubbing my sore wrists. His must feel the same. I swallowed my anger and pride like a poison. "You were right. My plan to escape would've failed. I owe the three of you my life."

Aiden looked away as if my gratitude made him uncomfortable, but Maz beamed. "You saved us valuable time with your little stolen key, lovely."

I bared my teeth in a smile. "Ah, yes, my thievery. If it weren't for my sleight of hand, Aiden might not have protected me from the jailer. Which I also thank you for," I added, glancing at Aiden.

His eyes met mine, hard and glittering. "I didn't know you had the key until I saw you shove it in your mouth *after* I pulled you behind me."

Lies, I wanted to scoff back. The poison bubbled in the back of my throat. No one put themselves in harm's way without wanting something back. He'd wanted to release the other prisoners. He'd saved Ruru from further maiming. He'd helped rescue me.

But there was always a further goal beyond a noble deed. Even if it was to simply assuage a guilty conscience.

Silence leaked through the room like water from the storm while Aiden and I glared at each other. Why was he making it so gods-damn hard to be friendly?

Finally, Maz cleared his throat. "Perhaps we should rest a bit, eh? Ruru, you'd best change your clothes."

"I gave them to Kiera."

"I told him he didn't have to," I said quickly.

Maz waved me off. "No matter. Can you dress yourself?"

Aiden's face went stony while mine flamed. "Yes," I snapped.

Maz chuckled. "Pity. How about everyone turns around, yes? Pick a wall to stare at and mind your own business."

I waited until the three of them faced away before I turned my back to them. Wriggling out of my wet clothes was a bit easier than my boots, but I was panting and sweating again by the time I was done.

"How's it coming, Kiera?" Maz called out.

"Got any more of that sleeping poison?" I grumbled.

Maz laughed, but it was Aiden who answered. "I have something that will help."

My stomach flipped over. "I'm dressed now."

We all turned around at the same time.

I frowned at Maz and Aiden. "You aren't going to change your pants?"

"Nah, we'll sleep without them," Maz said.

My eyebrows shot up.

His smile turned playful. "What, do you sleep fully clothed, princess?"

"Don't call me that," I snapped. Gods, that was the *last* nickname I needed. "As a bodyguard, I had to be ready at a moment's notice. So, no, not a lot of time for lounging in bed naked."

"Well, now's your chance—"

"Enough, Mazkull." Aiden's voice lashed like a whip. "You forget."

Instead of arguing, Maz glanced at him, and they had a strange, wordless conversation between themselves. Something I'd been able to do with my brother and sister when we were younger.

Maz abruptly nodded, facing me again. "You're right. Forgive me, Kiera. That was brutish of me, considering what you've been through."

Aiden must have told him the story about Julian. I waved away his apology. "Nothing to forgive. I . . . I think I just need to rest." And not say anything else I'd regret.

"Of course," Maz said quickly. "Take one of the hammocks."

Aiden stepped closer to me. "First, let me check your ribs."

I wrapped my arm protectively around them. "No."

"I need to make sure they aren't cracked."

"Let him, Kiera," Ruru spoke up from the corner where he'd made a nest of blankets to curl up in. "He knows healing."

"Learned from the best." Maz slapped Aiden on the back, clearly forgetting Aiden's wounds until Aiden winced. "Fucking Four, sorry, brother."

"See?" I said, pointing at Aiden. "You need to take care of yourself first."

A muscle pulsed in his jaw. "Have you ever had to heal cracked ribs?"

I pursed my lips. *No.* I doubted they were little more than bruised from what my probing fingers could tell. But he might leave me behind if he thought they were worse.

"Fine," I agreed, not meeting his gaze.

Never let an enemy see how wounded you are.

But an ally would, and that was what I needed Aiden to think we were.

His next words sent a tremor through my body: "Lie down."

CHAPTER 8
KIERA

I GRITTED MY TEETH, TRYING TO HATE THE COMMAND DESPITE ITS soft delivery.

Ruru tossed me a blanket, and I shook it out over the damp earth. Hiding less of my pain, I crumpled onto the blanket and stretched out.

Aiden knelt beside me, his broad shoulders and salty scent filling my world. I turned my head away and stared at the post near my head.

Warm, roughened fingers slipped under my shirt, grazing the skin on my stomach. I twitched but didn't move away. His touch traveled over my rib cage in firm strokes. Like a healer's would. Pursuing facts rather than feeling as a lover might. I relaxed.

"No breaks, no cracks," he murmured. "May I see your skin to check the bruising?"

"Yes," I whispered.

My shirt glided upward as if drawn by a breeze. He made a low noise in his throat that made me tense again.

"What is it?"

"You're going to be quite sore for the next few days." He paused, and I snuck a glance at his face. Rage, like what he'd shown as the Wolf was chaining me to the wall, harshened his features. "Renwell did this?"

"And the jailer."

His eyes flashed to mine, and that ominous heat crawled back into my belly. "They will pay, Kiera. I swear on my soul."

I shivered. Holy Four, how did he do that? "I'm no one to you," I whispered.

"You are everyone," he whispered back. "Everyone I'm fighting for."

I blinked. What in the deep, dark, wandering hell did that mean? Fighting whom for what? Was he admitting to being a rebel?

His thumb stroked my skin, and I forgot everything else.

Before I could react, he glared down at my skin and jerked his hand away as if appalled it had done such a thing. He pulled down my shirt and walked away without another word.

I stared after him, thoroughly confused.

Maz and Ruru filled the room with their snores, a noise I had somehow missed in the last few moments.

Maz had slumped against the wall next to Ruru, but Aiden kicked his boot. "Take the hammock. I'll keep watch."

Maz grunted and slung his bulk into one of the hammocks. Aiden dug something out of the crate and stalked back to me.

He thrust a flat tin into my hands. "Salve for your bruises. It'll ease the pain and help you sleep."

I opened my mouth to ask what was in it, but he cut me off. "You can try to sleep in the hammock, but it will probably make the pain worse. I recommend staying where you are." He untied the empty hammock and draped it over my lap. "That's the best I can do."

"Thank"—he turned away and slipped out the door— "you."

Was my presence truly so repulsive that he couldn't even stay in the room? He likely regretted bringing me here. I wondered of his plan—and if I'd already managed to fail my task.

Questions burned through my mind until they were wisps of smoke I couldn't see in the darkness of exhaustion. If only I could chase after him and demand answers. But if torture and imprisonment hadn't worked, neither would demands.

I pried open the tin. A yellowish jelly-like substance gleamed inside. It smelled bitter with a hint of spice I couldn't name. I smeared a thin layer of it across my rib cage and noticed an immediate coolness to my skin. I nearly whimpered with relief.

Maybe I could wait for him to come back. Make sure he didn't do anything without my knowing. Maybe . . .

A door slamming startled me awake. I tried to sit up and immediately fell back.

"Gods damn it," I moaned, the pain in my ribs crackling to life. I rubbed the grit out of my eyes and licked the dried salt from my lips.

"A pleasant afternoon to you as well, little thief."

Memories came flooding back to me at the sound of his voice—the same one that had haunted my dreams. I managed to push myself to a sitting position. Light peeked through the cracks in the door, filtering around Aiden's figure.

What did he look like in true daylight? He was wearing the same clothes as before and was still barefoot. He looked like any other bone-rattler who'd rolled out of a hammock after a long night of celebrating. I cringed to think how I looked.

I glanced around, if only to avoid Aiden's prying gaze. "Where are Ruru and Maz?"

"Maz is getting food and water and checking to see if anyone is on high alert for escaped prisoners. And Ruru had things to do, but he told me to tell you goodbye."

My gaze jumped back to his. "Goodbye? Will I not see him again?"

Aiden leaned against the door, my only way out. "No."

I nearly growled in frustration. "Why not?"

"Because you set sail in two hours on the evening tide."

Anger pumped blood and energy through my veins. I shot to my feet. "I'm not sailing anywhere."

He gave me a long, emotionless look. "Yes, you are. To Eloren. My captain will drop you at a friendly port where you can live your life, free and without pursuit."

What? Was that what he'd been doing while I slept? Booking me passage on a ship out to the pirate-infested isles?

"But first, you will tell me everything you know about the High Treasurer's vault."

My heart sang with triumph that he'd taken the bait even as my pride bristled. "I *will?* Is this the payment required for my safe passage?" Not that I would be going anywhere. *Never leave the city* had been another of Renwell's rules.

He frowned. "No. You will have safe passage, regardless."

I folded my arms over my chest. "Then perhaps you should ask me instead of commanding me. I don't work for you."

A slow smile curled his lips. "Would you obey me then? Because it sounds as though you weren't any better at following orders from those you did work for."

He meant Julian. I looked away. "There are some commands that I will never obey."

"And you are stronger for it."

I glanced at him in surprise. No one had ever praised me for disobedience. Quite the opposite. It was strange. He provoked my temper so quickly, yet he could soothe it to embers in the same argument. I couldn't figure him out as easily as I could others.

Which made him the most dangerous.

A heavy thump sounded against the door. Aiden opened it to let in Maz, whose hands were full of a few loaves of bread and a jug of water. An orange bulged out of his pocket.

His blue eyes lit up when he spotted me. "Lovely, you're awake!" He looked between the two of us. "Did I miss something?"

I smiled sweetly. "Aiden was just about to *ask* for more information concerning the High Treasurer's vault."

A snort of derision came from Aiden, and Maz narrowed his eyes at him. "You said you would wait for me."

"And I have," Aiden said. "She's told me nothing more."

Both men looked at me, but I was distracted by the smell of freshly baked bread.

"Food first," I said.

We settled on the floor. Maz broke the loaves into pieces and passed them out. One loaf was sweet with cinnamon, the other riddled with herbs and garlic. Was the choice lucky or purposeful? Perhaps an attempt to bolster my good will.

Either way, I didn't question it. I gobbled down every morsel they handed me. Washing down the warm bread with cold water tasted better than the finest banquet I'd ever had at the palace. I savored the orange's juicy flesh like I might never taste one again.

"Anything?" Aiden asked Maz as they also devoured their portions.

Maz shook his head, his cheeks bulging. "Not a whisper."

Aiden's gaze went distant, thoughtful.

"Is that strange?" I asked. "Wouldn't they alert the day guards and the harbor towers?" Unless Renwell was keeping it quiet because of me. But that only looked more suspicious.

"One can never be too sure with the High Enforcer," Aiden said. "He's always playing one game or another. It could be that he thinks we're dead. Or he can't admit to anyone outside the Den that two prisoners escaped his legendary clutches."

The hatred in Aiden's tone sent a chill down my spine. Was it simply because of what Renwell had done to him in the Den?

"I say it's a boon from Mynastra," Maz announced. "Now, let's talk about the gold."

I almost smiled at his eagerness. He would be crestfallen when whatever plan they had failed. Renwell would never allow them to steal from Father. I just needed the plan to take long enough to discover what Aiden was *really* doing in Aquinon and then escape before they found out who I was and what I'd done.

That thought brought me comfort as I spread my hands wide. "What do you want to know?"

Aiden's eyes pierced me, his relaxed posture belying the intensity in his eyes. "You said you watched Asher show the vault to the prince and princesses. But did you see how exactly he opened it? How many guards were there?"

"Only one guard because Asher thinks the door is unbreachable. He keeps the key around his neck at all times. Never takes it off." I paused. "And the vault door has several false locks that, if tripped, will require a key from the king to unlock."

"Do you know which is the right keyhole?" Maz asked.

I swallowed hard and nodded, the door gleaming in my memory. "Yes . . . if I saw it again."

"And how would you do that?" Aiden demanded.

"By helping you unlock it, of course."

Maz grinned and eased back against the wall, licking his fingers, while Aiden leaned forward with a glare. "Absolutely not."

"Why not? You need someone who can get close enough to Asher to steal the key without tipping him off. And you need someone who's seen the vault door to unlock it. That's *me*." I tapped one of my sore cheeks. "What is it again you like to keep calling me? Oh, yes. Little thief. Well, Aiden, it appears you have need of one."

Maz hooted with laughter, slapping his thigh. "Ah, fucking Four, I'll take her on if you don't, brother."

The fury in Aiden's eyes scorched the air between us, and I basked in the heat. I'd neatly played him, and he knew it. *Looks like I win again.*

But then his expression shifted, calmed. My skin prickled in warning.

"If you are telling the truth and if I allow you to join us, you will be working for me, obeying my orders." He gave me a serpentine smile. "Is that something you can do?"

My stomach turned over. I hated the idea of being under his thumb. But it was the only way. "I will never harm anyone for you. Or allow harm to come to myself beyond what I deem necessary."

Disgust hardened his face. "I wouldn't command anything of the sort."

"Then it shouldn't—"

"*But*," he cut in, "I would require you to live with us and be under our watch at all times."

I balked. How would I ever report to Renwell? "Why?"

"I don't trust you." He gestured to the door. "And if that's a problem, then you can leave now on a ship bound for Eloren. You will be safer there."

Safer for you. I knew things now that he didn't want me to know. About Maz, about this hideout, about *him*. I could turn them all in. He was right not to trust me, but I had to convince him he could. Otherwise, I would never find out what he'd been doing in the Den or why he was so desperate for gold.

"I have no money," I said carefully, "and the only skills I possess would land me in other unsavory jobs. All that in a foreign world. How is that safer?"

His jaw clenched. "A city where the High Enforcer and his Wolves will be hunting you is far more dangerous than the unknown. Especially when you plan to steal from another High Councilor."

"If it's so dangerous, then why don't you leave?" I demanded, jabbing my finger at both Aiden and Maz. "*You* stole from them and killed two Wolves."

Maz threw up his hands as if to defend himself, but Aiden beat him to it. "I *can't* leave," he snarled. "I've evaded them for years while you've never lived outside the palace. You won't survive here."

"Not without you," I reminded him bitterly.

"Even then, I can't promise anything." Aiden sat back into the shadows. "You would be safer far from here, Kiera."

He would give up his chance at the gold to keep me out of Aquinon? What game was this? I frowned and glanced at Maz, who shifted uncomfortably.

"What he means is, we've seen a lot of suffering and death," Maz said. "We don't want to see you get hurt."

Or you simply want me out of the way to conduct your crimes.

"I'm staying," I said. "I want my fair share of the gold. I want to take it from the bastards who did this to me." I swallowed. "To Julian."

"Then you'll leave right after the heist," Aiden replied. "That gold will buy you a life anywhere you want . . . and your silence." He stood and slowly extended his hand from the shadows. An offering, a promise.

I rose to my feet and stepped into the shadows with him. "Deal."

I placed my hand in his, and he gripped it as hard as I did.

"Then we have work to do, little thief."

CHAPTER 9
KIERA

I HATED WAITING. AND YET, HERE I WAS, DOING IT AGAIN.

Aiden and Maz had left hours ago, and Ruru had taken the position of my keeper instead. The boy had been elated that I was staying, and he was a much nicer jailer than my last one. But that didn't change the situation.

From one cell to another, I thought grimly, lying on my dirty blanket. I doubted Aiden would appreciate the sentiment.

He'd told me to "rest and heal" as he left me here under Ruru's cheerful watch. More like "keep quiet and out of the way as I handle matters I don't want you to witness."

Earning Aiden's trust would take time, but by the Four, I would have him wrapped around my finger by the end of this. Then his secrets would be mine for the taking. If he was a threat to the safety of my family or the security of my kingdom, it was my duty to destroy him.

I glanced at Ruru, who was busy tying knots into a length

of rope. Perhaps I could keep him out of whatever consequences befell Aiden.

After the cries of seagulls faded with the light, the door finally banged open. Ruru jerked upright, his knotted rope tumbling to the floor.

I merely glanced at Aiden's dark features from where I rested. But a tremor of anticipation curled through my chest at his appearance. He wore a long cloak over his shoulders, the hood drawn up over his dark hair. The hem fluttered around dark, scuffed boots. He held another cloak in his fist. For me?

His eyes flickered to me first, as if to make sure I was still there, then focused on Ruru.

"Sophie's got dinner for you," he told Ruru.

"Thank the Four," Ruru said, scrambling to his feet. He waved at me. "Be seeing you, Kiera."

I gave him a stiff smile. "I'm sure."

He disappeared as I clambered to my feet. Aiden watched me carefully. A strange, tense silence enveloped us like thick, sticky honey. Gods, I was hungry again.

"No dinner for me?" I quipped.

"Not yet. We have somewhere to be first." He handed me the cloak. "Are you rested enough for a long walk?"

"I've had all day," I said dryly. I pressed my fingers to my ribs. They still ached, but the pain was less sharp. "What was that salve you gave me? It worked wonders."

He didn't answer immediately. He always seemed to be weighing the risk of giving me information, even as innocuous as this. Unless I provoked him. Which I certainly looked forward to doing again.

"People call it Viridana's Kiss in honor of the goddess," he said. "Made from certain root powders and plant sap, it numbs the skin and speeds the re-gathering of blood."

I blinked in surprise.

The ghost of a smile played over his lips. "In other words, it heals deep bruises quickly."

"How do you know so much about healing? And where did you did get this medicine? I've never seen it before."

His face shuttered. "Never mind that. Are you ready?" He cast his gaze over me from head to toe.

I'd changed back into my dried clothes and laced my boots on my feet while I'd waited. I'd also combed my tangled, salty hair with my fingers and braided it down my back.

"Where are we going?"

"To corroborate your story," he said, yanking the door open.

My breath stilled. My story about the vault or about who I was? It had to be the vault as he would have no way to investigate the other. Unless he checked the city prison for recent executions or had someone inside the palace who could tell him if I'd really been a bodyguard.

Gods damn it. Renwell had assured me such a thing wouldn't be possible. But what if it was?

"What story?" I demanded, throwing on the cloak he'd given me.

He looked down at me. "About Asher and the vault."

Relief washed over me. "It's not a story. It's the truth."

"All the same," he said, gesturing out the door.

Ah yes, you don't trust me. I pulled my hood over my head, feeling a sense of ease in its shadow.

I slipped past him and caught a whiff of soap and mint.

Had he bathed while I was stuck in this hole? Perhaps if I started to stink enough, he would see fit to let me out of his sight for a few moments to savor a bath for myself.

Together, we stepped into the sultry twilight of the Docks Quarter. I took a deep breath of the briny air and glanced up at the violet sky already salted with stars.

"The Wolves won't be out yet, but we should hurry," Aiden said, his words stealing the warmth from the air.

I nodded, and we strode through the tangle of streets until we came to the bottom of the cliff road.

I suppressed a groan, looking up at the steep path ahead. A few supply wagons and pedestrians dotted the rocky edges.

Aiden didn't wait for me, just kept marching.

He probably has the thighs of a god if he does this trek a lot, I grumbled to myself, remembering the very detailed sculpture of the gods Terraum and Arduen in the palace. As young girls, Delysia and I had giggled over their muscled physiques and bulging manhoods.

My eyes darted involuntarily to Aiden's lower half as he walked ahead of me, but his cloak covered up anything interesting.

Not that you should be thinking anything *of the sort.*

I forced my gaze away and looked out over the harbor instead.

Torches and lamps were already glowing as the sun melted on the ocean's horizon. I studied the ships bobbing at the dock. Which one was I meant to be on? Had Aiden told the captain I wasn't coming? And why had he said "my" captain?

A short, sharp whistle made my head swivel back to Aiden

who stood some distance ahead. The shift in focus made the world wobble for a moment.

"Eyes forward," Aiden said as I drew even with him. "People have fallen over the side when they get distracted."

My stomach roiled, remembering the woman tumbling over the bridge. "Understood. It's just . . . rare that I get to see a view like this."

He kept pace with me as we walked on. "The views from the palace weren't beautiful enough for you?"

I darted a glance at him, but there was no malice in his face or his voice. "They were beautiful," I said slowly. "I could see the sea, the sky, and the city, but they felt so far away. Untouchable. A mirage."

"Like they didn't truly exist but in your mind. Or a memory," Aiden said softly.

My heart tripped. "Yes. Yes, exactly." It was one of the reasons I'd started sneaking out when I was eighteen. That and I was tired of sitting around grieving for Julian—the real Julian. I wanted to feel something again.

I'd wanted to feel the city I stared at so often from my windows. To see how it'd changed since the rebellion. I'd wanted to rub shoulders with the people I watched like ants. In my wildest dreams, I wanted to discover what was beyond the city walls. But not by sea.

My churning stomach had more than its fill of the sea last night.

"Why are you smiling?"

I glanced up to see Aiden watching me. I whistled and jerked my chin. "Eyes forward, Aiden."

His eyes widened, then he tilted his head back and laughed. Warmth fluttered under my skin. His laugh was rich and deep and too short. He cut it off as if surprised he'd done it at all.

"As you say, little thief," he said. "If you tell me why you were smiling."

Holy Four, was he *flirting*? Or he just couldn't stand to give something without getting something.

But talking to him made me forget the growing burn in my legs and ribs. I normally had reasonable endurance from Renwell's training, but I would gladly sink this road to the depths of the Abyss.

"I was smiling because I was thinking of how I got much too close of an experience with the sea last night," I said. "Enough to last me a long, long time."

"Ah, the true reason you wish to remain here. Your fear of the waves."

I scowled at him. "Being rich would go a long way to calming that fear."

"It had better."

We lapsed into silence once more. It seemed we couldn't get into any sort of conversation without our words becoming knives we used to chip away at the truth. Until he trusted me, *wanted* me to stay, we would continue to circle and stab at each other.

At long last, we crested the top of the cliff and passed through the gate into the Market Quarter.

The quarter was much busier this time. Vendors selling off the last of their food or haggling down final deals for their wares. Wagons loading or unloading supplies. Women beating the day's dust from rugs. Children chasing each other through the chaos.

I kept close to Aiden's boot heels as he wove his way toward the Noble Quarter gate. I hesitated as it came into sight. He must have a very well-connected source if he was going to verify my information in there.

I used to have connections as well. When I started sneaking out of the palace, I had made friends with some of the bridge and Noble Quarter gate guards who would look the other way. A few of them I became quite a bit more intimate with. When Father found out, he commanded Renwell to "take care" of the guards. I hadn't seen them since.

Soon after, on one of the rare occasions I'd beaten Renwell at Death and Four, my prize was the answer to what happened to those guards. He refused to say anything other than that they'd been demoted to border patrol. For simply looking the other way or for the crime of touching me without Father's permission.

I didn't speak to Father for weeks after that.

But perhaps Aiden had struck up a few friendships of his own among the guards.

The gate was ablaze with light from a dozen torches, giving the guards a clear view of who was coming and going. They stopped each person, demanding their name and business in the quarter.

"Gods damn it," Aiden hissed, coming to an abrupt halt.

I caught up to him and peered to where he was staring at the guards. I didn't recognize any of them, but he seemed to.

"We can't go through the gate," Aiden muttered, shuffling me off to the side. Away from the small knot of people the guards were preventing from entering. "They must have already done the guard change. And if those men have descriptions of two escaped prisoners on the loose . . ."

I swallowed hard. "Right. What can we do then?"

"We'll have to go the other way," Aiden growled and shoved me down a dark, narrow alley.

"What other way?" Holy Four, there was another way in and out of the Noble Quarter? Did Renwell know about this? Possibilities rampaged through my mind.

Aiden glared down at me, his glittering green eyes vivid even in the shadows. "We can't wait for another guard change. The Wolves will be out soon. My guard won't be back on shift for days. I need the truth tonight, little thief."

I held my breath at the battle raging behind his words, the reluctance lining his taut shoulders.

"But I can't let you have this secret. Not fully," he continued, his words growing quieter. "I'll have to blindfold you."

Instinctively, I stepped back, right into a wall. He didn't pursue me.

"Why?" I rasped.

"I feel it is necessary to protect the heart of what I do. But I won't do it without your consent."

I bit my lip. He'd never hurt me or tricked me, even when he had the opportunity. He'd rescued me, healed me, fed me, kept me safe. If I ever wanted his trust, I would have to offer a slice of my own.

"I'll allow it."

He nodded. "Don't move. I'll be back."

He was gone only a few moments, reappearing with a silky

purple scarf threaded with gold. He must've bought it off one of the merchants.

He stepped forward. Close enough that I could smell him again, that salt and sunshine mixed with soap and spice. His scent and his nearness seemed to have a habit of nudging my heart into a gallop.

But I wasn't afraid.

"Turn around," he said in a husky voice.

I tried in vain to calm my breathing as I faced the cracked clay wall. He tugged the hood from my head. Silk whispered over my skin as he wound the scarf over my closed eyes. Could he feel the tremble that slithered from my head to my toes?

He finished knotting it, trailing his fingers over the ends. "Bearable?" he whispered in my ear.

No. He was torturing me. Albeit a different kind of torture than one would find in a prison. This kind incited a riot of goosebumps on the back of my neck.

I nodded, not trusting my voice.

He drew my hood back up over my head and threaded my arm through his, like we were strolling through a royal ballroom instead of shadowed alleys.

"What if someone sees us?" I murmured.

"They will not question a man leading his blind wife home." Aiden's voice sounded deeper and richer in my darkened world. And the words he spoke . . .

I stiffened. I could *not* let him think he affected me. He would use it against me, surely.

My boot struck a stone, and I clutched his arm to keep from sprawling. "How long will this take?"

"Not long."

We walked for some minutes, turning far too many times to be necessary. But I didn't comment on his misdirection, focusing instead on keeping my balance. Eventually, I stumbled less and less. I anticipated his movements by each subtle turn of his body. Like we were dancing. Gods, I hadn't danced in years.

What would it be like to dance with him? I slapped the thought away. Our story could only end in betrayal and death, not dancing.

"Wait a moment," he whispered, then dropped my arm.

His warmth disappeared. I threw out my arms to gain my bearings but met air. There was the *snick* of a lock opening. Aiden grunted as he shoved against something heavy. The croak of door hinges.

What if the blindfold were to slip just for a moment? Would he kill me for peeking? I hadn't seen any weapons on him, but that didn't mean he couldn't have concealed one somewhere. His boot or the back of his waistband, perhaps.

He'd also shown me he could cause plenty of harm without one.

Before I could decide, his hand wrapped around my arm again. "In here. Three steps down. Good. Hold still now."

I froze, not daring to move. Instead, I listened. He had moved farther away from the scraping and creaking of heavy objects being moved around.

Dust suddenly tickled my nose, triggering a violent sneeze. The sound echoed as if we were in a large, enclosed space.

"Try not to announce our location to every Shadow-Wolf in the area."

I sniffed and scowled in the direction of his wry voice. "They can't catch up to us that quickly in the Old Quarter."

His voice was suddenly so close I jumped. "Figured that out, did you."

I shrugged. "It wasn't hard. This must be an old warehouse from the feel of it. Since we need to get to the Noble Quarter, we must be in one of the warehouses located near the wall in the Old Quarter."

His breath was a warm breeze on my forehead. I tilted my chin to blindly meet his gaze.

"You can see through the scarf," he said flatly.

"No."

"Then how did you know there were warehouses here?"

"I studied maps of the city as part of my training." Which was true. "If the city was ever compromised, I needed to know where to take the royals. I remember this cluster of large warehouses near the wall."

There was a long silence, but I could still feel him inches away from me.

"I would very much like to know," he said in a deadly quiet voice, "what else was on those maps."

A tricky request. I licked my dry lips. "I can assure you that your tunnel was not on them."

"Why do you think it's a tunnel?" he asked sharply.

"What else could it be? We can't go over the wall because it's too high, and no rooftop is close enough. So, we must be going under it."

Another silence. I waited, my heart hammering in my ears.

"Clever little thief," he murmured.

"Does that mean I can remove this blindfold?"

"No." He grasped my elbow. "You may have figured out a few things, but I still have secrets to keep." He led me on a jagged path across the soft floor. Most likely avoiding obstacles. But what kind?

"Mind the stairs. Five small ones."

I edged closer as his grip tugged me downward, into the tunnel. The air grew damp and still, every sound muffled. Even though my eyes were closed under the scarf, I could *feel* the heavier darkness press around me.

How long had this tunnel been here? Aiden must use it for more than sneaking in and out of the Noble Quarter.

"Wait for me," he whispered.

My lips parted to beg him not to leave me, even for a moment in this abyss, but he was gone. Shutting the entrance behind us.

My heartbeat spun out of control, fear clawing at my throat and my insides. "Aiden?" I didn't care that my voice trembled.

Warm fingers slid around my arm. "Kiera."

"Can I take it off *now*?"

"It won't make a difference in here. But I can't let you see where we come out."

I sighed. "Just don't . . . don't let go."

"As you wish."

He pulled me forward, but we had to walk somewhat sideways to stay connected without rubbing against the uneven walls of the tunnel. Dirt and pebbles crumbled over my shoulders. The earth could swallow us whole down here. I doubted even the gods would find our souls in this pit.

I bit my lip and slid my arm through Aiden's grasp until my hand gripped his.

His steps faltered for a moment before moving faster. But he didn't let go of me.

"Why did you reveal what you knew?" he asked suddenly. "You could have said you had no idea where we were, where the tunnel might be."

"Because I have no reason to lie," I whispered. "I want you to know what sort of person you're dealing with. Just as I wish to know you."

"There is no need. We may not live long enough for it to matter, as you said last night."

"That was in a prison cell. We're free now. We could get rich and never spend another moment in dark holes as we've been in the last day."

His fingers twitched in mine. "There are darker places than this."

"Where—"

"We're here," he cut me off. "Five steps up." I followed him.

There was some scuffling and a quick curse from Aiden.

"What's wrong?" I whispered.

"It's stuck." More heaving and grunting.

Something landed on my shoulder and started crawling up my neck. I yelped and batted it away. "What was that? A spider? Holy Four, open the gods-damn door!"

"It's gone," Aiden rasped. "You're fine as long as it's not a black moss spider."

My fingers itched to rip off the scarf, Aiden's secrets bedamned. I crowded up against him, desperate to get out of this spider-infested tunnel. Something crashed, and I was jerked forward. For a moment, I was falling, still clutching Aiden's hand. I felt him twist, and we landed in a heap, my body splayed over his.

My blindfold came loose.

CHAPTER 10

KIERA

STARTLED GREEN EYES BLINKED AT ME. MY SORE RIBS PROTESTED at being crushed against Aiden's hard stomach.

A low whistle sounded. Instinctively, I turned to look, but Aiden caught my chin, forcing me to keep looking at him. My breathing grew ragged. Slowly, he lowered the scarf back over my eyes.

"Maz," he growled, "quit gawking and shut the door."

Maz chuckled, and his heavy footsteps trailed by. "What can I say, you two put on a good show. The blindfold is a particularly nice touch. What was the shrieking about?"

"An ill-timed spider attack," Aiden answered, a hint of mirth in his voice.

Cheeks warming, I quickly rolled off him, landing on a plush rug. The musty smell of the tunnel faded under the scent of melted wax and rose petals. It vaguely reminded me of Renwell—a thought that sent a rush of vigilance through my veins. I swayed to my feet.

"Not so fast," Aiden said, grabbing my biceps. He turned me in a few circles. "Now you can take off the blindfold."

I peeled the scarf away and stuffed it in my pocket, blinking in the soft candlelight. A large sitting room slowly came into focus. A gold chandelier wreathed in fat candles. Thick crimson rugs over a gleaming wood floor. Wall tapestries stitched with stories too small to decipher.

Low couches draped in silks and furs were strewn around the room. Maz lounged in one, looking as though he'd never gotten up. Aiden stood, watching me, by a slender table cluttered with glass decanters.

Where was the door we had come through?

I spun in another, slower circle but found no sign of one. It must be behind one of the many tapestries.

"Look all you want," Aiden said. "It will do you no good unless you plan on tearing this room apart."

I gave him a lethal smile, the impression his body had left on mine still disturbingly present. "Is that permission?"

His lip curled. "You wouldn't make it far."

"Can't blame me for wanting to know all the escape routes."

"Not this one," he gritted out.

I glanced at Maz. "Is he always this stubborn?"

Maz barked out a laugh. "You're just scratching the surface, lovely."

A door opened at the far end of the room, and a tall, beautiful woman stepped inside, tucking a key down her generous cleavage. Distant laughter and conversation filtered through the door before she shut it.

"You're late," she called as she glided across the room to

join us. Blue silk and gossamer gold chains swayed over the curves of her body. A mass of long, curly black hair spilled over her shoulders and down the exposed back of her silk dress. Her dark skin was flawless.

She couldn't have been more than a few years older than me, but she held herself like a queen.

"Apologies, Melaena," Aiden said. "We had to take the longer route."

"I see." Eyes of the clearest cerulean blue met mine. Her observation of me was quick and business-like. Then she smiled. "Kiera, is it? Maz told me I'd be meeting you tonight."

I nodded, trying not to look nervous. I didn't recognize her, but that didn't mean she hadn't caught a glimpse of me somewhere.

But there was only kindness in her eyes. "Welcome to my club, *The Silk Dancer*."

"You *own* this place?" I blurted out. I'd heard of *The Silk Dancer* but had never entered, figuring I would have less chance of getting recognized when I snuck out to rowdy taverns near the city gate.

I hadn't expected it to be run by someone so young. Or so pleasant, given the circumstances of our meeting.

Her smile widened, making her features glow. "Yes. I inherited it from my parents. I rather enjoy running my own business."

"And you do a beautiful job of it," Maz declared, inclining his head to her from where he sat. "I was heartbroken to miss your Mynastra's Tide performance last night."

"Yes, we understand how very busy you must be, Melaena," Aiden cut in. "So, we'll make our business quick."

She smiled at him, a fondness in her eyes that curdled like cold gravy in my stomach. "You always do," she said.

"Kiera used to be a palace guard and witnessed Asher opening the vault where he keeps a large portion of Weylin's wealth," Aiden said. "Have you seen it?"

I stiffened at how easily he gave away details to Melaena. He must trust her a great deal.

But she took it in stride. "Yes, once. He made a grand show of paying me directly from his hoard."

"How did he open it?" Aiden demanded.

"A key from a chain around his neck. But he didn't let me watch him open it. Said that was only for High Councilors and royals to know."

See? Believe me, I silently commanded Aiden as he frowned.

"Is there anything else we should know about it?" he asked.

Her red lips quirked to the side. "I've heard he sometimes keeps other things in there like important documents, payroll, sunstone, even fireseeds."

Maz bolted upright, a feral look on his face. "Fireseeds, you say? Probably stole them from Dag traders, the bastard."

The seeds were precious, harvested from the fireflowers on Arduen's Mountain once a year. Depending on how many Asher had, he could fetch a high price for them. As well as for the sunstone. Father had built much of his wealth on the highly restricted sale of the gods-given rocks.

I glanced at Aiden. His face was hidden by his hood as he paced the room. Gods, to be a fly on the wall of his mind. I'd learn everything I needed to know in a heartbeat.

He stopped and faced Melaena, every thought safely tucked away. "How is his security?"

"Tight. His mansion is walled off from the rest of the nobility with high fences and guards all around the perimeter. But there's never more than a few guards inside and only one outside the vault."

"See? I told you Kiera was telling the truth," Maz said, standing and slapping Aiden's shoulder. "How are we going to do this, then?"

I stayed quiet, my focus on Melaena. She didn't bat an eyelash at where the conversation was headed. Did they plan this sort of thing a lot?

Either way, she was the key. My gut told me that any plan from her, Aiden would take.

"If you're planning to do what I think you are," Melaena said, "then you should know that Asher is having a party in about two weeks' time. A luxurious affair for his birthday with many guests and additional hired help. He also wants us to put on a special show for him, which I agreed to. I also happen to know the woman in charge of preparations." She quirked a manicured eyebrow at Aiden. "If that helps."

"It does," he said, his eyes flitting to me. "I thought we could steal the vault key from Asher here, as I know he's a devoted patron of this club, but that presented some logistical problems. Problems that would be solved if we used his party as cover instead." He didn't look away from me as he asked, "Could Kiera join your dancers for the show?"

I gaped at him. "You must be joking. I can't be in a show." *This* was his plan? It was almost like he'd heard me thinking about dancing with him as he'd led me around blindfolded.

Melaena turned to me, giving me a more scrutinizing look. "Why not? Even if you've never danced before, I'm sure I could teach you well enough to blend in. Besides, you're beautiful, even dirty and marked up as you are. But I'm guessing a bath and a few of Aiden's healing salves would fix that."

"And we need you to get close to Asher," Aiden said, folding his arms over his chest. Something akin to disgust flickered in his eyes. "He lets Melaena's dancers get . . . very close."

My stomach rolled over.

"But you don't have to touch him," Melaena added quickly, shooting a stern look at Aiden. "We have rules here. No one does anything they don't want to do."

I threw up my hands. "Even if I could fit in with the dancers, he could recognize me."

"Never mind that," Melaena said. "I have a theme in mind that will use masks and makeup with very little clothing, so I'm sure he won't be looking at your face too closely."

Gods damn it, to be so exposed . . . dancing in front of strangers . . . pulling off a heist.

I had barely started one mission to be thrust into another within that. So many disguises, so many lies. But I supposed this was the life of a spy. I'd started myself down this path with the ill-conceived bait of Asher's vault, and now I would have to keep to it until the end or risk all the progress I'd made.

But *two weeks*? I hadn't thought how much time I would have to ingratiate myself with Aiden and his crew to discover their purpose, but now I wanted more of it.

I shook myself. It didn't matter. Once I found a way to tell Renwell what they were planning, he would put a stop to the heist—perhaps giving me more time to steal their secrets.

Aiden's jaw clenched, his eyes hard as gemstones as he stared at me. "We can find another way."

"No," I said. "It . . . it's just a lot to take in."

Someone knocked on the door. "Melaena? We're ready to start," a woman's voice called.

"Be there in a moment, Jayde!" Melaena called back. "Keep them entertained!"

"Ah, Jayde's working tonight?" Maz asked eagerly.

Melaena smirked at him. "Yes, but I'd think twice about approaching her. She knows about you and Tullia."

Maz grimaced.

"Maz's labyrinth of a love life aside," Aiden said, "what's your answer, Kiera?"

I took a deep breath. "I'll do it. But could I watch the dancers for a bit? To get an idea of what I'll be doing?"

Melaena beamed and squeezed my hands. "Absolutely! Aiden can show you where to stand without being seen." She released me, heading for the door. "I'll give your name to the gate guards, so they'll let you through for training tomorrow. Noon. Don't be late. Aiden, we'll talk more soon. And don't bother my dancers, Maz. We have a private wrap party after our show tonight that I want *all* my dancers present for."

She hurried out the door with Maz trailing her, muttering something about not being a bother backstage.

"After you," Aiden said, gesturing me out the door.

I couldn't look him in the eye as I passed. My emotions and thoughts were tangled in a thorny mess. I wanted to be alone to sort through it all, but that would never happen if Aiden had his way.

Outside the room, another door stood across the hall. But

Aiden turned down the dim corridor, and I followed him as he walked most of the way down. He swung aside a heavy tapestry to reveal a small door that looked like nothing more than a broom closet.

"This is it?" I asked in disbelief as Aiden let me inside.

"You'll see."

I scowled and swiped away a cobweb that brushed my shoulder. No spiders here, at least.

At the end of a short passage was a tightly wound staircase. We climbed to the top and reached a small balcony that clung to an upper back corner of a huge room. More candle chandeliers hung from the ceiling. It felt like I was floating above a sea of flames. A large stage draped with a crimson curtain stood opposite our balcony.

I peered over the edge where Melaena's glimmering clientele lounged on couches or around tables. Was Asher down there tonight? Or anyone else who might know me?

The balcony was clever as no one in the room below could see me unless I leaned too far over the railing while they looked straight up.

"Holy Four," I breathed. "Are there usually this many people?"

Aiden rested his elbows on the railing, gazing down at the crowd below. "Yes. Melaena's entertainments are quite popular. As well as her exceptional wine and food."

"How did you meet her?"

His gaze cut to me. "All you need to know is you can trust her."

Only as much as I can trust you. Questions burned behind

my lips. Were they friends or lovers? Was it purely professional? They clearly had a deep bond. But over what?

"Do you still want to do this?" he asked, shattering my thoughts. "Knowing your role in what is to come?"

The curtain lifted, and Melaena swept onto the stage to thunderous applause. Her voice echoed up to us, welcoming everyone.

"I do," I said. "It won't be easy. It's not a role I'm used to playing, but I learn quickly."

"I have no doubt," Aiden murmured.

I ignored him—and the flutter in my chest—and watched four other women join Melaena. Unseen drums and flutes filled the club with sweet, seductive music. As the tempo increased, the dancers twirled and leaped across the stage, spinning silk scarves around their lithe bodies. Their movements were as precise as the ones Renwell had taught me to fight.

Just with much less clothing. And a smile.

My scarred fingers curled into fists. I could do this. It was simply training. And all the while, I would be learning everything there was to know about Aiden, Melaena, and what they were up to.

"I've seen enough," I announced as the dancers left the stage to weave through the crowd. "Back to the tunnel?"

Aiden smirked down at me. "Not a chance. I don't want you —or the Wolves—seeing anything near there. We'll take the gate. The guards don't question people leaving the Noble Quarter, only those entering."

My hands swept over my hips, searching for knives that weren't there. "Will they be a problem?"

"The Wolves? One never knows. You were trained to keep silent and unseen, weren't you?"

"Yes."

His eyes glowed with a challenge. "Then let's see how well you dance with the shadows, little thief."

WE LEFT *THE SILK DANCER* VIA A SERVANT'S DOOR OFF THE MAIN lounge and quietly funneled through the Noble Quarter gate with our hoods lowered.

I wanted to ask where we were going but felt that, in doing so, I'd be failing some sort of test. Instead, I trailed a whisper behind the flap of Aiden's cloak.

He left the main road almost immediately, plunging us into a labyrinth of alleyways. I'd studied maps of the quarters but not nearly to the detail of pinpointing where I was.

My lip curled. That was probably exactly what Aiden hoped to accomplish with his twisted path.

Darkened clay buildings that had existed since the Age of Gods still radiated with the heat of the day. Doors and windows were shut tight, not even allowing a candle flame to light our path.

Shadow-Wolves patrolled the city at night, and Father always said they did an excellent job of keeping the peace. But this didn't feel like peace. This felt like silent terror. It clung to the air like a mist.

The empty dirt pathways glowed under the stars and partial moon. The silver light was tricky and elusive, the indigo shadows reigning supreme.

But just as with the tunnel, Aiden didn't falter. How long had he lived here that he knew every corner and bend of this city? Jealousy nibbled at my heart. After all, knowledge banished fear. And I wanted to not be afraid. Like him.

My boot struck a bottle, which skittered into a foul-smelling gutter. The sound was like a rock thrown through a window, shattering our illusion of safety.

I froze. As did Aiden, his hood whipping in my direction.

Gods damn it, I'd been too preoccupied with him to watch where I was going. I was used to being alone.

Moments passed, but nothing swooped in on us from the shadows. The whole quarter seemed to hold its breath, waiting.

Aiden jerked his head forward, and we continued on.

We must be getting closer to the heart of the Old Quarter. It was the largest of the four, a wide swath of pebbled dirt from above. From within, a forest of buildings one could easily get lost in. I'd heard of travelers getting lost in the dense trees and foliage of Twaryn, never to be seen again. Perhaps the same was possible in Aquinon.

Aiden pulled up short, and I skidded to a halt to keep from toppling into his back. I glanced around, eyeing the distant rooftops and window ledges, the shadows that bruised every wall. Nothing.

Then I heard it.

A scrape, a shuffle.

The hair rose on the back of my neck. My fingers desperately, fruitlessly searched for my knives again.

A low groan.

Aiden's head snapped in that direction, a sliver of a dark

alley. The shadows were a writhing mass. And they were headed our way.

Aiden seized my arm and flung us back the way we'd come, but the murmur of soft boots was too close.

A shrieking howl shattered the night behind us.

An answering scream seared my throat, but I bit down on my lower lip to keep it from escaping. Bitter blood wet my tongue.

Aiden dragged me off the path into a deep, dark corner. The crux of the buildings cradled my spine. But there was nowhere to go. Nowhere to run. My heart fought against my chest. If they found us, we would die like rats in a trap. We had to leave. *Now.*

I tried to escape Aiden's grasp, but he shoved me back and pressed his whole body against mine, fanning his black cloak around us to meld with the only thing hiding us. Darkness.

"More come," he breathed in my ear.

I peered over the edge of his cloak. Shadow-Wolves. Two of them. No, four. They were hard to count, as they were little more than walking shadows. They dragged something large and heavy between them. Something that moaned in pain.

I squeezed my eyes shut. Gods, what had this man done to be captured? Had Renwell ordered it or had the man done something to anger the Wolves?

"Jerell? Oh, blessed Four! Jerell!"

My eyes flew open at the woman's hysterical voice. *No.*

Aiden's body stiffened. I dug my fingers into one of his arms that caged me.

Never interfere with my Wolves. We could do nothing but wait. And watch.

A young woman in a simple dress rushed forward on bare feet, tears streaking down her pale cheeks. She glowed like a white flame amid so much black.

"Please," she sobbed. "Please, don't take my brother! He's all I have left! He's done nothing wrong. Please, I'll do anything, any—"

The silent slice of a black blade, and a weeping line marred her throat.

I reared back, hardly noticing Aiden's hand clamping over my gasp of horror. The woman fell like a wisp of cotton that quickly became soaked in an inky puddle.

The man—Jerell—began to shout garbled words, but the boot of a Wolf silenced him. Then the Wolves continued to drag their prize as he trailed his sister's blood.

Moments drifted past like dust in a wild storm. Chaotic, biting, fleeting.

Was this why Renwell kept me away from them? Why he told me to never interfere with them? Because they would *murder* me if I did?

Slowly, Aiden released his hold on me, his features edging into my vision. But I only saw her. A woman trying to defend her family. A woman who got in the way. A woman who was now silenced forever.

"Kiera," he whispered.

I didn't want to hear my name on his lips. I didn't want to hear that there was nothing we could've done. Or that he was gods-damned right that I might not survive without him in this city.

I tore away from him, stumbling toward the woman. I fell to my knees at her side. She laid there in the moonlight, her pale hair and limbs strewn about in defeat. She looked like one of the lullaby lilies Mother had loved so much. But crushed, broken.

I brushed my fingers over her cheek as a familiar, soul-deep pain unfurled its wings inside me.

Mother had looked like this woman when they brought her body back to the palace. Except she had been tucked away under a sheet, as if she were sleeping. But the cold marble skin, the rusty tang of blood that stained her clothes, her soul drifting ever further away from me. Those were the same.

"Kiera." Aiden knelt beside me.

"I know," I snapped. "We need to leave."

His voice turned harsh and guttural. "No."

I finally met his gaze. His eyes were like shards of green glass, sharp with silvery edges. It felt as before, in the prison, like I was finally seeing beneath his mask. Fury, grief . . . guilt? Or perhaps I was merely seeing my own emotions mirrored back to me.

"We're not far from home," he said. "I'll lead you there and come back for her."

My eyebrows slammed together. "What are you going to do with her?"

"I'll give her what little peace I can offer."

"Then I'm coming with you."

His jaw hardened. "I can't carry her and protect you. If we run into more Wolves—"

"—then I will protect us both," I said. I held out my hand, the one that had touched the woman's cheek. "Give me what weapons you have, and we'll see it done."

He stared at me. I stared back.

This was an argument he wouldn't—*couldn't*—win. He was just going to have to trust that I wouldn't stab him in the back.

Something shifted in his gaze like a key twisting in a lock, and he reached under his cloak to draw two curved knives out of his belt.

I breathed steadily through my nose as he slowly placed them in my hand. I clenched one in each fist, feeling their weight and balance. They were longer than the law allowed. Shined and sharpened steel meant for slashing and stabbing. They were not my usual short, spearhead-shaped throwing knives, but I knew how to use them. In training. I'd never severely harmed or killed someone before.

But Aiden didn't need to know that. I said I would protect him, and I meant it.

I slipped the blades into my belt. "Let's go."

CHAPTER 11
AIDEN

CARRYING BODIES NEVER GOT EASIER.

The heaviness that sagged in my arms, the dullness that ached from no spark of life, no tautness of muscle. Like a sack of grain. That was what our bodies were reduced to.

I shifted the woman's weight as I walked, Kiera a vigilant shadow at my side. I'd nearly reprimanded her when she'd kicked that bottle earlier. Clumsiness got one killed.

But now she glared into every dark corner we passed, as if every shadow held an assassin. Her hands never strayed from my knives in her belt. I'd noticed how she seemed to reach for unseen weapons out of habit. What weapons did her fingers miss?

This was the first time I'd seen her the way she must've been before we met. A guard. Someone trained to notice everything, to be prepared for anything. A tightly pulled bow string ready to spring into action.

But I could also see the fear and the horror of what had happened pulling her shoulders tight, her spine straight. The wildness in her eyes when the woman died. It pierced a part of me that had long since grown numb.

Maybe that was why I'd handed her my knives. Because, for the moment, I finally, fully believed every word she said. But these moments would run dry, like a deserted well. Trust rarely lasted. As anything did.

I glanced down at the pale woman in my arms.

Too many bodies . . .

We didn't speak a word until we reached Floren's dwelling. Kiera read the carved sign above the door.

"A pyrist? Won't he ask questions?"

"His business is burning the dead, not how they got there."

Kiera's lips pressed in a grim line, but she knocked on the door.

Within moments, Floren opened it, his bald head shiny with sweat. He glanced at the body in my arms and sighed. "I was about to catch a wink, but I suppose I can do one more."

"Busy night?" Kiera gritted out.

Floren barely spared her a glance, ushering me inside. "Not terribly. But I do think I'm coming down with a malaise."

I gently laid the woman on the table he gestured to. "Shall I ask Sophie for a tea, Floren?"

He sniffed. "That would be lovely, thank you. Now put those young muscles of yours to use and stoke the fire."

I obliged, skirting around Kiera who was eyeing Floren the way a falcon would a mouse. The "pyre" wasn't much more than a stone furnace, built to hold several bodies at once. He had baskets of wood and skins of oil to feed the fire and a large barrel to sweep the ashes into.

For the luckier folks who had families around to care, they would take their loved one's ashes and release them to the sea, the air, or the earth with prayers that the gods would find their souls.

Everything given must be returned. Everything lost must be found.

The reason I came to Floren was because he had a kind heart, never turned a body away, and, when his barrel of ashes was full, he would bring it to the sea. The lonely and the forgotten drifted home on his small mercy.

I tossed wood into the slumbering fire and sprinkled oil to speed the flames.

"She's ready," Floren announced.

He had washed the blood from her skin and coated it and her hair with flower-scented oil. He was the only pyrist I knew who did that. When I'd asked him about it, he'd simply said, "It smells sweeter than death."

"This feels wrong," Kiera whispered as we stood around the woman's prepared body.

My fingers twitched, as if to reach for hers, but I curled them into a fist instead. "It's the best we can do."

Kiera didn't take her eyes off the woman. "What's her name? What if she had more family? What if—"

"She said her brother was all she had. And we can't drag her body around, asking for details. Her brother, if he's still alive, would thank us for this."

"Thank us, yes." She laughed bitterly. She hesitantly grasped the woman's hand and squeezed once. "I suppose if she were my sister, I'd want the same. If all I could hope for was a fast fire and the prayers of strangers, then it's better than nothing." She backed away from the table. "Do it."

Floren startled, as if he'd fallen asleep standing up. Which he probably had as I'd seen him do it before. A pyrist kept odd hours and slept where they could. Not unlike me.

He bustled to the furnace, opening it to test the heat that poured from its maw. Nodding, he gestured for me to bring the woman to him.

Carefully, we slid her body into the furnace and closed the heavy metal door.

"May the gods find your soul," Floren murmured, then left to clean his workspace.

"May the gods find your soul," I echoed.

Kiera's shoulder brushed mine as she stood vigil beside me. "May the gods find your soul. And your brother's. May you join your family across the Abyss."

The ache in her voice called to the ache in my chest.

Memories blinded me. Pyres stacked high with bodies. The night ablaze with my failure. The few living crying out for the many dead.

With a shudder, I yanked my mind back to the present. Sweat trickled between my shoulder blades.

"Do you think what she said was true?" Kiera glanced up at me, her honey-brown eyes beseeching mine. "That her brother —Jerell—had done nothing wrong?"

"I believe it."

"Then why would the Shadow-Wolves take him?"

I threw a stray wood shaving into the carnivorous flames. "They don't need a reason. They just do what they're told."

She bowed her head, but not before I saw her grimace. "If we hadn't been there . . . if we hadn't witnessed it . . . what would've happened to her body?"

"Birds, beasts, or street sweepers. But a street sweeper would've just tossed her body into whatever fire burnt the rest of the trash."

Kiera's shoulders jerked. But I didn't bother to comfort her. Why spin lukewarm falsehoods when I wanted her to be afraid. I wanted her to understand why I didn't want her here.

Her arms wrapped around her middle as if protecting herself. "Would no one else have done what we did?"

"Did you see a door or window crack open? Others must have heard her. Yet they will do nothing when the Wolves have done such a marvelous job of keeping them silent and afraid." A circumstance I could hardly blame the people for. I could only fight for a better life for them.

"You're not afraid," Kiera said. "You stopped. You brought her here."

"I have enough blood on my hands without adding hers. Or yours."

"My blood is not your burden to carry."

Our eyes met and held. Something churned in the space between us, like waves crashing against a stone wall neither of us wanted to tear down.

"It's not always a choice," I said softly. "And I'll have my knives back now."

Her chin notched higher in a way that made me want to seize it. Again. Her jaw feathered as she searched my face. For a moment, she looked as though she might refuse.

But then she slipped them from her belt, flipped them over, and passed them to me hilt-first.

"I'll be needing my own in this gods-damned city," she said.

"Noted."

I slipped Floren a few coins and promised to bring him a tea soon. The short journey to my rooms was uneventful, if tense. I abandoned the idea of taking too many false turns in favor of speed. Kiera didn't let on if she suspected where exactly we were. Sooner or later, she would. I just preferred it to be later. Not that I hid much in the few rooms I rented out of a large building that looked the same as a thousand others.

I did a quick check to make sure we weren't followed. We trod up the smooth stairs carved into the side of the building to reach my rooms near the roof. The height was a necessity.

The moment I pushed open the door, it was yanked from my grasp, and I was dragged inside.

A lone lamp illuminated Maz's bearded face twisted in a snarl. "Where. Have. You. Been?" He noted the blood on my shirt and hands. "Fucking Four, Aiden, what happened?"

"It's not my—" I started.

"Is Kiera—"

"I'm here, Maz," Kiera said wearily behind me.

He pulled her into one of his bone-crushing hugs, surprising me. It surprised her too, from the wide-eyed look she sent me over his shoulder.

I shrugged at her. It was Maz's way.

He released her, and she patted him awkwardly on the shoulder. "Have you been drinking?" she asked, sniffing the air.

"Not enough," he grumbled, stalking back to a small wooden table that we used for eating or cleaning weapons. An empty mug sat next to a partially drained brown bottle. "I'm guessing we all might need a cup for the story you're about to tell?"

"I doubt whatever you've got will help," Kiera said, glancing around the room, taking in our two cots, a few shelves of food, and a battered wardrobe. A thin door closed off the next room, which looked almost the same.

"Mead can fix almost anything," Maz said. "As does a good song or story."

"This is not a good story," I said, tossing my cloak onto my cot and pouring a cup of amber liquid that reminded me of Kiera's eyes. I drank deeply, then settled into a chair next to Maz.

"Hence the mead." He poured Kiera a cup as well and gestured her to the chair across from me.

She sank onto it with a sigh and gulped her drink.

I recounted what happened while Kiera stared into her cup. When I reached the part where we hid, she interrupted me.

"How did you know there were more coming?"

"Do you remember the howl behind us?" She nodded. "That's their signal to any nearby patrolling Wolves to join them."

"Lovely," she muttered. "They certainly like to play into their nickname."

Maz tipped his chair back on two legs. "It's also what makes them hard to evade. Their signals are difficult to imitate, and they never patrol alone but in random packs."

"That's how I got caught in the Den," I said. "Renwell must arrange their numbers in a specific way, or I wouldn't have revealed myself by trying to join an already assigned group leaving the gate."

Kiera's eyes narrowed, and I frowned. The mead must've loosened my tongue more than expected. I set my cup aside.

"How did you get the uniform, the mask?" she asked.

"How do you imagine?"

Her eyes widened at my harsh tone, and she looked away, chewing her lip.

We'd stalked Shadow-Wolves for the past two years, trying to learn their ways. Early on, a patrolling pair had snuck up on us, and we barely survived the fight. One of their uniforms was damaged beyond repair, but we'd taken the other one, as well as their masks and knives. We purposely hadn't used them until it felt like we had no other choice.

"What happened then?" Maz asked, drawing my attention back.

I finished the story in a crisp tone. I left out Kiera's reactions and our conversation, stating only the facts.

Maz bowed his head. "May the gods find their souls."

I nodded, weariness seeping into my bones. "We should get some sleep. Kiera, you can take one of the cots in the next room. Sometimes we have others who sleep in there, but it's empty now."

Kiera blinked at me as if her mind had been far, far away. "Thank you, but what of food?"

"You're welcome to anything we have," I said, waving a hand to our shelves. "Otherwise, Sophie usually has something cooking down in the courtyard."

Her gaze fell. "I don't have any coin to pay for that. Or my bed."

Maz clapped his hand to her shoulder, his mood bright once more. "Don't you worry, lovely. You're with us now. We take care of our own."

But she didn't look at him. Only me. "I want to earn my way. Like Ruru. He said he works for you."

"Because he can," I said. Kiera stiffened, but I continued, "I thought you didn't want to work for me, anyway?"

"Aren't I already?" she shot back. "You made it very clear who's commanding our venture."

Gods, this woman. Did everything have to be a fight? "Then what need have you to get more coin?" I growled. "If everything goes right, you should be rolling in it soon enough."

"Because I don't want to owe you anything. You have enough power over me as it is."

I rose to my feet, bracing my fingertips on the table. "And what is it you think you can do for me? I have no need for a personal guard, and I'm already using you for your skills as a thief."

She stood and matched my posture. Her eyes burned with determination, sending a crackle of heat through my blood. "I can do what Ruru does—run errands, carry messages, and the like."

"And you think it's that easy, do you? That you can just ask for a job. That I'll just let you into my business. Ruru works for me because I *trust* Ruru. I don't trust you."

"Then what's the alternative?" she snapped. "You said I would never be left alone. Are you going to assign a guard to sit with me day and night when not accompanying me to Melaena's club? That's a waste of two able bodies."

I snapped my mouth shut, hating her logic. But I couldn't just accept it. She was unforeseen. A scribble in my carefully inked plans.

She wouldn't be stupid enough to turn us in since she'd be condemning herself in the same breath. Melaena had confirmed everything Kiera had told us about the vault.

Yet, I still found myself looking for the lie.

And she clearly didn't trust me, either. But I needed her just as much as she needed me. Perhaps we simply had to meet in the middle for this to work.

"I'll think on it," I said gruffly, straightening away from her.

Maz grinned at both of us. I'd nearly forgotten he was there. Kiera seemed to have a disturbing effect on me where my surroundings narrowed to only her.

"Best get some sleep, lovely," Maz said. "I'll show you to your room."

Kiera obliged. My shoulders relaxed the moment her gaze broke away from mine.

Restlessness burned in my veins. Unable to think of sleep yet, I simply stared out of our one small window. We were high enough that I wasn't worried about intruders. And I needed it. For the fresh air—even in a storm—and the light. To remind me of my freedom.

The city looked still and peaceful from here. Silvery buildings as silent as the starry sky above. Was this like what Kiera had seen from her palace windows?

But I knew—and she did now, as well—that the silence

wasn't peaceful. It was a held breath while waiting for another blow to land.

Very soon, I would tear that silence to shreds. I would seize the revenge that had eluded me for years. I would give the people of Rellmira a better life.

Kiera was right. I couldn't afford to guard her every move.

I needed to visit the Temple at dawn. I had weapons to create.

CHAPTER 12
KIERA

THE MEAD PUT ME IN A FITFUL SLEEP. THE KIND WHERE MY BODY desperately needed rest, but my mind couldn't stop racing with fear and anger.

I dreamt of ever-shifting white labyrinths. Every time I thought I knew where I was going, I reached a dead end— one that held the bloodied body of a woman. The shadows that pressed in on me were sharp. They stabbed at my heels, making me run faster and faster until I fell down a dark hole.

And woke up, gasping and sweating.

It took me a moment to remember where I was as I stared at the domed ceiling. Aiden's place. The windowless room had little light of its own, but the sunlight that pierced the cracks of the door told me it was day.

I rubbed my hands over my face.

Maz showed me the water basin and soap last night, so I was at least able to scrub most of my skin clean. My hair I simply tied in a knot. It would have to keep until I could have a proper bath.

He'd also handed me more of Aiden's salve for my ribs and jaw. And praise be Viridana, my beating from Renwell was healing much more rapidly than any other injuries I'd ever had.

Good enough to dance, certainly.

I rose and poured fresh water into the chipped basin. After splashing my face and pulling on my boots, I opened the door.

Maz sat at the table, eating an apple with his sleeves rolled up over his massive, tattooed arms. But Aiden was gone.

Spotting me, Maz smiled and waved to a chair. "Take a seat, lovely, and have some breakfast. Courtesy of Sophie."

I slid into the chair and snatched up a thick slice of brown bread. "Will I ever get to meet this amazing woman?" I devoured the bread in two bites, my stomach already crying for more.

Maz chuckled. "Undoubtedly. Hardly a soul around that doesn't know Sophie. But be warned, she's as suspicious and protective as a mother bear."

I barely remembered to chew the three hunks of pale yellow cheese I grabbed. So creamy, so nutty. Gods, food was the best.

"I've never seen a bear," I mumbled through a full mouth.

Maz's ice-blue eyes brightened. "Of course, having lived in a gods-forsaken palace all your life. But you should see Dagriel one day. The snow-tipped mountains, the rapid rivers full of fish, the pine trees that smell sweet in the rain and spicy in the sun . . ." He trailed off with a dreamy look on his face, juice from his apple dribbling down his wrist.

I swallowed. "Will you get to go back one day?"

He refocused on me, the light in his eyes dimming. "Gods willing. But I carry home with me wherever I go," he added, gesturing to his tattoos.

"Like the mountain on your back?"

His voice softened. "Yes. The mountain is a symbol of our people, across all clans. Of our strength, of our endurance. The mountains have been our home since the first dawn and will be until every age has passed."

Before I could ask him more, the Temple bells rang. He took a final bite from his apple and tossed the core out the window. "Best hurry along. Can't be late for your first rehearsal."

I listened to the bells ring the eleventh hour while cramming bits of dried salted pork in my mouth. I washed it down with a mug of water from a green bottle, which I sniffed first to be sure it wasn't mead again.

"Where's Aiden?" I asked as Maz stood up and unfurled his shirt sleeves to cover his tattoos.

"Busy." Maz flashed me a smile, as if to make up for the curt answer. "But I assure you, I'm an excellent guide."

"You mean guard."

He pursed his lips. "I don't see it that way."

"Aiden does," I muttered, brushing crumbs from my mouth and pants as I stood up.

"Be patient with him, lovely. He has good reason not to trust so easily."

"And you don't?"

Maz stroked his bearded chin. "I suppose I would rather treat someone as a friend until they prove otherwise. Aiden tends to feel differently. He would rather not be surprised when someone betrays him. In my experience, the more times one is betrayed, the more one comes to expect betrayal."

I frowned. The idea that I was more like Aiden in that regard was discomfiting. And that he was not wrong about me. But who else had betrayed Aiden? And what had happened to them?

The food soured in my stomach. Maybe I didn't want to know.

The moment we stepped outside, I thanked the gods I'd left my cloak behind. The humidity immediately enveloped me in a sweaty hug. Mynastra's storms hadn't cooled the air but rather thickened it.

"Gods damn this Rellmiran heat," Maz grumbled, his thin sleeves flapping in a sluggish breeze as we hurried down the steps and through the Old Quarter.

I'd known no other kind of weather, so I didn't comment.

The twisting pathways looked and felt so different from my frantic journey last night. The weathered brown buildings warmed in the sun. Shutters and doors were thrown open to let in whatever breeze that stirred. Cooking fires flavored the air with meat and spice. Everywhere people bustled about their business—hanging colorful bits of laundry on the rooftops, carrying parcels, gossiping with their neighbors.

As if death didn't hunt their streets at night.

Maz led me to the main road via a different route than last night. Or else I would've seen the crimson stain, like an ominous mark on a map.

I needed to talk to Renwell. Soon. We'd come up with a way for me to reach out to him should I escape the Den with

Aiden. But I couldn't leave my mark, let alone have a clandestine meeting, while my every move was watched.

I could only hope that Aiden would agree to letting me work for him. The more he loosened his grip, the easier it would be to slip away for a while.

Patience, Renwell would tell me. But why did everything in this job require so much *patience*?

Here I was going to a dance rehearsal for a heist that would never happen instead of backtracking to find that warehouse to look through the crates or hunting down Aiden to see where he went and who he spoke to.

Patience. Play the part. Perhaps Melaena knows more of Aiden's plans.

I darted after Maz's tall figure as he plowed his way through the thick crowd toward the Noble Quarter gate. There, we had to wait long minutes in a line of people waiting to be allowed into the quarter. Most were turned away. Only nobles and those in clothing stitched with noble insignias were gestured through.

I held my breath as we approached the red-faced guard. His leather uniform creaked as he wiped sweat from his eyes. But I didn't recognize him, and he barely looked at me, focusing on Maz.

"Name and business," he grunted, his fist tightening around one of the long spears only the day guards were allowed to carry.

"Kiera, one of Melaena's dancers at *The Silk Dancer*," Maz answered.

The guard finally glanced at me with a frown. "No, she's not."

"I'm new," I said quickly. "And running late."

When the guard continued to stare at me without answering, Maz straightened to his full height, towering over the guard. "Melaena said she would give Kiera's name to the guards. Check the list and let us be on our way."

The guard glowered, but he sauntered over to consult with another guard that held a ledger. After a minute of conferring, he nodded and waved me through.

Maz started to follow, but the guard blocked him with his spear. "Just her."

Maz looked as though he were going to snap the guard's spear in half, but I forced a smile and waved him off. "Go on. I'll be fine. See you after."

Maz hesitated for a moment, no doubt thinking Aiden might take issue with letting me loose. But he had little choice. He nodded, and I hurried onward.

The flow of traffic was much different on this side of the gate. Much less pushy and dirty. Sparkling fountains, pristine cobblestone streets, and strolling nobles in their silks and satins.

It felt like a lifetime ago that I'd been one of them, albeit in the lonely halls of the palace.

Melaena's club sat closest to the wall on the west side of the street. The domed building was built with white stone that glittered in the sun. Wide, polished steps split around a bronze statue of a dancing girl mid-spin and draped in silks. Parts of her were worn glossy and smooth—probably from enamored fingertips. But her carved smile was still serene and untouched. A matching bronze plaque under her feet read *The Silk Dancer*.

Gathering my breath and my courage, I opened one of the heavy wooden doors and slipped inside.

The entrance was more like a lounge with guests sitting in overstuffed armchairs, sipping iced drinks and enjoying light refreshments. Melaena's patrons were all nobles. Men and women who held quiet conversations in dim corners or played friendly games of Death and Four on marble tables.

It certainly wasn't like the taverns I used to sneak into with beer-soaked tables, knife-throwing, and occasionally violent games of Death and Four.

Gods, I missed that.

I hurried past the daytime patrons, none of whom noted my passing. Down a crimson-wallpapered hall, I pushed open the double doors at the end, ignoring the "Closed for Rehearsal" sign on the handle.

At the far end of the cavernous room, Melaena was already on stage instructing her dancers. I strode past the staff cleaning the dozens of tables and couches, trying not to look as sweaty and uncouth as I felt.

That feeling only worsened when I noticed that all the dancers, including Melaena, wore a variety of silk dresses in a bouquet of colors. I hadn't even thought about what to wear since I only had one set of clothes. Clothes that probably smelled like the street and Aiden's salve.

One by one, the dancers' eyes widened as I approached the stage. They began to whisper behind their hands. A few seemed curious, others looked outright scornful.

Melaena stopped talking and turned to smile at me. "Ah, and here she is! Ladies, as I was saying, this is Kiera. She'll be joining us for Asher's celebration."

I tried to smile past my nerves that buzzed like flies in my ears.

Melaena waved to her dancers. "I'll introduce you to everyone in a moment, Kiera. How about we find you something to wear that will be easier to dance in? Ladies, start your exercises."

The dancers obediently snapped to formation and began to twist and bend, warming their muscles.

Melaena beckoned me. "Come, the dressing room is backstage."

I climbed the stairs on the side of the stage and followed Melaena behind the gold-painted backdrop.

She nodded to it as we passed. "Usually, we have much more detailed scenes depicted because I like to incorporate a story into our shows. But since Asher's celebration will be at his house, this will do for practice."

"Does he have a stage as well?"

She laughed, the silvery chains threaded through her hair twinkling. "He probably wishes he had one as grand as this. But he does have a very large ballroom where we will dance in the middle before dispersing into the crowd." She sobered. "I suppose that is when you will need to get close to him. Do you have much experience with men?"

My cheeks warmed as she guided me past a mess of ropes and pulleys. "Some, yes."

"Excellent. That will make my job much easier." She led me to the back wall and through the only door. "Here's the dressing room."

My eyes widened, taking in the numerous outfits hung on a dozen racks around the room.

"It also has a bathing and makeup area," she added, pointing to a row of mirrors atop tables littered with paints, powders, and brushes. A tall screen mostly hid a large bathtub in the corner.

"Most of my dancers live in the rooms I keep through there." Melaena nodded to a door at one end of the room. "The sitting rooms—like the one you first came through—are on the other side of that door." She gestured to a door at the opposite end.

"I had no idea this place was so huge," I admitted, running my fingers over an exquisite silk costume. Dyed violet with clusters of gold beaded flowers sewn around the waist and bodice, it was one of the most beautiful things I'd ever seen. It was much more revealing than anything I'd worn as a princess, but that made it even more alluring.

Melaena's smile softened. "This place was my mother's pride and joy, and my father took diligent care of it when she died. Now it's my turn to continue their legacy."

I released the dress, rubbing my fingers on my pants as if the dress had dirtied me instead of the other way around. "So, you've lived in the Noble Quarter your whole life?" Had she known Julian? "How did you meet Aiden?"

Her blue eyes turned cautious. "Yes, I have. I met Aiden through a friend, and we quickly became friends as well." She tilted her head to the side, studying me. "We're not lovers, if that's what you're wondering."

"No!" The word burst out of me, and I tried to laugh it off. "No, I was just curious because this doesn't seem like the sort of place he frequents."

She gave me a knowing look, but smiled. "Indeed. He

usually deems himself much too busy to enjoy something as simple as a dance."

Busy doing what? And what "friend" had introduced them? But I didn't want to push her too hard. I was supposed to be earning her trust as well.

"I'm sorry about your parents, though," I said softly. "You must've cared for them a great deal to take such good care of their legacy."

"Thank you, and yes, I miss them every day." She hesitated. "Are your parents still alive?"

My heart froze for a beat. "I . . . I never knew my father. And my mother died a few years ago."

"Oh, I'm so sorry. May the gods find her soul. Was she in the palace with you?"

Suspicion crept in. "Why do you want to know? Did Aiden tell you to ask me these questions?"

Her black eyebrows arched in surprise. "Of course not. I was simply curious. I thought . . . perhaps . . ." She pressed her lips together.

My body tensed. Oh gods, did she recognize me somehow? Had she heard something about me? "Perhaps what?"

"I thought perhaps you might need a friend." She sighed. "I know how Aiden can be. And after what you went through," —she paused to grasp my hands in her own.—"I just wanted you to know you're safe here. A few of my dancers came from terrible situations and found their peace and a family in my club. You're not alone."

A lump suddenly swelled in my throat at her words and unexpected kindness.

I wasn't alone. Not physically. But in allies? Safety?

Yes. I was very much alone. Melaena would make an excellent ally and resource, but I couldn't afford friends in this life. Even if the risk felt worth it at the moment.

I squeezed her fingers. "Thank you, Melaena. I hope I can repay your kindness and generosity one day."

She squeezed back before letting go. "There is no debt in true kindness. Now, go try that dress on. It looks like the perfect size, and the colors will complement your eyes and skin tone."

"Are you sure?" I asked, my fingers already reaching for the violet dress I'd grasped.

"Absolutely. Join the rest of us as soon as you're ready." She smiled at me over her shoulder before closing the door behind her.

I quickly stripped out of my dirty clothes and boots and kicked them into a corner. I pulled the dress over my head, and it floated down my body like a glittering purple cloud. Cinching the laces in the back tightened the gown around my frame like it was made for it.

I stepped in front of a floor-length mirror, swallowing a gasp. Gossamer sleeves swished down to my elbow. The dress fell in layers to my knees, barely opaque enough to cover my skin from my breasts to my thighs. It turned my body into an illusion, a mystery.

Excitement swirled low in my belly, and I grinned. This job had just gotten its first perk.

I eyed the doors at either end of the room. Would anyone notice me roaming the halls? I could find that sitting room again and try to discover the entrance to the tunnel. But it would have to wait until after rehearsal.

Deciding to leave the room barefoot as I'd seen the other dancers, I padded back to the stage.

Holy Four, don't let me fall on my face.

Two hours later, I was certain Melaena regretted agreeing to let me dance with her. Sweat stained the lovely silk that clung to my body as I completed what felt like the thousandth spin.

Melaena watched me with her brow furrowed. "You're still wobbling a bit. And your arms need to float about as if weightless. When you hold the dancing silks, they need to flow like water. Like this." She demonstrated the turn, looking as graceful as a flower. "Again."

"I had no idea dancing could be this painful," I grunted, trying again.

"You'll thank me for it later," she sang. "Don't forget to *smile.*" She flashed a pearlescent smile at me.

I bared my teeth at her as I spun again and again, my muscles burning. Years of training with Renwell had *not* prepared me for this. Fighting was about speed and power. Throwing knives needed focus and accuracy. Looking pretty was definitely not a factor.

Melaena had dismissed the other dancers an hour ago. They had picked up Melaena's choreography in moments, their movements already beautiful. I had an excellent memory, but that didn't equate to performance.

We'd spent the last hour going over the basics, as she called them. Leaps, twirls, sinuous arm movements, and hip flourishes.

I finally bent over with my hands on my knees, breathing hard. "How . . . how do you do it? You make it look so easy."

Melaena gave me a playful smirk, executing a flawless leap just because she could. "Practice. I have no doubt you'll fit in with the rest of the dancers by performance time."

I groaned. "And if I don't? Will Asher not look twice at me?"

"Oh, he will. Asher appreciates beauty because he finds security in the appearance of flawlessness. And what is more beautiful than joy?" Her smile turned serene as she twirled in a flourish of silks. "Find the joy, and he won't be able to take his eyes off of you."

I gave her a weak smile even as my heart fell. When was the last time I'd found that sort of joy?

The doors at the entrance opened, and a young boy in a crisp white shirt and pants scurried toward the stage.

"High Councilor Garyth would like to speak with you, my lady," he said.

I stiffened, averting my face on the chance that the High Councilor would enter. Why would Garyth want to meet with Melaena?

The calmness on Melaena's face rippled away under concern. "Tell him I'll be with him in a moment, Elias."

He bowed and hurried back the way he came.

"Excellent work for today, Kiera," she said. "After you've changed, you can wait for your escort in the front lounge."

I nodded, my thoughts racing too fast to form an answer. If she was meeting with Garyth in the front lounge, then that was the last place I wanted to be. Being a High Councilor for years, he had frequented the palace enough to remember what Princess Emilia looked like. I couldn't have him wondering what I was doing here when, as the princess, I hadn't stepped out of my rooms since my mother's death.

But why was he here in the middle of the day? And why did Melaena look so worried?

I walked back to the dressing room and changed in a daze. The other dancers had long gone.

I hesitated at the door. I could wait here or . . . I could poke around that sitting room and find the entrance to the secret tunnel.

Swiping a few hairpins from a makeup table, I hurried to the door Melaena had pointed at earlier. It swung open soundlessly and let me into a familiar hall—the same one I'd walked with Aiden last night. Which meant the door opposite me led to the sitting room.

Glancing up and down the hall to make sure I was alone, I inserted the pins into the lock. The tumblers fell into place within moments. Ever the same, a smile curved my lips at the sound.

I doubted Melaena would be amused if she knew one of my little joys was lock-picking.

I opened the door and closed it quietly behind me. A soft *snick* told me the door had locked itself behind me. Good. That would slow someone down, even if they had the key.

The room was darker than before, with no windows and the candelabra unlit. Only a small oil lamp on a low table shed any light. But that would have to be enough. Snuffed candles left smoke and scent.

Leave no trace, Renwell's voice instructed me from a dozen memories.

Willing my eyes to adjust to the shadows, I approached the

wall that likely faced south, toward the Old Quarter and, therefore, the tunnel. I gently pushed tapestry after tapestry aside, skipping the ones that were blocked by couches or tables. My fingers painstakingly crept along the surface underneath. But I found nothing but smooth wall. No cracks. No indentations. No weaknesses.

I huffed in frustration, gazing around the room and trying to remember. Aiden and I fell when we'd exited the tunnel. My blindfold had slipped. What had I seen before he forced my attention back to him?

Feeling only a little ridiculous, I laid on my stomach on the plush carpet. Something fluttered in my chest at the memory of lying on his chest. I'd felt his heartbeat. His breathing. His firm grasp on my chin as I stared into those unnerving green eyes.

I shook myself. *Focus.* Someone might enter this room at any moment.

I turned my head at awkward angles until . . . *there!* I'd caught a glimmer of the strange, clawed foot of a sofa when I fell. Which meant . . .

I repositioned my body to put the clawed foot to my left, meaning my feet were now pointed at the tunnel.

My sore muscles protested as I flipped over and approached the west wall. I dug under the nearest tapestry. My fingertips brushed over a sliver of a crack. A grin split my face. Yes! This was it! My fingers traced the line as high as I could reach while my other hand searched for its twin.

My heart pounded with triumph. This was the door. But there was no handle, no latch.

Frowning, I swept my hands over the whole wall. Nothing.

Gods damn it! There must be a trigger of some kind out here, not as close as I'd hoped. Gods alone knew how long it would take me to find *that*.

Muffled voices filtered through the locked door. I grew still as stone. The jingle of keys.

Someone was coming in.

CHAPTER 13
KIERA

CURSES EXPLODED THROUGH MY MIND AS I LET THE TAPESTRY fall back to the wall and dove for the sofa in the darkest corner.

I dropped to my stomach again just as a key embedded in the lock. I shimmied under the couch, hugging the wall as much as possible, praying my boots weren't visible.

The door opened, and footsteps whispered over the rug. Light flared as someone turned up the oil lamp.

"You know better than to cause a scene in my lobby," Melaena said, her voice low and tense.

I scrunched my eyes shut in horror. If she was here . . .

"Forgive me, Melaena," a familiar voice said. High Councilor Garyth. "My worries for my family and myself overtook me."

Melaena sighed. "Have a seat, Garyth, and tell me exactly what happened."

A rustle and a creak, then Garyth said, "Someone searched my study."

I winced, my heart drumming harder.

"How can you be sure? Perhaps your daughter or a maid moved a few things around?"

"My daughter is not allowed in my study, and the maid doesn't clean there unless I'm present. The papers in a secret compartment in my desk were disheveled in such a way that someone must've put them back in a hurry."

By the Abyss, did he have to have such an eye for detail? I had been as careful as I could manage under the circumstances.

"But nothing was missing?" Melaena asked.

"Nothing, and everything is encoded, but . . . but if someone saw the insignia or cracked the code . . . I'm a dead man. My family as well."

My stomach twisted at the utter certainty and hopelessness in his voice. Surely Father wouldn't execute Garyth's wife and child if they knew nothing of his traitorous sympathies?

But he would. He had done it to others.

Bile rose in my throat, but I swallowed it and the memories back down.

"Do you have enough to condemn him?" Melaena asked.

My brow pinched. Condemn who? My father?

"Not yet. Dracles has been blocking my attempts to gather more information. His gods-damn soldiers patrol the entirety of the river, and getting close to the mine has been impossible. He's definitely hiding something."

Melaena and Garyth continued speaking in hushed murmurs that I couldn't make out.

Did he mean the Medria River? It was the largest river in Rellmira and ran west to east from Twaryn, splitting north to the small mining town of Calimber and south to Aquinon. I didn't know much about the Calimber mine itself, other than that it was where Father's precious sunstone was carved out of a cave deep in the cliffs.

He protected it more fiercely than his own family—that was no secret. But why would he keep Garyth—his Master of Commerce—from the river and the mine, which were his purview as overseer of Rellmira's trade resources?

I shook my head. None of this made sense. Perhaps that was why Renwell had wanted me to sneak into Garyth's study —he suspected Garyth was doing some spying of his own.

But for what purpose? Was Garyth gathering information and supporters to overthrow Father? Why would he even want to bring back the People's Council, if that was his goal?

After all, they were largely to blame for the Pravaran rebellion getting out of control, forcing Father to take extreme measures.

If the council had simply calmed the angry masses in Pravara, instead of insisting that Father give in to their demands of overturning multiple laws involving taxes, food quotas, and army conscriptions, so many lives would've been saved.

Was Aiden also mixed up in this conspiracy?

My fingers clenched in frustration. I hated having so few threads of what felt like a much larger story. Regardless, I needed to tell Renwell what I'd heard. If I could ever find a way to contact him.

"But when?" Garyth's voice grew louder. "We can do nothing if he doesn't succeed. And quickly. If Renwell and his dogs start baying for my blood, it will crush what little hope

I've managed to inspire in the others. Those gods-damned executions after the rebellion were a crippling blow."

Julian. I bit my lip, fighting back the wretched memory. Who was Garyth waiting for?

"We *all* felt the pain of those executions," Melaena said icily. "And he *will* succeed. In the meantime, how long can you hold off Renwell?"

"Not long if it was him or one of his spies in my study. My family—"

"—will be protected. Stay the course, Garyth."

A heavy silence followed.

Gods, Renwell would devour this information. But how would he act on it?

"Focus on your daughter's birthday celebration," Melaena said in a soothing voice. "The gift you ordered should be here in a few days' time."

Garyth heaved a weary laugh. "Why my little girl wants a lizard, I'll never know. But I can hardly wait to see her smile."

I couldn't help a smile of my own at the thought of my innocent accomplice getting the scaly pet she yearned for. Strange that he'd asked Melaena to get it for him. But my smile drooped at the thought of the danger Isabel's father was putting her and her mother in.

"You'd best get back to her," Melaena said softly. "We shouldn't be seen together too much."

Garyth grunted in agreement.

Just then, something stirred in the shadows, creeping toward me. A spider, dark and furred.

I clenched my teeth to keep from screaming. Every muscle in my body locked. Except my eyes, which followed the little beast as it tiptoed closer. Was it the same one from the tunnel last night? It must've slipped through. Probably hunting my scent. Could spiders do that?

Gods, if it really was one of the poisonous black moss spiders . . .

Melaena and Garyth were taking their gods-damned time rising from their couches and saying goodbye.

Fuzzy legs nestled in the top of my hair. And climbed. Inching its way to my forehead. I squeezed my eyes shut, fear pounding in my throat.

"One moment, Garyth." Footsteps padded over and stopped right next to my boot heels. "How did this get knocked astray?" Melaena muttered under her breath, adjusting some-thing—probably the tapestry I'd let fall.

A cold, furry body scraped over my forehead. Searching legs tapped near my eyelids.

A shudder tore down my spine, but by some miracle, my body didn't utter a sound.

Melaena's footsteps faded away with Garyth's. The moment the door locked behind them, I slowly slid out from under the couch. Too much movement and the spider might sink its fangs into me.

It crept over my eye and down my cheek.

I whipped my head to the side while slashing at the spider with my hand. I felt it sail away from me.

I finally opened my eyes. Where in the deep, dark, wandering hell did it go? A discordant shadow scurried back toward the couch. I stomped it with my boot. The sickening crunch made me wince.

But then regret hummed through me at the gory mess on my boot heel and the rug.

Leave no trace.

Gods damn it. Renwell would be disappointed. He'd trained me to keep calm in any situation, yet a spider had rattled me enough to leave a mess.

Fingers shaking, I used a hairpin to scrape the spider's remains from the rug. It wasn't perfect, but I was running out of time. Maz was probably waiting for me by now. He might even come looking for me.

I wiped the hairpin on the underside of the couch, then shoved it in my pocket. That would have to do. Hopefully, a maid would clean the rugs before Melaena noticed and questioned two oddities in this room occurring in a short span of time.

I hurried out of the room and back into the dressing room, which was blessedly empty. Walking more slowly, I passed through the showroom, down the hall, and into the lobby.

Melaena and Garyth were nowhere to be seen, but neither was Maz.

Shifting away from the curious glances of Melaena's patrons, I left the club. Heat simmered from the streets in the mid-afternoon light. I skirted the bronze dancer statue and dubiously approached the gate.

Where was Maz? Could I find my way back on my own? Or could this be my chance to leave my mark for Renwell?

A low three-note whistle caught my attention.

A lone figure leaned against the city wall, out of sight of the guards. Familiar green eyes flashed at me from beneath his low hood.

Swallowing against my dry throat, I drew closer.

"Survived your first rehearsal, I see," came Aiden's low voice.

A thousand questions crowded my tongue. About what I'd just witnessed. About where he'd gone off to. But I couldn't ask any of them.

"Where's Maz?"

The skin around his eyes tightened. "Busy."

I didn't know whether to laugh or curse that both men used the same one-word excuse.

Aiden shifted away from the wall. "Hungry?"

"Always."

A smirk flickered over his mouth. "Do you play Death and Four?"

I gazed up at him, keeping my face a smooth, blank canvas. "Not well."

His light chuckle warmed my skin. "Liar. Follow me."

CHAPTER 14
AIDEN

THE CROWD AT THE WEARY TRAVELER WAS LOUD AND IN GOOD spirits as their night of drinking, eating, and gambling began.

Light poured from the candle chandeliers and a few iron braziers. Men and women, dressed in clothes stained from work or travel, flocked to the scarred tables. Smiling barmaids delivered pitchers of beer and bottles of wine to cheery shouts or grumbled thanks. The scent of roasting meat made my mouth water.

I'd always felt much more at home in places like this over somewhere like Melaena's club. The restrained conversations and side glances from the rich patrons rang false.

But here . . . here people celebrated another day lived or wallowed in their sorrows out in the open.

Tercel's sharp eyes immediately spotted me, and he jerked his chin to an empty table. His bushy eyebrows lowered when he noticed Kiera trailing behind me. I rarely brought people here except Maz and occasionally Ruru. But I was always welcome. Mostly because of the mutually beneficial business deals between us.

Where ideals didn't earn allies, money usually did.

"Friend of yours?" Kiera muttered as Tercel's gaze followed us to the table near the dead hearth.

"Of a sort. Have you ever been to a tavern before?" I unclasped my cloak and draped it over the chair with its back to the stone wall.

Her eyes halted their perusal of the crowded tavern to dart to me. "Yes. I . . . I snuck out of the palace a few times when I was younger. Before I was a guard."

She sank into the chair opposite me and drummed her fingers on the uneven tabletop. I kept finding myself fascinated by those fingers. The thin scars that decorated them. Their deftness. The way she had grasped my knives so tightly last night, as if she never wanted to let them go.

Clearing her throat, Kiera tucked her hand under the table.

I lifted my gaze to meet her guarded one. "Did you get caught?"

"Yes."

"How did you sneak out?"

"Is this why you brought me here?" she asked sharply. "To interrogate me? I thought we were here to eat and play a game."

I smiled, relaxing my posture and lazily waving down one of the barmaids. "We are. I was merely curious." The barmaid bustled up to our table, her arms full of empty mugs. "Hello, Iris, how's the new baby—Farah, was it?"

She beamed, her cheeks like shiny apples. "Farah, yes. Oh, she's much better now after that tonic. No more coughing! I

thank the gods every day that they led me to you. I can't . . . I
can't imagine—" Her eyes suddenly welled with tears.

I shook my head desperately. "I'm glad to help." I gestured
to Kiera. "But my companion and I are incredibly famished
and were hoping you could help us out."

Iris dabbed her eyes with her damp apron. "Of course, of
course! Anything you want!"

"We'll take a platter of whatever you've got roasting tonight
and two mugs of Sunshine. Oh, and some of Tercel's biscuits, if
he has any left," I added with a glance at Kiera, who looked
taken aback.

Iris nodded and hurried away.

"Are you some sort of healer for the city?" Kiera asked, her
tone less guarded than before.

"Not exactly. I help where I can." I pulled open a small
drawer under our table and fished out a bulging pouch.
"Ready to play?"

Anticipation gleamed in her eyes. "What are the stakes? I
haven't got any coins. Unless you'll let me work for you alongside Ruru." She gave me a saccharine smile. "Delivering teas
and tonics, it sounds like."

I shook out the Death and Four tiles as a prickle of admiration for her relentlessness stirred in my gut. "I still haven't
decided."

"Perhaps that should be our wager, then. If I win, you give
me the job."

I cocked an eyebrow. "And if you lose?"

"Then I suppose I'll just have to owe you some coins from
our other job."

"Nice try. But I'd rather play for something else."

Immediately, Kiera was on her guard again. "I have nothing else."

I smiled slowly, wickedly. "Yes, you do."

I paused to let her—and my—imagination run wild. As if we were just two strangers who had met in a tavern and wanted to enjoy each other's company until dawn. It had been a long time since I'd allowed myself to even entertain such a simple, yet complicated, pleasure.

And I had no intention of truly doing so with Kiera.

But a dark, yearning part of me wanted to see her squirm in her seat. To catch a little spark of the heat that seemed to flare between us at odd moments. To see something other than fear or suspicion in her beautiful eyes. Like the way she was looking at me now.

I crushed my thoughts into meaningless dust. "Answers," I said abruptly. "I'll play you for honest answers."

She seemed to mentally shake herself. "And if we choose not to answer?"

I dipped my head in agreement. After all, there were a great many things I could never tell her. "Then we will keep asking until there is a question we can answer."

"How do I know the answer you give me is honest?"

"If you can't figure that out, then you needn't worry."

One of the strategies in Death and Four was bluffing. If she couldn't decipher my lies from truths, she wasn't likely to win, anyway.

And I'd been lying my whole life.

Challenge flared in her eyes. "Deal."

We flipped tiles to see who would go first. Kiera unveiled Mynastra's fierce visage while I unveiled a lowly three.

Kiera selected her tiles first. I didn't draw mine until after she'd peeked at hers. Her expression was as carefully blank as it'd been when she'd lied to me about playing well.

I picked up my four tiles, rubbing them between my fingers. The wooden squares were smooth and thin, with each number or deity burned into one side. I'd played with many sets over the years, including one of solid gold and another of animal bone.

I didn't so much as twitch a muscle at the two, eight, ten, and the god Arduen with his headdress of burning flowers I'd drawn.

Not a bad hand. Only one of each of the four gods existed in the game, as well as the skull of Death. Hence the name Death and Four. The numbers one through ten had three tiles each.

I nodded at Kiera to take her first turn. *Let's play, little thief.*

We were a silent island in a sea of laughter and conversation as we took our four turns, discarding and swapping tiles or passing.

Then we came to the Duels.

She laid a tile facedown between us. "Ten," she told me, her jaw tight.

Liar. Trying to make me to give up a higher tile early in the game, are you?

I placed a seven facedown between us. "You lie," I said evenly.

She scowled, and we flipped our tiles. My seven beat her six, but I didn't gloat. Playing off emotions was also a handy trick.

I laid down another tile. "Mynastra."

She grinned with triumph, slamming down her tile—the true Mynastra tile. "Liar."

I flipped my tile, and Death leered up at us. "So eager to prove me wrong," I said, unable to help a smirk at her incredulity.

"Shut up," she growled, "and keep playing." She plunked down another tile. "Eight."

I chuckled. "Truth, I think. It seems the angrier you get, the more honest you are."

I won the Duel with a nine.

She clenched her last tile as if she were wishing it was a dagger she could throw at me. Instead, she tossed it to the table in defeat as I'd won three of the four Duels. My Arduen would've beat her ten, anyway.

Four tiles, four turns, four Duels. The gods must have really liked the poetry of their number when they invented this game to play with humans.

"Ask your question," she said, violently crossing her arms and legs as if to ward off an invasion.

But I didn't want us to be enemies.

Before I could ask anything, Iris swept in with a platter of cinnamon-glazed ham and tender root vegetables, two mugs of golden Sunshine mead, and a plate crowned with three steaming biscuits as big as my palm.

Kiera immediately relaxed, her fingers snatching a biscuit the moment the plate touched the table. She quickly took a bite. I hid a smile as her eyes rounded like gold coins.

She let out a muffled groan that unfurled strange ribbons of heat through my stomach.

I looked away from her to thank Iris.

Iris grinned and winked at me. "I believe you've found the way to that girl's heart," she whispered conspiratorially in my ear.

I clenched my jaw. Gods, that was the *last* thing I wanted to do. Such attachments never ended well in my world.

Oblivious to my chagrin, Iris pattered away to answer the call of another customer.

Meanwhile, Kiera had inhaled her biscuit and was reaching for another.

I batted her hand away. "There are only three, little thief. You'll have to play me for the third."

She scowled. "It will be cold by then. I'll Duel you for it."

"Fine." We turned all the tiles facedown and shuffled them around. She drew Terraum's regal, bearded head, and I drew Viridana's smiling, doe-eyed impression.

"A draw," I said. "We could split the biscuit."

Kiera shook her head. "Again."

This time, I drew a two, and she flipped over Death.

"Ah, Death wins the biscuit," I said, graciously passing it to her.

Surprise and a hint of gratitude flickered in her eyes as she took it from me. After several moments of staring at the moist, flaky bread, she sighed and tore off a chunk for me. Not half. But something.

My lips quirked. "Thank you."

She didn't look at me as we devoured our biscuits. Her gaze pinned to a far corner of the tavern where Tercel had fashioned a target from a wooden barrel top and nailed it to the wall. A few men shouted and laughed as they competed with throwing knives.

"What weapons did you used to carry with you?" I asked her.

She glanced at me. "Is that the question you choose as your prize?"

"Yes." I wanted to know what she'd been like before her arrest. Last night had turned that curiosity from a prickle to a burn.

"Knives," she said, confirming my suspicion. "Small ones for throwing. Better than what they're playing with." She nodded at the men in the corner.

"Do you miss them?"

"Aren't you supposed to play me for the answer?" she asked dryly.

I shrugged, giving her a charming smile. "Humor me."

Her brows pinched together, and she took a sip of Sunshine. She smacked her lips. "Mmm, that's good. Why is it called Sunshine?"

"Because it tastes like sweet drops of sunshine," I said.

She gave me a dubious look before turning to stare at Tercel's perpetual frown. "*That* man named it Sunshine?"

I laughed. "No. A customer did, and it stuck. Sometimes I order it just to see his face turn sour. But people love it, so he won't stop making and selling it."

"It is very good," Kiera said, taking another swallow. She stared into her mug. "And I do miss them. The knives. I feel . . . exposed without them." Her eyelashes fluttered. "Last night, before you gave me your daggers, I was so afraid. If they had caught us, I would've fought to my last breath. But there's a difference between knowing you will certainly die and thinking you have even the slimmest chance of surviving. Knives give me that chance."

"I understand," I said softly.

I'd had to do terrible things to survive. Things that might drag my soul into the Abyss to wander through the Longest Night. Even vowing to never again put myself in a position to have to make those choices didn't heal the wound.

She mixed the tiles again. "My turn to win."

We set up another game as we chewed the sweet, hot meat and savory carrots and potatoes. Our plates were empty by the time she did indeed win the next game by the skin of her teeth.

She grinned as though she'd just won a fortune.

"Not subtle, are you?" I teased her as we drained the last of our mead.

"I still won, didn't I?" A golden drop of Sunshine slipped from her mouth, and she caught it with the tip of her tongue.

Warmth fizzled and popped in my blood. Probably from the mead. "Winning looks beautiful on you." Gods damn it, I should never drink around her.

She blinked at me, her cheeks flushed. "You think I'm beautiful?"

"Is that your question?"

"No! I . . . I . . ." She looked flustered, which gave me my own sense of triumph. "Where are you from?"

I grimaced. That was not a question I wanted. "Everywhere. Nowhere."

"That's not a real answer. I gave you—"

"Yes, yes." I held up my hands to stop her angry tirade. I sighed. "I was born on a ship on the Niviath Sea."

"Yes, in a storm, you said. I remember. But where did you live *before* you lived here?"

"Many places. You've already figured out a few."

She nodded. "Twaryn. Dagriel, with Maz, I assume. Is that all?"

"I've answered your question enough," I said through gritted teeth.

"With things I already knew!"

"Then ask me something else."

She hesitated, thinking for a moment. "How did you meet Maz?"

I shook my head. "Try again."

She growled in frustration. "You're impossible! I could ask you a thousand questions and get no answers."

"There are lots of things you could ask me. My favorite . . . color."

"I'm not wasting my win on something so trivial."

And I was glad she didn't, or I would've had to tell her that my favorite color was rapidly becoming the unique shade of golden brown in her eyes.

I glared into my empty mug. What kind of truth-telling, flirtation-inducing drug did Tercel put in the Sunshine tonight?

"Have you ever been to the sunstone mine?" she asked.

I froze. "Why would you ask me that?"

Her brow furrowed at my demand. "I don't know much about it. You seemed to have traveled a lot, so I simply wondered . . ."

The scar on my back burned with memory. "It's not a place you want to know. The closest a person can get to the Abyss in this world. Prisoners mine the sunstone. Soldiers guard the mine. No one gets out. It's a place of death." I flicked the Death tile away from me. "So I've heard."

"Prisoners? From where?" she whispered, her eyes full of horror.

Bitterness snaked into my voice. "You've lived in the palace all your life, and no one ever mentioned the mine?"

"They did. But never . . . never many details."

"Did you never wonder how Weylin carted in wagon after wagon of his precious sunstone? Did you think the miners were paid or even voluntary for a job that killed most people within a year of work?"

Kiera shook her head continuously as if to dislodge my words buzzing around her like flies.

I should stop. But I couldn't. Years of unsatisfied rage cast words like sparks from my throat. "It wasn't that way when the Falcryns ruled Rellmira. King Tristan and his father before him offered wages and the safe, clean town of Calimber to live in. But Weylin's greed is too great for such fairness."

My lips curled into a snarl as I drove my point home. "Where do you think we were headed once Renwell was done with us in the Den? Where Jerell is probably headed right now if there are enough working pieces of him left?"

"No. That can't be true," she said fiercely. But doubt clouded her eyes and crumpled her chin. "I would've heard about it. More people would know. People would—"

"Would what? Stand up to Weylin? Fight? Look what happened last time they did that. No one wants that to happen again. No one wants to be the woman we burned last night. *I* can't let—" My throat caught, snagged on guilt and secrets. I swallowed. "It's the way things are."

Silence sat between us like a cage, trapping all the things I'd said and couldn't take back.

"What if the People's Council came back?" Kiera whispered so quietly I almost missed it.

My gaze clenched hers as if I could pull her closer just by looking at her. "Who speaks treason now?" I rasped.

CHAPTER 15
KIERA

FEAR ALMOST SWALLOWED MY HEART.

What had started as a ploy to claw more information from Aiden's lips, to answer one of the many questions that had roiled in my mind since the conversation I'd overheard between Melaena and Garyth, became dangerous. Deadly.

Who speaks treason now? I would, if I must. To understand.

"The people would be more protected, would they not?" I asked.

But I had overplayed my hand, it seemed. Aiden slowly drew back, his gaze still never leaving mine, but the heat of it —a burn I felt on my very soul—was muted.

"I believe we have lost sight of the rules of our game," he said coolly. "Shall we play again?"

I wanted to scream with frustration and wring the answers I so desperately sought out of that gods-damned tongue of his. That tongue that distracted me with words of wit and comfort and charm.

How I loathed it.

Patience.

But I couldn't be patient for much longer. Time would run out quickly once I spoke to Renwell.

I nodded stiffly, and we played another game. Iris came by to fill our mugs once more, but we both asked for water instead. Cold, clear water to wash away the Sunshine.

There was no more teasing or banter. We played for victory. For a shield from the other's questions.

Aiden won. Barely.

Unwilling to draw his attention back to my fingers, I tapped my nerves out on my thigh. "Well?" I asked, anticipating a heavy strike.

And he delivered. "Tell me what you know of Weylin and his children."

My fingers tapped faster. "That's not a question."

He threw me a look that loudly protested my nitpicking. I threw him one back that stated *he* was the one worried about the rules.

"What do you know of Weylin and his children?" he growled. "What they're like, their habits, friends, enemies."

My fingers stilled. My stomach churned with dread. "Why do you want to know that?"

"Are you refusing to answer?"

I hesitated. If I refused to answer, as he had done several times, it would look like I had something to hide. While he didn't seem to mind hiding things from me, I held the lower ground here. I needed him to trust me, to tell me his plans. To do that, I would have to give, give, give.

I could lie. But he'd already shown himself to be quite adept at knowing when I was.

Or he was testing me. Seeing if I really had worked in the palace and was matching my information to his, as he had done with Melaena.

"I guarded the princesses as I told you," I said finally, feeling strange talking about my family—and myself—in such a way. "Emilia and Delysia. Sweet girls, if naïve. I spent all my time around them. I only saw Weylin occasionally at dinners. Same for the crown prince."

"Did you like Prince Everett?"

I frowned. "What is your interest in the prince?"

"I'm merely curious about the heir who never leaves the palace. Weylin has gone to great lengths to ensure his family has the only claim to the throne, so it makes me wonder why he hides the prince."

My eyes narrowed. "He's not hiding him. He's protecting him. Especially after his mother—" I broke off, swallowing hard.

Aiden's face darkened, and a thought struck me.

"You said you and Maz have been in Aquinon for years," I breathed. "Did you know of Queen Brielle?"

"Yes, I'd heard of her kindness," he said stiffly, his gaze dropping to where his long, callused fingers tightened around his mug. "The death of another innocent Weylin and Renwell should've protected is always tragic."

I gulped more water to soothe my aching throat, trying to read the contempt that pulsed in every muscle of Aiden's face. "Did you see anything that night? Hear anything?"

One pounding heartbeat. Two. Then three, and he finally

looked up at me as if coming out of a daze. "Maz and I were working elsewhere that night. Ruru told us about it in the morning."

"What did he say?" I asked desperately. Almost too desperately.

Renwell had told me what he'd seen, but perhaps Ruru had gleaned something more. My mentor would despise me asking, wouldn't want me to risk exposing my personal stake in the matter. But he wasn't here.

Aiden's mouth twisted to the side, as if he were trying to remember. "He saw the burning building near the Temple. He couldn't get too close because of the many Wolves, but he watched them carry the queen's body out of one of the rooms."

Tears pricked my eyes, and I had to stare down at the cluttered tiles. Renwell had told us the assassin killed my mother and somehow burnt a hole in the roof to climb out and escape when the Wolves surrounded the building. I'd wanted to see for myself where she was murdered, but Renwell said the building was destroyed. That there was nothing left.

"Is it gone now?" I asked, not daring to meet his eyes yet. "The building?"

"Yes. The fire consumed it, and the rubble was cleared out. Thank the gods it was an old, abandoned building, so no one else died."

Then Renwell had told the truth. Even if I went looking, I would find nothing new. I would never know who killed her or why.

A familiar frustration coupled with helplessness roared to life like a ravenous beast. It had nearly devoured me many times, but Renwell had encouraged me to keep training, to keep fighting, to keep honing myself into a weapon that could defend my family. Which usually kept the beast quiet, but never satisfied.

Aiden cleared his throat, bringing my gaze back to him. "You haven't answered the rest of my question."

"Your question was layered with many others. That is not a fair question."

"Yet I have also answered many of yours that weren't part of our wager."

The questions about my mother. Anger dug its claws into my gut. Those answers had cost him nothing and hadn't given me any new information.

What I *had* learned was of his hatred for Weylin and Renwell, of his disgust over the sunstone mine that he clearly knew much more about than I did. Which only sparked more questions like, why hadn't my father continued the same treatment of the miners as the Falcryns had before him? It seemed a prudent way to avoid another uprising.

Aiden also didn't want to speak of the People's Council. It sounded as though he didn't want to repeat the Pravaran rebellion, which was good news, but it made me wonder all the more what he was really after.

In return for these paltry details, he wanted information on my family like they were nothing but tiles in our game. Things he could use or discard. And I had to play along.

I would make a poor High Enforcer if I couldn't even stomach this task.

"The royals eat, sleep, and shit like everyone else, except they do it in a palace," I spat out. "The prince and princesses are kind but have few friends and innumerable, unknowable enemies because of who their father is. Weylin is quick to punish and never forgives. Why else do you think I'm here?"

Aiden was staring at my fingers again. Fingers I hadn't realized I was drumming against the table to the frantic pace of my heart. I crushed them into a fist.

When he looked up at me, his green eyes flickered with sympathy. "You must have cared for him a great deal."

Him . . . Julian. His memory would never stop haunting me either, it seemed. "I do," I said tightly. "I did." But I cared more for who I'd left behind in that palace.

"Let us call a ceasefire on Death and Four." Aiden jabbed his thumb at the knife target. "How about a different game instead?"

Savage relief flooded my veins. "Yes."

Aiden swept the tiles back into the bag while I rose from the table.

A heavy hand clamped on my shoulder. Without thinking, I threw my elbow backward into a taut stomach, eliciting an "oof!" Then I wrenched the thick wrist away from me.

"Whoa, easy there, lovely," a familiar, deep voice rumbled over my head.

I released Maz and turned to see his blue eyes wide with surprise.

He backed up a step. "Forgive me, I should've announced myself." He grinned. "That was a gods-damned quick response, though. Fierce little warrior. My sisters would love you."

I caught my breath, willing the fight to recede from my quivering muscles. The tavern, which had gone silent at our quick scuffle, resumed its hum of activity. A few women at the bar smiled at me appreciatively before turning those smiles on Maz.

"You have sisters?" I forced out. "How many?"

"Three. All younger, but any one of them could take me in a fight."

I managed a weak chuckle. "I suppose that's the best compliment you could give them."

"Of course." Maz drew up to his full height and puffed out his chest, winking at the women by the bar.

I rolled my eyes. "Does nothing damage your ego?"

"I wouldn't know. Haven't found anything strong enough yet."

I laughed along with him, finally relaxing. Maz had that strange, elusive power few did to make a friend of anyone. Even people like me and Aiden, who usually preferred to be left alone with our secrets.

But that didn't mean we didn't want to be found occasionally. And Maz seemed to like finding us.

"You already ate?" Maz asked, staring at the remnants of our meal, crestfallen.

I nodded.

"We were about to throw knives," said Aiden's voice behind me. "Grab your food and drink and join us."

I twisted my head to see Aiden giving Maz one of those significant looks. About me? About something else?

Then his gaze dipped down to me, and for a moment, nothing else existed. His black hair fell nearly to his beautiful green eyes, their contrast stark and mysterious. The shadow of his stubble merely enhanced his bronze cheekbones and embraced his lips like a gift.

He was the most attractive man I'd ever seen. Even with the threat he posed. Even when I was furious with him for the position he put me in.

He'd called me beautiful twice now. But he was only charming when he wanted something. I couldn't trust his little sympathies or his warm smiles. And I certainly couldn't trust the way he was looking at me now, as if I, too, were the only person in the room.

"After you," he said, tipping his head.

I pursed my lips and made my way to the target. The two men throwing were getting increasingly sloppy as their empty mugs piled higher. They didn't deserve those knives. I did. I *needed* them.

The men's bloodshot eyes looked me up and down and dismissed me.

I stepped closer. "Best of three. Winner names their price."

The bigger one guffawed, his knife hitting well outside the bullseye. He wore leather boots and a wide-brimmed hat, both caked with dust. He smelled of livestock and cheap beer. A cattle driver from the province of Winspere. Likely spent a lot of time in the saddle, playing with his knives.

I'd played many a friendly game with others from that rough, wind-swept province, but these two had a nasty look about them. Which would make this all the more satisfying.

The second man wore similarly stained clothes, but his sneer, like his nose, was sharper. "You don't even have knives, girl."

I shrugged. "I'll borrow yours. Advantage to you."

Beak Nose spat on the floor. "What do we win?"

His friend elbowed him in the side. "She said whatever we

want. I know *exactly* what I'll be takin' as my prize." He licked his lips as his beady eyes crawled over my body.

A wall of warmth crowded my back. "Not if I take your life first."

Aiden's growled threat stripped me of my contempt, leaving me cold with shock.

The men's faces paled. *Him* they believed. *Him* they feared.

I spun to face Aiden, finding his exposed collarbone inches from my mouth. His bristled chin scraped my forehead.

I jerked backward. "Leave this to me," I hissed.

He looked down at me, rage swirling like storm clouds in his eyes. "Beat them, or I will."

I didn't need his rage. Only mine. These men were never going to claim any prize from me. They were simply a means to an end. Arrogance and lust only made them more stupid.

And Holy Four, did I want this win more than ever now. I'd lost control back at that table. I'd shown vulnerability. I'd gotten distracted.

But here, with knives in my hand, I would feel right again.

I pointed at Beak Nose. "Give me your knives. I'm playing your friend first."

He started to sneer again, but then glanced at Aiden towering behind me and handed them over. Something quieted in me as I held them.

Five simple steel knives with wooden hilts that had been handled to a shine. Nothing so nice as Aiden's or my old ones. But they would do.

I'd played around with any knife I could get a hold of as a child. Earned myself plenty of scars in those early years. But

I'd gotten very good. And Renwell had made sure I was even better.

Beady Eyes ripped his knives out of the target and backed out of the way. "The lady may go first," he said in a mockingly subservient tone.

I lined up with the target, drew back my arm, and threw. Third ring.

A muffled groan came from Aiden, who leaned against a high table, effectively caging in our little group.

Beady Eyes and Beak Nose cheered and slapped hands with each other.

I suppressed my own smile and threw four more times, hitting the third and second rings twice each. Aiden grew quieter with each one while my other two targets grew louder.

Maz showed up on my last throw with a hunk of meat in one hand and a full mug in the other. His brows scrunched together. "What's happening?"

Aiden gave him a low, rapid explanation as Maz's face took on the same stormy look. I ignored them both.

Beady Eyes had better throws than mine and practically fell over with giddiness, jumping around like a buffoon.

This time, I did smile, holding up my bouquet of knives. "Yes, you win that round. Now, you throw first."

He did, a few of his knives going very wide in his elation, but he just waved his filthy hand. "Psh, won't matter, won't matter. She's got nothin'." He leered at me, leaning close enough to show me his brown teeth.

I slipped one of my knife tips under his weak chin. "Stand clear, or you'll lose every piece of flesh I can reach."

He scoffed but took a begrudging step back. I had no idea if

I'd ever make good on such a threat, but sometimes threats were enough. Even if they were lies.

Out of the corner of my eye, I noticed Aiden and Maz looking murderous.

I threw my knives, calculating just enough for a win. But now, Beady Eyes was serious. His so-called prize was in jeopardy. He couldn't lose in front of all these men—and a few women who had crowded closer.

Maybe now there would actually be some sport to it.

I gestured for him to lead again, and he did. Hit the bullseye once with four hits to the second ring.

A few of the men, including Beak Nose, cheered and clapped him on the back. He grinned, all doubt gone.

I grinned back and threw one knife. Then the next. And the next until I'd flung all five. All while beaming into his slack-jawed face.

A loud cheer rose around me. Each of my five knives quivered in the bullseye, nearly obscuring it. Maz pushed Aiden aside to wrap me in a huge hug and bounce me up and down. I laughed as other hands reached forward to pat me on the back and voices called out praise.

But I sought Aiden's gaze.

His smile was quieter than the others, more reserved, but his eyes glowed with admiration. Somehow, I knew that he'd guessed my game and stayed silent while I hustled the cursing oaf behind me.

I pried the knives out of the target and waved them at Beady Eyes. "These are my prize."

He clenched his fists. "You cheated."

"No. I simply have more skill than you."

He growled, stalking toward me, but stopped abruptly when two pillars of muscle flanked me.

"Careful, cow herder," Maz warned.

"Touch her," Aiden growled, "and we'll strap you to the target where she'll show you just how much skill she has."

I blinked at such rage, such violence, on my behalf. Only Renwell had ever been so protective of me. But it felt different coming from two men who knew me so little. The sensation was uncomfortable, yet not altogether unpleasant.

Beak Nose tugged on his friend's arm. "Let the girl have my cheap old knives. Come on, there's more sport to be had at *The Broken Coin*." With one last nasty look over his shoulder, Beady Eyes allowed himself to be dragged from the tavern.

Another round of cheers went up, and Iris filled everyone's cups.

More contenders offered to play me, and before another hour had passed, I had a small purse of coins, a few free drinks, and a jaunty, feathered cap from a fletcher who nearly beat me. Maz kept stealing the hat from me and belting out drinking songs with the ridiculous peacock feathers bobbing in his face.

Flushed with success and Sunshine, I pressed a few coins into Iris's palm. She tried to wave me off, saying Aiden had paid her already, but I insisted. I hadn't realized how good it would feel to pay for something.

As others competed against each at throwing, I settled onto a high stool next to Aiden, who hadn't thrown once. He nursed a single mug of mead as if he couldn't have another.

I brushed my sweaty hair off my forehead and smiled at him, jingling my purse. "Care to challenge me as well?"

"Maybe some other time. I would like to offer you a job instead."

My eyebrows arched. "You'll let me work with Ruru?"

He nodded slowly, as if still coming to terms with his decision. "I have a job I could use some help with, but in the meantime, I'm sure Ruru won't mind sharing the work he picks up around the city as a courier. He'll show you the ropes, and the two of you can work side by side until you're ready to be on your own."

I flipped one of my newly won knives over and over. "You realize you'll have to tell me what your business is."

"I work in shipping. I send and receive cargo, which is then distributed to its buyers."

Shipping. I blinked at how easily he divulged his work. But shipping made sense. He had a warehouse full of crates. He'd mentioned "his" captain. Skeevy or Skully or something. People seemed to come to him for things.

But it seemed so . . . ordinary for a man who'd snuck into the Den and killed Shadow-Wolves.

"Do you ship things for Melaena?" I asked, piecing together more information.

"Yes, she's my main business associate. A lot of what is in the warehouse is hers."

"Does that mean I get to visit it without a blindfold this time?" I teased him.

But his expression hardened. "Let me be clear, little thief. I'm offering you this job because you've shown you're capable. And you were right. I don't want to always assign a guard to you to ensure that you are behaving yourself. You may help Ruru with his work, but you are not privy to all parts of my business. If I feel that you have endangered my operation or my people in any way, I will have Skelly drop you on the farthest island in Eloren with only snakes and rats for company."

"Death, then," I said flatly, clutching my knives.

"A chance to survive." His words echoed my earlier ones.

Without warning, he stole one of my knives and whipped it between the two men currently throwing. It slammed into the bullseye dead-center.

Everyone turned to stare. Maz chuckled and shook his head, the peacock feather drooping into his cup.

"Don't try to hustle me, Kiera," Aiden said, his mouth set in a grim line. "You'll regret it."

Not as much as he was going to regret ever meeting me.

CHAPTER 16

KIERA

THE NEXT FEW DAYS BEGAN TO TAKE ON A NEW RHYTHM.

Ruru and I ran messages and packages through every quarter but the Noble. Which was just as well, since very few people outside the upper class might recognize me. For once, my restriction to the palace worked in my favor.

We delivered things like cloth and thread for seamstresses, wood for carpenters, letters for soldiers' wives, beer and food for tavern keepers. He even delivered a toe fungus powder to a jailer from the city prison while I watched from afar with my face covered.

Some of the items and messages came from Aiden, but many others came from the same ordinary folks we delivered to.

Under Ruru's cheerful tutelage, I learned more of the city than I ever could've staring at maps in Renwell's study. He showed me where to walk and who to talk to. We never ran at night to avoid the Wolves. But he told me plenty about the day guards, who seemed much less vicious—and therefore, less feared—than the Wolves. I worried what that might mean if I were to gain control of them one day as High Enforcer.

We walked past the city gate that I'd never been outside of —and neither had he—and past the Temple and the city prison that I gave a wide berth. The few memories I had of those places were painful enough.

But for the first time in a week, I didn't feel so lost.

I handled every package, coin, and message with the utmost care, especially Aiden's. He had no reason to suspect me of any wrongdoing.

That didn't mean I didn't lift the sealed envelopes to the light to discern what was written inside. But what I read was nothing more than business transactions for the items we carried. No mention of Garyth or the People's Council.

We also ran errands for our landlady and personal cook and laundress, Sophie. A short, cantankerous woman with frizzy gray hair, she had yet to say a single word to me outside of barking orders. But she fed me, washed my clothes, and let me pay a pittance.

So, I ran her tea to Floren and delivered her food to pregnant mothers and fetched her deliveries from the market.

But the days were slipping by too quickly. I wasn't gleaning any more of Aiden's secrets. I didn't know where he disappeared to or why he needed so much gold when it seemed his business was prosperous enough.

I had thought to ask him about the gold again—as one of my prizes during our game of Death and Four—but he'd already refused to answer that question once. I didn't want him to get suspicious of my interest.

I'd asked Maz once, in passing, what he planned to do with his share.

He winked and said, "Buy myself a beautiful axe. Made by Dags, of course. The best there is."

"Surely Aiden is letting you keep more gold than that."

He shrugged. "Perhaps we'd just like to buy ourselves a new life of freedom. Same as you."

Then he hurried out the door, claiming the heat was muddling his brain, and he needed to go for a good soak in a bathhouse.

Clearly, Aiden and Maz had much bigger plans for the gold than "a new life of freedom." They wouldn't risk infiltrating the Den or stealing from the High Treasurer if they didn't. I just couldn't figure out what those plans were. If he didn't want to incite a rebellion, what did he want? And what would they do if their plan for the heist failed?

I needed to follow Aiden more closely instead of running errands for pocket change. But between working with Ruru and my daily rehearsals with Melaena, I had little time to spare. Which was probably part of Aiden's reasoning for letting me work with Ruru. I had no time or energy to pry into his affairs.

The few times I saw him at night back in our rooms, he seemed distracted and worn out. Maz seemed similarly occupied, albeit in a less brooding way. More . . . eager.

I asked Aiden once if he needed any help preparing for the heist, and he said it was taken care of, that he would give me the details later. That all I needed to worry about was rehearsing with Melaena.

188 • LEAH MARA

Which frustrated me, working so hard to prepare for a heist that would likely never happen.

Because once I told Renwell about it, he would put a stop to it. Ruru gave me enough leeway to easily slip away and leave my mark for Renwell. But I didn't want to until after I finished tonight's job.

Aiden had agreed to let me help deliver his ship's goods to his warehouse, saying it should be easy for me with my skills as a "guard."

I took that to mean my job would be to protect while staying quiet and out of the way. But I didn't care. I wanted to see what cargo needed protection and what else was in that warehouse.

Perhaps he was smuggling weapons or poisons or explosives —things that might be passed through Melaena's hands to Garyth and his shadowy allies. He might not want a rebellion of poorly armed Pravaran farmers, but a war? An assassination? He could also be making foreign allies with his shipping business.

But the ship was late.

Ruru and I sat on the sea wall—the quarter's last defense against a heavy tide—while Aiden and Maz paced the docks. Other ships had docked and unloaded their cargo, and their bone-rattlers were already crowding the many taverns.

Another hour tolled by before a large ship sailed into harbor. Its white sails plumed like clouds against the purple twilight.

"About bloody time," Maz grumbled, tossing another rock into the only empty berth.

Aiden didn't cease pacing until the ship—*Mynastra's Wings*

—threw down the anchor. A gangplank slid down to the dock. Aiden all but ran up it and disappeared.

"Tell me, where did *Mynastra's Wings* fly from this time?" I asked Ruru, passing him a bag of roasted nuts we'd bought from the market earlier with some of our wages.

Ruru tossed a nut in the air and caught it in his mouth. "Eloren, I believe. Skelly frequents several ports through the isles. Anywhere he doesn't have hefty gambling debts."

I frowned, watching as Aiden reappeared carrying a crate. Several barefoot sailors with their chattering ropes of bones passed down more crates and barrels while Aiden and Maz loaded them into two wagons pulled by two pairs of large horses. Floren had rented them to Aiden for tonight.

"Doesn't that concern Aiden that his captain has money problems? Could his loyalty not be easily bought and sold?" I asked.

"Not ole Skelly's. Aiden takes care of his sick wife, you see. And his daughter. Skelly wouldn't turn against Aiden for all the money in Lancora."

He had found Skelly's weakness, as Renwell would say. Yet, instead of using his debts against him, Aiden cared for his family.

There it was again. That little flicker of warmth for Aiden. I'd felt it several times.

When he'd protected me. When he'd healed me. When he had spoken of my mother with kindness and sorrow.

Sometimes it was difficult to think of him as my enemy. As someone who might have gruesome plans for my kingdom. I'd seen him kill two Shadow-Wolves, but from what I'd seen and heard, those men had probably committed much worse crimes.

Even Aiden's threats were born of a desire to shield others from harm.

I needed the truth, once and for all. To quiet the storm in my mind. To put the shadows back where they belonged.

A red-faced dock official hurried up to Aiden, who handed him a piece of paper. The man barely glanced at it before scribbling on it and scurrying off again.

I frowned. "Why didn't the official check the cargo?"

Ruru shrugged. "We have a deal with him. We get our cargo off his docks immediately, and he doesn't look too closely at it. For a few extra coins, of course."

Of course.

"All right, catch this, and I'll give you a copper," Ruru said with a grin.

Without warning, he lobbed a nut into the air, and I flung myself backward to catch it. I lost my seating and barely caught myself from falling to the ground. My boots stuck up in the air with my ass sliding down the other side of the wall.

Ruru roared with laughter, spilling our nuts every which way.

"Be quiet," I grunted. "Pull me up, you little monkey."

He clasped my hand and helped drag me back up the wall. Cheeks flaming, I noticed Maz laughing at us, along with the sailors. Aiden's face was shadowed by his hood, but it was turned in our direction.

Perfect.

"Give me those." I snatched the paper bag from Ruru's hands.

"Fine." He smirked. "But I'm keeping my copper."

"Stake it for another round of Death and Four," I challenged.

His expression soured. "Not a chance. I'll never understand that game." His brown eyes brightened. "Teach me more knife-throwing?"

Ever since Maz had told him of that night at the tavern, Ruru had begged me to show him how to throw. In between deliveries and in quiet alleys, I showed him the basics. He was a quick learner. He told me he wanted to be a soldier one day. Maybe even High General.

My heart ached to think of him turning into someone as cold and ruthless as High General Dracles. But perhaps my brother would choose someone different when he became king.

A sharp whistle cut across the deserted docks.

Ruru and I both stiffened, looking toward Aiden, who waited next to the fully loaded wagons. The bone-rattlers had disappeared, either onto their ship or into the packed taverns behind the sea wall.

Aiden gestured to us, and we hurried over.

"We'll drive as quickly as we can since we have little time left," Aiden said grimly, then focused on me. "No one is allowed to move cargo through the city after dark. Once the Wolves are out, they will certainly stop us if they catch us. Ruru with Maz. Kiera with me."

My heart beat faster. I whisked my fingers over the four knives tucked into my belt and the one in my boot.

Maz took the first wagon with Ruru, and I climbed onto the

seat next to Aiden. The moment I was settled, he snapped the reins over the horses' backs.

The streets were as empty as the taverns and inns were full. No one wanted to risk a run-in with a Shadow-Wolf. Even the sea was fairly quiet, just the gentle hush of waves. I'd overheard Maz telling Aiden last night that the Wolves had gotten particularly violent in this quarter since our escape. Perhaps they thought we might still be here.

Suddenly, I wished Aiden would urge the horses into a gallop.

"Steady, little thief," he murmured as I looked over my shoulder for the tenth time. "We'll make it."

The horses strained as we mounted the cliff road and began the long, back-and-forth journey up the cliffside. I clung to the edge of the wagon seat, forcing myself to keep my eyes open. But I didn't dare look over the edge of the road as the wagon swayed and rattled. Our cargo groaned under the ropes that secured it to the bed.

I lifted my eyes to the sky, my heart sinking with the last ribbons of pink and scarlet that trailed after the sun I could no longer see.

"Gods damn it," I breathed. "Why was Skelly late?"

"Storm. He lost two of his men."

I winced. "May the gods find their souls."

"May Mynastra collect their bones."

"Is that what sailors say? When one of them dies?"

Aiden nodded as his eyes remained pinned to Maz's wagon. "They sink the bodies to the sea floor, where it's rumored Mynastra's own bones lie."

Death always won. It had even come for the gods and

goddesses when they left this world to us humans. Thus began the Age of Peace. Although peace had dwindled in the centuries after the gods died. When those who weren't alive to remember the wars became restless.

"Fucking Four," Aiden cursed harshly.

A small box had worked its way free of the ropes mooring it to Maz's wagon and fell to the ground. Aiden yanked on the reins, bringing the horses to a snorting halt. He whistled for Maz to stop.

I leapt off my seat and raced for the box before Ruru had even turned his head. I seized it. Something skittered inside, and I nearly dropped it.

A howl rose from the Docks Quarter below us. My stomach plummeted. I peered over the edge but saw nothing in the shadows. But they were there. They were hunting.

"Move, Kiera!" Aiden commanded.

Instead of trying to shove the trembling box back onto Maz's wagon, I sprinted to Aiden.

"Go!" I gasped, jumping into my seat.

Aiden whistled again, and Maz's wagon jolted forward the same moment ours did. Slapping the reins, Aiden urged the horses faster. Sweat shone on their dark coats as they strained over the last stretch of the cliff road.

I released a deep sigh of relief as we passed under the torch-lit gate. We weren't safe yet, but we could lose ourselves in the labyrinth of the city before the Wolves reached the gate.

We didn't speak again as the wagons rolled into the alleys of the Old Quarter. I knew where we were going this time. Aiden's warehouse. But the likelihood of peering into a few of his crates was miniscule with Wolves snapping at our heels.

The wooden wheels scraped against the narrow alley walls, and I clutched the box in my lap tighter. Whatever was inside had quieted. Perhaps I could risk a peek once we stopped.

We drove directly to the warehouse this time. Aiden likely knew I had no trouble locating it by this point. We rolled to a stop in front of one of the many long, low buildings that huddled in the shadow of the high city wall. The same wall that cut off the Old Quarter from the Noble Quarter. The one Aiden tunneled under. No soldiers patrolled this wall—only the edges of the city.

We were alone. For now.

Aiden faced me, only his mouth and chin visible under his hood. "Keep a lookout with Ruru. Whistle if someone comes. If it's them, run, hide. Don't let them capture you."

I forced a tiny smirk. "Can't break me out of prison twice?"

"You would never make it to a cell."

I swallowed hard, remembering the woman. Her brother.

Aiden disappeared into an alley where I guessed the door was. Maz started unloading crates from his wagon. Ruru waved at me from his seat, but my hands were locked around the box.

The box.

I pried my fingers away from it, noticing the holes cut into the sides. I carefully lifted the top. Something rustled inside. Whatever it was, I couldn't risk it escaping. A thin, scaley tail suddenly whipped through the crack, and I slammed the top closed.

Some kind of lizard? Who in the deep, dark, wandering hell would smuggle in an exotic creature from—

I nearly laughed. Garyth's daughter, Isabel. So, this was the birthday present Garyth had ordered from Melaena. Aiden was Melaena's—and therefore, the nobles'—supplier of illegal goods. But was that the extent of it? Or did he supply more than just unique pets?

Gods damn it, if only I could poke around the warehouse. I wasn't even going to be able to get inside. All I'd managed to see was a girl's lizard. Hardly a secret worth telling Renwell.

Aiden strode to Maz's wagon and began wordlessly helping him unload it. Then they carried their crates toward the warehouse.

Biting my lip and keeping an eye on the back of Ruru's head, I set the lizard box beside me. I pried the lids off one, two, then three crates to see inside. Boxes of tea, casks of liquor, and tins of spice. Fat bags of rice with their weight and origin stamped on the burlap leaned against the barrels. All from Eloren.

Nothing from Dagriel. Nothing from Keldiket. No sign of weapons or armor or anything that might hint at whatever Aiden or Garyth were planning.

Why was Aiden so protective of his business then? Why did he keep so many secrets?

I quickly sat forward when Aiden and Maz came back for another load. I did my duty and studied every twisting alley within sight. There were no windows and doors along this alley, aside from the other warehouses. But all was quiet.

It took two more trips for Aiden and Maz to empty the first wagon. Then they started on mine, taking the lizard first.

Unease prickled at the back of my neck. I looked behind me, but nothing moved in the shadows.

I quietly clucked my tongue, making my horses' ears twitch but also catching the attention of Ruru, who turned immediately. I beckoned him over. He hopped down and rushed over to my wagon.

"You see something?" he whispered, his owlish eyes blinking.

"No, but what's the sense of guarding an empty wagon when we can stand watch together?"

He grinned. "I like the way your mind works. Got any more nuts?"

I picked a few from my pocket and handed them to him. "What was in your boxes? Anything interesting? I think I had a lizard in one of mine," I said with a smile.

"We get lots of strange requests like that." Ruru lowered his voice further. "Spices that make you see things. Berries that cost ten gold coins a handful. Jewelry that changes your mood."

My nose wrinkled. I'd never heard of such things. "You jest."

"I swear by the Four. Melaena gave a bracelet of yellow jewels to a woman who had lost her husband and—"

"Quiet!" I grabbed his elbow.

Something was wrong. The skin on the back of my neck crawled once more. Just as I heard the barest whisper of sound. A soft boot brushing over stone.

I slowly turned my head, glancing around the edge of my hood. My breath stuttered and died on my lips.

Two dark figures walked in tandem, steadily approaching from behind. Moonlight glinted off their demonic masks.

"Wolves," I choked out.

"Face forward," Ruru whispered. "Hold on." He snapped the reins and whistled a merry tune as we slowly pulled away.

"What are you doing?" I demanded. "Aiden said to run."

"We can lose them if we make it to the southern end of the quarter, closer to the taverns." Fear trembled in his voice. "Or at least give Aiden and Maz a chance to lock themselves in the warehouse."

We slowly rounded a bend.

"Are they still following?" Ruru asked.

One moment. Two. My clammy palms gripped the side of the wagon as I darted a glance behind us.

"They're gaining," I gasped.

The two Shadow-Wolves loped toward us as if they could catch us easily but didn't want to. Yet.

Ruru snapped the reins again, and the horses trotted faster. The wagon's rattling shook my very bones, my teeth clattering together.

But still, the Wolves came closer.

"It's not working." I tugged on Ruru's arm. "We need to abandon the wagon."

Aiden's words howled through my mind, *Run, hide, don't let them capture you.*

"Not yet. Do you know how much this cargo is worth?" Ruru gritted out, turning the wagon down a narrow alley.

"Less than our lives," I snapped. "We need to run. Now!"

Ruru glanced over his shoulder, and his eyes widened. I didn't need to look to know how close they were. The light rhythm of their boots in a matched pace told me everything I needed to know.

They were close. They were faster. And they wouldn't tire for hours.

"Fucking Four," Ruru swore, then jerked the reins to the side, making the horses swerve.

The wagon careened sideways to block the alley. Ruru and I leapt out the other side and sprinted. Muted thumps signaled the wagon had only slowed the Wolves for a moment. They didn't want our cargo. They wanted us.

Terror tore at my heart as we raced.

Ruru tugged me down one alley, then another. I was lost, my panic and the shadows rendering the city strange and deadly. Like my nightmare.

"No. No!" he shouted as he came to an abrupt halt.

Our alley ended in a pile of rubble. One of the buildings had collapsed and effectively crushed our exit.

Ruru leapt forward, trying to scramble his way up the loose rock and broken wood.

Behind us, the boots had stopped.

I turned, my heart a caged, thrashing animal in my chest. Two snarling metal masks faced me. Glittering black daggers rested in gloved fists. They stood utterly still. They knew we were cornered.

"Ruru," I said in a hollow, unrecognizable voice. "Can you make it?"

He appeared at my side, panting. "N-no. There's too much . . . I can't . . ."

Blood snaked down his arms from where debris must have sliced his skin. But he pulled the pathetically small knife I'd trained him with from his belt and crouched low.

"They won't take us, Kiera. I won't let them," he said.

My heart stuttered. I'd known this boy a handful of days, and he was willing to die trying to save us? There was no way he could fight two Shadow-Wolves and live. Even I would be hard-pressed—

I froze.

I couldn't fight them either. Renwell had been very clear—*never interfere with my Wolves.*

But had Renwell ordered them to spare me, should they happen upon me? Or had he assumed I wouldn't be anywhere near them on my mission?

No. The Wolves had hunted us, cornered us. They meant to take us. But I refused to be that woman who died begging for a life. I would die fighting for it. For both of our lives. And this time, I had the knives to do it.

I exhaled slowly and untied my cloak before tossing it aside. The Wolves didn't even seem to breathe as I unsheathed two knives.

"Ruru, when I say run, you run."

His head swiveled toward me, taking in my knives. "Wh-what? No, Kiera! They will kill you! Or take you! They've taken my friends, my brother—"

I thrust him behind me, flipping one knife to grasp the tip. My best chance was to take one Wolf down before dealing with the other.

"Ready?" I whispered to Ruru, bouncing on the balls of my feet.

The Wolves dropped to identical crouches, their blades lifted.

The left or the right?

Sweat rolled down my cold neck.

Whatever happened in the next few moments would stain my soul or take it.

The one on the left shifted the tiniest bit, tracking Ruru.

My arm lashed out like a whip. Silver streaked, and the Wolf fell backward, my knife in his throat.

The world suddenly felt made of glass, fragile and silent.

And the Wolf's body hitting the ground shattered it.

Ruru shouted as the other Wolf charged me.

I barely avoided his first swing. He slashed at my ribs. I pivoted and seized his fist, driving my second knife to his neck.

But he whirled and kicked me in the stomach. I flew backward, landing in a heap. My knife clattered somewhere out of reach. But our positions had switched.

Ruru stepped forward as if he were going to take my place, but I struggled to my feet and shoved him. "Run, you idiot!" His footsteps raced back the way we'd come.

I pulled out two more knives as the Wolf attacked. I blocked his strike, and my knife shattered with that same sickening shriek of metal. Like Maz's axe.

He stabbed again. I dropped and rolled out of reach. I flung my knife, aiming for his neck. The surest kill.

He twisted at the last moment, my knife simply grazing him. A low hiss came from behind the mask. My mind blanked with fear. I had one knife left.

My fingers plunged into my boot just as he charged. I wrenched to the side, catching his wrist. I slammed my elbow into his lungs and my heel into his groin. His grip slackened. I kicked his legs out from under him while using his weight and momentum to fling him over my shoulder.

I ripped the knife out of my boot and drove into the nearest bit of him—the wrist of his knife hand.

He screamed and thrashed. I backed away, defenseless. He

tore my bloody knife from his wrist and flung it away from him. He transferred his sunstone blade to his good hand.

Gods damn it. I had nothing left. No more knives. I couldn't—

Something caught the corner of my eye. My knife in the other Wolf's throat.

But my remaining enemy noticed it too. He charged. I dropped to my knees and spun under his slashes, ripping my knife out of the body. My stomach heaved, but I forced my fingers to grip the bloody knife tighter.

I brought the knife down to the Wolf's chest, but he caught my arm, placed a boot on my chest, and crushed me against a wall.

I gasped, my ribs groaning, collapsing. The air shimmered around me.

Gods, I couldn't breathe.

Use your knife.

I limply stabbed at his ankle until he jerked away, and I slid down the wall.

Get up. Get up! Do not die like this!

My mother's body flashed through my mind. Stabbed. Lifeless. Unavenged.

Groaning, I shakily rose to my feet. The Wolf waited for me, blood leaking from his injuries.

Me or him.

Each breath rasped through my lungs.

"No," I whispered. Then louder. "You—" I pointed the bloody knife at him. "—will be joining him."

He didn't make a sound. He simply stilled and slowly shook his head once.

We struck at the same time. I stabbed his shoulder. His knife sliced across my chest. Fiery pain drew a cry from my lips. I twisted backward, his next strike whistling past my cheek.

I slashed in a frenzy, barely scraping his arms and legs. But I couldn't reach . . . he was too fast . . .

Gods, the pain.

There was no air. Anymore.

I clumsily ducked another swipe, but he swung backward, catching my temple with the hilt of his knife.

I collapsed.

Someone shouted. My name? It didn't matter.

Darkness consumed my last sky. And that knife made of stars.

CHAPTER 17

AIDEN

I HEARD THE WHISTLED TUNE FIRST.

I waved my arm at Maz and nodded toward the door of the warehouse.

He stilled and listened. "Gods damn it," he breathed.

Kiera.

Fear slithered through my body and nested in my stomach. Would she remember my instructions? Would she stay with Ruru?

I gently closed the hatch on the smuggler's hold, sending up a cloud of dust. I swallowed hard to keep from coughing. Maz darted around stacks of crates and barrels to get to the door. The whistling faded away, as did the sound of the wagon wheels.

Maz peered into the empty alleyway. "I don't see anyone. Should we go after them?"

I frowned. "Ruru wouldn't be foolish enough to take the

wagon if it was Wolves. Perhaps it was just a random passerby."

But the doubt on Maz's face mirrored the one in my gut. No one but us was desperate enough to be out here with the Wolves.

"Gods damn it, Ruru," I muttered, then louder, "We can't do much else without a wagon to unload, anyway. Move the other wagon out of sight, then we'll follow."

Maz nodded and raced for the empty wagon while I quietly locked the warehouse.

Fucking Four, little thief, I hope you heeded my warning.

I strode in the direction I'd heard Ruru whistling, Maz quickly catching up with me.

"Rooftops," I commanded, finding a low building to scale.

A scrape behind me told me Maz was following, but I didn't wait. I sprinted across the rooftops.

My feet didn't falter as I leapt from one building to the next, dancing around debris. I slid over domed roofs and ducked under laundry lines. Despite the needles of fear in my chest, my senses were sharpened to a clarity I craved. Even if the cost was steep.

Something caught the corner of my eye, and I skidded to a halt. Maz caught up a moment later, breathing hard.

"The wagon," I said, pointing to where it was turned sideways in a narrow alley.

"Cargo's still there," Maz grunted.

"Kiera and Ruru must be on foot." My gut twisted. "Or their pursuers caught up with them."

"Gods damn it," Maz swore softly. "Which way would Ruru take her?"

He would head south toward more populated areas with more places to hide. "This way." I jumped over a narrow alley, tucked my body, and rolled onto the next roof. Guilt gnashed at my heels, making me run faster. I had to find them.

Kiera had knives, but could she use them against Shadow-Wolves? How many were there? I'd heard no howls.

My chest burned. I wanted to roar at the night sky, but I needed every last breath to get to her. To them. I couldn't bear more deaths on my soul.

"There!" Maz shouted and swung down to the street.

We landed in front of a fleeing Ruru. His eyes were wide with panic, and he was covered in dirt and bloody scrapes.

"What happened?" I demanded. "Where's Kiera?"

He gulped for air, gesturing wildly behind him. "Back . . . back there. Two Wolves."

A thousand curses flooded my mind. "Show me," I bit out.

We ran through a twisted mess of alleys until the sounds of a struggle reached my ears. The next moment, I jerked to a standstill at the scene before me.

A body in black on the ground.

Kiera slashing and stabbing at a Wolf who tried to cut her down with equal fervor.

She was alive. But hurt. Her movements weakening.

My blades were in my hands before I could think. I charged just as the Wolf hit her on the side of her head. She crumpled.

"Kiera!" I roared.

The Wolf's attention shot toward me. But I didn't hesitate. I leapt at him. Sank one blade through his weapon hand and the other into his throat, pinning him to a wall.

The sunstone knife clattered to the ground. The Wolf gurgled, shuddering on my blade.

I ripped his mask off. His heavy, scarred face sneered at me even as he choked on his own blood.

As the life left his eyes, I whispered, "May the gods never find your soul."

I wrenched my blades out of his body, letting it slide to the ground. I hurried over to where Ruru knelt next to Kiera. Maz stood over them both, his face stricken, axe in hand.

"Don't touch her," I snapped at Ruru.

He backed away, his eyes cast down. The rage in my blood cooled. I set aside my knives and laid a bloody hand on his arm. "Forgive me, Ruru. This isn't your fault."

He looked up at me, silver lining his dark eyes. "She's still breathing."

I inhaled sharply, turning my full attention to Kiera. Her body was so still. Only a slight rise and fall in her chest.

I turned from warrior to healer. I pressed my fingers to her neck. A faint pulse. I traced her body from head to toe, checking for broken bones and swelling. She had a shallow but nasty cut across her chest and a large lump on her temple. Her limp fingers still held a bloody knife.

"Stay with me," I murmured to her.

I worked the knife out of her grasp, wiped it off on the dead Wolf, and shoved it in my boot.

"They came out of nowhere." Ruru was babbling. "They wouldn't stop coming. I tried to lose them but . . . but the alley." He gestured weakly at the pile of rubble.

"Did they howl for help?" Maz demanded, stalking a perimeter around us.

"No. She . . . she killed that one quickly." Ruru pointed at the body lying deeper in the alley. "And I heard nothing from the other one, even after she told me to run."

"Thank the gods," Maz breathed.

"Don't thank them yet." I stared down at Kiera's bloodied body. Memories battled for my sanity. Darkness crowded my vision. How did I always end up standing over the body of someone I should've protected?

With a growl, I tore myself away from the edge of that particular cliff. "Maz, take care of the wagons and the warehouse while Ruru and I get Kiera to safety. If you see even a flicker in the shadows, abandon everything and save yourself."

Maz gripped his axe tighter. "I'd rather stay with you, brother."

I shook my head. "We'll manage. Right, Ruru?"

The boy wiped the tears from his cheeks and straightened his shoulders. "I would do anything to protect her."

As will I, it seems.

I nudged the thought away and got to work.

MY HEART DIDN'T STOP POUNDING UNTIL WE REACHED OUR rooms.

I gently laid Kiera on her cot while Ruru hid the stolen Shadow-Wolf gear under a loose floorboard. We'd taken the uniform of the Wolf Kiera had killed, but the other Wolf's was too shredded to be of use. We also gathered up their masks and knives. A choice I might come to regret.

But a part of me wanted to know that when Renwell

found his dead Wolves, they would be unmasked and unarmed. A feeling I hoped he would understand intimately soon enough.

I also collected Kiera's knives and cleaned them. Whether she'd want them after all this, I didn't know. But at least they would be here.

My years of training in Twaryn took over as I removed her boots and grabbed our medical supplies and a bowl of water. I cleaned her head wound and the cut on her chest. I had to remove her bloody shirt, Ruru aiding me with tight-lipped efficiency. She wore a tight band around her breasts, but I averted my eyes, anyway.

We didn't have the herbs that would've worked best for her head wound, but I made do with a different poultice that would at least slow the bleeding and ease the swelling.

The knife wound was more difficult.

A Wolf's sunstone blade had jagged edges due to only being sharpened on more sunstone. The cuts were never smooth. Skin gave way to sunstone like torn parchment.

While I was creating a sealing paste with my precious few clawberries, Maz returned.

"How is she?" he asked immediately.

"The same." I carefully pinched her skin together and slathered the thick, sticky paste over the seam.

"It's my fault," Ruru whispered, staring at Kiera's pale face with a look I knew all too well. "If I hadn't led her to that alley . . . If I knew how to fight better . . ."

"Thinking of every possibility but the truth only makes it harder to accept." I finished dabbing the last bit of paste on her cut, her chest now a mess of green gunk. But no blood. "And the truth is it's not your fault, Ruru. Shadow-Wolves did this. They alone are to blame."

He sniffled while I pulled the blanket up over her chest. Enough to keep her warm but well away from the paste.

Now she just needed to wake up. I'd seen people with head injuries who slept until death. I prayed the knife hilt hadn't caused more damage than I could see.

It was one of the reasons I never wanted to be a true healer. Too many times, healing coupled with hopelessness in a way I couldn't bear. Even for strangers.

Yet I maintained what skills I had to be of use when I could. My way of bringing a little light into a world I'd smudged with darkness.

My throat grew tight as I gazed down at Kiera.

Wake up, little thief. Don't let them win.

Don't leave me.

I blinked at the startling thought. Clearing my throat, I left Ruru holding Kiera's hand and began to clean up the mess I'd made.

Maz leaned against the doorframe between the rooms and watched as I repacked the medical bag, tossed the dirty water out the window, and poured some fresh water in the basin. I set it on our table and washed my hands, then raked my fingers through my hair. The cool water trickled down my scalp.

"Aiden—" Maz started in that calming, understanding tone that tore through my defenses like knife through muscle.

"Did you secure the warehouse?" I cut in, staring out the window. *I am free. I am alive. As are Maz, Ruru, and Kiera.*

"Yes." A chair creaked as Maz eased into it. "I saw no one,

heard nothing. The cargo is accounted for. I grabbed the pack of darts and venom Skelly brought me, but left everything else. The horses and wagons are back at their stable."

"Good." I slowly sat in another chair and gave Maz a weary nod. "Thank you, brother."

He nodded back. "Any news from the Temple?"

"Librius is still making good progress, and training is going well."

"Any word from Nikella?"

"No. But she'll be here soon enough."

Maz leaned forward, stroking his short beard. "And what of our little dancer? Will she be ready, do you think?"

I looked toward the window once more. Dark clouds hid the moon and stars. The fitful breeze that drifted in smelled of rain. "If she wakes up," I said in a rough voice.

Maz grasped my arm and squeezed. "She will, Aiden. She's a fighter. Don't mourn what you haven't yet lost."

I met his solemn gaze. I envied his ability to have hope, to shed the weight of fear. But I also thanked the gods for it.

"I'm assuming you want first watch?" he asked, heading over to his cot and tugging off his boots. "Though you might have to knock Ruru unconscious for the privilege."

My lips twitched with a spark of humor. "I'll barter with him. Sleep well, Mazkull."

"Watch well, Aiden."

By the time I convinced Ruru he could have the next watch if he got some sleep, Maz's snores thundered from the other room. Ruru could barely keep his eyes open as he cleaned the scrapes on his arms and coated them with the hornleaf sap I gave him to fight infection. He collapsed on my cot and was breathing deeply in minutes.

I dragged the extra cot next to Kiera and sat on it. I hated this windowless room with its low lamplight and stale air, but I needed to be at her side if she woke.

When she woke.

As the hours dragged on, I found myself studying what I could see of her. The strong set of her shoulders dusted with freckles. The shine of her hair in its tangled braid. Those scarred fingers. Light, thieving, deadly. Would she hate what they had done? Would she hate me if I held her hand as Ruru had?

I wanted to. Gods damn it, I wanted to clutch her hand, touch her skin, gather her up in my arms. Anything to anchor this fierce woman to life.

But I resisted.

Instead, I memorized every detail of her face. The dark brown curves of her eyebrows and the stillness of her long lashes. The delicate sweep of her cheekbones and jawline. Her smooth, defiant chin. The flare of her straight nose. And her lips . . . curved and pink. And a little dry.

I rose quietly and dipped a rag into the pitcher of water in her room. I brushed it over her lips. They twitched, parting.

Elation pounded in my chest. I rushed back to the pitcher to fill a cup with water. Cradling her head in my hand, I nuzzled the cup between her lips.

"Drink," I murmured to her.

After a moment, she took a sip, then another. She swallowed and began to gulp greedily.

I drew back the cup. "Easy. Go slow, little thief."

She whimpered, and I dripped more water into her mouth. Finally, her eyes fluttered open. There. That was what I'd been missing. Those beautiful amber eyes that glowed with the light of her soul.

Even if it quickly dimmed as she remembered.

"Aiden?" Her voice cracked. "Where's Ruru?" Tears beaded in her eyes.

My heart softened, as if she'd caressed it. "He's safe, sleeping in the next room with Maz. You saved his life."

Her face crumpled with pain and exhaustion. "Everything hurts. What—" She lifted her hand toward her chest. "What is this?"

I grabbed her hand, gently guiding it back to her covered stomach. "Don't touch it. You have a long gash across your chest, but my paste will heal it."

Her eyes widened, and she tucked her chin to look downward. "You . . . you took my shirt."

"We kept you covered as best we could. No leering. I swear on Maz's three sisters who would cut out my eyes if I were lying." Though I had been admiring everything else I could see.

She nodded, her relief fleeing under the current of more pain. But she didn't reach this time. "My head," she whispered.

"He hit you hard, but you're awake and talking and remembering, which is the best we could hope for."

She closed her eyes. "It doesn't feel that way." Her chin scrunched, and she turned her face away from me.

The muffled sound of her crying nearly undid me.

Whoever this woman was, whatever reason she kept her path twined with mine, her heart was good. And I found myself yearning for a piece of it. But how could I want that when I had nothing to offer in return?

I handed her a dry rag. "Don't disturb the paste," I reminded her.

She slowly dabbed at her face. "He was the first person I've ever ... ever ..."

Killed. I ground my teeth together.

Fucking Four. Why had she insisted on staying in Aquinon? I'd warned her. Death followed me. Death was everywhere. And now it clung to her too.

She faced me again, her eyes shining with misery. "Does it always feel like this?"

My whole body clenched. "No."

She winced, but I didn't elaborate. How could I possibly explain to her that each life I'd taken had left a different stain on my soul? No two lives were the same as no two deaths were.

"What happened to the other one?" she asked, not meeting my eyes.

"I killed him." And I didn't regret it.

"Two more dead Wolves," she murmured, almost to herself. "Renwell will be furious."

"The alternative was worse."

"Was it?" Her mouth twisted as if the words tasted bitter. "You could've left me there to die. Reclaimed your wagon and hid your cargo. Then the remaining Wolf would've taken the only criminal he had."

I sat back, not fully comprehending her words. "Was that what you expected from me? Do you really think I would leave you to such a fate?"

"You did for that other woman."

"There were *four* Wolves that night. Fighting them would've gotten all of us killed. If I could've saved her, I would have." I gripped the edges of her cot and leaned into her face. "But I will *not* be the reason you die, Kiera."

She studied me for a moment, her gaze poking and prodding at mine. Then it softened. She lifted her hand slowly, haltingly, giving me time to pull away.

But I didn't.

I let her brush my cheek with those fingers I craved. She cupped my jaw in her palm, and I closed my eyes. Just for one moment. One thread of connection. One beat of unity.

"I believe you," she whispered, then let me go.

I pulled away from her. My heart contorted oddly in my chest. As if trying to figure out how to keep beating among these dangerous feelings.

What are you doing to me, little thief?

CHAPTER 18
KIERA

I KILLED A MAN.

And caressed Aiden's face.

The first seemed as though it should be more significant than the other. But that one, warm, tender touch might prove to be more damning than murder.

What a strange life I led that affection was more dangerous than the knives I carried. But Aiden was the enemy. He just didn't know it. And in moments like these, he didn't feel like it.

But the Wolf . . .

Bile rose in my throat. I swallowed against it, but the acid remained. My eyes stung again. My head groaned under the sudden pressure.

I'd killed a Wolf and nearly killed another.

What was Renwell going to do when he found out? He would figure out it was me in that alley. He was the one who'd taught me to aim for an enemy's throat with my knives. Probably didn't expect me to use them on his Wolves.

Which meant I hadn't just broken one of his rules. I'd obliterated it.

Fear crawled like spider legs over my skin, and I shivered.

"I'll fetch you another blanket," Aiden said, quickly disappearing into the other room.

I hated that he left, if only for a moment. But I kept quiet.

A dark, brittle part of me yearned to touch him again, to pull him closer, to see how it would feel to be wrapped up in his arms. To feel safe in the chaos I'd leapt into.

But what I wanted was an illusion. Whatever emotion I desired from those green eyes, whatever comfort I sought, would be fleeting, and ultimately, false.

I believed him when he said he didn't want me to die. But that didn't mean there weren't other lies between us. Including my own.

No one could truly protect me except myself.

"Here," Aiden said, draping his cloak over me. "Maz and Ruru are using the other blankets, so this is the best I can do."

"Thank you," I whispered. *For everything.* "How long will my wounds take to heal?"

He rubbed the dark bristle along his jaw, right where I'd touched him. "A few days, perhaps. Your head will mostly heal on its own with a little ointment. But you must tell me if you get dizzy or start to vomit."

I grimaced. Gods, I really hoped I wouldn't vomit in front of him again. "And my chest?"

"The clawberry paste knits skin back together without needle and thread. It's also less likely to scar and sustain infection."

My eyebrows shot up. "I've never heard of such a thing.

That's . . . that's remarkable. Is it also from Twaryn? Why don't more people have it?"

"It's a very old remedy created by Viridana herself. The clawberries used to be very plentiful but were gathered nearly to extinction for their usefulness. Under the stringent care of the Twaryn forest dwellers, the berries have regrown in number."

"Do you know the Twarynites well? I hear they only bow to the gods."

Aiden nodded. "Especially to Viridana. It's her forest, after all. I had a peaceful life among them. For a while."

"Then what happened?"

A shadow darkened his gaze. "That's a story for another time."

A story he didn't want to tell. Strangely, I hadn't asked because I wanted to collect his secrets and use them. I simply wanted to know more about who he was.

"I should go," he said quietly, rising.

"Why? Where?" I blurted out.

Gods, I sounded like a child. But the sudden roar of desperation in my chest was a beast I was too weak to tame at the moment.

Gods damn your little weaknesses.

"Do you wish me to stay?" he asked.

He was probably exhausted. I had no idea what part of the day it was. He should rest.

"Please," I whispered. "Just a little longer."

He immediately sat down. Keeping his enigmatic green gaze on me, he slipped one of his hands under mine and held it. Much as he had when he'd blindfolded me. My world felt darker now than it had then.

His callused thumb brushed over my scarred knuckles, the ridges in our skin nipping and tugging at each other.

Something about that simple touch unlocked a chasm of emotions inside me.

I stared at the dusty ceiling as tears escaped my eyes and trickled into my hair.

Suddenly, I didn't care if this warmth between us couldn't last. I wanted it. I *needed* it. I embraced this little weakness. Because it didn't feel like a weakness at all.

Instead, it gave me the courage to admit a secret of my own. "I wanted to give up," I said, the words rough and raw. "In that last moment, when I thought death was coming for me, I wanted to die so I could see my mother again."

Aiden's thumb paused for a moment before continuing to stroke my skin. "I've wished for the same thing. A time or two, it was almost a relief that death was going to win over me."

My heart stilled at the thought of him dying.

"Isn't that what we all want when we reach the dark Abyss?" he continued, his voice sounding far away. "Someone we love reaching for us on the other side."

A weak hope kindled in my chest. "Do you truly believe that's what will happen?"

"Some people close to death have claimed to hear their dead loved ones speaking to them from across the Abyss. Whether that was a wishful memory or a happy truth is a mystery. One we won't understand until it's our time to cross." He squeezed my hand. "But not yet."

"Not yet," I whispered.

Especially not when that moment of thinking about my mother was followed by agonizing fear. Fear of losing the life I had. Of being separated from Everett and Delysia. Of being thrown into a furnace and turned to ash.

No, I didn't just fear death.

I feared disappearing.

So, I fought the darkness, even as it continued to hover around me.

At some point, I drifted off to sleep, and when I woke, it was Ruru's deep brown eyes that looked down at me.

"Kiera," he breathed, shoving his dark hair out of his eyes. "Aiden said you woke last night, but I almost didn't believe it. How do you feel? Do you need water? Sophie sent some broth. You didn't vomit, did you? Aiden told me—"

"Hush, Ruru," I croaked. "Water first."

He leapt to his feet and retrieved a full cup. I drank it in moments, the cool water like liquid silk over my tongue and throat.

"Where is Aiden?" I asked. "How long was I asleep?"

Ruru jerked a thumb toward the other room. "He's sleeping. It's about noon. He woke me a few hours ago and told me and Maz that there must always be someone awake by your side should you need anything. Maz said he'll be back soon with some of those biscuits you like." Ruru grinned. "He promises he has a boatload of stories to entertain you with, since Aiden said you can't move until the paste is done."

I smiled, my stomach rumbling at the thought of food. My heart warmed at their kindness, even as it whispered a warning against getting too attached.

Not being able to move for two days was daunting.

Someone would need to tell Melaena why I was missing rehearsal. I also needed to leave my mark for Renwell as soon as I could slip away. Time was running out. And after two more dead Wolves, I didn't want *him* to come searching for *me*.

Over the next two days, Maz and Ruru kept me company, as they promised. Maz regaled me with stories of growing up in Dagriel—about his sisters, his parents, and his clan. Ruru fed me sweet treats from the market and gossip from his messenger duties.

I rarely saw Aiden.

He came in briefly to check my head and my chest, and I caught him sitting with me once when I was sleeping. I wondered if he'd chosen that time on purpose to avoid speaking to me.

When I woke up on the third day, a leather brace lay next to me. It looked just like the one I'd left behind in the palace. This one was also full of knives. Not the knives I'd won, but real, spearheaded throwing knives made of sharpened steel. The hilts molded to my fingers. The weight was perfect.

No one said a word about where they'd come from. But I knew.

Aiden had left my other knives under my cot, but I couldn't bring myself to look at them anymore. Somehow, he must've known.

I strapped the new ones to my waist after he'd announced the clawberry paste had done its job and left.

Someone knocked on the door as I finished tugging on my boots.

"Come in!" I called out.

Ruru burst inside. "Aiden just told me the news! You can move again!"

I laughed as he bounced forward and gave me a ginger hug. "Yes, very exciting."

"Want to go get breakfast with Sophie? She made apple oatmeal!"

I shook my head. "Aiden brought me some earlier. I have one goal right now, Ruru, and that's to take a gods-damned bath."

I'd been taking baths at Melaena's after rehearsals, but after lying in my stinky, sweaty clothes for two days, I wanted nothing more than to wash off all the paste, ointment, and grime.

Ruru's face fell. "Are you sure that's a good idea? I mean, I could go with you . . ."

I leveled my fiercest stare at him, my hands wrapped around my new knives. "I'm going alone, and you're not going to stop me."

He blinked, then bobbed his head once.

I hated to push him like this, leaning on the guilt I knew he harbored for leaving me behind in that alley. I'd told him he owed me nothing because I'd *wanted* him to leave. But the debt still lingered in his eyes.

"I'll be fine, Ruru," I said more gently. "It's daylight. No Wolves. I have my knives and my impressively bad smell to ward off any danger."

His grin broke out easily. "That's true. Well, once you've washed up, maybe we could get some sticky bread from the market."

"I'd love that. I'll be back soon."

I stepped outside and inhaled deeply. I'd listened to a few rain showers while I lay on my cot, and now the air was crisp and fresh. Clouds danced over the sun, giving warmth and coolness in turns.

I doubted I would ever wander this city after nightfall again.

But at least I'd earned the ability to walk around by myself.

Keeping my head low, I hurried to the tavern Renwell had told me about. *The Crescent Moon.* I ducked into a grooved alley and tread across the thin stream of water and piss to the west wall. After clearing away a pile of broken crates, I carved two diagonal slashes in the worn stone near the ground.

Now all I had to do was check back.

Was Renwell already waiting for my mark? How often had he checked this wall? Or did he have someone else watching it?

I glanced up and down the alley but saw nothing.

Apprehension roiled in my gut like a black-cloud warning as I made my way to the nearest bathhouse. Ruru had shown me three scattered around the Old and Market Quarters.

I passed one of my last copper coins to the attendant at the front. His nostrils flared as he took in my bedraggled appearance, but he handed me a clean towel and a sliver of honey-scented soap without comment.

The bathhouse felt like a cave of sorts—a large, cavernous stone building. Dim and quiet. A few lit braziers gave the room a soft, sleepy glow. The pool was half the size of the one in the palace, but steam still rose in tantalizing curls above the water. A furnace—not unlike the one the pyrist used—heated the fresh river water from a room below as it was funneled in through an aqueduct.

And I had it all to myself.

I nearly whimpered with relief.

Men and women were allowed to bathe together, Ruru had told me, but not allowed to touch. I'd dreaded climbing into a crowded pool with leering men. Unless the snooty attendant came to check on me, I'd be free from prying eyes.

I chose one of the curtained nooks in the farthest corner and stripped naked. I untied my hair and tried to shake it out. If only I'd thought of bringing a comb . . .

I bundled my knives into my clothes. Hopefully, no one would be foolish enough to paw through my belongings.

With the towel wrapped around me and armed with my soap, I padded over to the water's edge. I dipped a toe in.

Oh, *gods*, it was so warm.

I dropped the towel and slipped into the pool.

The water hugged my sore body, promising relief. With my eyes half-closed in bliss, I dragged the soap over my skin until naught but a pebble was left. Not quite enough for my hair, but I didn't care.

I gently scraped off the dried clawberry paste with my nails. Bits of green floated away from me before dissolving.

It was hard to see in the steamy, low light, but I couldn't make out much of a scar. My fingers, however, could track its thin line across my chest. If I stretched it too much, the skin tugged uncomfortably. Melaena wouldn't be pleased with my stiff movements later.

The thought made me smile. She had sent me a basket of fruit and crackers that hadn't lasted a day between the four of us. She'd also included some oils she said her dancers used to soothe aching muscles. I had yet to try them, wanting to wait until my skin was clean.

I missed Melaena, despite her apparent role in Garyth's and Aiden's schemes. I even missed our rehearsals. I'd started getting better, and the other girls had been a bit friendlier.

I hated to think that progress had been cut short by a Wolf's blade.

Would Renwell also cut my mission short?

After everything that had happened, everything I'd done, would he pull me out? If he did, I would probably never see Aiden, Maz, Ruru, or Melaena again. Or if I did, it would be under unpleasant circumstances.

A lump formed in my throat.

I slid lower in the water until it closed over my head. Silence and darkness pressed around me like a warm pillow.

My mind conjured the image of a sunstone knife plunging toward my chest.

I jerked upright, gasping for air. My eyes blinked water away as they darted around the shadowy room.

There was no one here. No Wolves. No knives seeking my death.

But then a shadow by the door moved. My heart seized.

"Kiera."

CHAPTER 19
KIERA

"Aiden?" I gasped, sinking lower into the water.

"Forgive me for intruding," he said, his gaze fixed somewhere above my head. "Ruru told me you went for a bath, but you didn't bring fresh clothes. So, I . . . I brought you some." He cleared his throat. "Sophie laundered them."

I blinked. Why hadn't he just sent Ruru with them? Holy Four, had he seen me leaving my mark for Renwell?

"How did you know which bathhouse I would be at?" I demanded.

"I tried the one closer to our place first."

I shrugged, trying to look nonchalant. "Ruru said this one was bigger." Which was true.

"Right. Well, then. Where shall I leave your clothes?"

Careful to keep my breasts underwater, I pointed toward my curtained alcove. "There."

He strode over to it and laid a canvas bag on top of my dirty clothes. "Do you need more soap?" he asked, still averting his eyes. "The attendant wouldn't let me in without paying for soap and a towel."

"Yes, thank you."

He knelt next to the pool and laid the extra towel next to mine. Then he handed me the soap. Our eyes finally met as our fingers touched.

Something burned in the depths of his gaze that stirred a nest of embers in my stomach.

We stayed locked together until the soap slipped from our fingers.

It fell to the floor, too far for me to reach. Ignoring it, and him, I turned away and dug my fingers into my snarled hair to comb it out. The scar on my chest pulled, and the tender spot on my head prickled with pain.

Biting my lip to keep silent, I dropped my hands back into the water.

"Do you need assistance?" His voice was like a deep, sensual song to my ears. Gods help me if he ever did sing as Maz was always trying to get him to do. His voice mesmerized me like it had that first night when he helped me with my boot and checked the bruising on my ribs.

I nodded.

"Give me a moment."

Clothing rustled. The embers in my stomach burned hotter. How many clothes was he taking off? His soft footsteps stopped behind me.

Gods, what was I doing? This was treading dangerously close to a line I couldn't cross. Not with him.

Bare, muscled legs lowered into the water on either side of me.

Heart in my throat, I whipped around. My eyes widened, trying to consume the naked man in front of me. Well, mostly naked. He still wore his undershorts. But the rest of him was like a living, breathing, heated work of art. His waves of black hair—damp from the steam—curled at the ends over his forehead and neck. Contoured muscles rippled under bronze skin as he pulled himself closer.

And I had been right before, on the cliff road—his thighs were magnificent. I wanted to place my hands on them and lift myself toward him.

His jaw tightened at the look on my face. "Turn around, little thief," he rasped.

What? Oh. My hair.

I turned around and closed my eyes tightly, my body quivering under the water. I heard him squeeze the soap between his hands. Then he trailed his fingers over my hair.

I bit my lip harder as he slowly worked through the tangle.

"How are your wounds?" he asked.

I had to swallow twice before the words came out. "Healed. Mostly. You seem to be doing that a lot for me lately."

He hummed. "You seem to get into trouble a lot."

I snorted. "And you don't? Do you not recall how we met?"

"When I helped you escape prison? Of course, I remember." There was a smile in his voice that I wished I could see.

I laughed. "That was a mutual effort, I believe." An effort that had left behind two other Shadow-Wolf bodies in that cave.

My humor dampened. Why did everything have to remind me of Renwell and what I'd done?

Aiden tugged on a hard knot, and pain shot through my scalp. I flinched.

"Forgive me," he whispered. His touch gentled, and for some reason, my heart ached.

Silence swelled and thickened like the clouds of steam around us as he continued to methodically comb and wash my hair. His fingers stroked my head and brushed my ears and my neck, building a delicious sensitivity. When he lightly raked his nails over my scalp, a moan escaped my throat.

His fingers stilled. Then he gathered my heavy hair and draped it over my shoulder. "Done."

But before I could turn around, he swore and seized my shoulders. I froze.

Fucking Four. I forgot.

"Who did this to you?" he snarled.

I tried to breathe calmly through my nose. I knew what he must've finally seen in the low light. A thorny mess of scars etched across my shoulders.

He turned me to face him. I recognized the fury blazing across his face. From when the Shadow-Wolves were chaining me in the cell. And when the cattle herder had leered at me.

My heart fluttered like hummingbird wings.

"Who gave you those scars?" he demanded.

"Does it matter?" I whispered.

"It shouldn't. Gods damn it, but it does."

"It was a long time ago. In truth, I forget they're there because I never see them."

"Who?" he bit out.

"Korvin." Saying his name was like pulling the cork from bottled memories. Memories that now flooded my mind.

Korvin's cold, dead eyes. His monstrous grin. That whip of shattered night.

Father ordered it. Renwell allowed it.

Mother begged Father to change his mind, but instead, he forced her to watch as Korvin flayed my back with his whip. And Renwell . . . Renwell never took his eyes off me. Then he collected me afterward. Cleaned me up. And swore he would never let Korvin hurt me again.

All because I fell in love with a boy my father considered a traitor.

"Kiera . . . Kiera?"

I heard my name as if from beyond the Abyss. Darkness clouded my eyes. I felt my body lifted with ease and quickly wrapped in a towel. Then I was being carried. Again. Safe. In these arms.

Aiden.

Aiden held me tightly, rubbing his hands over my shuddering body. "Breathe, Kiera. Breathe. Focus on my voice. Listen to my words." His lips pressed to my forehead, a warmth that branded my soul through my skin. "Come back to me. You are not there anymore. You are here. With me. Breathe."

Slowly, the darkness faded. Air returned to my lungs. In and out, like calm waves.

Aiden cradled me in his lap in the curtained alcove surrounded by our clothes. My cheek was pressed into his neck. My fingers dug into his shoulders.

Tears burned behind my eyes, but I refused to give any more to that monster.

"I'm sorry," I whispered.

"You have nothing to be sorry for. It's him who should feel this pain. I pray that I am the one to inflict it on him one day."

All dignity forgotten, I burrowed my face deeper into his neck. "I don't think a monster like him can be defeated. Not like I can." My words grew fragile. "You said I wear victory beautifully. I'm afraid I don't wear defeat quite as well."

He grasped my chin and lifted my gaze to be devoured by his. "I'm beginning to think there isn't a way you are not beautiful."

My breath caught.

And I was beginning to think that repeating my history was more than a dangerous possibility.

But I couldn't let him destroy me this way. I could choose to resist this . . . this lure between us. The pull of his gaze as it dropped to my lips. The breathless urge to surrender to what my whole being cried out for.

I needed a distraction.

My fingertips brushed over a patch of uneven skin on his shoulder. Of course. His scar.

"What is this from?" I asked softly, hiding from his gaze by peering over his shoulder.

The skin looked deeply burned with odd divots and whorls in it. The image of a falcon in flight had been inked over it with the breast of the bird embodying the scar.

For a moment, I didn't think he would answer. A part of him seemed to withdraw from me even as he continued to hold me.

"The mine," he finally said. "They brand all prisoners in such a way by heating up a chunk of raw sunstone and pressing it into the prisoner's shoulder."

My jaw dropped. "The Calimber mine? But you said that no one ever left there except in death."

A muscle in his cheek twitched. "We escaped."

Understanding dawned on me. "Maz. That's where you met him. He has the same scar."

Aiden nodded. "He arrived a few months after me. We shared a cell."

Suddenly, many things made sense. Why he hated being shackled more than beaten. That he'd been in darker places than the tunnel. Why he and Maz were so close.

I pressed my hand over the scar, the bird in flight. "Did the Dags give you this tattoo after you escaped?"

"Yes. Maz has a bear—the chosen animal of his Yargoth clan—over his scar. It was our way of commemorating our victory in survival."

I traced the wing tips of the falcon. Aiden sighed deeply into my hair, but he didn't stop me.

This must be another of his reasons for hating my father. Being imprisoned and forced to work in a mine. Why had they put him there?

And why hadn't Renwell mentioned the connection? Surely he had noticed during his "thorough" interrogation. He would've known what this scar meant, having been to the mine many times.

Unless Aiden was lying.

But something deep in my gut told me he wasn't.

I couldn't promise him revenge as he had done for me upon seeing my scars. He'd already avenged the one across my chest. But I wanted to give him something. A moment of peace. As he'd given me.

I leaned forward and pressed my lips to the middle of his scar, inhaling his warm, spicy scent.

His body tensed around mine. His hands fisted in the towel separating our skin.

I pulled back. The dark, hungry look in his eyes made my heart take flight.

"Be careful what you steal, little thief," he growled. "Or I might take back what's mine."

A shiver ricocheted down my spine. My breath turned ragged once more. But this time, it was a wild excitement rather than fear. A desperate desire.

Perhaps destruction wouldn't feel so terrible with his lips on mine.

Our noses brushed together. Our mouths were a few frantic breaths apart.

A loud crash shattered the moment.

We jerked apart as a clamor of voices entered the bathhouse.

"Do you have to be such a gods-damned bumbler?" a male voice grumbled. "If you broke a single one of my jars—"

"Eh, quit your griping, old man. Your precious oils are intact. You'll still smell like a peach in summertime for your wife."

The men kept sniping at each other as they splashed into the water.

I looked at Aiden and clapped a hand over my mouth to keep a hysterical giggle from bursting out. His eyes brimmed with mirth as he grinned back at me.

He looked so beautiful in that moment it made my heart hurt.

"I should get dressed," I whispered.

He nodded. "I'll move to another alcove so we don't get banished for . . . touching." My cheeks burned. "I'll wait for you outside."

He gathered his clothes and slipped around the curtain.

I tied my hair into a knot on top of my head and dressed myself in moments. After shouldering the bag full of my dirty clothes and making sure my knives were hidden under my cloak, I stepped out.

Neither of the two men soaking in the pool looked up as I walked past.

Outside, Aiden leaned against the wall, resting in the shadows. His eyes warmed when they spotted me.

That subtle change unnerved me.

Even though we were now both fully clothed, I felt like I'd exchanged a piece of my armor for his, leaving me vulnerable. The more he knew me, the more he could use against me. But I could do the same to him.

I wasn't sure I wanted that power.

"Headed home?" he asked.

Home. I had no home. "I told Ruru I would meet him for a treat at the market."

Aiden dipped his head. "I will leave you to it, then."

I blinked in surprise. "You're not going to follow me? Have I finally earned your trust?"

"Trust." His expression twisted as if he didn't like the taste of the word. "Trust is knowing the sun has risen thousands of times, yet never being sure of tomorrow. It's a promise, yet always a question."

"Then you don't trust anyone, truly. Not even the sun."

His cheeks furrowed with a small smile—one so bitter-sweet my heart prickled. "I can hope for sunlight while still guarding my own flame should I find myself in the dark."

His words soaked into my mind like ink into parchment. Like a letter written from his heart to mine. Words that I understood without having to think of them.

"Then I will do what I can to be a light," I said.

Even I didn't know if that was a lie.

Aiden simply nodded, his features stern. But his fingers brushed mine as he walked past me.

I stood there for a moment in a daze, unsure of which way to go. But eventually, my boots tread back to where they knew I had to be. In the alley behind *The Crescent Moon*.

Every other thought abandoned me as I stared at the wall where I'd left my mark.

A horizontal line was slashed through it. Deeper and longer than my scratches. The ferocity of it made my stomach quiver with unease.

I had to meet Renwell tonight.

CHAPTER 20
KIERA

THE CROWD AT *THE CRESCENT MOON* WAS VERY DIFFERENT THAN that of *The Weary Traveler*.

Dim candlelight shone over the sparse tables and hushed conversations. Curtained booths provided some privacy for the small groups of hooded customers shuffling to and from the bar.

I peeked into one booth where a woman sat in the lap of a man nearly as tall as Maz but twice as wide. She whispered in his ear, and he chuckled. He started to turn his head, and I darted away before he could see me.

Why in the deep, dark, wandering hell had Renwell chosen this tavern? He hadn't specified much, other than I was to wait for him inside. My nerves felt like dry twigs ready to snap.

After everything that had happened, this meeting was not going to go well.

My fingers shook as I climbed onto a stool at the end of the bar and waved down the bartender.

"Coin first," the grizzled old woman rasped.

I tossed her a copper—one I'd just earned from doing an errand for Sophie. My cover for being out alone. Aiden, Maz, and Ruru hadn't even been home when I left. After meeting with Ruru and a short, painful rehearsal with Melaena, I'd sat with Sophie until she'd given me work to do.

The bartender passed me a pitiful mug of brown ale. Her gaze lingered on me for a moment. Probably wondering who I was meeting since it seemed everyone else was here for one illicit affair or other. I scowled at her until she looked away, then drained the whole mug.

The ale was weak and tepid, but gods, I wanted more. Anything to stop my racing thoughts.

When Renwell and I had made this plan, I'd been so certain I would have heaps of information to lay at his feet. Then he would gift me a rare smile and a few short words of praise that would tell me I had succeeded. That I had protected my family, done my duty, and was well on my way to being an excellent High Enforcer.

But now I wasn't sure what to tell him.

For two years, he had been my guide, my mentor, my only escape from grief and a life I no longer wanted. He had been a constant in some of the darkest moments of my life. He had shaped who I was.

But I couldn't let him be the only window through which I saw the world.

Ten days in this strange life had already fractured that view.

Cracks formed between what I believed and what I saw. My intentions and my actions. Most of all, my fondness for Ruru,

Maz, and Melaena and my growing feelings for Aiden warred with my duty to destroy them if they threatened my family or my kingdom.

My view had become distorted. Strange. Uncertain.

What would happen when that window shattered?

"Room six," the bartender's voice wheezed.

I lifted my head, almost having forgotten where I was.

The old woman took my empty mug and wiped the bar top under it as if I'd left a mess. She jerked her head toward a staircase. "He's waiting."

I nodded woodenly, sliding off my stool.

How had he gotten there without me seeing him? Perhaps there was a back entrance. Renwell always remained unseen when he wished.

My boots sounded too loud, too slow, up the stairs and down the narrow, dark hall. Most of the rooms were occupied, if the noises within were any indication.

The ale had done nothing to calm my nerves. If anything, it sloshed harder in my empty stomach, making me feel sick.

Room six. I stared at the dented brass number nailed to the door. Renwell was on the other side. Waiting for me. Growing impatient with me. He was likely already furious after everything that had transpired.

Sweat prickled along my spine. The thin scar along my chest seemed to tighten and tingle—evidence of my disobedience.

Something creaked on the other side of the door, as if a body had shifted. Then the door slowly swung inward, revealing a dark room.

Lifting my chin, I slipped inside.

The door eased shut. A bolt scraped.

I whirled around. I couldn't see him, but I could smell him. Always the same. Melted wax and candle smoke.

A tiny flame flickered to life in an oil lamp overhead. Renwell's hooded face and dark eyes loomed over me. His gaze was like a scavenging crow, devouring me from head to toe.

"Hello, Wolf slayer," he murmured. Then his gloved fingers seized my throat. He slammed my back against the door.

I gasped, but he only clenched harder. I tried to tear his hand away, but his grip was like the sunstone blade at his waist.

Unbreakable.

My other hand scrabbled for my knives, but he snatched my wrist and crushed it against the door by my head.

Tears leaked from the corners of my eyes as he brought his face within a breath of mine.

"You disobeyed me," he hissed.

I choked and spluttered. Shadows pillowed around my vision, around him. Gods, he already knew. How—

"One of my sources told me of a woman who looked just like you disappearing into an alley with two of my Wolves. Did you think I wouldn't find out?"

I tried to speak, but he snarled. "And don't lie to me, Kiera. I *will* know."

He released my throat and my wrist, and I gulped the air between us. He watched me without a drop of remorse in his eyes.

"I . . . I was going to tell you. I had . . . no choice."

"No choice but to disobey me?" he demanded. "Has our prisoner won your loyalty so quickly?"

Warnings pounded through my head. I needed space from him to gather my thoughts and my breath. But he gave me none.

"No," I snapped. "But I had to earn his trust, otherwise I never would've been able to come here tonight."

His eyes remained hooded with suspicion.

"Do you think I wanted to kill those Wolves?" I hissed, yanking down my shirt collar to expose part of my scar. "They hunted *me* down. They almost killed *me*. Would you have preferred they did?"

His nostrils flared as he stared at my bare skin.

Heartbeats thundered past, and he didn't answer.

I tugged my shirt back over my scar, my throat dry. "Do you want me dead, Renwell?"

His gaze pierced mine. "No."

"Then why didn't you tell your dogs to stay away from me as well?"

"They would've let you be if you were alone. Their job is to clear the streets of criminals. Anyone out after dark who shouldn't be. And since you're entangled with such—"

"Entangled on *your* orders." Jerell and his sister flashed through my mind. "And they don't only hunt criminals."

"What do you mean?" Renwell asked sharply.

I drew in deep breaths, trying to steady myself. I had to know. "The night after we escaped, four of your Wolves dragged away a man named Jerell and . . . and killed his sister without cause."

"Without cause?" he whispered, wrath tightening every line in his face. "They do nothing without my order."

I flinched.

"Was this woman interfering with their business?"

"She was trying to save her brother."

"And paid the price. As you almost did."

"What was Jerell's crime? What did you do with him?"

"That is my business," Renwell said in a soft, deadly voice.

I didn't heed the warning. The rising rage in my gut crashed into every other ugly feeling that had grown fangs and claws in the last ten days. "Does Father know how you conduct your *business*?" I spat. "Killing innocent women to keep them quiet while you steal their kin?"

"What tale do you want, princess?" he snarled. "Perhaps something to soothe those little weaknesses that fester inside you like a slow death."

My heart jerked. I felt as though I were bleeding from wounds I couldn't see. "Don't call me that. That is not who I am anymore."

"Then why do you still act like it? 'Father,'" he spat the word from his mouth like venom. "He is not your father. He is the king you serve. And I am your commander. You answer to me. Unless that has changed for you?"

I couldn't speak. He'd never been this furious with me.

Renwell drew back a step. His eyes turned cold and calculating, not unlike his beloved torturer's. "Has it, Kiera? Or do you now prefer to answer to the man who infiltrated my Den, helped you escape, killed the other Wolf in that alley to protect you, and healed your wounds?"

"How do you know that?" I whispered.

Renwell brandished a jagged smile. "I took the bodies and gave them to Korvin. You know how he likes that sort of thing."

Memories shivered in a corner of my mind—crusty tables,

jagged tools, that glittering whip, and jars of nightmares. If I hadn't fallen apart with Aiden earlier, I might've now. But remembering his whispers, his touches, kept the darkness at bay.

"He told me which one was your kill. The punctured throat, just like I taught you. He was impressed."

A wave of nausea rocked me back on my heels.

I didn't care for the man I'd killed, but death felt different after dealing it out in a moment's decision. After I'd stared into the face of my own. What had that Wolf seen in me when I killed him? Had I been no less of a monster than Korvin?

Renwell watched me, noting every fear and weakness I tried to hide. But he didn't steady me, didn't draw me into his arms to comfort me. I used to hope he would, after that night he'd rescued me from a different attacker in another alley. Foolishly, I'd soaked up every glance and every effort he made to protect me, thinking it meant the most dangerous man in Rellmira cared for me.

But he'd never shown any affection to me.

Instead, he loved to scratch and poke at my fears as if hoping they'd bite back.

"But the other body," he continued. "The other one was interesting, Korvin said. Multiple cuts and a few deeper wounds, delivered by a weak arm. I told him how I found the body, crumpled against a wall, a blood trail smeared down the length of it. Your protector impaled my Wolf's hand then pinned him to the wall with a blade through his throat. He—"

"Saved my life, yes," I rasped. "Why are you telling me this?"

"What's his name?"

I balked. It was probably the easiest bit of information I could give him, yet even that one word felt like a betrayal.

Renwell's gloved fist wrapped around his knife hilt. "His name, Kiera."

"Aiden."

"Aiden," he murmured. "Do you feel you owe Aiden your life, your loyalty?"

My heart hid from the truth. "No. I told you. I used the incident to gain his trust and immediately left my mark for you. I owe everything to you, Renwell."

In many ways, I did. Even though there were times, like now, when I hated owing him so much. But I buried those feelings.

A glimmer of triumph and something else—something darker and uglier—brought life back to Renwell's gaze. "Yes," he murmured. "To me."

He let the heavy words hang in the air between us as we stared at each other.

Unbidden, a memory slithered through my mind. Of a moment I'd tried hard to forget.

Months ago, I'd been changing clothes in my room when Renwell had swept in without knocking. We'd both frozen— me in my breast band and undershorts and him fully clothed. But for one searing moment, his gaze was utterly naked with desire.

Before I could take another breath, he stormed out of my room, and I didn't see him for two days. We never spoke of it, and he'd never looked at me that way again.

But I'd taken to locking my door, even when I was inside, and sleeping fully clothed.

The memory faded as thumps and amorous cries suddenly rose from the room next to ours.

My stomach churned at the unfortunate timing, but I pointed my chin at the source of the noise. "Why did you choose this tavern as our meeting spot?"

His smile grew into something sinister I'd never seen before. "I needed a place where no one wants to look you in the eye. Nor are they sleeping or listening in."

"Surely there were other places," I grumbled. I wanted to move away from the trembling wall, but that would've brought me closer to the small, bowed bed. And to Renwell.

"And if you were followed," he added smoothly, "then they would assume you're doing nothing more illicit than meeting a lover in the dark."

My heart stopped. I'd assumed I hadn't been followed since no one was home and I'd been on an errand for Sophie, but . . .

What if Aiden came looking for me and saw who I was with?

A laugh scraped past Renwell's lips. "Tell me, Kiera, are you more worried that someone will see me as your lover or you as a traitor?"

I glared at him, his strange behavior making him ever more unpredictable. Was it because I'd killed one of his Wolves? Or because of Aiden?

"I can't risk either," I said, "and I shouldn't stay much longer. Do you want to know Aiden's plan or not?"

Renwell leaned against the far wall, his expression back to its usual mask. "Tell me."

I told him of Aiden's need for gold, despite his shipping

business and smuggling for nobles, and how I'd offered the idea of stealing from Asher's vault as a way to tempt him.

"That was a dangerous move. One the king will not like," Renwell said, but his eyes gleamed.

"Does it matter? We can't let it happen."

"Why not?"

"Because," I spluttered, "they could take that gold and disappear or use it for gods only know—"

"Have you learned *why* he wants it?"

I ground my teeth. "Not exactly."

Disappointment harshened every line in Renwell's face.

I thought quickly. "But I overheard something else. Something that might be related."

My words tumbled over each as I told him about the conversation I heard between Garyth and Melaena. I only left out the details of Garyth suspecting someone had searched his office and found his papers. I didn't want to turn Renwell's fury on me once more. As I spoke, he paced the room like a caged animal.

"That gods-damned fool is meddling where he shouldn't," Renwell muttered.

"What's happening at the mine?" I asked carefully.

His voice lashed out. "Nothing that concerns you."

I didn't want to push him, but I hated being in the dark. "Does it have something to do with the People's Council? With the letters I found?"

"I searched for them, but they were gone."

"Are you going to arrest him?"

"Not yet."

Gods, I hoped for Garyth's sake that he forgot about the

People's Council and the sunstone mine and whatever else he was meddling in.

I hadn't considered the lives that would weigh on my conscience with this job. I thought the lines between good and evil were carved in stone, not sand. Father would call Garyth a traitor for even *wanting* the People's Council back. But Garyth was also a good father, a loving husband, and, from what I remember, a decent man.

Holy Four, what if it was like the Pravaran rebellion all over again? Those days had been filled with terror so potent I could taste it in the air, like a brewing storm. Renwell hunting down my father's enemies in Aquinon and serving them up for execution. Friends and family betraying each other to save themselves. Enemies taking their revenge by naming supporters.

And through it all, I had believed—with all my sixteen years of wisdom—that love would be enough to save Julian, if not his family.

But he refused to give up his cause, even for me.

"You're certain Garyth said, 'We can do nothing if he doesn't succeed?'" Renwell asked, ceasing his pacing.

I nodded. "And Melaena assured him *he* would."

I hated bringing Melaena to Renwell's attention like this, but I hated the idea that she could be plotting against my family and my kingdom even more. But did she deserve condemnation any more than Garyth did?

"Then your mission has become more important than ever." Renwell pinned me with his sharp stare. "This heist will be the key to solidifying your place among these people, so you have more time afterward to find out who *he* is and what *he* plans to do."

"But what of the gold? Fa—the king will not want to lose it."

"We will win it back tenfold when you uncover the conspiracy and all its makers. Everything they have will be forfeited to the crown."

Panic bubbled under my skin. "Aiden expects me to be on a ship sailing away with my cut after the heist."

"You're not leaving this city," Renwell growled. "Unless you plan to disobey me again."

"Then how—"

Renwell slashed his gloved hand through the air. "If he cares enough to kill for you, then he'll care enough to keep you. Use that."

My body grew cold. He wanted me to weaponize the flicker of trust that had just sparked between me and Aiden.

I had already betrayed Aiden in so many ways, yet this one felt the worst.

"I will do what I can," I said in a hollow voice.

"Excellent, now tell me the plan for the heist."

I told him my part as a dancer stealing the key from Asher and opening the vault for Aiden.

Renwell nodded along, as if it all made sense. "How will you keep Asher and the other attendees from recognizing you?"

"I'll wear a mask and makeup along with a . . . distracting costume. Melaena says he's partial to her dancers."

Renwell sneered. "Asher and his many weaknesses. Simply

act the sweet, playful admirer, and you could steal his very soul if you wished."

I frowned. I knew there was no love lost between the two of them, but he seemed to care little for the position we were putting a fellow High Councilor in.

"Do you remember which lock it is?" he asked.

"Well enough."

"Come here." He emptied a pouch of gold coins onto the bed.

I stood opposite him, but he shook his head with a smirk and pointed. "Next to me, Kiera."

I steeled my spine and walked around the bed to stand next to him.

"Imagine this is the vault door," he said. "And these"—he placed the coins in a familiar pattern on the coarse bed linen —"are the locks. This is the one you want." He placed a gloved finger on one near the top-right corner.

I might've gotten it right without his help, but I committed the position to memory. I couldn't risk making a mistake now that I was officially going through with this.

Holy Four, I was actually going to have to *dance* in front of the nobles and *steal* from the High Treasurer.

Sweat beaded along my hairline. I needed to rehearse much, much more. I needed everything to go smoothly so that Aiden and Melaena would see me as an ally they wanted to keep—and to trust.

Renwell swept the coins off the bed and put them back in his pouch, his elbow brushing mine.

I quickly put some distance between us, pressing my back

against the now-quiet lovers' wall. "Do you really think I can do this?" I blurted out.

Renwell faced me, his gaze unfathomable. "You did well, Kiera, bringing me this information. You have earned trust and loyalty from dangerous people by simply using your wit and tenacity. This was only your second mission, and your first undercover one. I stand by my initial assessment."

From the bridge. When he was convinced I would succeed even though my father didn't.

This was more of the Renwell from my training. Harsh but empowering. After all, if he didn't think I could succeed, he wouldn't have given me the task.

"But what if innocent people get hurt?" I asked, thinking of Ruru, of Garyth's wife and little Isabel. And even though I doubted they were innocent, my chest tightened at the idea of harming Aiden, Maz, and Melaena.

Renwell's brow furrowed. "Innocent people always get hurt." He reached into his boot and pulled out my mother's sheathed knife.

My breath snagged on something sharp in my throat. He had kept it like he said he would.

"Your mother was innocent, was she not?" he asked in a deadly quiet voice, slowly sliding out the black blade. "As is Everett. Delysia. Would you be so worried about these *criminals* if you knew they were plotting the murder of your innocent siblings?"

I stared at him, everything blurred and muffled as if I were underwater. Drowning in fear.

That couldn't be what Aiden was planning. Nor Garyth

with Melaena and their talk of the mine and the People's Council. It just couldn't be.

I barely noticed Renwell step closer until he pressed the tip of my mother's blade to my collar. He eased it down to reveal my scar once more.

I stilled, a strangled gasp escaping my numb lips.

His gaze jerked to mine, but he didn't move the knife. "Steal the gods-damned gold, Kiera. Figure out what the traitors are plotting. And *never* disobey me again."

He tore the knife away without drawing a drop of blood.

But I didn't wait another moment. I fled.

CHAPTER 21

AIDEN

"To the best shot in Aquinon!" Maz announced.

I chuckled as Ruru's ears turned red with embarrassment.

We tapped our mugs together over a table at *The Weary Traveler*. Nearly every table was full, and no one paid us any mind.

I sipped my Sunshine while Ruru messily gulped his watered-down ale.

Maz laughed and clapped him on the shoulder. "Look at the boy! So proud he can barely drink past that grin!"

Ruru wiped his chin, wincing a little at the burns on his hands.

"I'll put some hornleaf sap on those as soon as we get home," I assured him.

He beamed. "They don't hurt much."

Maz ruffled his hair, and the two of them began to reprise every moment of our evening at the Temple. I was proud of

Ruru for working so hard, but always, there was a stab of fear. For getting him involved. For asking him to take such a risk.

He'd wanted to. Begged me to let him help. And if all went according to plan, he wouldn't be too much in harm's way.

But when did anything go according to my plan?

A pair of honey-colored eyes teased my mind.

Gods, had it only been this morning that I'd seen her at the bathhouse? It felt like an age had passed. How quickly that beautiful thief stole my thoughts, my peace. I'd thought of little else all day.

The change of clothes had been an excuse to follow her. At first, because I was worried about her on her own so soon after recovering. Then, when I saw her soaking in the steamy water, I didn't want to leave.

I'd given her space over the past few days, letting her recover, letting Maz and Ruru bolster her spirits with theirs. I didn't want to add my tormented feelings to her own.

Instead, I'd focused on preparing for the heist. I had everything we needed now—guard and servant uniforms, a wagon with horses, and false-bottom barrels. Melaena had procured Asher's seal to get us through the gate, as well as a crude map of Asher's house.

All the while, I'd wondered how Kiera fared beyond her wounds.

Nothing distracted me from my work. *Nothing.* Distractions ended in death.

But I couldn't resist her.

When I'd knelt to hand her the soap and she'd looked up at me, the water lapping at her bare shoulders, everything else faded away. My previous torment evaporated like the steam around us.

When I undressed to wash her hair and she gaped at me with raw desire, my own desire shone hard and bright, as if it'd always been there. Waiting. Until the clouds of fear and distrust shifted away.

But what had truly unraveled me was finding those scars on her back. Seeing her in such pain over that monster, Korvin. Holding her shivering body in my arms until she calmed.

She hadn't told me why she'd been punished in such a way. Probably over some small infraction in her life as a personal guard—fell asleep on duty or looked at Weylin the wrong way. Whatever it was, it certainly didn't warrant Korvin's whip.

Perhaps it'd been foolish of me to share what I did about the mine and my scar. From the moment I met her, she'd carved my secrets from me, piece by piece. But this time, I wanted to let her. I wanted her to see more of me. I wanted to know what she would do with it.

When her lips had touched my scar, it made my heart twist with agony. Because, for the first time in a long time, I wanted to let someone else in. But my heart knew I didn't deserve the kindness she showed me. She didn't know what I'd done to earn that scar. Or what I'd done since then.

Soon—too soon—it wouldn't matter. She'd be gone with her gold, and I . . . I would disappear as well. One way or another.

"Well, look who it is!" Maz's loud voice roused me from my thoughts. "Hey there, lovely!"

My gaze latched onto the very object of my distraction.

Kiera had frozen in the middle of the crowded tavern. I drank her in, from hood to boot, pleased to see my sharp little gifts strapped to her waist.

But she looked at me as if I were the last person she wanted to see. My smile fell.

Oblivious, Maz waved her over, yanking another chair to our table. "Come, come, sit. Hey, Iris! Some Sunshine, if you please!"

Kiera trudged over and sat down next to me. Even though she angled as far away from me as she could get, our knees still brushed under the table.

She nodded a greeting to Maz and Ruru, but avoided my gaze with her head lowered. Iris appeared between us with a full mug of Sunshine, which Kiera seized with thanks. The mead sloshed over the rim.

I frowned. Was she trembling?

She took several long gulps of mead, eliciting raised eyebrows from Maz.

"Where have you been?" I asked, rougher than I meant to.

Her shoulder twitched next to mine. But she kept her chin tucked. "I . . . I just finished a task for Sophie. It was nearby, so I thought I would stop for a drink." *Alone*, was what she didn't say.

"An errand without me?" Ruru asked, his mouth bent in a frown.

Kiera drank more. "I waited, but Sophie said it was urgent. Medicine for the pregnant wife of one of the guards."

"You went to the barracks?" I demanded.

She nodded.

"Gods damn it, Kiera, look at me!"

Three pairs of eyes widened at me, but I only cared for hers. Shadows hovered in them, and her face was drawn and pale.

I tried to gentle my voice. "What happened? Is it your wounds?" My gaze darted from her head to her chest.

She shook her head. "I think I just overexerted myself is all."

It wasn't all, but I didn't want to push her. And I'd frightened her by behaving like a gods-damned brute.

"Forgive me," I murmured. "Are you hungry?"

An emotion I couldn't name flickered in her eyes before she nodded and looked away. I rose and went to find Iris instead of Maz bellowing for her again. I also needed a moment to calm the protectiveness that seemed to turn me into a wild beast where Kiera was concerned.

I found Iris coming out of the kitchen, carrying two platters of food. I asked her for some of everything and to hurry if she could. After slipping a handful of silvers in her apron pocket, I headed back to the table.

Just as Maz was saying, "I believe he's brooding over a woman, but he won't tell me."

Her eyes flicked to me. "How do you know it's a woman?"

Gods damn it, Mazkull. I sat down with a glare.

He grinned and winked at me. "I always know when it's a woman. I understand women intimately, you see."

"Is that so?" I quirked an eyebrow at him. "Lorel."

"Ah, yes, a beautiful woman with the biggest pair of,"—he glanced at Ruru's rapt expression—"ah, *eyes* that I've ever seen. She adored me."

"She burned your tent to the ground."

Kiera laughed, and I instantly forgave Maz.

Maz waved his hand in the air. "That was an accident. She was merely trying to start a cooking fire."

I smirked. "*Inside* your tent. To roast you and . . . what was the name of the other woman? Bertha?"

"Bella." Maz grimaced. "She didn't know Bella was in my tent."

I sent a laugh up into the rafters. "By the Four, she did. I also recall we moved camps quickly after that."

"Call it what you will," Maz said with a chuckle, "but all I take from that story is how much I've learned about women. To prove my point," he added, dipping his head at Kiera.

She grinned. My shoulders relaxed. Perhaps we could chase away whatever demons haunted her tonight.

Iris arrived with a platter of sticky bread pockets filled with sliced beef, onions, and tomatoes. She also set down a pot of baked beans and a plate of biscuits.

"Gods, you're the best, Iris, thank you," Kiera said, already reaching for a bread pocket. "Did you three not eat yet?"

We all shook our heads and dug in like a pack of wolves.

With each bite, a few more of the shadows disappeared from Kiera's eyes. She caught me studying her and wiped her mouth with the back of her hand. Our gazes linked in a way that felt like holding hands. Was it my imagination, or did she lean the slightest bit toward me?

"Tell us another story," Ruru piped up, licking butter from his fingers. "From . . . from *Dagriel*," he whispered.

Maz grinned. "How about the time I blindfolded Aiden, tied his hands behind his back, and left him in the forest overnight?"

Ruru's mouth fell open, and a soft laugh escaped Kiera's lips.

"Now this is one I definitely want to hear," she said. "I hope something worse than a spider hunted you when *you* were blindfolded."

I grinned, nudging her shoulder. "How about a mountain lion?"

"What's a mountain lion?" Ruru asked.

Maz guffawed and described the large, sneaky cat, then told everyone the story, embellishing a few details here and there. Kiera and Ruru gasped and laughed in the right places, and Maz glowed with the happiness of telling a good story. If not for the smoky tavern, we could've been back around a roaring fire in the mountains of Dagriel.

Soon, Maz. I'll get you home. I glanced at Kiera and Ruru. Perhaps my actions would also make Rellmira a home worth having. Maybe then Kiera could come back.

I had to bring up her travel plans again. Skelly's ship was nearly reloaded for his next run to Eloren, and Kiera would have to be on it.

But it didn't feel like the right time to discuss it.

Over the next few days, it never seemed to be the right time.

Kiera threw herself into rehearsals as if making up for lost time. She stayed with Melaena most of the day, running errands with Ruru less. But she did practice pickpocketing with him late at night. She was already fairly adept at it—given how easily she'd stolen that key from me in the prison.

Ruru showed her a few more tricks for stealing a necklace from someone's neck, and she quickly perfected them.

I suddenly hated how she was going to have to steal the vault key. If there were any other way . . .

The night before the heist was stiflingly hot as the four of us crowded together in my room. Ruru sat on Maz's cot, playing with one of Kiera's old knives. I paced the room while Kiera and Maz sat at the small table. She wore the purple silk scarf I'd blindfolded her with around her neck. She said she'd been using it to practice outside of rehearsal. It seemed strange that she kept it around her neck instead of in her pocket like I had, but I didn't question her.

Maz was shirtless and sweating as he laid out his new darts and cleaned his whistler.

"Is this for the vault guard?" Kiera asked, reaching for one of the needle-like darts.

Maz seized her wrist before I could. "No touching, lovely. That's a death dart."

Her wide eyes blinked at me. "You're going to kill him?"

"No," I said, raking my sweaty hair away from my neck. "Maz has sleeping ones as well."

"Like the ones you used in the sea cave?"

Maz nodded. "Skelly brought me both. See, the death darts have little red feathers, and the sleeping darts have little green feathers."

Kiera studied them, biting her lip as if she were still concerned. "What happens if the guard wakes up or remembers who shot him with a dart?"

Maz waved his hand. "He won't. Aiden will be in a guard's uniform, and I'll be in a servant's uniform. We'll drag him back to his post when we're done and give him a half-gone tankard of ale to make it look like he was simply drunk."

258 • LEAH MARA

Tension simmered in the room like heat over the cracked clay buildings.

I ceased pacing and faced them. "Let's go over the rest of the plan one more time."

Maz groaned, but Kiera and Ruru nodded wearily.

"Kiera, after your dance, you'll get close to Asher and steal the key."

Her fingers tapped on the table. "Without him noticing, yes. Then I'll meet you and Maz in front of the vault. After I unlock it—"

"And you're positive you remember which lock?" I interrupted.

Irritation flashed over her face. "Yes. After I unlock the vault, I'll stand watch while you and Maz load up the barrels and cart them toward the servant's entrance."

I crossed my arms over my chest. "And if you hear someone coming before we're done?"

"I'll knock on the door. After you two have closed the door *most* of the way, I'll pretend to be lost until whoever it is leaves." She narrowed her eyes at me. "Remember, don't close the door, or you'll have to wait for me to unlock it again."

My skin crawled at the idea of being locked inside a vault. "Trust me, I'll remember."

"Once you two are clear," she continued, "I'll return the key. Then I'll go with Melaena to *The Silk Dancer*, where she'll send me through the tunnel."

"To the warehouse, where we'll be waiting," I finished for her.

"I don't have much of a job," Ruru muttered, flipping the knife end over end.

Maz looked up from his work. "You'll be keeping a lookout on our escape, little brother. That's extremely important."

"Yes," I said firmly. "We can't have another incident like we did last time."

Ruru glanced at Kiera, who was staring out the window. "I'll make sure no one knows we're there. Then I'll take the wagon and horses back."

"Good, good. Now—"

"What if I get caught?" Kiera asked. She faced me, her chin lifted in a show of fearlessness I didn't believe. "What if I don't make it back to the warehouse?"

The air seemed to still, as if everyone in the room was holding their breath.

"You won't get caught," I told her. Then, more softly, "But I will come for you. If you're not in the warehouse by dawn, I'll find you."

The scarf shifted around her throat as she swallowed. She tugged on it and went back to staring out the window.

Not long after, she and Ruru went to bed, shutting the door behind them.

Maz gathered up his darts and whistler and stowed them in his pack while I stretched out on my cot and closed my eyes.

"You should tell her," he grumbled.

I didn't open my eyes. "Tell her what?"

"Come off it, Aiden. Tell her how you feel. That you want her to stay."

My eyes snapped open, and I glared at him. "Quiet," I hissed, glancing at the door.

Maz shook his head and sat down on his cot. He lowered his voice to his version of a whisper, which was really just a lower rumble. "Tell her before it's too late. You have enough regrets, brother."

My fingers curled into fists. "I'll tell you what I told her. I will *not* be the reason she dies. If she stays—"

"You don't know what's going to happen."

I shot upright. "No, I don't, Mazkull. But I can't—I won't—" I stopped, the words for what I feared getting lost in a storm of memories.

His face fell as he stared at his boots.

"There's already so much at stake," I whispered. "Don't ask me to add another life to that burden."

After several long moments, Maz nodded, but his eyes pierced me across the room. "You've given up everything but your life for this, Aiden. I just want you to have something to live *for* when this is all over."

With that, he laid down and fell asleep.

I sat in the dark, my mind spinning.

Could I ask her to stay? She seemed to love Maz and Ruru. She seemed to feel . . . something for me. But would that be enough?

No. No, it would be selfish to ask her to stay for me. To put her in further danger.

I had to protect her. And to do that, I had to let her go.

CHAPTER 22
KIERA

THE KNIVES WERE SLIPPERY IN MY HANDS.

Blood and sweat dripped down my arms. How many times had he nicked me?

"Again," Renwell's voice floated to me through a haze of pain, exhaustion, and fear.

I heaved myself to my feet, trying to hide my wince. The silky blindfold covered half my face, but he would still see me weakening.

I shifted into a ready stance. His voice echoed around me as if he paced the large training room.

"You're still hesitating," he said. "Do you think I can't stop your knife even if you manage to throw true?"

I rotated on the spot, following his voice. I didn't speak because we both knew the answer. We both knew I was afraid.

"Pitiful." His voice edged closer. "Your mother's killer didn't hesitate. He *wanted* to kill her."

My heartbeat throbbed in my throat. *He's trying to get in your head. It's part of the training. Duress. Focus. Calm.*

"He trapped her first." Renwell's voice softened. Not with sympathy, but with a cold malice. "Only the gods know what he did to her in that room, all alone."

My fingers shook. I gripped my knives tighter. "Stop," I whispered. *Stop, stop!* My mind screamed at the images he painted there.

"When he knew he was surrounded, he didn't hesitate." Renwell's voice drifted in and out. "He took her dagger, her only protection against a man like him."

"S-stop!" I stumbled, weaving like a drunkard trying to track his voice.

"He drove that dagger straight into her heart. He watched the light leave her eyes. Made certain she took her last breath. He wanted to be sure we couldn't save her. He—"

"*Shut up!*" I screamed, slashing at his voice.

"Make me," Renwell growled in my ear.

A ribbon of fire sliced through my back, and I howled. I whipped around and threw my knife with every ounce of strength I possessed.

A dull, wet *thunk*. The muffled sound of a body hitting the floor.

Silence.

My heart outpaced my breathing in a wild race. With my free hand, I ripped off the blindfold. The purple silk fluttered to the ground.

"No," I whispered. "Gods, no. Please."

My mother—my beautiful, kind, loving mother—lay in a

tangled heap on the floor. Blood soaked her pale skin and her long golden hair. The knife in her heart—it wasn't hers.

It was mine. One that Aiden had given me.

A sob tore from my throat. I dropped to my knees and crawled to her. "Mother . . . Mother, what did I do? I didn't . . ."

Her eyes were closed. Her chest still.

She was gone. She'd left me. No, she'd been *taken* from me. I didn't do it. *I didn't do it.*

Her eyes flew open. "Kiera."

I gasped and woke up.

My heart pounded so loud in my ears I thought the walls were crumbling around me. Sweat beaded over my cold, clammy skin. My sore throat ached with each rasping breath.

Slowly, the nightmare bled away, leaving the four walls of my room and Ruru's soft snores nearby.

My shoulders crumpled as I hugged my knees. Part memory, part monstrosity. I'd had nightmares like that before. But this one felt so real, so true.

Perhaps because I was failing my mission. I still didn't know why Aiden needed the gold. I hadn't found a way to stay after the heist. The final day was upon me, and I had already failed.

I felt as though there were a thousand hooks digging into my skin, tugging me in a thousand directions. What to do, where to go, who to trust? Any choice would be painful. But I had to choose.

Aiden hadn't brought up my supposed imminent departure after the heist. Perhaps he didn't want to think about it either. He'd been hanging around more often the last few days.

Offering to eat breakfast with me, walk me to *The Silk Dancer*. Watching me with Ruru.

What if all I had to do was ask?

Unless this was his way of spending time with me before he said goodbye.

If he cares enough to kill for you, then he'll care enough to keep you.

But did he care? If he did, it felt wrong to use him that way. Especially when I might share some of those feelings. But perhaps that was what would make it so believable. The best lies were always knotted with strands of truth.

I slipped the silk scarf from my pocket. How uncanny that it played a role in my nightmare. I wound the scarf around my neck to hide the finger-shaped bruises Renwell had left on my skin.

The bruises would likely cause an uproar among the men I shared rooms with, and I didn't want to answer questions. The idea that there would even *be* an uproar sent a strange warmth through my blood.

I rose and washed my face quietly. After tugging on my boots, I left the room. Tiptoeing past a snoring Maz and a turned-away Aiden, I snagged an apple from the bowl and hurried into the pink dawn.

I arrived at *The Silk Dancer* to an unusual level of chaos as the seven other dancers and Melaena fluttered to and fro. The girls swept armfuls of makeup from the tables into bags while others took quick baths in the corner. A few were already curling their hair and perfuming their skin. Melaena oversaw a few servants packing our delicate costumes, barking orders and redoing work.

I hurried up to her, breathless. "How can I help?"

She thrust a lacquered box into my arms. "Pack only the gold jewelry. Enough for all of us. Did you bathe?" she asked with a quirked eyebrow. She didn't know how I could stand to live with three men and one bathroom for the whole building.

I grinned. "Last night, before I left here, like you told me to."

She brightened. "Ah! Yes, because I told you the bath would be busy this morning. See what happens when I'm right?"

"You're always right!" I called over my shoulder as I loaded the box with shimmering gold earrings, necklaces, and bracelets.

Several hours later, several gilded, curtained carriages arrived to carry us through the Noble Quarter to Asher's mansion. I hated having to leave my knives behind, but I was a dancer today in a simple silk dress. I'd added a black silk mask that fluttered over most of my face. None of the other dancers questioned me.

And neither did any of the guards when we arrived at Asher's mansion.

We stepped out of the carriages to meet two guards who opened Asher's gates and ushered us inside. A high, spiked wall surrounded the meticulously crafted lawns that rolled out like a green, bushy rug from the street to the mansion. At least six more guards patrolled the grounds.

Asher's mansion sat at the north end of the Noble Quarter, closest to the city wall and the river. Its domed roof and small spires were reminiscent of the Temple on a much smaller scale. Even so, three of the other townhouses lining the street could've fit inside this little palace.

The other girls squealed and pointed at the pearlescent peacocks and the gold lotus-shaped fountain. But I kept my focus on the guards as I hovered in the middle of the group.

More gasps peppered the air when the guards opened the double doors and whisked us inside Asher's enormous atrium. Light flooded the white marble floors from the glass ceiling. A wide, sweeping staircase poured from two hallways high out of sight.

Workers in stiff, violet uniforms pattered across the marble, carrying embroidered cloths, silk ribbons, and vases of fresh flowers. An old man, who was perched on a ladder with wheels, scrubbed every gold-and-glass brazier to a sparkle.

A short woman with a battle-weary look snapped her fingers at us. "This way, and don't touch anything."

We herded along until she led us to a large suite of rooms that had its own bathroom, several large mirrors, and an assortment of gilded lounge furniture.

"Keep the noise down," she ordered us, then shut the door with a snap behind her.

Immediately, the girls broke into a stream of chatter.

I simply breathed a sigh of relief. Until Jayde and Tullia approached me with pots of gold paint, a few horsehair paint-brushes, and gold chains.

"This will take a while," Tullia sang, waggling her brush at me. She tossed her long red hair over her shoulder. "But first, let's do your hair."

An hour later, they had brushed my hair to a gloss and

braided in gold chains dripping with gold shards that flickered when I moved. I praised their handiwork even as my scalp winced from the weight.

"Clothes, off," Jayde commanded, snapping her fingers in an impressive imitation of Melaena. The statuesque blonde was formidable but well-meaning. I could see why Maz fell for her and Tullia's differing charms.

Keeping my eyes averted from theirs, I undressed behind a screen, keeping my breast band and underwear on. I relinquished my scarf to the pile. My hair covered the scars at my back—for now—but Jayde's blue eyes immediately fastened on my neck.

She scowled. "Wait here."

Tullia remained uncharacteristically quiet, her eyes darting to my neck once, while she set up her paints.

Jayde returned with Melaena. Jayde looked incensed, but Melaena was calm.

"Is there something you would like to tell me, Kiera?" she asked.

"It wasn't Ai—any of the men I live with."

Jayde's eyebrows lifted, and Tullia trembled next to me, no doubt bursting with questions.

Melaena blinked in confusion. "The thought never crossed my mind. I just want to know if you're safe. If there's anything I can do."

My skin heated with all the attention. "I'm fine. Just a mishap with a guard." I hesitated. "Don't tell him." *Aiden.*

Melaena studied me for a moment, then nodded. "We'll cover it with paint. No one will know." Then she left.

Jayde crammed her brush into a pot and started stroking

glittering gold paint down my arm. "I hope you gutted him for it."

"The guard?"

"Or turned him in," Tullia added.

Jayde scoffed. "If he's a city guard, they won't punish him. Best do it yourself."

I glanced at her. Was she one of the women who had come from an awful situation, as Melaena said? It was an unspoken rule not to ask a person's history at *The Silk Dancer*. But everyone wondered all the same.

Tullia giggled nervously. "Oh, Jayde, don't be so grim. Let's just focus on the dance, shall we? I mean, look where we are!" She threw her arms wide, flinging a drop of paint on the pristine white wall. "Oops."

Jayde rolled her eyes and wiped it off. "Focus, Tullia. We have five more girls after this without you painting the walls."

The girls bickered and gossiped in turn as they slathered me. I joined in where I could, but my nerves were slowly tightening to the point of choking me.

What if someone recognized me? What if Asher caught me trying to steal from him? What if I forgot the dance routine and shamed the entire group?

"Try not to sweat, dear," Tullia said, fanning my skin. "Your paint will run."

I took a sip of water from the glass Melaena had brought me and tried to remain calm. When Tullia and Jayde lifted my hair to paint my back, they paused again. I imagined the two of them sharing a look behind my head, wondering what sort of life I'd led. But neither of them said a word and continued painting.

Soon, they proclaimed me finished and ordered me not to sit or smudge myself until rehearsal.

I carefully shimmied into my costume—a twisted silk breast band with a long, flowing silk skirt, through which my gold legs were clearly visible. A few bits of jewelry brightened my ears, neck, and wrists.

I meandered around the room, helping where I could, until one by one, the rest of the dancers and Melaena looked like they'd been dipped in liquid gold as well.

The snippy woman from before poked her head into the room to tell us we had an hour to rehearse. Everyone secured their masks and crowded out the door.

Last to leave, I donned my stiff gold mask, which covered me from nose to forehead and boasted flowers and flames spreading from the edges. Then I finally looked into one of the mirrors.

A laugh slipped from me. I looked like the very gold I was here to steal.

I was unrecognizable. A creature fit for the god Arduen himself. It was one of his stories we would reenact tonight.

I hurried to join the others, my eyes darting over every face I passed by. Were Aiden and Maz here yet? Would Aiden watch me dance?

My skin prickled under my thick paint. It didn't matter who watched me tonight. As long as they believed every lie from my lips and every swish of my hips, they would never catch me.

"Kiera."

I peered into the shadowy hallway as Melaena edged her way between painted dancers, twittering about in their silks and masks. We waited outside a pair of engraved doors for our cue. Conversation and laughter rippled from the other side, at distinct odds with our tense silence and my pounding heart. The ballroom must have filled quickly after our short rehearsal.

Melaena finally reached me and pulled something from her hair. "Take this," she whispered, handing me a knife shaped like a hairpin. "I have a feeling you'll need it more than me tonight. May Mynastra's luck be with you."

Words of gratitude clustered in my throat, but none escaped. I gave her a tremulous smile and stabbed the knife into my gilded hair.

She smiled back. "Remember what I said before, Kiera. Find the joy, and you'll find the power you seek."

I tucked her words away in my mind as a light scratching sounded on the door.

"That's our warning," Melaena hissed. "Positions."

Everyone slipped into line like we'd practiced dozens of times.

A loud voice boomed out an introduction, then the doors were swept open. The massive ballroom had been darkened. A few servants holding candelabras lit our path through a crowd of craning necks.

Out of sight, a low drum beat started. Like a heartbeat.

We lifted our arms, silks tied to gold bracelets, and floated into the room. Our bare feet tapped, and our bodies swayed forward with each beat.

The drum picked up tempo as we approached the center stage—a slightly raised platform with a large bronze brazier in the center. I caught a glimpse of a man lounging in an alcove draped with silks. Asher.

Focus.

We circled the brazier, undulating and spinning like restless flames.

I deftly freed my fiery silks from my wrists and whirled them around me. Somewhere in the back of my mind, Melaena's voice counted the beats of the routine. But my body simply danced.

My muscles were fluid and warm from our rehearsal earlier. The idea that no one knew who I was left me utterly *free.* I wasn't Emilia. I wasn't Kiera. I wasn't a princess or a spy or a guard.

I was one of Arduen's flames begging to be unleashed.

We kicked our pointed feet high, twirling our skirts like golden clouds. Faster and faster, the drums pounding until—

They cut off, and Melaena flicked her hand over the brazier. Two tiny fireseeds fell on the slumbering embers. The flames roared to life. Gasps and applause rumbled through the room, but we weren't done.

Now that we had "awakened" Arduen—the god of fire, love, and the arts—we danced through an old story. The drums picked up again, joined by a flute and a fiddle.

Melaena played Arduen wearing a gold crown dripping with long strings of beads while I played his human lover. I mimed pleading with her for a fire of my own. She graced me with a beautiful flower—its petals colored to look like the real glowing fireflowers. I plucked the seed at its center and tossed it into the flames, which rose higher.

We twirled, trailing our silks like happy flames, as I held the flower aloft, silently praising Arduen for his gift.

Light blazed back into the room as servants uncovered the torches along the walls and lowered a magnificent candle chandelier through a hatch in the wooden ceiling. Shards of crystallized glass reflected rainbows of light over the similarly glittering crowd.

Cheers and another round of applause thundered through the air.

I smiled at the crowd. My heart felt raw with happiness after the thrill of performing. No wonder Melaena called this powerful. I felt like I could accomplish anything.

We gathered four each to Melaena's side and bowed to Asher, who was on his feet, clapping hardest of all.

"Excellent!" he called. "Marvelous!" He was wearing a headdress similar to Melaena's on his dark blond curls. His linen shirt and white pants were embellished with gold thread. Layers of gold chains rippled from his neck to his chest. A gold satin cloak completed his godly ensemble. "Come, come!" He waved us over.

We strolled hand in hand through the crowd until we reached his alcove. A few men and women were perched atop large pillows scattered around the floor. They smiled at us with stained lips and soft eyes. Small tables held gold plates of food and drink that made my stomach rumble.

Thankfully, Asher didn't seem to hear it as he beamed at us. "Splendid performance, truly. When I first came to

Melaena with my ideas, even I couldn't have imagined such beauty."

We smiled and curtsied, murmuring our pleasure.

Asher's brown eyes fixed on me. "I believe we originally planned for seven dancers besides Melaena. You were quite the stunning addition, my dear."

My heart stopped as my earlier confidence vanished. How could he possibly know I was the new one with our costumes, masks, and makeup?

I bowed my head to hide my panic. "You honor me, High Councilor."

He stretched out two fingers and lifted my chin. His gaze was warm, if not a little playful. The faint lines in his skin hinted at a life of smiling. "When someone calls me that, I still look for my father. Please, call me Asher. I would like to get to know you better."

I blinked. The rumors of his womanizing and expensive tastes were clearly not far off. But he also wasn't quite the pompous fool I remembered. Apart from the one time he'd shown us his vault, I'd never interacted with him. He'd become the High Treasurer three years ago, taking over from his father.

And now I would have to steal from him.

A smile grew on Asher's clean-shaven face. "Why don't we start with your name?"

A few titters echoed around the alcove, and my cheeks warmed.

"K-Katerina," I stuttered, cursing myself for not being prepared.

Another name. Another disguise. Another lie.

None of the dancers around me so much as frowned over my made-up name. Perhaps they also used other names.

"Katerina," Asher said, pressing a smooth kiss over my fingertips. A few flecks of my paint clung to his lips.

I smiled. "Asher, forgive me, but you have some gold just here," I said, tapping my own lips.

"Do I?" He released me to find more gold streaked over his fingers. He chuckled and swiped it over his jaw. "Luckily, it's my favorite color. Perhaps I could take over for Melaena and play Arduen for my lovely dancers," he said.

We all laughed and agreed. He was a bit ridiculous, but not unkind, at least.

He insisted we sit with him, ushering us to different cushions. He led me by the lightest touch to the cushion next to his. "Wouldn't want to mar any more of that beautiful gold," he said with a wink.

Melaena sat behind me with an encouraging smile. I tried to return it, but my nerves were back.

It was perfect. He sat so close to me. Close enough that I could see a thin gold chain among the ropes of other gold necklaces. The key had to be dangling from that one under his shirt. Tantalizingly out of sight.

Act the sweet, playful admirer, and you could steal his very soul if you wished.

But I didn't need to steal his soul—just the key from around his neck.

CHAPTER 23
KIERA

ASHER POURED SCARLET WINE INTO A GOLD CUP AND HANDED IT to me. "How long have you been with *The Silk Dancer*, Katerina?"

I took the tiniest sip, still managing to leave gold paint on the rim. "Only a few weeks."

His eyebrows arched. "Melaena must have quickly recognized your deep talent."

"That and her drive to work hard," Melaena said with a fond smile.

I relaxed a little. "At first, I thought my body would give out from the number of turns she forced me to practice."

"I told you the torture would be worth it. You were lovely. You even remembered to smile."

I laughed, and Asher leaned closer. "And even lovelier when you laugh, Katerina. I do hope you'll stay on at *The Silk Dancer*. I would love to see you dance again."

A part of me wilted, while another part celebrated such an easy take. "Of course, if she'll have me."

"Friends are always welcome," Melaena said quietly. "Please excuse me. A few of my patrons wish to speak with me."

She gracefully rose and melted into a crowd of admirers.

I bit my lip, watching her go. Gods, if only she knew how far from a friend I was.

Asher tsked, gently pulling my lip from my teeth. "Tell me what troubles you, darling."

I hid my shiver and slipped back into my role of sweet seductress. "I—I've never been to a party like this before. I'm nervous I'll say or do the wrong thing."

His shoulder brushed mine as his warm brown eyes asked me to trust him. "You have nothing to fear with me. Stay by my side, and I'll make sure this is a night you remember forever."

I smiled and tentatively initiated the first touch, catching one of the beaded strings from his crown and rolling it between my fingers. Ruru had said that was important, to get my mark used to my hands being near him.

Asher was completely enraptured and didn't feel my hand slip under his cape. No weapons. Shirt tucked. I would have to change that. His desire to wear so many other, heavier necklaces tonight might actually work in my favor. If I found the right clasp on the first try.

"I've heard you have the *best* food at your parties," I said, still playing with his beads.

His nose dipped close to mine. "I do. Would you like some?"

I nodded shyly, leaning away.

A wicked gleam entered his gaze, but he turned and called out to a few servants standing nearby.

They quickly brought forward platter after platter of food. Skewers of smoked meat and chubby balls of white cheese drizzled with oil and herbs. Whole fish stuffed with a rainbow of vegetables. Heaps of rice with thick curls of butter melting through them. Whole corn cobs from a distant field in Pravara were fried in a delicate crust of cheese and spice.

Those corn cobs used to be my favorite. Father had them served at the palace every summer. Even during the Pravaran rebellion. I'd lost my taste for them since then.

Everyone else in the alcove partook of the expensive delicacies while I chewed a bit of bread soaked in honey to settle my stomach. I made sure to keep refilling Asher's wine glass. He asked me a few more questions, but I steered the conversation into talking about him, which he was only too glad to do.

I didn't know how much time had passed, but surely Aiden and Maz were waiting for me by now.

Any moment someone might realize Aiden wasn't really a guard or the real guard could wake up or Asher might grow tired of me . . .

"Gods, it's getting warm in here," I said, fanning myself with one of my silks. I leaned back on my hands, pushing my breasts forward. "Don't you agree, my lord? I mean, Asher."

He grinned, his cheeks flushed from the wine, as his gaze dipped to my barely covered breasts. "Indeed, I quite like it. Makes one relax, I think. But I could have my servants bring fans—"

"No," I said quickly, curling closer to him and pressing my hand to his stomach. "I'm simply thinking of you. You're wearing so much more than I am. Would you allow me to . . . loosen a few things?"

His eyes glazed over as I tugged his shirt from his pants. I danced my fingers over the back of his neck, feeling for the smallest clasp.

I brought my lips close to his ear. "After all, didn't Arduen prefer decoration over clothing?"

Asher shuddered just as I unclasped his cloak and his necklace in the same moment.

His gold cloak fell into a puddle of gold—and a small metal key landed in my waiting palm under his shirt. Heady with triumph, I nipped Asher's earlobe as I stowed the key with its chain in my breast band.

He groaned and seized my wrist. "You tease me, Katerina."

I smiled at his torn expression. "I have not even begun to tease you, Asher. Shall we play a game?"

"I would love to play with you," he whispered, his wicked smile returning.

I tapped the end of his nose. "Eat, dance, flirt with anyone else you can find. If, by the end of the night, you are still interested in me, I will dance for you again. *Only* you."

Desire flared in his gaze. "The end of the night can't come too soon."

Yes, it certainly can.

I slipped from his grasp and gave him one last heated look over my shoulder as he watched me leave.

But Asher evaporated from my mind the moment I turned away. I took pains to walk slowly through the crowd. The little key felt like a branding iron pressed to my skin, marking me as a thief for all to see.

I passed by nobles I'd known since birth but hadn't seen in years. A few of them smiled and congratulated me on a well-done performance. Others looked down their noses and gave me their backs.

But one day, they would all know who I was, and they would heed my power as High Enforcer.

My footsteps quickened as I left the glittering nobles behind closed doors. I hurried across the silent atrium, the moonlight making the marble glow like a second moon.

Following the map in my head, I navigated several hallways and stairwells until I was in the bottom southeast corner of the mansion. Wall sconces were few and far between, leaving long shadows in the hallways. Not unlike the Old Quarter at night.

I shivered. My bare feet didn't make a sound on the plush carpet, but the gold in my hair tinkled merrily.

A guard stepped into the hallway, blocking my path. I froze until my eyes locked with Aiden's under the shadow of his feathered helmet.

"Aiden," I breathed.

He looked strange dressed as the guards I'd seen on the grounds. Absent his usual dark colors and cloak. But I experienced the same familiar rush as his green eyes raked over me. They darkened when he saw the streaks in my paint where Asher's hand had clasped.

His lips parted as if he were going to say something, but then he shook his head.

"Did you get it?" he asked roughly.

A kernel of disappointment lodged in my chest. "Of course."

I pulled the key from my silk breast band, and his nostrils flared.

But then Maz sidled up wearing the plain servant garb stitched with Asher's insignia. He grinned. "Fucking Four, you're even more beautiful than Aiden said you were!"

My head whipped toward Aiden, but he merely scowled at Maz. "She's late."

I glared at him. "It's not so easy to seduce a man *and* steal from him in a crowded party."

His eyes smoldered like green fire. "Liar. He simply didn't want to let you go." He stared pointedly at my smudged wrist.

Maz shouldered his way between us. "You can have your lovers' quarrel later. Aiden, go back to your post. I'll grab the cart. Kiera, unlock the gods-damned door."

Aiden growled something under his breath and stalked off.

I gave Maz a light shove. "We are *not* lovers," I hissed.

He smirked. "To quote your lover: 'Liar.'" He poked my ribs, and I smacked his hand away. "Lovers are often of the heart and mind before they are of the body," he added.

I snorted. "Who said that? A poet?"

"My grandmother."

That surprised a chuckle out of me. "Figures," I muttered.

"Maz!" Aiden called sharply.

Maz waggled his eyebrows at me and disappeared down the hall. I took a deep breath and joined Aiden by the vault door.

He said nothing as I surveyed the ten keyholes set into the ornate metal door. Swirling gold leaves hammered over iron and steel.

Second one down from the top right. I slid the key into the hole.

Holy Four, please be the right one.

I twisted it, and several tumblers clanked inside the door. Holding my breath, I pushed down the steel lever, and it gave easily.

Air whooshed out of me in relief. The corner of Aiden's mouth hooked in a tiny smile.

"Told you I'd remember," I taunted him, stuffing the key back into my breast band.

"We wouldn't be here if I doubted you." He glanced down the hall. "We should wait for Maz before we open the door, in case someone walks by."

I nodded. We stared at each other in silence.

"Where's the guard?" I asked.

"Closet."

I nodded again.

Lovers. Maz couldn't be more wrong. Aiden was angry with me. Again. Because I'd meddled with his plans. Again. He might feel sorry for me. He might see me as his responsibility. But we weren't *any* kind of lovers.

Were we?

Aiden's eyes flared, as if he'd read every thought that crossed my mind. I swallowed hard. "You watched me dance."

He nodded.

I traced a finger along the edge of my mask. "How did you know which one was me?"

He slowly stepped closer to me. I didn't move a muscle. Even with a vault door temptingly ajar beside us, I wanted to see inside his mind more.

"This." His fingers captured the ends of my hair, stroking them like he had when he'd washed my hair. "And your smile," he murmured.

"My smile?"

He edged even closer, placing his thumb at the corner of my mouth. "You were the brightest light up there, my little thief. So bright, you stole the very shadows from my heart."

My stomach swooped hard and low. Lightning sizzled through my veins and curled around my spine.

His lips were so close. Had I pulled him forward? Gods, I wanted a taste. I wanted to trap those beautiful words between our lips and never let them go.

"Hey now, lovers! It's not the time for that either!"

I jumped away from Aiden as Maz pushed a servant's dining cart down the short hall, a smug grin curling through his golden beard.

"We—we were just—"

"No need to explain, lovely," Maz said. "Did you get it open?"

"Of course she did," Aiden answered, but I didn't dare look at him. His words were still busy crumbling the walls around my heart.

Maz did a little jig. "What are we waiting for?" He grabbed the handle and heaved back on the door.

"Fucking Four, how much does this thing weigh?" he grunted.

"More than the gold, I imagine. Asher's guard seemed to have no trouble with it the last time I was here," I teased.

He bared his teeth and pushed harder. Aiden wrapped his

hands around the edge and helped him drag it the rest of the way open.

I seized the lamp from its wall holder and slipped inside. Just for a quick peek.

It was ... emptier than I remembered.

Dozens of chests lined the walls, but many of them were only half-full of coins or less. Only one small barrel of fireseeds. The glass cases that had been stuffed with jewels and expensive trinkets now looked picked over. Was this Asher's fault or my father's?

I winced when my bare foot landed on something sharp. I picked up a heavy gold ring, pointed wings extending from it like a bird. Squinting, I could see two tiny sunstone fragments for eyes and a beak.

"No jewelry," Aiden said, appearing in front of me. "Only coins."

He held out his hand for the ring, something strange flickering in his eyes, smothering their earlier warmth.

I dropped it in his palm. "I'll go stand watch." I gave Maz the lamp, but glanced over my shoulder as I left.

And saw Aiden slip the ring into his pocket.

I frowned. Had he simply wanted it for himself? Or did it mean something to him?

He started to face me, so I rushed down the hallway and peered around both corners. Still empty and silent.

I paced the hallway, my skirt swishing with each step. The only other sound was the faint tinkle of coins. How much were they taking? We'd never discussed numbers. I'd spent so long assuming the heist would never happen that I'd never thought about it.

But it didn't matter. Renwell would never let the gold escape Father's clutches for long.

Come dawn, I would ask Aiden if I could stay with him. Plain and simple. After what he'd said, surely he wanted me to stay?

I bit my lip as butterflies danced through my stomach. *My little thief.* Did he want me to be his?

Sudden longing struck in a deep, dark crevice of my heart, growing roots, taking hold, drawing strength from hope.

At long last, Aiden and Maz pushed the cart out of the vault.

Just as voices echoed down the hall.

Panic flooded my bloodstream, and I waved wildly at them.

Their eyes widened, and they struggled to shove the cart back into the vault.

The voices came closer. Gods damn it, they would be here in moments.

Lost. I was supposed to act lost. Should I run out and greet them before they reached the vault hallway?

Aiden and Maz strained to close the door with Aiden on the *outside.*

What are you doing? I wanted to scream.

My fingers dove into my hair and pulled out the hairpin knife Melaena had given me. Just to be safe.

Voices. Male. Footsteps. So close. More guards?

Aiden raced up to me, whipping off his helmet, his eyes blazing with determination.

I gaped at him. "You shouldn't—"

"Don't stab me," he whispered.

Then he kissed me.

CHAPTER 24
KIERA

THE WORLD HAD FROZEN TO A SHOCKED CALM AS AIDEN'S SOFT lips pressed against mine. Somewhere, in a different world, there were voices and the feel of the knife slipping from my fingers.

Then a beautiful, raging storm exploded inside me.

I flung my arms around his neck and kissed him back.

He groaned and wrapped his arms around my waist and pressed me into every hardened muscle of his body.

I gasped as my feet left the ground, but his mouth chased mine, stealing it once more.

Fucking Four, I wanted to be stolen.

His kiss was as demanding and desperate as mine. I clung to him as if my life depended on it, afraid I would shatter if our lips ceased to touch. My hands flew over him, tunneling into his silky hair, yanking on his shirt collar, raking over the stubble on his jaw, clutching his face to mine.

The tip of his tongue kissed mine before stroking into my mouth.

Gods, he tasted like apples and cinnamon. Like sweet wine that blurred my thoughts and quenched my thirst.

Like chaos and destruction.

A strangled whimper rose from my throat. He answered with a hungry growl, wrapping my legs around his waist and pinning me against a wall with his hips.

A deep, pleasant warmth coated my insides like honey.

But then something small and hard bounced off my leg.

Aiden growled again, as if ordering me to ignore it. But it happened again.

My eyes blinked open the same moment our lips parted. His panting breaths soothed my swollen lips. My heart thundered in my ears.

Another projectile bounced off my shoulder.

I tore my attention from his gold-streaked mouth and found a sweaty Maz standing in front of the closed vault with the loaded cart, a handful of gold coins, and an expression somewhere between elated and exasperated.

"Gods damn it, you two," he said, shaking his head. "I will personally donate twenty of my gold coins to rent the best room in Aquinon for you to devour each other. But can we *please* finish stealing the coins first?"

A high-pitched giggle burst out of me, and I slapped a hand over my mouth.

Aiden glanced down at me with such a smoldering grin that I would've melted to the floor had he not been holding me. He looked *wrecked*. My gold paint was streaked over his face and neck. Gold flecks winked at me from his tousled black hair.

Slowly, he eased me back on my feet and picked up one of the coins Maz had thrown at us.

He flicked it at Maz, hitting him in the chest. "Only if you stop throwing them at us like we're your entertainment for the evening."

"Do forgive me," Maz said dryly, picking up the fallen coins as he wheeled the cart toward us. "But I thought that's exactly what you were doing—putting on a show for the two servants who walked by. Or did you forget about them? And me? And the heist? And—"

"Enough!" Aiden cuffed him on the back of the head as he passed.

Maz ducked away, whistling and wheeling our stolen treasure down the hall.

But it was like a cloud had passed over, dripping cold rain into our warm bubble.

"Was he right?" I whispered. "Was that just for show?"

Aiden's face turned solemn, but his touch was gentle as he stroked my cheek with his thumb. "Not for a single moment."

Relief coated me like his clawberry paste—sealing the wound that had already begun to hurt.

He kissed me once more. A tender, heart-wrenching kiss before he ripped himself away with a harsh sigh. "We have to go. I have to get the guard before he wakes up."

"But . . . but your face." I tried to dab off some of the paint from his lips with my silks. "Everyone will know—"

He caught my wrist and leaned into my palm. "Let them. If

I had my way, I would end the night wearing every speck of your paint."

My blood hummed with desire until the realization hit me. "Gods! My paint! I'll have to fix it before . . . before . . ." *Going back to Asher.*

Aiden's jaw clenched. "Go, then. Do what you must. I'll be waiting for you."

I had fled only two steps when he called out, "Kiera!"

He caught up with me, his helmet tucked under his arm, and pressed my hairpin knife into my hand. "Thank you for not stabbing me."

A lump formed in my throat as he spun around and marched in the other direction. The dangerous truth was, I couldn't bear the idea of stabbing him.

But betrayal cuts deeper than a blade.

My heart twisted, afraid. With trembling fingers, I jammed the sharp hairpin back in my hair.

Instead of going back to the party, I raced up the stairs to our dressing room. I stood in front of the mirror, trying not to stare too hard at the streaks in my body paint—a map of Aiden's desire for me.

I quickly slathered on more sparkling gold paint and made sure my mask was secure. Then I slipped into the decidedly more drunk crowd. The musicians continued to play in their corner as if people were still paying attention.

Melaena's bright eyes found me as she spoke with several nobles. One of whom was Garyth. Were they sharing secrets again?

I gave her a tiny nod and kept moving.

Asher still lounged in his alcove, completely oblivious to his missing key and the robbery that just took place in his vault. Tullia and Jayde and several other dancers were sprawled around him on cushions now stained with food and wine. They laughed loudly at something Asher said, and my heart lifted with hope.

Perhaps he had found another who interested him. Perhaps he wouldn't require me to dance for him. After all, I only needed to get close enough to clasp his key necklace around his neck.

Tullia spotted me first, and her whole face lit up in a smudged, golden grin. "There you are! Where have you been, K—"

"Just playing a little game, Tullia," I spoke over her loudly in case she forgot my new name.

She giggled, waving her skirt at me. "Come join us!"

"Yes, please do," Asher said in a deep, slightly slurred voice. "Then I can tell you I've won our little game."

My stomach clenched, but I maneuvered through the mess and sank down next to him. "And how is that, High—Asher?"

"I want that dance," he murmured in my ear, his breath hot on my cheek.

I swallowed. "And you shall have it. At the end of the night."

He grinned, somehow looking ten years younger. "Fine, fine. Until then, we drink!"

The dancers cheered, and a servant carrying a jug filled everyone's cup. But I continued to take small sips. Asher's glazed brown eyes blinked slowly, as if sleepy.

Dear Mynastra, if only I were so lucky.

"I have decided!" Asher announced, startling Jayde, who sloshed more wine on her skirt. "You will all spend the night here!"

Gasps echoed around the alcove as my heart sank.

"Yes! Oh, that sounds lovely! How kind of you!" the women chirped over each other.

Asher grasped my hand in his sweaty palm. "Please say you'll stay." He threw back his head and laughed. "Gods, I should've been a poet! Yes?"

I smiled weakly and nodded.

"Yes! She'll stay! I've . . . gotten my way!" He beamed proudly.

I took another fortifying sip of wine.

"Yes, everyone can take a hot bath," he continued. "And I assume you all have other clothes with you? If not, I'll send for some. Oh, this will be perfect. And breakfast in the morning!"

I gritted my teeth.

Why in the deep, dark, wandering hell did he have to be a chatty, overly friendly drunk? There was no gods-damned way I was taking a bath or changing my clothes here. This costume was the only thing keeping him, and others, from recognizing me.

A minute later, Melaena glided over and smiled at Asher. "A truly marvelous evening, Asher, but I must get my dancers home soon."

He brightened and told her his plan and that we had all agreed.

Her eyes darted to me. "All of you wish to stay?"

I tried to silently signal her with my eyes that I had *not*.

She gestured to me. "I'll just take this one back. I need her assistance at the club."

Asher pouted, throwing his arm around my shoulders. "But she's promised me a dance, and I intend to collect."

Melaena's eyes widened the slightest bit. Tullia looked confused, while a few of the other dancers—the ones I didn't know very well—scowled at me.

My stomach hollowed out. Gods, he made it sound more salacious than I meant it.

Melaena cleared her throat delicately. "Very well." She glanced at me. "A word."

I rose and followed her to an empty corner of the room. No one gave us a second glance as some guests had departed already and others were indisposed in alcoves.

"What is going on, Kiera?" she whispered through a tight smile.

I turned my back to the room, unable to keep my expression relaxed. "We were successful, but I still need to get the chain back around his neck, which is more complicated than taking it. A private dance will help. Otherwise, one of the women will notice my fumbling."

"I understand." She sighed. "I'll leave the back door of *The Silk Dancer* open for you. Will you be able to sneak out of here and get to the club unseen?"

"I'll manage. The Wolves rarely come through this quarter, so I shouldn't run into any trouble."

Melaena nodded. "Very well. But be careful. Asher is . . . not a bad man. He's used to getting his way, but he won't force you. Just don't make promises you can't keep."

I suppressed a shiver, the heat of Aiden's kiss still lingering on my lips. "I won't."

"Wake me when you get back, and I'll take you to Aiden." She stepped forward as if to embrace me, then remembered our painted skin. Instead, she squeezed my hand with an encouraging smile.

We headed back to Asher, and Melaena said her goodbyes.

Once she was gone, Asher clapped his hands. "I think it's time we also settled down for the night, yes?"

Everyone eagerly agreed. We flocked out of the ballroom and followed Asher upstairs.

"A few of you may use this bath," he said, pointing to the room we'd used to get ready. "The bedrooms and additional bathrooms are down this hall." He waved his arm at the glossy wooden doors lining the dim hall.

Amid sighs of gratitude that escalated to squeals of excitement as the dancers opened every door, Asher extended his arm to me, swaying a bit. "Come with me?"

I swallowed, my throat dry as parchment, and threaded my arm through his. We walked to the end of the hall and turned left, traipsing another hall that lined the back of the mansion.

He stopped in front of a set of gold-tipped doors painted with his insignia. His bed chamber.

My heart tapped against my breastbone like a caged bird as he flung the doors open.

A fire burned merrily in a hearth larger than the room I shared with Ruru. It cast a warm glow over a bed chamber the size of a small house. An enormous bed with four wooden spires and lush violet curtains was wedged into a corner near a floor-to-ceiling window. Another set of double doors was carved into the glass, leading out to a wide balcony that over-looked more gardens at the back of the mansion. I could almost see beyond the city wall from here.

Aware of him staring at me, I thanked the gods my mask hid half of my expression. "It's beautiful, Asher."

He shrugged, a loose grin on his handsome face. "It is. But you are more so."

He reached for me, but I seized his hand. He blinked at me curiously.

I tugged him over to his bed and gently guided him to sit on the edge. "Would you like to watch me from here?" I whispered.

Understanding dawned on his face, and he nodded eagerly.

Trying to breathe evenly through my nose, I sauntered backward, keeping my eyes locked on him, a small smile on my lips. When my bare feet brushed over the warm stones in front of the hearth, I stopped.

Was this a terrible idea? What if Melaena was wrong about Asher's nature?

Don't make promises you can't keep.

But still I hesitated. For one wild moment, I wanted to bolt through those doors and drop the key somewhere for Asher to find it. But Aiden wanted him to be oblivious for as long as possible.

Aiden.

Perhaps if I pretended this dance was for him . . .

Closing my eyes, I drifted back to that hallway . . . Aiden's hands caressing my body . . . his mouth making love to mine . . .

Heat pulsed through my veins. I opened my eyes.

No music, but I didn't need it. I freed my silks from their bracelets and began to weave them around my body as I'd practiced with Melaena hundreds of times.

I stepped forward, twisting my hips. I lifted my arms and gently twirled. I thought of Aiden's smoldering grin instead of the entranced look Asher displayed.

An easy smile curled my lips, and I sank to the floor with split legs, one in front of me and one behind. Thank the gods and Melaena my flexibility had improved.

Asher was gripping the bed with white knuckles now, leaning forward, his heavy necklaces swinging. But it was Aiden's muscled chest I saw. Those green eyes that played tricks on my mind.

I swayed forward and back, exposing my throat to the ceiling, my breasts to him. My silks floated around me like lazy flames.

Carefully rolling, I twirled to my feet. I danced closer and closer to him. My chest heaved with each breath. Sweat gathered under my heavy hair. My skirt brushed his knees.

But then the wrong hands gripped my waist. The wrong scent—rose oil and mint—snapped me out of my wishful haze.

Asher's wet lips were a breath from mine when I stumbled away from him.

"Forgive me," I gasped. "I—I forgot myself."

He shook his head, his smile kind even as disappointment flickered in his eyes. "I am the one who needs forgiveness. I fear I have done the very thing I promised I wouldn't by frightening you."

When he continued to sit there looking like a wounded puppy, my anxiety slowly calmed. Melaena had been right. As usual.

I smiled and sat next to him on the bed. "Of course, you're forgiven. It's easy to get caught up in the heat of the moment."

"Indeed," he murmured, rubbing his temple. "Also, a bit more wine than I'm used to, I think."

"Here, let me help you," I said, grasping his Arduen crown. "May I?"

He nodded wearily. I eased it off his head and set it aside. An idea struck me.

I scooted back on the bed's satin covers. "Lay your head in my lap, and I'll try to ease your pain."

"You're very kind," he mumbled, obliging.

My heart winced. No, I wasn't. I simply wanted access to his neck.

Once he was settled with his head propped on my crossed legs, I began to massage his neck and shoulders. "Close your eyes and relax," I whispered.

He sighed heavily, already half-asleep.

While slowly rubbing one of his temples, I eased the vault key on its chain out of my breast band.

I gently nestled the key among his other necklaces and guided the two ends of the chain around his neck.

His deep breathing shifted the key the tiniest bit, and it clinked against the other necklaces.

I froze, waiting, a dozen excuses filling my mouth. But his eyes remained closed. I circled my thumbs over his neck while catching the dangling chains. Holding my breath, I pinched the two ends together. The clasp slipped through my sweaty fingers.

Gods damn it! Fucking Four! Help me!

I dug my knuckles into his neck, bracing against him to fumble with the clasp again.

Asher bolted upright, yanking the chain from my fingers. I gasped. He twisted to face me, his eyes wild.

And the key tumbled from his neck to land between us.

CHAPTER 25
KIERA

"Are . . . are you all right?" I cried. "I'm so sorry, my lord. I was rubbing your neck, and your necklace snagged on my bracelet. I would never—"

"Hush, hush, my darling." He patted my knee, his voice creaky with sleep. "You did nothing wrong. I've been prone to nightmares since I was a child. I didn't mean to startle you." He scooped the key and its chain into his palm. "This gods-damned chain is so old; I need to replace it, anyway."

"I feel terrible," I whispered, pressing my shaking hands to my cheeks. "I was trying to comfort you, and instead, you had a nightmare . . ."

Asher smiled, but it didn't reach his eyes. "It's not your fault. Hazard of my job, I'm afraid."

I frowned. Did he not like being High Treasurer? It wasn't easy working with my father, but Asher seemed so carefree. Guilt nipped at my conscience. What would Asher do when he discovered the theft? Would he be punished?

"Don't you worry your pretty head about me," Asher said, tucking the key into his pocket. "But I feel I'm not the best host at the moment. I would like a second chance soon. If you'll grant me one?"

I nodded. Melaena would have to make up some story about why he'd never see Katerina again.

"You're welcome to stay with me. I have the largest bath in the mansion if you would like to use it."

"Thank you, but I think I should return to the others."

"Of course. I can walk you, if you'd like."

I slid off the bed, eager to flee. "That's kind, but not necessary. I wish you more pleasant dreams, Asher."

He gave me a wan smile. "Perhaps I'll dream of you."

I smiled back but said nothing. *I hope you forget me.*

I slipped out the door and all but ran back to the dressing room. A splash told me someone was still in the bath, but I didn't look. I threw on my cloak and tugged down the hood as far as it would go.

From there, it was a simple matter of empty halls and well-oiled doors. A sense of elation rose in my chest as I closed the mansion door behind me. The outside air never smelled sweeter. I smiled back at the grinning moon and took off down the gravel path.

The guards barely glanced at me and opened the gate. Perhaps they were used to letting out late-night visitors smothered in cloaks.

I darted through the sleeping quarter, the dark alleys familiar and less threatening than those the Shadow-Wolves roamed.

Melaena had left the back door of *The Silk Dancer*

unlocked, as she'd promised. I let myself into the dark dressing room.

I felt my way toward the lamp on the wall, grazing the porcelain tub as I did so.

Melaena had wanted me to wake her when I arrived, but surely she—and Aiden—wouldn't begrudge me a quick bath to finally rid myself of this paint.

I turned up the lamp and twisted the knob to fill the tub with water. I ripped off my mask and shimmied out of my dirty silks. Groaning with relief, I lowered myself into the tub and scrubbed every inch of my skin clean.

Picking the ornaments from my hair was much less fun, but it was worth it to feel like myself again. I carefully placed Melaena's hairpin knife on a makeup table.

By the time I was divested of my glamor and dressed in my old clothes and knives, exhaustion pulled at my bones and my eyelids. It must be close to dawn. Was Aiden waiting for me in the warehouse like he'd said? I couldn't get through the tunnel myself without picking the lock and searching for the hidden mechanism to open the tunnel door. Which left waking Melaena.

But perhaps I could let her sleep a while longer. Catch a few winks myself, as Ruru would say.

After all, I wasn't sure of everything that awaited me once I reached Aiden.

I turned down the lamp and used my cloak and a few old dresses to make a nest for myself in a deep corner behind racks of clothes.

Just a few winks . . .

A door slammed. My eyes flew open. A soft light filtered through the forest of clothes I laid in.

"Gods damn it, Aiden!" Melaena hissed. "You scared me halfway to the Abyss, standing over me like that! And look, the door is still unlocked, and she's not here. She must be with Asher."

My breathing hitched. Aiden had come for me. Like he said he would. It must be past dawn.

Aiden growled with frustration. "I can't believe you let her stay with him, Mel. We had a plan."

"What was I supposed to do, drag her out? She said she had it handled. I trust her, and so should you."

"I just don't want her to get caught," he snapped. "If Asher realized at any point—"

"We would've heard something. You can't storm his mansion looking for her."

"I will if I have to." My heart danced at his conviction. "But I'll wait here a little longer first."

Something creaked as if he'd sank onto one of the makeup chairs. I shifted, preparing to reveal myself when he spoke again.

"I brought your cut, by the way." Coins jingled as if in a bag. "And I wondered if you could keep this safe for me."

Melaena gasped. "Oh, Aiden, was this in the vault?"

"Yes." His voice turned cold and harsh. "Weylin must've stolen it from my father's finger after he stabbed him in the back."

A wave of horror crashed into me, drowning out every other sound.

Weylin—*my father*—stabbed Aiden's father in the back? He *killed* him? And stole—what, a ring?

Another wave knocked me backward.

The ring from the vault. The one Aiden slipped into his pocket. That was his *father's*?

Why would my father kill his? Why was this ring so valuable?

I shook my head to clear the buzzing in my ears, desperate to hear more.

"...found it on the floor?" Melaena was asking.

Aiden snorted. "I doubt Asher knew who it belonged to. It was probably just another piece of jewelry for his collection."

"I can't keep this, Aiden. Garyth said Renwell searched his house. What if he came for me next? I can't afford to lose this place. These women depend on it."

I leaned forward, my fists clenched in my makeshift bedding. *Why?* What was so dangerous about a ring? And how would Renwell recognize it?

Aiden sighed. "Very well. I'll find somewhere safe to keep it."

There was a beat of silence where I didn't dare to breathe or move a muscle, even as my mind screamed.

"He wants to meet you," Melaena said. "Garyth."

"It's too risky."

"But—"

"We're so close, Melaena. After *years*, we've almost reached our goal. I'm not going to throw all that away to soothe a noble's fears. That's why I have you. Deal with him."

"You are not the only one who has sacrificed for this,"

Melaena snapped. "I have lived here all my life, unlike you, and seen much worse."

Aiden's voice softened. "Forgive me, Mel. It was not myself I thought of. I will never forget what you've endured here. You, nor anyone else who has fought or died, hoping for a better world."

"I will never understand why you hide who you are," she said, her voice breaking. "You have all the power you need to unite this kingdom—"

"I will never be king. The Falcryn line ended with my father. Betrayed by his gods-damned closest friend. I want no part of a life where I'm nothing more than a crown to steal."

My heart stopped. My vision blurred. *No.*

But even as every fiber in my being tried to deny it, images flashed through my mind.

Falcryn. The house name inked on the royal history of Rellmira. The name just before the house of Torvaine. Falcryn, a falcon insignia. The inked falcon on Aiden's shoulder. The gold falcon melded to a stolen ring.

Aiden mentioned the king when we played Death and Four. He'd respected the king's treatment of the miners as well as his title. King Tristan Falcryn—his father.

Aiden was the original heir to the Rellmiran throne. Even if he didn't want it. And if what he said was true, my father had lied to an entire kingdom about the circumstances under which he became king.

Which was why he'd slapped me when I said he'd gotten the crown by chance.

My cheek burned with the memory, and my lips curled

into a sneer. Pulling off such a betrayal certainly would've taken a great deal of work.

What had he told me once? *"We were dear friends—Tristan and I. He trusted me implicitly. Which is why he wrote into law that I would inherit the throne if he passed without heirs."*

Without heirs. Had he known of Aiden? What happened to Aiden's mother?

My world shifted further. It tipped and spilled a darkness over me like an overturned ink well. My entire life, and everyone in it, was stained with lies.

Aiden and Melaena were quiet now. I didn't know what other conversation I'd missed. But I couldn't reveal myself now. I didn't know what in the deep, dark, wandering hell I was supposed to do with this.

I sank against the wall, rustling a few dresses hanging over me. I stilled.

Silence.

Then, "I'm sure Kiera will be back any moment," Melaena said. But her voice sounded oddly shaky. She cleared her throat. "Perhaps we should wait elsewhere? Would you like something to eat?"

A rustling noise, then a door opened and closed.

I waited. More silence.

I'd need to sneak out the back door and then come in, pretending that I'd bathed at Asher's.

Hands and feet numb, I crawled out of my hiding place.

"Hello, little thief."

CHAPTER 26
AIDEN

THE RELIEF I FELT AT SEEING KIERA ALIVE AND WELL DIED A quick death.

The panic on her face punched me in the gut. Her eyes dropped from my face to the dagger I held casually in my hand.

I had expected *someone* to come crawling out of their hiding place. But not her.

For the past few hours, I'd done nothing but relive our kiss. I'd paced the dusty warehouse, unable to sleep, waiting for the moment I could pull her back into my arms. For however long I could have her.

It was foolish to hope.

"You have mere moments to explain yourself," I said softly.

She slowly rose to her feet, never looking away from my blade. Then she began easing her way toward the door.

"Kiera, don't—"

She bolted for the door, but I leapt forward and slammed her against it before she could reach the handle.

Melaena gasped behind me, but I ignored her.

Kiera flailed beneath me, probably reaching for her knives. I wrapped my arm around her, pinning her arms to her sides. I slid my knife under her chin and lifted it.

"Why were you eavesdropping? What did you hear?" I snarled.

Her eyes were wild with fear, her skin bloodless. "Please," she whispered. "Please, Aiden."

It felt like she'd taken my knife and stabbed me in the heart. I stumbled backward. The knife clattered to the floor. My vision blackened at the edges like burning parchment. I blinked to clear it.

Please, Aiden.

I am not a monster. I am not a monster.

But you've done monstrous things . . .

Melaena hurried over to Kiera and guided her to a chair, then sat next to her. "Let's just sit and talk for a moment. *Calmly,*" she added firmly, with a glare in my direction.

I picked up my knife and shoved it in my belt. But I didn't sit down.

"Now, Kiera, why were you hiding?" Melaena asked.

Kiera shook her head vehemently. "I wasn't hiding! I—I came back and took a bath, but I was so tired and didn't want to wake you, so I curled up in a corner back there to sleep for a bit." Her eyes pleaded with me. "Go check if you don't believe me."

Grateful to look anywhere but at her, I peered inside the tub to find a few gold paint streaks. Kiera's discarded jewelry and costume were also nearby. Then I tunneled through the clothes where she'd appeared and found a mashed pile of dresses in the corner.

I reemerged and gave her a short nod. "Fine, but you still haven't answered my other question. How much did you hear?"

"Nearly everything," she whispered. "I was going to come out and reveal myself, I swear. But then . . . then I was scared to."

Gods damn it, I should've been more careful. Only a handful of people knew my true identity—Maz and Melaena among them. That knowledge in the wrong hands could get me killed—or worse, ruin my plans.

As for the other tidbit . . .

Not many people knew what Weylin had done the night he became king. Some might have guessed, but kept their mouths shut. But I heard the real story from one of the few living witnesses.

More people *should* know what kind of murderous traitor sat on the Rellmiran throne. But a propaganda campaign would be messy and chaotic.

My way was easier. Simpler.

"Why would my identity and the true history of our kingdom frighten you?" I asked.

"Because that's the kind of information someone would kill to keep secret," she said, staring at me as if that were my plan.

The truth tumbled from my lips. "I could never kill you."

She searched my eyes in that way of hers. "Maybe not. But you would put me on a ship bound for a deserted island, right?"

I rubbed my jaw. I didn't know *what* to do with her. She was never supposed to have this information. I never wanted her to get this involved. I couldn't let her leave now. But I also couldn't risk my plan in her hands.

I didn't trust anyone's but mine.

"How about she stays with me?" Melaena offered tentatively. "She can live here and dance until . . . until . . ." She blanched, glancing between me and Kiera.

"Until Aiden kills the king," Kiera finished for her in a flat voice. She fixed me with a hard stare. "That's the plan, isn't it? That's the only thing that makes sense." She shook her head and continued, almost to herself, "You hate Weylin. He murdered your father and stole your throne. He obliterated the People's Council and put you in prison. The smuggling, the heist—it was all just a means to an end. Assassination."

Melaena's eyes widened, clearly shocked at how much Kiera knew.

But I was . . . relieved. Almost. That she understood why. But she didn't have all the pieces.

"You'll die," she whispered. "They'll kill you before you ever breach the palace."

"Does the thought of my death sadden you?"

She hesitated, looking down at her fingers twisting in her lap. Then so quietly I wasn't sure I heard her, "Yes." Her head jerked up. "What of the royal family? My—my charges, the prince and princesses? Are you going to kill them as well?"

"You truly do care for them, don't you?"

"Yes. They shouldn't be executed for their father's crimes."

"I remember you said as much. That night at the tavern, playing Death and Four."

She straightened in her chair, her gaze fierce. "I stand by it. They are good, kind people."

"It's strange to see such loyalty for people who didn't try to save you from your cell."

"Nothing can stop Weylin when he's made up his mind," she said harshly. "Surely you know that." She rose and stalked toward me. "If your plans include the slaughter of innocents, then you'd better kill me now, because I will do *everything* to stop you."

I inhaled her scent, honey and lilies, as I basked in the heat of her rage.

Gods, I wanted to yank her into my arms and crush my mouth to hers, taste all that sweet fury.

I leaned closer until we were nose to nose. "That is *exactly* what I wanted to hear," I breathed.

Confusion rippled over her features.

"I have no plans to murder the royal children," I said. "But the crown prince, Everett, does have a part to play."

I watched a few more pieces thread together behind her eyes.

"You said you don't want to be king. You're going to put Everett on the throne." The realization knocked her back a step.

"I've heard many counts of his good nature, yours included."

"And mine," Melaena added. "From what little I recall of him."

Kiera paced the room, her brow furrowed.

I waited, my arms folded over my chest. So far, she'd

KEYS TO THE CROWN • 309

proven herself true. An ally. But whatever she said next could seal her fate.

Finally, she stopped. "I want to help you."

My eyes narrowed. "You want to help me kill Weylin?"

She swallowed hard, drawing my attention to a few dark smudges on her throat. Leftover makeup, perhaps. "To help you put Everett on the throne."

I mulled it over in my mind. I'd never considered that she might *want* to help me since I couldn't stand the idea of letting her.

Melaena caught my eye, giving me a subtle nod. Of course, she wanted to keep Kiera. She seemed oddly protective of her. But then again, Melaena collected women like Kiera, giving them a home and a purpose, a new joy in life.

But Kiera wasn't fleeing an abusive home or a life of poverty. She had escaped Renwell's prison, stolen Asher's gold, and was now offering to help me stage a royal coup.

She could die for this. An excruciating traitor's death.

If she was telling the truth. *If* I trusted her not to betray us.

"I'll think about it," I said.

She nodded. "Where's my cut of the gold?"

Gods, the heist seemed like it'd happened days ago instead of hours. "Safe. Did you return the key to Asher?"

Her cheeks turned a light pink. "Yes."

I scowled. "He didn't suspect you at all?"

"No. We parted ways on friendly terms."

Friendly. Jealousy slithered through my stomach.

"You're having your dancer party tonight, yes?" I asked Melaena. She nodded. "Good. Kiera, you will remain here for that while I sort out a few things. I'll return for you in the morning with your money and my decision."

Kiera's mouth dropped open. "You're leaving me here? And holding my gold hostage?"

"Are you going to run?"

She scowled at me. "No. Where would I go?"

"Nowhere I wouldn't find you," I murmured. "All the same, I want to ensure you're still here when I get back."

Something flickered in her eyes. For a moment, we were back in that hallway, wrapped around each other, desperately wanting to get closer. Maz had teased me about the paint streaks on my face and hands, but I'd only wanted more. More of her. More of this feeling.

Kiera looked away from me, breaking the moment.

My chest tightened. "Melaena, would you unlock the sitting room for me?"

She nodded and led me out of the room. I didn't look back.

CHAPTER 27
KIERA

MY FATHER WAS GOING TO DIE.

Or at least, I had to pretend that I wanted him to. While trying to figure out a way to keep it from coming to that. I'd already had one parent die by someone else's hand. Despite his crimes, I didn't see the sense in further bloodshed.

There had to be a better way to put Everett on the throne.

I spun ideas around and around my head while Melaena stuffed me with fried eggs and toast and insisted I get more sleep. I barely spoke to her.

I tossed and turned in one of the beds in the dancers' sleeping quarters. Sleep brought nightmares. Consciousness offered little better.

But I was alive. I'd convinced Aiden I wasn't a spy, although he seemed to burrow closer and closer to that truth. Would he kill me then?

The skin at my throat tingled as if remembering the cold edge of his knife there. Gods, I'd never felt so vulnerable and afraid. But then he'd seemed to come back to himself, horrified by what he'd done.

His remorse should have brought me some level of peace, but nothing about this brought me any.

Triumph, maybe, that I finally knew his intentions without a doubt. Really, that had been the only answer I was left with.

Frustration, because I still didn't know his whole plan. I had yet to even see the gold, let alone see what he did with it. Was that one of the things he had to "sort out?" But he'd essentially imprisoned me here until he was ready.

And fear . . . fear of discovery, fear of what I'd agreed to, fear for my family.

It was strange how my goal of seeing Everett on the throne mirrored that of Aiden's. Although, I hadn't planned on murdering my father to see it done.

There had to be another way. But would Aiden listen? Would my father? Would anyone?

Aiden sought revenge for a lifetime of injustice. I understood that. But killing a king . . . so many things could go wrong. My father had planted many allies in the ranks of the nobles and the army—anywhere he believed held power. He'd had decades to establish himself.

What kind of crumbling kingdom would my brother be ruling amid my father's supporters?

Someone knocked on the door, and I sighed, throwing off my twisted blankets. There were four beds in each room, and Melaena had given me the only unclaimed one. A few of the dancers had wandered in throughout the day, dumping their stuff or taking quick naps. But Tullia and Jayde weren't among them. They must live in the other room.

I trudged barefoot to the door and opened it to see Elias, Melaena's servant boy. The nervous one. He held out a sealed envelope, which shook like a leaf in his hand.

"F-for Katerina," he said.

"Katerina," I repeated blankly. "Who told you that name?"

"Th-the messenger who came to the front door. He said this was for Katerina, the new dancer." The boy's eyes begged me to take the envelope as if it were burning his hands.

Only Asher knew that name. Why would he send me a message?

I gingerly took it from the boy's hands, and he fled.

The envelope was heavier than I expected. And lumpy.

I closed the bedroom door and took it back to my bed. A single blob of gold wax sealed the envelope, imprinted by something round and flat. No insignia. A coin maybe?

I broke the seal and pulled out a single piece of thick white parchment.

Join me for a late dinner tonight.
—A.

Something shifted in the bottom of the envelope. I shook it out.

My heart dropped.

Death's skull leered up at me.

Renwell's token. The one I used to get in and out of the palace.

This message wasn't from Asher. It was from Renwell. He wanted me to come to the palace tonight. He must've heard that I was at *The Silk Dancer*. I shuddered to think how.

I picked up the Death and Four tile, rubbing my thumb over its etched black-stone surface.

The messenger had said, "Katerina."

Only Asher could've told Renwell that name. Could've told him of our connection last night.

Which meant . . .

Asher knew he'd been robbed. And Renwell had taken him to the palace. To my father.

I clutched the token in my suddenly sweaty palm. A command from my father was the only reason Renwell would risk my cover now.

Something was wrong.

MELAENA'S AFTER-PARTY WAS STILL IN FULL SWING WHEN I TOOK my leave, claiming I was exhausted. She watched me leave the entertainment hall with sad eyes as the other dancers continued to eat and laugh and do silly dances on the stage as if they hadn't a care in the world.

I felt as though I were preparing for battle.

I changed from my party dress into my plain black shirt, pants, and boots. I cinched my knives around my waist with a grimace. My cloak and neckcloth turned me into a complete shadow. Last, I tucked Renwell's Death token into my pocket. I'd fed his note to the hearth fire moments after reading it.

I stuffed my bed with pillows and blankets to look like a sleeping body, then strode to the large, curtained window in the room. I'd already tested the latch.

After checking the street outside, I slipped out the window, easing it closed behind me. The sleeping quarters were on the second floor, situated above another set of sitting rooms. But no one should be using those tonight. *The Silk Dancer* was closed to outsiders for the party.

My fingers and boots clung to the ridges in the stone wall. I crept along, praying no one was passing by this late at night. It reminded me of escaping Garyth's study. At least there was no rain tonight. But instead of escaping, I was running *to* danger. I feared what awaited me more than I feared this climb.

I passed under Melaena's window, then navigated around the corner to the back of the building where I'd noticed a servant's ladder when I'd done a quick study of the building.

Most of the noble houses had these ladders for servants to climb to the roof for maintenance. I'd used one to find a perch to spy on Garyth from.

I hurried down the ladder and landed in the back alley. The moon was hidden behind clouds, but I didn't need it as I scurried along with the rats.

Eventually, I had to swerve out into the main road. Two guards waited by the torch-lit gate, the waterfall roaring behind them. They clenched their spears tighter as I approached. I took a deep breath and flashed them the Death token. They didn't relax, but they let me through the gate.

As I crossed the bridge, the glowing palace ahead of me, I glanced down at the waterfall—something I hadn't dared to do in years.

It was strange, knowing what was hidden beneath it. The Den. The caves. The tunnels. Only two weeks had passed since I'd clawed my way out of there with Aiden and Maz.

So much had changed. What would Aiden do if he could

see me now? Especially after I told him I wouldn't leave the club.

I climbed the dozens of white steps to the palace doors. There were nearly as many guards as there were steps. They watched me with gleaming eyes, armed with knives, spears, and clubs. Torchlight shone over their polished bronze armor.

This didn't feel like a battle. This felt like walking to my own execution.

I nearly tripped over the last step, catching myself just in time. Two guards shoved open the heavy doors. They'd been expecting me, it seemed.

A lone figure swathed in black, just as I was, waited on the other side. The large hood only revealed a dark eye and half of an ominous smile.

Renwell.

I held my breath, waiting for him to say something, but he merely stretched out his hand. I dropped his Death token into it. He clenched his fist and sauntered toward the next set of doors, more ornate than the last. The throne room.

Heartbeat frantic, I stepped up behind him as he opened one door wide enough to slip through. I followed, and someone —a guard, probably—shoved the door shut behind me.

The sound echoed through the cavernous room, which was large enough to hold hundreds of people. But right now, it only held four.

Light from torches and chandeliers around the room made it feel brighter than day. Columns stacked on top of columns soared to the painted dome ceiling. A black marble dais led to a gold throne where my father sat amid deep purple cushions, his gold and sunstone crown firmly in place on his iron-gray hair.

It'd only been a few weeks since I'd last stood in front of him. I felt as though a dozen knives had reshaped me since then. Yet, I recalled the sting of his palm against my cheek as if it were a mere moment ago.

Asher, dressed in an embroidered jacket and pants, stood at the foot of the dais. His curls were disheveled, and he fidgeted with a broken button on his cuff.

He shot a frightened look over his shoulder at the sound of our footsteps, but he didn't dare turn his back to Father.

I had to force my legs to keep walking. An animalistic instinct to survive gnashed at my muscles, telling me to run away. But I didn't stop until I reached the dais. Renwell stood between me and Asher.

We bowed.

Father tilted his head, his gaze scraping over me like the sharp edge of a knife.

"Katerina, Your Majesty," Renwell said.

Asher's head whipped toward us, peering around Renwell with wide eyes. "N-no. That can't be her. She's one of Melaena's dancers. A sweet girl who couldn't have—"

"Take off your hood and mask," Father barked at me.

I obeyed.

Asher paled, swaying a little on his feet. "You . . . you . . . you're—"

"Yes, yes," Father said with a nasty smile. "From princess to spy to thief and seductress. Emilia, Kiera, Katerina—you can't make up your gods-damned mind, can you, girl?"

I flinched. Asher continued to stare at me, his mouth opening and closing like a fish.

"Renwell informed me of your little heist this afternoon," Father continued. "What in the deep, dark, wandering hell possessed you to go through with such a *foolish, treasonous plan?*" he roared the last three words.

Even though he remained seated, his fury rose to fill every corner of the room. Every flame seemed to gutter under its weight.

I could barely breathe past my tightened throat, as if a fistful of the stolen coins was wedged there. Why hadn't Renwell told him about the heist earlier, after we spoke at *The Crescent Moon*?

"It was the only way," I whispered. I cleared my throat and spoke louder. "I offered it as a ruse to discover the . . . the criminals' intentions."

"See? She knows where it is," Asher babbled. "We can—"

"Silence!" Father snarled. "Or I'll cut out your tongue and feed it to your kin—the sewer rats."

Asher's throat bobbed with a hard swallow, but he stayed quiet.

Father's eyes cut back to me. I hated those eyes. I hated that they were a mirror of mine. But most of all, I hated the disgust and contempt in them when he looked at me.

"Tell me how you did it," he said, his ringed fingers clawing into his gold armrests. "Every. Detail. Do you understand?"

I nodded, fear crawling over me like a thousand ants. What had Asher told them? Already my mind tried to cut out the memories that weren't too damning, to offer the pieces that might save my own skin.

Haltingly, I told him about the dance, about getting close to Asher and stealing the key, about remembering which lock to open. I forced Aiden's and Maz's names from my lips, told Father of their disguises and their plan to get the barrels out. But I refused to tell him of the kiss. I would die with that memory locked in my soul.

My words came faster after Aiden's and Maz's roles were over. I tried to lessen Asher's gullibility and my fumbling, but by the end, Father was nearly apoplectic with rage.

"You," he spat, jabbing a finger at Asher. "You call yourself my High Treasurer. A position your father held for my entire reign before you. And you let a *girl* steal my fucking gold!"

Asher stumbled back a few steps, gasping. Renwell matched pace with him as if to keep him from running, but he didn't reach for the crumbling noble.

"P-please, Your Highness, Merciful Majesty. I didn't know —I'll get it all back—I would never—"

"Are you telling me you know where it is?" Father asked.

"No!" Asher's wide eyes rolled, like a panicked horse's. "But she does! Ask her!" He fell to his knees before me. "Please," he whispered. "Tell him."

Tears stung my eyes. My body shook uncontrollably. "I-I'm sorry. I don't know—"

Asher's face slackened.

"No one fails me twice," Father said. He jerked his head at Renwell.

"Wait!" I screamed.

Renwell stepped up behind Asher and slit his throat.

CHAPTER 28
KIERA

A FOUNTAIN OF ASHER'S BLOOD SPLASHED OVER MY PANTS AND boots as my scream echoed its last.

Renwell tossed his body aside, wiping his sunstone blade on Asher's soiled clothes. There wasn't a shred of emotion on his face. His dark eyes swept over me then returned to his king.

I felt empty. An emotionless husk. Not in the way of Renwell. But like my blood had spilled out with Asher's. My skin cold as his would be. As if the Abyss had started to swallow my soul, piece by piece.

"Give the body to Korvin when we're done." My father's words were like bees burrowing under my skin. "Tell him to send back the head, and he can keep the rest. A gift from his king."

Bile surged up my throat, hot and acrid.

Gods damn your little weaknesses.

I clenched my teeth and swallowed it back.

Father smiled at me as if he knew exactly what I was trying to hide. "Tell me of this Aiden."

You murdered his father. Stole his crown. Imprisoned him. He's clever and good at Death and Four. He healed me and saved my life. He makes me laugh and feel desired. He tries to protect everyone and hates when he can't.

He is a better man than you.

"He plans to kill you," I said.

Renwell inhaled sharply, probably incensed I hadn't told him first.

Father merely chuckled. "So, he's a lunatic."

I nearly laughed, remembering how I'd called Aiden something similar when I first met him. But Aiden was no madman or fool.

"How?" Renwell demanded.

Feeling a bit mad with carelessness myself, I shrugged. "He hasn't told me yet. I was too busy convincing him to let me help."

"*What?*" Father bellowed.

I sneered. "How else am I to learn his plans, *Your Majesty*? I wouldn't be alive if he thought me less than loyal."

Only the gods knew if that was a lie or the truth.

Father glared at me in a way that should've made me cower, but I felt nothing.

"Watch your tone, *servant*," he said. "And find out where my gold is before it leaves the gods-damned city."

"I thought you would be more concerned for your life," I retorted.

"He would need an army to reach me here." Father leaned forward. "Is *that* what he's buying with my gold?"

I hesitated. It was barely plausible. Where would he find enough trained fighters?

"Impossible," Renwell said, echoing my thoughts. He narrowed his eyes at me. "Perhaps he's buying his way into the palace."

Gods damn it, that made more sense.

"I'll have every guard re-vetted," Father said, slamming his fist on his armrest. "Anyone who doesn't pass will be fed to Korvin while the others watch."

Ah yes, your favorite punishment, Father.

He studied me beneath furrowed brows. "Or you simply tell me where this street scum is hiding, and I'll send Renwell and his Wolves after him."

The first spark of fear flickered back to life. "No."

"*No?*"

I rushed on, "We don't know how far this conspiracy goes or who else is involved. You could have countless traitors within your ranks. Your gold might find its way into any number of pockets in Aquinon or beyond." I took a deep breath. "You need me on the inside to learn all his secrets."

"I agree, Your Majesty," Renwell added swiftly. "It will win you no favor to burn the city to the ground looking for your gold. Some might say it hints of incompetence."

Father's face twisted. "Are you one of those people, Renwell?"

"Never, Your Majesty. I'm thinking only of what's best for the most powerful king in Lancora. You must retain power by showing no weakness."

"I have no weaknesses," Father snarled. His gaze pierced

me. "Report to Renwell the moment you find any useful information. If you haven't found every stolen coin and every traitor in this conspiracy in a month's time, I will do so by fire and blade. And you, little nameless one, will suffer the fate of those who fail me." He nodded to the crimson puddle that surrounded Asher's body.

Scars under and over my skin seemed to pulse with warning.

I said nothing. No placating words. No groveling promises. I was caught between two men who wanted each other dead. There was only one way this game ended. Death always won, after all. But whose would it be?

I could make that choice with a few words. But not tonight.

"Leave." His last command finally freed my muscles.

I walked out of the throne room, my spine straight, my chin lifted, ignoring the squeak of blood under my boots.

Instead of leaving the palace, I turned and walked down the hall toward my old room.

A fist closed around my shoulder and whirled me around.

Renwell. Of course.

Anger cracked through the shell that had shielded me in the throne room. I knocked his hand away.

"Are you trying to get yourself killed?" he growled, his eyes darting to the guards at the far end of the hall.

"Afraid you'll be my executioner as well?" I snapped.

"It won't come to that," he said, as if the decision were up to him. "But if there's something else you need to tell me, do it now. Let me help you."

I stared at him. My mentor.

He could've warned me what I was walking into. He could've defended Asher, saying the game was rigged against him. But he did nothing but murder a decent man and let my father threaten me.

Why should I tell him my secrets when I knew he was keeping his own? He'd said nothing to my father about the heist until *after* it happened. He made no mention of Garyth or the People's Council. Renwell played his own game, and I didn't want to be part of it.

I shook my head and gestured to my stained clothing. "I have pants to change, and you have a body to mutilate—forgive me—to *gift*."

I spun on my heel and charged away from him, something I'd never dared to do. He didn't come after me.

I tried to open my door. Locked. And I'd given up the key.

Fucking Four! Why? Why can I do nothing right?

Yanking the hairpin out of my braid, I shoved it in the lock. It took me twice as long to pick it with my trembling fingers and blurred vision.

At last, it clicked open. No flush of success this time. Just a whirlwind of emotions that couldn't be held back any longer. I threw myself inside my room and locked it behind me. I didn't make it two steps before I collapsed on the dusty floor.

Sobs wracked my body. I tried to keep them quiet, but I was suffocating. I closed my eyes, gagging.

Gods, Asher pleaded with me like I was his only hope. If I'd known where the gold was, would Father have spared him?

I would never know.

Instead, guilt speared through my chest. I'd lied to Asher,

stolen from him, and in his last moments, I'd taken away his final hope.

The bile exploded back up my throat, and I vomited in the corner of my room. Everything I'd eaten at Melaena's party, every drop of water I'd consumed—my stomach wrung itself dry.

Tears streamed down my face, and I curled into a ball on the floor.

Moments passed. Heartbeats drummed onward. Emotions bled out.

I couldn't stay here.

I rose and searched through my wardrobe to find another pair of pants. I traded them for my stained ones. No boots. I'd have to wash them somehow.

My head pounded, and my mouth tasted like sewage. But that would all have to wait. Gods, my room at *The Silk Dancer* felt miles away. Had the girls noticed I wasn't in bed?

And what if they didn't? I would simply lie, lie, lie my way back in.

My life was nothing but lies now.

I opened my door to find Everett on the other side, his fist raised.

"Kiera?" His pale face tightened with concern.

My face crumpled, and I threw my arms around him. He hesitated for a moment, then hugged me back.

"It's all right," he murmured. "It's going to be all right. I know."

I sniffled, looking up at him. "Know what?"

He nodded solemnly. "I watched from the peephole—you

know, the one in the north wall? I didn't hear much, but I saw what happened to Asher. May the gods find his soul."

"It's my fault," I whispered.

The corners of his mouth turned down as he shook his head. "We should talk somewhere more private."

"Not my room," I said quickly. *I don't want you there if Renwell comes back.* "It . . . stinks." *From my vomit.*

"Right. Then follow me."

He led me halfway down the hall, checked both directions, and pulled a sconce. A latch clicked, and a door popped open in the wall. We slipped through it and sealed ourselves in the hidden passage.

The smell of dust and stale wood reminded me of my childhood. Playing games in these corridors with Everett and Delysia. No maps existed, so we challenged each other to see who could discover the most passageways.

Delysia was usually too frightened to explore much on her own, but I'd thrived on the adventure. Everett had proven a stout competitor with his studious mind. Perhaps he knew more about them now than I did.

Mother said the passageways had existed since the Age of Gods—probably built into the palace by the god Terraum himself. He'd had a great love of tricky carpentry and was an excellent architect, having built the four Temples of Lancora as well.

We often wondered if the Keldiket or Eloren Isles palaces had such secrets. The fortress-like castle in Dagriel had been destroyed in a clan war over a hundred years ago.

Likely, we would never know.

Murky light leaked into the narrow hall from hidden vents

and peepholes. We brought lamps with us as children. But Everett's footsteps didn't falter once.

We didn't speak until he stopped at an exit panel. One I recognized.

"Everett, are you sure?" I breathed.

"It's fine. She's alone."

He unlatched the door and opened it a sliver. After checking the hall, he opened it all the way and waved me out. We hurried to Delysia's door and let ourselves in.

A fire burning low in the hearth of her sitting room illuminated the achingly familiar light pink furniture. The same furniture that had filled this room when it was our mother's. Delysia had wanted it after her death, and seeing as how I'd chosen to become Renwell's apprentice, I'd been in no position to argue.

Not that I wanted it, anyway. The memories were too close. Each tufted velvet chair carried Mother's floral scent. The back window was still filled with the potted plants that she'd nurtured into a tiny forest.

Paintings of me, Everett, and Delysia filled the walls. Her favorite vase full of fresh flowers sat on the mantle.

The whole room felt as though Mother might walk in at any moment. A thought that flung shards of grief at my weak heart.

"Ev? Is that you? What's—" Delysia scurried out of her bedroom, a pink dressing gown belted around her curvy figure. Her mouth dropped open when she spotted me. "Kiera?"

Her big blue eyes, so like our mother's, filled with tears as she rushed toward me. She threw her arms around me, but then just as quickly backed away with her nose wrinkled. "You stink."

I let out a choked laugh. "It's good to see you too, Lys."

She smiled, and I nearly wept at how much Mother shone through her face. Delysia had changed in the last few years. Her features had matured, her golden curls were longer than ever, and a newfound seriousness lingered in her eyes.

"Don't sit down yet," she ordered. In a cloud of pink satin, she hurried to the door and flipped the lock. "That won't stall Father for long, but enough to hide if he comes to check on me."

I frowned. "Does he do that often?"

"He says it's to make sure I'm safe." Delysia pursed her lips. "But it's really just to spy on me, so speak softly and don't stoke the fire."

I remembered the soldier entering her room the night I left. "Seems you've had a lot of practice at hiding secret visitors, Lys."

Her cheeks flushed as she grabbed my hand. "That's none of your business."

"Trust me, Kiera, I've tried to talk sense into her," Everett spoke from where he sat in a high-backed armchair near the fire.

Delysia continued to try to drag me to her bathroom, but I pulled back. "I don't have time for a wash, Lys. But I'll take some mint leaf if you have it."

"Fine, but take off that dirty cloak before you sit down. I can't explain away mud stains. And let me get you a wet cloth for—for—" She trailed off, staring at my boots in horror. "Is that blood?"

I winced. "Not mine."

"That's what we were going to tell you, Lys," Everett said, staring into the dying fire. "High Councilor Asher . . . he's dead."

I stared in shock at Everett. When did he start telling our little sister things like this? Normally, he refused to talk about the things Father did.

Delysia sank onto a plush foot stool with a gasp. "No! He was just here at the palace a few days ago! What happened?"

"I can't tell you everything," I said quickly. "But it's—it's my fault. The work I'm doing . . . it got Asher killed."

"Executed," Everett mumbled while Delysia gaped at me as if truly seeing me for the first time.

"How?" she asked.

"Does it matter? I'm trying to keep you safe," I snapped, but the platitude felt like the dried bile in my throat.

A hardened expression I didn't recognize stole over Delysia's face, and she shot to her feet. "It *does* matter. Lies only protect the liar. Keeping me in the dark doesn't keep me safe. It just makes me easier to manipulate. Henry taught me that."

"Is Henry your soldier lover? Did you learn *nothing* from my mistakes, Delysia?" My voice cracked. "Shayn, the guards Father sent away . . . Julian."

Her face softened. "I can take care of myself. Henry is a captain in the army. He's above suspicion—"

"No one is above suspicion when it comes to Father. That's why Asher was killed."

"And I pray that the gods find his soul." Delysia lifted her chin stubbornly. "But I'm not letting go of Henry. We're in love.

And he's not being watched as closely now that he's stationed in Pravara instead of Calimber."

I stiffened. "He was in Calimber? Why was he moved?"

Delysia shrugged, going to her bathroom and rummaging around. She brought back a mint leaf and a wet, soapy rag. I stuck the mint leaf in my mouth, and after removing my cloak, sat on a sofa to first clean my face, then my boots.

"Orders," she said. "He told me conditions in the town and the mine were awful, and he was glad to leave." Her mouth twisted in thought. "He did mention that he was surprised General Dracles ordered him to move because there were more workers than ever. They were expanding the town and building something on the beach."

"What were they building?" Everett and I asked at the same time.

Delysia shook her head. "His letter didn't say. Even though we have a trusted source smuggling our letters, he never wants to reveal too much in them."

My head spun. Garyth had said Dracles was keeping him away from the mine. Was this why? Did he not want Garyth to see what Father was building out there?

Did Aiden know about this?

The mere thought of Aiden sent a frisson of worry through me. If my absence were discovered at *The Silk Dancer* . . .

But I had one more question. "Do either of you know how Father became king?" I asked carefully.

Delysia waved her hand. "Of course. King Tristan wrote him in as successor before his early death. They were great friends. No other heirs. You know all this, Kiera."

I shook my head, watching Everett. He looked deep in

thought, as if he were back in his library trying to sort out the problems of the world with books.

In the silence, his serious gaze met mine, and he nodded.

My throat tightened. "What do you know? Who told you?"

"Mother," he rasped, his throat bobbing. "About a year before she died. She didn't want me to tell either of you."

Delysia sent me a sharp look as if this proved her earlier point about hiding things.

I ignored her, desperate for answers. "Please, Ev. I need to know."

His gaze turned hollow. "She told me I should know so that when I became king, I would have the truth of our past. Father was High Advisor until he murdered King Tristan and Queen Rhea—his pregnant wife." Delysia gasped again, her hands flying up to cover her mouth. "Mother didn't see it happen because she was pregnant with me and couldn't leave her bed, but Father told her what he did.

"He took the throne in a coup so strategic that most of Rellmira didn't question his succession. The ones who did mysteriously died or disappeared. Three days after his coronation, I was born the official heir of a stolen kingdom," Everett finished bitterly.

Aiden had been telling the truth. Except he hadn't mentioned his mother. Or how he survived. How did he find out who he was?

I peered at my brother's distraught face. Should I tell him that he had supporters outside of the palace, working to put him on the throne?

But even that tiny bit of information might risk his safety, might make him ask questions I couldn't answer. Whatever Delysia thought, sometimes secrets *did* save a life.

I stared down at the stained rag in my hands. Everything was stained. My family's legacy, my view of the world, my soul.

Oh Mother, what do I do now?

I rose to spit out the mint leaf and rinse my mouth with a glass of water from Delysia's refreshment table. "I need to leave."

Delysia blinked, her face still pale with shock. "You—you can't leave. I've just discovered my whole life has been a lie, begotten by murder. *Please* . . . don't leave."

The tenuous hold I had on my emotions trembled with the added weight of hers. "I can't, Lys. If I don't get back . . ."

She buried her face in her hands, her shoulders shaking. "I can't take this anymore. Everyone lies to me. Everyone keeps secrets from me. And the one person who doesn't is a hundred miles away." She ripped her hands away from her face, angrily dashing away tears. "You know what? Fine! Leave, Kiera! You're so good at it. But don't think for one moment that you're doing any of this for me."

My jaw dropped. That was the one thing she'd gotten from our father—his quick temper.

I wanted to stay. I wanted to comfort her. But what did I have to offer? I felt as lost as she did.

Everett stood. "I can get you to the gate."

I shook my head. "It's easier if I go alone."

I squeezed his hand, then reached for Delysia's, half-expecting her to push it away. But she grabbed my hand and clung to it fiercely, her crumpled face turned toward the fire.

I released them, leaving a little piece of my heart behind, and disappeared back into the hidden passageways.

By the time I climbed through the bedroom window of *The Silk Dancer* and crept into bed amid the heavily sleeping, probably drunk dancers, I was certain of two things.

First, I couldn't let Aiden kill my father. The assassinations had to stop. For Aiden's sake as much as mine and my siblings'.

Secondly, I wasn't going to do it Renwell's way. Or my father's way. Or even Aiden's way. I needed to do this *my* way with as little bloodshed as possible.

Which meant being the perfect rebel.

CHAPTER 29
KIERA

AIDEN DIDN'T COME FOR ME UNTIL I WAS FINISHING BREAKFAST with the dancers.

Tullia and Jayde had dragged me out of bed, thinking my haggard appearance was from drinking the night before. They cheerfully passed around scrambled eggs, sausage, apple fritters, and coffee and caught me up on everything I'd missed at the party.

Jayde was telling me of a salacious song Tullia had performed when Melaena entered the entertainment hall where we all ate.

"Kiera? A moment, please." But the tension in her eyes told me he was here.

I swallowed the last of my buttered toast and followed her out a side door and down the hall. Her pale blue dress whispered around her ankles as we walked.

"What about my knives and my cloak?" I'd left them in my room for breakfast.

"I brought them to the sitting room." She gave me a side-long glance. "I'm truly sorry for how you were drawn into this, Kiera. I'm sorry if you feel that you don't have a choice."

I almost snorted. I had choices. But hardly any of them were good.

She stopped in front of the sitting room door but faced me instead of opening it. Her cerulean eyes were bright with sincerity. "What I said before is still true. You have a home here. A safe haven, should you need it. And if you so wish, I'd love for you to keep dancing here, even if you can't perform again."

Gods damn it, I didn't deserve her kindness. Thanks to me, she and her business would be under Father's scrutiny. Even if I tried to steer his attention away, Melaena would never truly be safe while Father was in power.

After everything, I'd at least managed to succeed at that part of Renwell's plan—earning a place with Melaena. But it didn't feel like success.

I tried to smile at her and nodded. "I would love to visit and keep dancing. If Aiden allows it."

Her look turned sly. "When it comes to you, I doubt there's much he wouldn't give."

My stomach rolled over as she unlocked the door. On the other side, Aiden stood in the middle of the room. My trai-torous heartbeat quickened.

He wore a thin, dark shirt unlaced at the top with the sleeves rolled up. His dark pants and boots were far cleaner than mine had been last night. His serious green gaze and locked jaw made my steps falter.

"Are you . . . well?" he asked.

I must look as ghastly as the girls had said. "Yes. I—I just didn't sleep well."

His brows lowered.

"I'm fine though," I added quickly. "Did you decide?" *By the Four, don't make me fight to stay.*

He nodded. "I sent Skelly on his way this morning. You're staying with us."

I let out a sigh of relief. "Will I be able to visit Melaena and the others here once in a while?"

He glanced at Melaena, who sent him a pointed look. He shrugged. "If Asher doesn't cause any trouble, and no one suspects the dancers' involvement with the heist, then I suppose you can."

Melaena clapped her hands twice, beaming. "Excellent! Now that's settled, I'll leave you to your business."

The moment she left, the air thickened with tension.

Aiden took a step closer, and my eyes darted to his waist to see if he still carried his knives.

He froze, his face stricken. "I'm not going to hurt you, Kiera. I never should have—" He growled, raking his hands through his hair. "I acted without thinking. Maz says I always assume the worst in people. But when I thought you were eavesdropping with ill intent, that you might be an enemy . . ." He dropped his hands, lifting them palm-up toward me. "I hated it. I didn't want you to prove me right. Forgive me."

Gods, that hurt. Worse than Melaena's words. He had no idea that I'd fed most of his plans to his worst enemies. He found trust so difficult, yet he extended a morsel of it to me— the person who deserved it the least.

Yes, he planned to kill my father. Yes, he had kept—and still was keeping—secrets from me.

But I had lied to him. Many times. And I wasn't even sure I was on the right side of the lie anymore.

"I forgive you," I whispered. Would anyone forgive me?

Aiden's hands fell back to his sides, regret still lining his face. "Thank you. We should go. Ruru and Maz are waiting for us. Your knives and cloak are over there." He pointed to a table.

I belted the knives to my waist and threw my cloak over my shoulders. It was probably terribly hot outside, but I didn't want anyone seeing my knives.

Aiden walked over to a carved wooden panel in the wall and pressed his thumb to the center of a sun. The tunnel sprang open behind the tapestry that I'd left askew the last time I was in here.

"Aren't you worried that I know the secret now?" I tried to tease him, but my voice came out uncertain.

He glanced at me over his shoulder. "If you're going to visit Melaena, you should know how to make a quick escape should Asher—or someone worse—come looking for you."

I bit my lip as I followed him into the tunnel. Asher would never come looking for me. But others might.

The door swung shut, leaving us in damp darkness.

"Shall I go first to scare off spiders?" Aiden's deep voice spoke ahead of me.

Perhaps we were both trying to ease the awkwardness.

I threw up my hood with a shiver. "Yes, please, and let's hurry."

This time, I trailed my fingertips along the uneven walls of the tunnel instead of holding onto Aiden. Then I remembered the spiders and unsheathed two of my knives to feel my way through instead.

Before long, we surfaced in the warehouse. I blinked dust from my eyes as I studied it. My imagination hadn't been far off when I'd come here blindfolded. A long, low domed building filled with an assortment of crates, barrels, and boxes. Shafts of clouded light pierced through small holes in the walls and the roof.

But my curiosity for this place had dimmed considerably after everything that had happened in the last few days. Unless . . .

"Is this where you're keeping the gold?" I asked.

"Only yours." Aiden hefted a small, bulging sack and handed it to me. "Your cut."

I weighed it in my palm. "It's heavier than I expected."

"You earned it."

My stomach soured. Earned it. And Asher paid the price. I doubted this would have been enough to appease Father. He would have killed Asher, anyway.

I glanced up to see Aiden watching me with an impenetrable gaze. "Is there somewhere I could keep most of this?" I asked. "Where it won't get stolen? Perhaps with the rest of the gold."

"The rest of the gold is gone. Spent." His smile made a brief appearance at my incredulous expression. "I told you I needed it. But there *is* somewhere safe you can keep your gold. It's where I put my father's ring."

I tried to crush my rising panic. If all the gold was already spent, there was no hope of me getting it back. Certainly not before Father's deadline. Gods damn it, I needed more time.

KEYS TO THE CROWN • 339

Which meant I had to keep this information to myself for now. Renwell could wait.

Aiden peered more closely into my eyes. "We don't have to go now if you would prefer to go back to the apartment to get some rest."

"No, no, I want to go." I really didn't want to carry Asher's blood money with me, and I also wanted to see where Aiden had deemed safe enough to hide his ring.

"I believe Maz and Ruru will also be waiting there," Aiden said, gesturing toward the door.

I tied the bag of coins to my belt and draped my cloak over it. "Then perhaps you can tell me about my role in your . . . plan?"

"Yes. Maz and Ruru are aware of what you know and that you're staying. I thought it best to discuss this with them." He gave me a half-smile. "They were much happier about it than I was."

My heart swooped high, then low. "You still wish I weren't here."

His eyes traveled over my face, lingering on my lips. "It's complicated."

My skin tingled under his taut gaze. Very, *very* complicated.

"Should we go?" I whispered.

He jerked his head in a nod, and I strode to the door. We left the stuffy warehouse and walked into an ocean of heat. Immediately, sweat rose along my skin. Holy Mynastra, even a cloud would be nice. I looked up at the clear, bright blue sky.

Aiden led the way, angling west, then south, following the wider road close to the west wall of the city. The same road Ruru and I had fled down not long ago.

But everything seemed so different in the daylight.

Carts, drawn by animal or human, rumbled along the road. Day guards joked and spat in the dirt from shaded corners. Children carried buckets of water from a wide cistern nearby.

"Gods, Maz must be suffocating in this heat," I grumbled, garnering a few strange looks from passerby at my heavily cloaked appearance.

Aiden flashed me a heart-stopping grin. "Days like this, he refuses to even step outside unless it's to a bathhouse."

A rusty laugh scraped from my throat. Aiden's gaze warmed. But then he nodded to a tower we were approaching. "We should skirt the city prison."

I skidded to a halt. "Where are you taking me?" I demanded, my voice high and sharp.

Aiden frowned. "To the Temple. Is that not . . ."

The rest of his words faded as memories swallowed me.

A rickety scaffolding erected in the square between the Temple and the city prison.

A line of prisoners awaiting execution. Julian's beaten face and sad eyes among them.

His gaze held mine until the last moment.

"Kiera? What's wrong?" Aiden gently pulled me to the side of the road. Then understanding dawned in his eyes. "Ah, I forgot. The boy. Julian."

I flinched.

"We'll take a route that will shield you from the square, Kiera. Unless you would rather—"

"No, it's fine. Let's just go around."

A cry arose from near the tower. A large crowd had gathered in front of it, near the execution square.

Aiden frowned. "Wait here." He strode off into the crowd, keeping to the edges of it.

I fidgeted for a moment, then darted after him. The crowd murmured around me while a few of them broke off and hurried away.

"Gods, when did this happen?"

"May the gods find his soul."

"I can't believe the king—"

"—no explanation—"

Somehow, I knew before I saw it—Asher's head on a spear in the square. A crude wooden sign with the word THIEF burned into it was laid at its base.

My stomach churned. This was why Father wanted the head sent back. As a message for everyone else. There was no explanation because the king didn't need to explain himself. He was simply threatening the city with their fate should they commit the same crime.

I trembled next to Aiden, who stared at the head with an expression of barely suppressed rage. Did he expect this outcome? Would he have done things differently if he had?

A slight breeze lifted Asher's limp curls, and I spun away, charging blindly through the crowd.

A warm hand closed around my arm and gently pulled me into a narrow alley.

Aiden didn't speak. He simply wrapped his arms around me and held me tight. I slipped my arms around his back and buried my face in his chest. His heartbeat pounded like thunder, and he smelled like salt and sunshine, sea and warmth. He rested his cheek on top of my head.

He had held me several times—out of comfort, desire . . .

threat. But this embrace felt fierce and desperate in a way that made me think he needed it, too.

We stood there for several moments, lost in our need to cling to an anchor in the storm.

"It's not your fault," he murmured.

A harsh laugh sputtered from my lips.

He drew back to pierce me with his furious gaze. "It's not, Kiera. It's Weylin's. He didn't have to execute Asher and display him like this."

I closed my eyes, unable to look at him. "Did you think this would happen?"

He hesitated. "No. But with Weylin, it's always a possibility. I thought we would have more time. I'd hoped Asher would be able to hide the theft if he discovered it. I only wanted to take what we needed—a pittance compared to what that vault should've held."

I opened my eyes to see the sincerity in his. And the guilt buried deep within.

I wasn't alone.

My fingers dug into the muscles of his lower back. His jaw clenched, and he nestled his forehead against mine, closing his eyes and breathing deeply.

"We shouldn't linger," he whispered.

I matched his breaths for one heartbeat. Two. Then I let him go.

He gave me one last penetrating look before walking further down the alley. The bell towers of the Temple and its massive white dome floated above the buildings. I didn't relish the idea of going there either. I'd never been able to go back after Julian.

Mother had asked me time and again, but I refused. Eventually, she'd stopped asking. If I'd just gone with her to the Temple the night she was taken and murdered, maybe she'd still be alive.

It wasn't the first time the thought had occurred to me. In my darkest moments, I'd had to wrestle with that gnawing guilt and reason it back into its cage.

But now, Asher's death also had a stranglehold on me. I couldn't bear the weight of any more. I *needed* to save everyone I could.

The alley spat us out in front of the Temple in all its sunbathed glory. Wide white marble steps rippled from the soaring doors to the cobblestones. A few people entered and exited the Temple while most bustled about their business under its great shadow.

I followed Aiden up the steps and let the heavy, ornately carved wooden door ease shut behind me. Instantly, all sound disappeared. It took a moment for my eyes to adjust to the dim interior, lit here and there by candles and braziers.

The smell of jasmine and wood smoke evoked memories of coming here as a child—for grand weddings, solemn pilgrimages, and joyful celebrations of the gods' days. Beautiful singing had filled the enormous, marbled hall. Teachers from around the world had traveled here to speak and share their knowledge.

But now only a few Teachers in their long, hooded robes moved quietly among the colorful pillars and sparkling statues of the gods, tending the flower offerings and polishing the Temple.

Father no longer allowed any celebrations here. After he'd

executed the High Teacher for aiding fugitives during the Pravaran rebellion and replaced her with an old, bitter man—Nefteus, the Temple was used for little else than its bells and its library.

And apparently hiding stolen treasure.

Aiden motioned me toward a side door, which led to a small, plain corridor lined with other doors. He opened the third one and gestured me down a steep flight of stairs.

The scent of parchment, ink, and leather instantly made me think of Everett. My eyes widened at the rows and rows of books in the underground library. They seemed endless.

Everett would probably weep with joy if he could stand here once more. Like me, he hadn't been here since he was a child.

A handful of desks with stools stood empty in front of the shelves. Piles of half-inked scrolls and books were stacked neatly at each one.

"Holy Four," I breathed. "*This* is where you hide things?"

Aiden smiled a little, shaking his head. "Further still."

I frowned. I'd never heard of a lower level to the library.

We walked past shelf after shelf of books until Aiden made a sharp turn down a row that looked like any other. We came to the end, and he faced me with his arms crossed over his chest.

"Nefteus has no idea this doorway exists. The old High Teacher claimed she had it sealed off and burned any evidence of its existence. You must swear to the Four never to reveal what you are about to see."

I mimicked his stance. "Must I?"

"Yes, I had to as well."

"Aren't you breaking that vow by telling me?"

"I had to get special permission." He quirked an eyebrow. "Well? Do you swear?"

"I swear to the Four I will not reveal what I'm about to see," I echoed him. *Unless keeping it secret will cost a life.*

Holding my gaze, he stepped on a stone floor tile, and something unlocked in the floor. He shoved the last shelf by the wall, and it swiveled easily, revealing a very narrow tunnel.

I grimaced, peering into it. "For someone who hates being underground, you sure spend a lot of time in it."

"I suppose that's what happens when someone lives most of their life in hiding," he said dryly.

I lowered myself into the passage, using the short wooden ladder someone had propped up at the entrance. Unlike the tunnel from *The Silk Dancer*, the walls of this one were stone. Ages old from the wear of them.

Aiden clambered down behind me, flipping a latch that swung the bookshelf back over the entrance.

He nudged me forward. "It's not far."

I could already see a faint light ahead. Quiet voices echoed toward us. I hurried down the passage and came out in a wide room. The floor was smooth stone, but the ceiling was like a cave—craggy and dark.

Several targets were set up at the far end of the room with a collection of weapons—bows and arrows, spears, and even two swords—near me. Perhaps the Teachers used to train here, back when they were allowed to teach the skill of combat.

A group of people hovered around a few tables against another wall.

One of them broke off and ran toward me. Ruru. His

beaming face made me smile as he folded me in a hug. He smelled like the sticky bread he was so fond of.

"Kiera! I'm so glad you're here! We were just catching up on the heist and—oh! Aiden, guess who showed up?"

But Aiden's eyes were already fixed on one of the strangers in the room. A woman.

Ruru waved to her. "Yes, Nikella's finally arrived!"

CHAPTER 30
KIERA

WITHOUT ANOTHER WORD, AIDEN STRODE OVER TO NIKELLA AND clasped forearms with her.

I followed at a more cautious pace while they murmured to each other.

Maz grinned at me from a chair where he was polishing his small silver axe. Standing behind one of the tables, a man with dark skin and a crown of white hair nodded at me with a warm smile. He was dressed in a Teacher robe.

But the woman. The woman was a mystery.

She was tall and built like a warrior. Long black hair with a few touches of gray was braided down her back. She wore a loose white shirt with short sleeves under a leather vest and dirt-smudged pants and boots.

As I drew closer, she looked away from Aiden and pinned me with a stare. I quickly swallowed my gasp. She was strikingly beautiful with her dark blue eyes and sculpted cheekbones. A thin scar ran from her left temple to her right jaw, splitting over her lips as if someone had dragged a knife over her face. As if someone had wanted to destroy her beauty.

That person failed miserably.

Her muscled arms were etched with even more scars— light and dark, twisted and smooth. She looked like she'd been through a dozen wars, yet Rellmira hadn't seen one in centuries. Perhaps they were from Dag skirmishes? Aiden had lived there for a while.

Something else haunted me about her face. A familiarity I couldn't quite place. But I'd never seen her before. And from the quick study she did of me, she didn't know me either.

My heart stilled. Was she Aiden's mother?

Aiden released her arms and turned to me with relief shining in his eyes. "Kiera, this is Nikella, my mentor."

Oh. I gave her a nervous nod.

She nodded back but said nothing.

"Did you have any trouble coming through the city gate?" Aiden asked her.

"No, but I had to smuggle in my spear," she said in a hoarse voice, as if she hadn't spoken in days.

I glanced down at the table to see a double-ended spear made entirely of steel with a wide leather grip in the middle.

"How did you do that?" Ruru asked in awe.

Nikella picked up a long hollow stick from the ground and shoved her spear into it. She capped it with a leather cuff. "Walking stick," she grunted.

Ruru's mouth fell open, and I had to blink a few times myself. How often did she have to disguise her spear?

"And this is Librius," Aiden continued with the introductions. "A Teacher here, and a good friend."

White stubble framed Librius's smile as he gave me a short bow. "Lovely to meet you at last, Kiera. The boys have talked about you a great deal."

My cheeks warmed, as did Ruru's. Maz winked at me, wearing nothing but an unlaced vest and rolled-up pants. Aiden simply studied the assortment of tins laid out on the table.

Nikella, however, looked unamused. Or perhaps that was just how she always looked. "Ruru tells me you helped Aiden escape prison," she said, her eyes as sharp as her spear.

"That's true," I said, wondering if there was a wrong answer.

"Stole the key to the chains right off the jailer," Maz added.

"Then you set Aiden free," Nikella continued. "Why?"

I blanked at the blunt question. I was also very aware of Aiden standing two feet away. "Because . . . I needed his help to escape. And . . . and he tried to protect me from the jailer. Which is more than anyone's ever done for me before."

Aiden's fingers stilled in their perusal of the tins. Then he continued as if I hadn't spoken.

Nikella subjected me to her unwavering gaze a moment longer. Whatever she saw must have convinced her of my truth, because she gave me a curt nod and slid her spear out of its disguise.

Aiden held up a tin of brown powder. "Looks like you have everything you need now, Librius."

The Teacher rubbed his hands together, rocking on his feet. "Yes! Nikella procured everything we asked for. This will allow me to finish the,"—his eyes darted to me—"er, items soon."

"It's all right, Librius," Aiden said. "You can speak freely about anything pertaining to Ruru's part in the plan."

My brow furrowed, but before I could ask, Ruru nudged me with his elbow. "Did he tell you? You'll be with me."

"He hasn't said much of anything yet."

Ruru glanced at Aiden. "Can I tell her?"

Aiden nodded.

Tugging on my hand, Ruru led me over to a simple wooden bow and a quiver of arrows. "On the night it happens, my job is to distract the Wolves."

"*What?*"

"No, no, we have a plan! See, I've been practicing with this bow." Ruru fit an arrow into the bow and pulled the string back to his ear. "We'll be high up on a rooftop, setting fire to a few abandoned parts of the city, to keep the Wolves busy chasing their tails." He released the arrow, and it flew to hit near the center of the target. "I've been practicing for weeks," he added proudly.

My eyebrows rose. Bows and arrows weren't allowed in the city, except for the guards on the wall. Renwell had a bow in our old training room, but he'd never taught me to use it. Said I'd never need to know.

"Do I have weeks to catch up to your skill?" I asked Ruru, sending a covert look over my shoulder where the other four had their heads bent close over the table.

"You don't need to catch up," Ruru said, his brown eyes sparking with excitement. "Aiden says I need a personal guard —someone to watch my back while I take the shots. He said you're the best, and I agree."

I smiled, ruffling his messy hair. Such confidence, such

stout support. Like a future commander, learning the ropes of leadership.

My heart warmed that *this* was the job Aiden had given me. Not thieving or killing—unless it was in defense. But guarding this dear boy.

I glanced over at the others again as Ruru readied another arrow.

This job was also going to be conveniently far away from whatever *they* were doing that night. Whichever night they chose.

"Do you know when it's happening, Ruru?" I asked quietly as he aimed his shot.

"Nope. Aiden said we were waiting on Nikella and for Librius to finish making our bombs."

I startled. "Bombs?"

Ruru released the bowstring with a *twang*. "Yep. Librius is a genius for that sort of thing. He knows how to seal a few fire-seeds into a can of brown powder. We stick the can in a pile of old wood and shoot it with a burning arrow that sparks the powder and the seeds, then *boom!*"

I blinked in horrified fascination. I'd never heard of such a thing. This was information Renwell—and Father—would probably kill to get their hands on. But it still didn't explain what Aiden and the others were up to. Father wouldn't care about a few fires and distracted Wolves.

"Do you know what the others will be doing that night?" I murmured to Ruru as he fired another arrow.

He shook his head. "Aiden said it's safer that way. Oh, and before I forget." His expression turned serious. "If we need to escape the city, there's a guard at the gate by the name of Gregor who will give us horses and let us out."

So, Aiden had at least one guard on his payroll. The bag of gold on my belt felt heavier than ever.

"And you support Aiden? In . . . killing the king?" I asked.

Ruru stood the bow on the ground, crossing his hands over the top. That missing thumb made my heart twinge every time I noted its absence.

"I don't like the idea of killing people," Ruru admitted, his eyes drifting over to Aiden. "But I believe in justice. A king should face the consequences he forces others to. My father used to say that."

I placed my hand on top of his. "You never told me about your parents."

He shrugged. "They died when I was little. Sickness. My brother—Daire—took care of me for a while. Then the Wolves took him too."

"I'm sorry, Ruru," I said, my throat tight.

He gave me a small smile. "It's all right. Everyone loses everyone eventually. But there are always more to find. I found Aiden. And Maz. Sophie. Librius and Nikella. Melaena. My friends around the city. And you."

Tears welled in my eyes, but I smiled back. "I'm so glad I found you too, Ruru." I quickly blinked back the moisture. "So, what happens now?"

His smile widened. "I've never had a personal guard before, but I think that means you start carrying my stuff for me. Want to practice?" He lifted the quiver of arrows.

I laughed. "That's most certainly *not* how it works."

"I disagree, but I'll also be showing you our route and helping you practice your climbing."

I sobered immediately. "Climbing?"

"We have to climb fairly high to stay out of reach of the Wolves. Then we'll have to run over a few buildings to get to the next spot, and so on."

My palms grew moist at the thought of flying over rooftops. "Then I'll need all the help I can get."

"Kiera! Ruru!" Aiden called and waved us over.

He hadn't called me "little thief" since he'd discovered me crawling out of my hiding spot. Certainly not *"my* little thief" as he had during the heist.

I shook the thought from my head as we made our way over. It didn't matter what he called me. It was a ridiculous moniker, anyway. One of many I held.

Father's voice taunted me, *You can't make up your gods-damned mind, can you, girl?*

Everyone's face was serious as we approached.

"I told them about Asher," Aiden said. He inclined his head at Ruru. "He's dead."

Ruru groaned.

"Stealing from the High Treasurer was ill-conceived," Nikella said.

Aiden cut her an irritated look. "We had to. What's done is done."

Her eyes flicked to me, but she didn't say anything.

"Well, it's a gods-damned shame—may the gods find his soul—but where does that leave us?" Maz asked, twirling his axe in one hand.

"The same place as before," Aiden said. "We just need to

tread more carefully. Librius will continue working with his new materials, aided by Nikella. Kiera and Ruru will continue training for their part—"

"—while Aiden and I relax and drink and wait for you all to be ready," Maz finished with a laugh.

Ruru and Librius laughed along with him while Aiden sighed. I thought I even caught a glimmer of a smile from Nikella, but it was there and gone so quick, it could've been a trick of the torchlight.

I nudged Maz's knee. "What has you in such a festive mood?"

He grinned up at me, his light blue eyes glowing like a cloudless day. "I get to go home soon, lovely. Figured I might as well start celebrating now."

"We're not there yet," Aiden reminded him sharply.

Maz waved him off. "Details, brother."

My gut tied itself into knots. Would Maz make it home after all this? I didn't want to be the reason he didn't. It wasn't just Aiden's fate I held in my hands. It was all of theirs.

Aiden jerked his head. "I'll show you where to keep your gold, Kiera."

He led me to a locked trunk nestled in a corner. Sinking to one knee, he fished a key from his pocket and opened it. "Librius usually has the key and will give it to you whenever you ask."

I knelt next to him and peeked inside. Two snarling Wolf masks gazed blankly up at me. A shiver rippled over my skin. The stolen uniforms and sunstone knives were there as well, alongside a few pouches that bulged as if filled with coins.

King Tristan's ring was hidden near the bottom. A packet of letters and—

"Is that *human hair*?"

Aiden chuckled. "One of Maz's braids. He was so upset when he had to cut them off that he brought one with us as a reminder of sorts."

I wrinkled my nose and tucked my bag of coins as far away from the blond braid—and the Shadow-Wolf gear—as possible.

Aiden closed the trunk and locked it. But he didn't get up. I suddenly realized how very close we were.

My breathing tightened.

"That gold is yours, Kiera, to do with whatever you want," he said quietly. "You don't have to worry about working as a messenger or a dancer anymore, unless you wish to." He took a deep breath. "When the time comes, I'll give you a warning so you can prepare. However this ends, I hope you can take this gold and use it to make a new life for yourself. A better one."

"What if I can't see a way to a better life?" I whispered.

His eyes softened, and I could almost feel his need to reach for me. Or perhaps that was only my own need. "You'll find one," he whispered back. "For the short time I've known you, you've always found a way to win."

Gods help me, I wanted him to win too.

"AGAIN," RURU'S WEARY VOICE FILTERED DOWN TO ME.

I grunted, hobbling in a circle on my sore ankle. "Give me a moment."

He sighed loudly, and I nearly threw a rotten apple from the gutter at him.

It'd been nearly a week since Asher's death and my induction into this gods-forsaken plan.

A week of training with Ruru—throwing knives while he shot arrows, running laps above and below ground, and this gods-damn climbing routine straight from the deep, dark, wandering hell itself.

He'd shown me the spots he was to shoot from, each one a small, flat-topped roof of a high building—a bathhouse, an old inn, and an abandoned apartment building. Our views gave us a direct line of sight to the closest web of alleys and our targets —a crumbling carpenter's workshop, an empty house, and a dilapidated stable near the prison.

Each target was chosen for its state of abandon and its separation from the surrounding buildings. We didn't want to start a fire that would spread to more parts of the Old Quarter.

Thinking of my mother, I made Ruru swear that we would triple-check that no people or animals were inside when we set the bombs. He'd already been stocking the places with old driftwood and broken furniture.

But to get to our perches?

We had to scale three buildings in a very short amount of time. Aiden and Maz had been timing the Shadow-Wolves' response to commotions for months. Everything had to work perfectly.

But I was used to the climbing walls Renwell had rigged in our training room, as well as the few places in the Noble Quarter I'd climbed. All of which had a myriad of footholds and handholds. And even then, I hated clinging to the side of a building like a moth. Except I had no wings and would plummet to the dirty street below.

These buildings were plainer, smoother. I had to rely on windowsills and small cracks in the storm-washed stone.

Gods, I wished I were back with Melaena completing a thousand turns with a smile over *this* torture.

"You're hesitating right before the jump," Ruru called down to me from the roof I'd been trying to leap to from the one next to it. "It's making you fall short."

I glared up at him. "You think? Any more helpful tips?"

A deep voice spoke from the other roof. "Perhaps you need more motivation."

I squinted past the setting sun to see Aiden's green eyes gazing down at me. We hadn't spoken much in the last week. I'd seen him with Librius and Nikella when I trained with Ruru; I'd eaten with him and the others at *The Weary Traveler*. He'd slept every night in the next room.

I followed him a few times to see if he was doing anything else, but each time, he simply went back to one of his usual places.

But he'd become withdrawn and restless. Prone to quiet, tense conversations I wasn't part of. Mostly with Nikella, who barely spoke to me at all. To be fair, I didn't try to draw her into conversation either. She never seemed to leave the Temple, anyway.

Every day that passed weighed more heavily on me. I didn't want to let Aiden assassinate my father, but I couldn't think of a way to convince him not to. And if I protested too much, he might cut me out of the plan entirely. A plan I still knew precious little about.

Father wouldn't step foot outside the palace, especially when he knew assassins were afoot. Which meant Aiden, Maz, and Nikella were going to infiltrate the palace while Ruru and I distracted the Wolves.

But *how* were they going to infiltrate with only the three of them?

I also hadn't reached out to Renwell to tell him anything I'd learned. I hadn't even checked *The Crescent Moon* for his mark.

I couldn't hide much longer.

"What did you have in mind?" I asked Aiden.

He flashed me a sharp grin. "How about I play the Wolf?"

CHAPTER 31
AIDEN

RURU'S FACE BRIGHTENED, BUT KIERA LOOKED DUBIOUS.

I didn't want to scare her again, but she needed to keep up with Ruru. And to do that, she had to make these jumps. Besides, I'd been slowly losing my mind to impatience over the last few days.

I'd grown used to being in charge, to always being in action. But now, I was waiting for Librius and Nikella to finish their work. The explosives I needed for my part of the plan were different than Kiera and Ruru's—more complicated. I couldn't call in the Dags until they were complete.

I'd spent nearly all the stolen gold on bribes for the gate guards, the special materials for the explosives, and to pay off Skelly's debts for the risk he'd be taking for shipping the Dags around. Maz's clan—the Yargoths—had suffered enough attacks from Weylin's border patrols and imprisonment in his gods-damned mine to staunchly support our plan. But I'd still insisted they take a small sum as well. In case things went poorly.

I was using every resource I'd gathered over the years. Which meant I would have very little chance of ever attempting something like this again.

Maz was content to eat and drink and idle these days away, but I felt as though my skin would peel off from restlessness.

I gestured toward their next and last destination, the old inn. "If you two beat me to the inn, I'll buy you both dinner."

"You buy us dinner all the time," Ruru called back.

"Fine, as much sticky bread as you can eat then."

"Deal!"

I glanced down at Kiera, noticing the way she favored her ankle. I'd winced, watching her fall short on the jump, scrambling for purchase, before awkwardly falling five feet.

She pointed her chin up at me. "Deal, but you have to start from the street like any Wolf would."

I grinned. *There's my little thief.*

I swung from the roof and landed gracefully on my feet in front of her.

She glared at me. "Play fair."

"Wolves don't play fair," I said, leaning closer until our noses almost brushed. "But I will for you."

The flush on her cheeks deepened, filling me with a sense of purpose I hadn't felt all week. "Up you get," I said, tipping my chin toward Ruru.

With narrowed eyes, she turned and used the stairs built into the side of the building to reach Ruru's rooftop.

"On the count of three," I said, dropping to a crouch. "One, two, *three!*"

They tore off across the roof and out of sight. I sauntered up the stairs after them, giving them a sporting chance. They raced across the roof, ducking laundry lines and evading rain barrels. When they came to the lip of the roof, Ruru flew off without a second thought.

But Kiera hesitated. And looked back at me. I used that moment to run full tilt at her. Her eyes widened. She backed up a few steps and took a running leap off the roof. She landed on the next one and staggered a bit but kept going.

I sprinted faster, relishing the wind in my ears and the flight of my feet. I soared over the gap as my quarries scrambled their way over more roofs.

Ruru pulled ahead of Kiera, nimble as a monkey I'd seen once in Eloren. He reached the inn and began climbing to the top. Kiera kept losing time on each jump she made. I got closer. And closer.

She came to the last jump and leapt. But not far enough. Her hands slammed down on the edge of the roof, and she hung there.

I hurtled over the gap and skidded to a halt on the other side. I knelt and extended my hand to her.

She was panting, her boots searching for a hold on the wall.

"Just take my hand," I said.

She huffed in frustration, her eyes a blazing gold in the setting sun. "But then you win."

I flexed my hand. "I already won, Kiera. But I can still save you the fall."

Her lips clenched tight, stubbornness fighting defeat. But then she locked hands with me, and I hauled her onto the roof.

"I won't be ready in time," she said. "What if I can't protect him?"

"You *will* be ready, and you *will* protect him." I gently moved a strand of her hair from her glistening forehead.

Her face softened. "How much sticky bread am I buying? I didn't know you even liked it."

I smirked. "I never said I wanted sticky bread as my prize. I'll buy some for Ruru, since he did beat me." I waved at Ruru who waved back from his perch. "But you . . . I want something else from you."

Her expression turned suspicious.

"Don't worry," I said. "There's only a slight chance of death involved."

"I TELL YOU I DON'T LIKE HEIGHTS, AND YOU FORCE ME TO CLIMB to the top of the Temple?" Kiera's annoyed voice echoed behind me in the tight stairwell.

I suppressed a chuckle. "Almost there."

When we stepped out of the stairwell, she gasped, her eyes going wide with wonder. She walked to the stone balustrade as if in a trance to gaze at the gathering night on the far eastern horizon over the sea. Her loosened hair danced in the calm breeze that smelled of the sea—and now her.

It was the most beautiful sight I'd ever seen.

I stepped up next to her. "The Teachers call this the bell tower balcony. It circles the whole dome with four short walkways to each bell tower." I nodded to the two that flanked us.

Statues—one of Mynastra and one of Arduen—adorned the tops.

"How did you find this place?" she whispered, her grip tight on the railing.

"Librius told me about it. He lets me come up here whenever I want."

"Because he knows who you are?"

"Yes. He knew Nikella. From before." I glanced over to see Kiera frowning in confusion. A little more of my story wouldn't hurt. "Nikella is a Teacher who used to train at this Temple."

Kiera's eyebrows arched. "I would never have guessed that."

"She isn't the friendliest person, but she's one of the best Teachers in the world. Taught me everything I know." I took a deep breath and looked back as the starry night sky slowly crept over the fiery day. "She was the one who rescued me and raised me."

"What happened to your mother?" Kiera asked softly.

"Remember how I told you I was born at sea in a storm?" I pointed toward the deceptively calm waters on the horizon. "My mother died giving birth to me on a boat out there."

"Oh, Aiden." Kiera slid her hand next to mine until our skin touched. "May the gods find her soul."

A lump formed in my throat. A knot of sadness for the mother I never knew. "Nikella was trying to get my parents out of Aquinon via boat, but my father never made it on. Weylin stabbed him in the back while my mother screamed from the deck. Then Renwell wounded her and Nikella as they sailed away. Between the pain of losing her husband, her wound, and labor, my mother didn't last the night."

Kiera's hand jerked away, and she stared at me, horrified. "Renwell injured a fleeing pregnant woman?"

"Yes." I glared into the invading night. "He tried to shoot my mother with an arrow, but Nikella stepped in the way. Took it in her shoulder. When she fell, he shot my mother in the chest."

Kiera stumbled backward. "Renwell . . ."

I placed a steadying hand on her arm. "You probably didn't see much of him at the palace, other than when he arrested you, but that man is just as much of a monster as Weylin is."

"Gods, that—that's awful. Then Nikella took you and raised you herself?"

"Yes. We lived in Twaryn for most of my life." Misty, thick forests filled my mind. "She taught in the villages there and told people I was her orphaned nephew."

"I thought you might've lived there a while," she said with a small smile. "When we first met."

"I remember," I murmured. I'd been so angry that she'd managed to pry those personal details from my lips. But here I was—letting them spill out of me. It felt more relieving than I ever could've imagined. "But I didn't bring you up here just to tell you stories."

She quirked an eyebrow. "Did you also want to scare me?"

"No. I wanted to help you try to make peace with your fear." I held out my hand to her again. "Let's visit the Four, shall we?"

She hesitantly placed her hand in mine, and we walked along the balcony to Mynastra's tower.

In full truth, I wanted to make peace between us as well.

I tired of spending day and night near her without being

able to touch her, talk to her, tell her everything. I longed to have her back in my arms more than I longed for food or sleep. But I craved her trust even more.

Each time I thought of getting closer, I remembered that stark fear in her eyes when I'd threatened her and again in the sitting room when I'd come to get her.

We stopped at the walkway leading to the bell tower. "Touch the bell with me," I said, tugging on her hand.

Kiera paled, gazing over the railing at the ground a hundred feet below, then at the narrow bridge to the bell.

She shook her head vigorously. "Why are you doing this?" she whispered.

"Because I want you to win," I said. "Once you've proven to yourself that you're stronger than your fear, you'll win every battle it wages."

Her erratic breath warmed my lips. "I watched a woman die once. She fell off the bridge to the palace during Mynastra's Tide."

Ah, that was why.

I drew her close. "I swear by the Four, I will never let you fall."

She closed her eyes and tried to calm her breathing, inhaling through her nose and exhaling through her mouth. My heartbeat galloped like a runaway horse, pounding blood through my body, as I savored her nearness.

My grip on her tightened, and she opened her eyes. "Let's go," she said.

The bridge was barely wide enough for the two of us, so I hugged her close to my body. She didn't seem to mind.

The wind pushed us a little harder out here in the open, and Kiera let out a whimper.

"Just reach out and touch it," I said, guiding her arm forward.

Her fingers trembled as she inched closer. Finally, she lunged forward and grazed the smooth brass bell. She made to flee back across the bridge, but I held her back.

"Go slow and easy," I instructed her. "We're safe."

The moment we reached the balcony, Kiera sagged against the smooth white dome.

I grinned at her. "That was excellent! Only three more to go!"

She gaped at me. "I take it back," she rasped. "You don't want to scare me. You want to *torture* me."

"Never." I leaned next to her against the dome. "It might feel like that at first, but you get used to it."

"Like with you being underground or in chains?"

I grimaced. "Admittedly, I've never shackled myself on purpose to overcome that fear."

A glimmer of amusement lit Kiera's eyes. "You let Maz bind your wrists for your night of survival in the Dagriel forest."

I chuckled. "That was different. I *could* have gotten myself out of those ropes. But the point was to prove that I didn't need my hands to survive."

Kiera smiled and looked up at the nearly violet sky. "Does being underground still frighten you?"

"Sometimes that fear will ambush me, yes. Especially if I'm already anxious about something. But I'm only ever underground because I have to be. Because there's something more important than my fear."

Her eyes narrowed in thought. "Perhaps that's what I'm missing in my training with Ruru. Instead of thinking about who I'm running from, I should think about who I'm running toward. The other end of the tunnel—or bridge—so to speak."

Gods, I couldn't agree more. For the first time in years, I was also beginning to see beyond the one thing I'd been running toward for years—vengeance against Weylin and his allies, giving a better life to all Rellmirans.

For the first time—just as Maz hoped—I also wanted something for myself. A life free of the darkness that had haunted it for so long.

I wanted her. She was the light beyond the darkness.

But we were still so deep in the shadows.

"Aiden?" she whispered, searching my eyes.

I'd leaned closer to her without realizing it. I cleared my throat, shifting away. "Who do you want to visit next?"

"Who's nearest the sunset?"

I led her around the dome, the air warmer here in the last of the sunlight. Crimson and gold painted the sky over the weakening sun. But she pulled up short when she realized what else she could see from here.

"The prison. Is—is Asher still down there?" She kept her head turned away.

I rubbed my thumb over her scarred fingers. "No. I heard someone stole his head several days ago."

"Stole? Who in the deep, dark, wandering hell would—" She stopped, narrowing in on my perfectly composed expression. "It was you. Why?"

"I gave it to Floren so he could bring his ashes to the sea

with the others. I doubt the rest of his body received the proper rites, but I did what I could."

Kiera threw her arms around my neck and hugged me tight. Like the day we'd discovered him in the square.

I hugged her back just as hard. Gods, the relief nearly crushed me.

"Thank you," she whispered in my ear.

A shiver coursed down my spine. Every muscle in my body grew taut, barely keeping from delivering her mouth to mine. Those lips had tasted like fire and honey, and they teased me every night in my dreams.

But what if she didn't want that anymore? What if she was still afraid of me?

She pulled away from me, breaking the moment. "I'm ready for Terraum's bell, I think," she said with a brave smile.

She touched Terraum's and then Viridana's with my help, getting more confident each time. For Arduen's, she placed a hand on my chest, telling me to stay put. Then she walked across the short bridge, arms aloft as if she were dancing on a stage once more. She laid a palm against the bell, smiling at me over her shoulder. I grinned, bursting with pride.

Then she came back to me and clasped our hands together. "Thank you," she whispered. "That felt amazing."

I bent toward her, but then someone cleared their throat behind us. I whirled, shielding Kiera.

Librius watched us from the stairwell with a knowing smile. "You said to tell you the moment we finished. This is that moment, Aiden."

My heart leapt. It was finally time to send word. There was no going back now.

CHAPTER 32

KIERA

"IT'S CLOSE TO SUNSET."

I smiled at Melaena, who lounged on the couch opposite me in the sitting room of *The Silk Dancer*. "There aren't any windows in here. How do you know?"

She popped another grape into her mouth and grinned. "I have a sense about these things."

I'd spent the last few hours dancing with the other girls, then had a late dinner with Melaena. She'd ordered roasted chicken and a pot of melted chocolate to dip fruit and cubes of cheese into.

It'd been two days since I spent the sunset on top of the Temple with Aiden—a memory I would keep close for the rest of my life. Being up there with him had felt so dangerous, yet exhilarating. Not unlike how I felt about Aiden himself.

After touching the last bell, I'd wanted to fly back into his arms and stay there all night.

But then Librius had interrupted us, and Aiden had

hurried me downstairs before disappearing with a whispered apology.

I swiped a bit of chocolate from the rim of the pot and licked my finger clean. "You know, I may have to live here now if you keep feeding me like this."

She shrugged. "Chocolate bribes always work with me. I thought they might with you too."

"You really think I'd be able to stay here and live with you after . . . after everything?"

"I do. With poor Asher gone and a new, benevolent king on the throne, you wouldn't have to hide anymore."

I chuckled dryly. "I'm still an escaped prisoner and a thief."

"All for the glory of a better Rellmira. At the very least, you should be a free woman, if not a hero."

The chocolate seemed to harden in my belly. "Do you truly think an assassin should be called a hero?"

She frowned, twirling a long curl around her finger. "Aiden's not doing what he is for the glory. Trust me, that man would rather disappear back into the forests of Twaryn than be paraded around as the savior of Rellmira. But sometimes . . . sometimes the only choices are ugly ones."

I leaned forward, hardly daring to speak the thought that had been spinning around my mind for days. "Do you think there could be another way? A way to get Weylin to leave peacefully? Exile, maybe?"

Melaena smiled sadly. "You know what he's done to stay in power, Kiera. You know what he did to attain that power. Do you really think he would step aside for his son? Or for the true heir?"

I growled, getting up to pace. "But aren't we just repeating history, then? How is this any better than what Weylin did to Aiden's father?"

"Aiden's father was a good man. Kind and fair. Many of the charitable initiatives he put in place were overturned by Weylin. As if he were trying to scour away every mark Tristan had tried to make." She shook her head, the ornaments woven in it tinkling. "This isn't a best friend lying and manipulating his way to the top, only to stab his benefactor in the back and take what was his. This is justice."

Justice. The word Ruru had used. They truly thought they were fighting for what was right. This was war for them, and Weylin's death was the victory. Or rather, Everett taking his place.

But was I any better?

I had lied and manipulated my way into this group. If I obeyed Father and gave him everything he wanted from me, I would also be betraying my friends, especially Aiden. They might also die because of me.

Fucking Four, I was no better than my father.

"Kiera? What's wrong? You look pale."

I blinked, the room coming back into focus. "I'm fine. Just tired, that's all. I should probably go."

"See? You know it's close to sunset too," Melaena said with a smile that didn't quite reach her worried eyes.

Someone pounded on the locked door.

I froze, whipping out two of my knives before Melaena called out, "Yes?"

A boy's voice spoke. "Miss Melaena? I'm sorry, there's a woman—"

"Melaena? It's Lady Helene! Please, I need to speak with you."

Melaena flew off the couch and flung the door open.

A woman and a young girl burst into the room past a flabbergasted Elias.

My heart sank. Lady Helene and little Lady Isabel. Garyth's family. Isabel clutched a wooden box with holes in it. She'd brought her gods-damned lizard.

The beautiful, laughing woman I'd spied on was now a mess of panic. Strands of auburn hair flew from her tight bun. Her eyes were red and watery with tears. She clutched a satchel in one hand, and her daughter's hand in the other.

"That will be all," Melaena told Elias, and shut the door in his face. "Please sit, Lady Helene. What's happened?"

Helene and Isabel took the seat I'd vacated with barely a glance in my direction. I quickly sheathed my knives.

"It's Garyth," Helene said, her voice cracking. "Renwell is arresting him."

No, no, no.

"Gods help us." Melaena sank to the couch.

Helene uttered a dry sob. "One of Garyth's allies tipped him off, said R-Renwell was coming for him with a unit of those awful guards of his. He told us to come here. That you would help us get out of the city. He—he—" Helene started to cry in earnest. But she opened her bag and shoved a handful of papers into Melaena's hands. "Th-those are everything he has from our allies. We c-can't let Renwell find those."

The letters. More than what I'd found in his hiding place. This was what Renwell was looking for. Evidence of those who wanted to bring back the People's Council—the same people who wanted to see my brother named king in place of my father.

These letters were going to be the death of Garyth. Just as the heist had been Asher's.

"Renwell was crashing into the house as we left," Helene said. "The Noble Quarter gate was barred and guarded, which means he'll know we're still here and will come looking for us any moment. We have to leave!"

Melaena nodded as the letters trembled in her hands. "I have to hide these. But if he comes here—if I'm not here—"

"I'll take the family," I spoke up.

All three of them stared at me as if remembering I was even here.

"Who are you?" Helene asked in a shrill voice.

Isabel studied me with suspicious eyes. Did she recognize me without my mask?

"Kiera . . ." Melaena breathed. "You don't know Renwell like I do. You weren't in the city when he was ferreting out rebel sympathizers. That tunnel you use"—she gestured behind me—"is the one my parents used to smuggle out the few sympathizers he didn't find first."

My heart twisted. Why didn't Julian use it then?

"I know what Renwell is capable of," I gritted out. After Aiden's story on the roof of the Temple, I wondered what other sort of dirty work my mentor had done for his king. "But you need someone to get these two out of Aquinon. You stay. Hide the letters and stall Renwell as long as possible."

Gods, what was I doing? *What was I doing?* Renwell would kill me for this.

My gaze dropped to the little girl clutching her ill-gotten pet.

But I couldn't live with myself if I let him take them too.

I stabbed the sun button with my thumb, and the panel creaked open. "Let's go," I snarled.

Helene staggered to her feet, hope and caution mingling in her desperate eyes. "How do I know if we can trust you? I don't even know who you are!"

I hesitated.

But Melaena spoke for me. "Her name is Kiera, and you can trust her. Go!"

That was enough to spur Helene into dragging her daughter toward me. As they climbed into the tunnel, I looked past them to Melaena.

"Don't get in his way," I told her. I could only protect her so much, and that killed me.

She nodded, her chin lifted and her spine straight.

I hurried into the tunnel and latched the door behind me.

"I don't like the dark!" Isabel's voice sounded so young and thin. "And neither does Captain!"

I pushed past them to lead the way. "Captain? Is that the name of your pet?"

"Yes, he's a lizard and loves the sun. He's scared."

Helene tried to hush and comfort her daughter. Gods, we didn't have time for this.

"Is he a pirate?" I asked, feeling my way through the tunnel. "Is that why you named him Captain?"

"Yes." Isabel sniffled. "I made him a little hat too, but—but I left it behind. With Father."

Pain clawed at my heart. I knew what she was feeling. What she'd be feeling for the rest of her life.

"You can make him a new one," I said firmly. "But he doesn't need one. It's not the hat that makes him a captain, it's how brave he is when he's scared. You'll have to show him how."

"I—I want Father," she whispered.

My throat thickened. But thankfully, Helene answered her. "I want him too, Izzy. But he wants you and me to be safe right now. We should do that for Father, yes?"

"Yes."

Gods damn it, how many mothers and fathers had been lost over a crown? Brothers, sisters, friends . . . It had to stop.

I sent up another silent prayer for Melaena just as we reached the hatch. I shoved it open with my shoulder.

We tumbled out into the warehouse, panting in the gloomy light. I closed the tunnel and laid a tarp over the top.

"Where do we go now?" Helene asked.

Could I simply take them to the city gate? Would they let us out?

Do not leave the city.

My fingers curled into fists. The sun was probably behind the wall by now. The Wolves would be out any moment. Renwell would be coming from behind us with more Wolves.

We had to keep going, and fast.

Gregor. Ruru had told me that was the guard who would let us out if we needed to escape after we blew up the Old Quarter.

Would he let us out now?

I mapped our route in my head. I could take the most direct one—the main city road. But what if Renwell had set guards to watch it? That meant slinking through the labyrinth of the Old Quarter, which would take us right by—

"Walk fast and keep quiet," I said. "Cover your faces if you can."

One of them whimpered, but they both drew hoods over their heads. I strode over to the door, twisted the lock, and ushered Helene and Isabel through. After I wedged the door shut, I hesitated. I could relock it using the pins I always kept in my hair, but that would take too much precious time.

"Gods damn it," I swore under my breath. Hopefully, Aiden would understand.

We plunged into the nearest alley. Everyone's doors and windows were already shut tight. The violet sky deepened to black like a bruise. I started to run.

Please be there. Please be there.

I raced up the stairs to our apartment and wrenched the door open.

Aiden and Nikella whipped their heads toward me from where they sat at the table.

I sagged with relief. "G-Garyth's been arrested," I gasped. "Need to get them out." I stepped aside to show Helene and Isabel bumbling up the stairs behind me. "Had to leave the warehouse unlocked."

Aiden sprang to his feet, his chair falling backward. "Never mind that." He seized his daggers and shoved them into his belt and threw on his cloak. "Renwell?" he spat out.

I nodded.

Nikella didn't speak a word. Simply grabbed her wooden staff from where it leaned against the wall and stuffed something from the table into the pocket of her Teacher's robe. She tugged the long hood over her head.

"Maz and Ruru?" I whispered to him.

"Temple. Find them and tell what happened and that we'll be back."

"No. I'm coming with you."

Aiden's eyes hardened. "Absolutely not. You're staying with Maz and—"

"*No.* I told these two I would get them out of the city, and that's what I'm going to do." My heart drummed at a frenzied pace, but I held firm. It was my fault they were on the run. It was my fault Isabel was going to lose her father.

"Let her come, Aiden," Nikella said sharply. "We don't have time for this."

My eyebrows lifted at the unexpected support.

Aiden growled, raking his hands through his hair. "Fine. Stick close together. Nikella, cover our backs."

Helene's eyes widened as Aiden stalked past her. "You're the one my husband talked about, aren't you? The one he never met."

Aiden's jaw tightened. "Let me handle all the talking."

Isabel huddled closer to her mother as Aiden led the way back down the stairs.

The shadows had grown longer, filling the alleys. Clouds drifted over the moon and stars.

We were out of time.

Aiden kept up a pace just shy of a run. I stayed close to

Helene and Isabel, knives in hand. Nikella drifted behind us, a silent guardian.

The journey felt interminable.

My heart jumped into my throat every time a pebble rolled or wood creaked. But no one appeared from the shadows.

Was Renwell still in the Noble Quarter? Had he searched *The Silk Dancer* yet? Thank the gods I hadn't told him about the tunnel. That little secret might save us.

A warm glow melted through the shadows as we neared the taverns and inns that crowded near the city gate.

Hope fluttered through my chest. We were almost there. We were going to make it.

We wove around shuffling pedestrians, trying to stay together. The enormous city gate stood halfway open. Guards lined the top and bottom of it, lit by bouquets of torches.

Aiden's eyes darted about until they fastened on a heavyset man between the gate and the stables. "That's him. I'll—"

"Aiden!" Nikella's cry slashed my hope like a cold knife.

We turned to see a dark figure galloping down the main road on a black horse. *Renwell.* A fleet of Wolves sprinted in his wake, their masks glistening.

Someone screamed, and chaos unleashed. People scattered and dove for open doors or dark alleys. Guards shouted. Someone plowed into Isabel, and she dropped her box.

Nikella snatched it and shoved it back in her arms. "Run! I'll hold him off!"

Aiden seized a shaking Helene and Isabel. "Kiera! Let's go!"

I held back, catching a fistful of Nikella's cloak. "Don't! He'll kill you, Nikella!"

She shook me loose, her scarred face taut with resolve. "No, he won't."

"Yes, he will! You don't know—"

"I do know." Nikella threw back her hood. "He's my brother."

Then she strode forward to meet him.

CHAPTER 33
KIERA

I GAPED AFTER HER. A LONE, TALL FIGURE WITH HER STAFF, facing Renwell on horseback and his Wolves.

It couldn't be true. Renwell was her *brother*? He'd never mentioned family. Never said where he came from. And I'd never asked.

She would have to be out of her gods-damned mind to lie about that.

Renwell spotted her, and his face whitened. He yanked back on the reins so hard his horse reared, whinnying. His Wolves came to a whispered halt behind him.

He mouthed something. Her name?

She ripped a container from her pocket and strew its contents in a wide arc in front of her. She grabbed a nearby torch—

"NIKELLA!" Renwell roared.

She threw it to the ground. A wall of fire roared up from the cracked cobblestones. I stumbled back with a gasp.

Hooves clattered behind me. Aiden rode toward me on a brown horse with another's reins clutched in his hand.

He pulled to a halt. "Get on."

The realization hit me like the heat wave at my back. "I don't know how to ride!"

He thrust his hand toward me, and I grabbed it without thinking. I leapt, and he swung me up behind him on the scratchy blanket that covered the horse's back. Nikella heaved herself onto the other horse.

With a kick of Aiden's heels, we jolted forward. I wrapped my arms around his waist and squeezed my arms and thighs, trying desperately to stay on.

Guards shouted and flocked to the barricade of fire while someone rang an alarm bell. They were too busy to notice Helene, with Isabel nestled in front of her, galloping out of the gate, with the rest of us close behind.

I twisted around for one last look and saw nothing but Renwell pacing behind the fire. I couldn't see his eyes, but somehow, I knew they were fastened on me.

The gods themselves wouldn't be able to save me from his wrath.

I shuddered, every bone in my body already rattling from the strange, rocking movement of the horse.

I had left the city. The realization made me forget everything else. I tilted my head back to look up at the open sky. It was the same sky I saw every night, but there was *more* of it. I was flying beneath it, flying away, and there was still ever more. The walls that had encircled me my whole life were rapidly fading behind me. Smaller and smaller, like a child's toy left by the sea. How had that city seemed so large before?

Miles of rolling fields stretched out before us. The road we galloped over curved and dipped toward a dark smudge on the western horizon. Woods, perhaps? Gods, I'd never been in the woods before.

A giddy laugh bubbled up in my throat, and I had to swallow it back. I was *free*. Perhaps this was why Renwell and Father forbade me from leaving. Because they knew I'd never want to come back.

I used to imagine what it would be like to leave Aquinon and explore the world. To be someone other than Emilia or Kiera Torvaine. Forsaking my name and legacy to roam the world with no expectations.

Like Aiden had.

Yet he'd come back.

Just like I would have to. I couldn't leave Everett and Delysia behind. Not unless they were safe. And now I had Maz, Ruru, and Melaena to worry about as well.

No. This was a short freedom. But that wouldn't stop me from enjoying it.

I breathed in the cool night air, scented with wet grass instead of the sea. What did the rest of the world smell like?

Mother's voice echoed in my head from a day we'd been walking through her garden as she showed me her herbs and flowers.

A thousand scents in one garden, Kiera. Each one presses a new memory to your mind. Imagine, a garden of a thousand memories.

If her garden had held that many, then a multitude could have existed outside our small world.

My chest ached, and I leaned against Aiden's back. He stiffened. I pulled away, but his hand reached back and gripped my knee. A silent reassurance.

I held him closer, inhaling his familiar scent. I wished I could tell Mother that a scent carried more than just memory. It could carry a whole heart's worth of emotions as well. Like every time I was in her old room, an ocean of grief and longing, love and guilt enveloped me.

And how, whenever I was this close to Aiden, I felt the crash of something similar. Not as deep and wide as the ocean. More like a hidden pool under a waterfall. It was new and secret. Feelings, like water, kept pouring into it.

I didn't know deep it went. I didn't know what else awaited me there. But being near Aiden made me want to jump in and find out.

After a while, the horses slowed to a walk. No one pursued us.

Helene and Isabel looked limp with exhaustion, but Helene held her posture well, as though she'd ridden before. Nikella was shrouded in her cloak once more, carrying her staff like the spear it held within.

I had so many questions—about her and Renwell, and whatever she threw on the ground. About where we were going.

But it felt wrong to break the silence. As if breaking it would alert the guards to where we were.

We rode until my muscles ached and my thighs burned. The rolling fields ended in a thick glade of trees with twisted trunks and chattering leaves. The Hollow, if I remembered my maps correctly.

The creak of old wood and the muted clop of the horses'

hooves made it sound like we were alone in this dense, gloomy world.

Until light emerged ahead. Lopsided buildings of wood and thatch were clumped together under the trees. A carved sign out front said Fairglen. A small village I'd heard travelers mention as a stop on their long journeys.

Hay-filled paddocks with horses, donkeys, and cattle looped around behind what looked like four inns and a tavern. Whoever lived here must run the only five businesses that made this a "village."

Even this late at night, everywhere seemed brightly lit and full. No guards. No Wolves.

Aiden maneuvered us next to Nikella. "We should rest," he murmured to her.

"No, we should keep going. They might not be far behind."

"*If* he comes after us," Aiden countered. His head turned to Helene and Isabel. "He already snagged his bigger prize."

Helene drew up near us. "We have a family estate. In the heart of Pravara. We could go there."

Aiden shook his head. "That will be the first place they check. We need to get you somewhere safe they don't know about."

Helene seemed to wilt, her last familiar refuge gone. Isabel looked too tired for tears. She simply clutched Captain's box and stared at me with hollow eyes.

"Food and something to drink," I said, nodding to Isabel. "Then we plan."

Nikella's eyes cut to me. How could I have not realized why she seemed familiar? Hints of her brother stared back at me.

I suppressed another shiver.

"Agreed," she said.

Aiden directed his horse toward a sprawling inn with glass windows and a sloping roof. *The Twisted Tail*, according to the painted board above the door. A running horse with a braided tail was painted next to the name.

Aiden slid off our horse, and I tried to follow, throwing one leg over and sliding as he did. But my muscles must've been beaten near to death by that gods-damned horse because I fell to the ground in a heap.

Aiden stretched out a hand to me, his lips pressed together as his eyes twinkled.

"Don't you dare laugh," I hissed, grabbing his hand and lurching upright. "Or tell Maz."

His smile snuck out as his thumb stroked the back of my hand. "Never."

The others dismounted much more easily than I did, with Aiden lifting Isabel to the ground. Perhaps I should've let him do the same for me.

A young boy sitting on the fence rails next to the inn took our horses for a tossed coin. We trudged inside to shouts of laughter and the smell of unwashed bodies and bean stew. A fire crackled in a stone hearth adorned with a wreath of cow horns. Roughly dressed men and women crowded the tables and the bar. No one looked up at our entrance, too busy eating, yelling, and playing Death and Four.

Helene hugged her daughter close, her eyes wide. But I was glad to be around strangers in a rowdy tavern. Much more comfortable than I'd felt in Asher's ballroom.

Aiden sauntered over to talk to the bartender while Nikella glared our way to a table by the hearth.

He came back with a basket of bread and a bowl of butter that he set on our table. He sat next to me, our bodies touching from hip to toe. I didn't move away.

Isabel snatched a brown loaf and bit into it like she was starving. Her box quivered on her lap. Helene stared at the bread as if she couldn't imagine eating. She'd tucked her satchel between her dainty, muddied boots.

"Bartender said the inns are full tonight." Aiden slathered a piece of bread with butter and ate it. "Cattle drive from Winspere and a host of farmers from Pravara for market day."

I slumped in my chair. I'd rather sleep on the roof than get back on that horse.

"I'll take them onward," Nikella said, ripping off chunks of bread. "I have allies not far from here who will keep them safe."

Aiden nodded. "Kiera and I will go back to Aquinon after dawn when the guards rotate, and the Wolves are gone. Maz and Ruru will be wondering where we are."

So soon. Part of me wanted to run and hide. Evade Renwell as long as I could. But things might only get worse.

A barmaid thumped down five bowls of stew with wooden spoons and left. Steam curled from the thick brown soup, brimming with beans and chunks of vegetables. She returned moments later with a pitcher of water and a handful of mismatched mugs.

Nikella stopped her before she could leave. "Bring me a cup of fruit or wet greens if you have it. For the lizard," she added to Isabel as the barmaid trotted off.

A glimmer of a smile appeared on the girl's face. "Thank you, Teacher."

Helene twisted her hands together. "I'd like to pay you all for this. For your help."

"Not necessary," Aiden said.

I looked away from the gratitude and grief shining in her eyes. I poured a mug of water and gulped it down. The barmaid came and went, dropping off a bit of lettuce and diced apple. Isabel slid a few pieces into the crate.

"Your husband is High Councilor Garyth?" Nikella asked.

My gaze shot back to her. How did she know that?

Helene nodded.

"Two months ago, I passed information to one of his men. Four days later, I found the man by the side of the road. Dead."

Helene gasped and covered Isabel's ears. "Please don't say such things in front of my daughter."

Nikella pressed her lips together, aligning her scar. She didn't say anything, but her silence spoke loud enough. There was very little Helene could shelter Isabel from anymore.

"What information?" Aiden asked in a low voice.

Firelight danced in Nikella's eyes. The dark blue was different than Renwell's, but they held the same hardness. As if they had known nothing but brutality. Yet, Nikella had raised Aiden. She was a Teacher. There must be a softer heart in her body than the one that beat in her brother's.

"About the Calimber mine," she said. "Garyth had his men poking around for months. They were raising suspicion, so I told one of them what I knew. That Dracles moved several patrols to guard the river where large shipments of wood float from Twaryn to the mine. Larger than usual. And they cleared out the village. It's nothing but Dracles' men now."

388 • LEAH MARA

It was the most Nikella had ever spoken, and several things became clear.

Nikella was a spy, not unlike me.

Delysia's lover was telling the truth. Father was building something near the mine, taking more than his share of wood from Twaryn. I'd heard him say once that the trees grew back, so Viridana shouldn't care how many he took from her forest.

But the kingdoms had signed a treaty before the gods disappeared, never to invade Twaryn and never to take more than their share of the goddess-grown trees. It was part of Garyth's duty as Master of Commerce to see that the treaty was enforced.

Why was Father breaking it now? And why had he kept his Master of Commerce in the dark about it? Had he suspected his true—and treasonous—alliance already? Because of Renwell. Because of me and my own poking around.

No one spoke after Nikella's news. Aiden scowled into his water as if more answers swam there. Perhaps he was hesitating to kill my father, not knowing what sort of nefarious plans Everett would be inheriting.

That could be my key to this particular lock. I could convince Aiden to capture my father and force him to tell us what he was doing. Get him to order Dracles and his men away from the mine. Maybe even replace Dracles with someone who would be loyal to my brother. Delysia's lover, perhaps?

"Weylin's plans will die with him," Aiden said.

Helene gasped again, and Isabel's mouth dropped open. I inwardly cringed. Nikella frowned.

Aiden sent Helene a piercing stare. "I'm only sorry it wasn't sooner. Then I could've saved your husband."

Helene's chin crumpled, and her gaze dropped to her untouched soup. "I wish that as well," she whispered.

Isabel snuggled into her mother's side, and they held each other, mired in a grief so thick no words of comfort would penetrate.

"We should carry on," Nikella said, dropping her spoon into her empty bowl. "We have a few more hours of riding ahead of us."

Helene nodded and ate a few spoonfuls of her soup before pushing the bowl away. Nikella stuffed the extra bread in her pockets while Isabel dumped the rest of the lettuce and apple chunks into her lizard's crate.

We all stood.

Helene stepped forward and awkwardly embraced me. "I will never forget your kindness and bravery. I pray the gods will protect you. All of you," she added, inclining her head to Aiden.

Isabel rushed forward and clutched my hand, pulling me closer to her. "Save my father if you can," she whispered in my ear.

I jerked back. Had she remembered me from the study?

But she gave no other hint of recognition. My chest burned as I squeezed her hand. "Take care of Captain and your mother. And yourself, Lady Isabel."

She nodded solemnly and followed Helene and Nikella out the door. I sank back onto my chair.

"I need to speak with the bartender a moment," Aiden muttered and disappeared.

I tried to swallow a few more bites of soup, but it felt like mud in my mouth. The clamor of the patrons that had been comforting moments before now felt like needles in my skin.

I stood abruptly, looking for Aiden. But I didn't see him anywhere.

I staggered away, the room blurring as my emotions threatened to overwhelm me. I bumped into someone who spilled their drink and cursed at me. Finally, I reached the door and flung myself outside.

The humid night air soothed some of the tightness in my chest. But it was still tainted by the sharp smell of livestock and the ruckus from the inns.

Without thinking, I wandered off the only road and into the woods. The soft ground muted my boot steps, and the heavy trees drew a curtain between me and the village. I'd never been somewhere like this in the dark without being frightened.

But nothing sinister awaited me here. A few small creatures skittered in the brush, but the rest of the woods breathed peace.

Something I desperately needed, yet rarely found.

I had an almost inexorable urge to run. To flee through these welcoming trees and bury myself so deeply in their embrace, no one would ever find me. The world would move on. I wouldn't have to face my guilt or my crimes.

I wouldn't have to face those I'd failed, as I'd just faced Helene and Isabel. Acting as if I deserved any of their gratitude.

Delysia's accusatory face surfaced in my mind. When she'd

told me to leave because that was what I was good at. I'd wanted to argue with her, but now . . .

I'd always looked for a way out when things grew difficult. I snuck out of the palace to drink and gamble and have affairs with charming men. I'd wanted to leave Rellmira when Father began planning my tactical marriage before Mother's death. And I'd disappeared into Renwell's shadow after she died.

Had I truly helped anyone by spying for Renwell? My first mission concerning Garyth. And this one with Aiden. Both only seemed to bring more death, more guilt, more pain. He claimed I was doing my duty, serving the crown, protecting it.

But sometimes it seemed the people needed more protection from the crown.

"Kiera," a deep voice said behind me.

No twigs had snapped, yet I'd known he would come for me.

Where would I go?

Nowhere I wouldn't find you.

CHAPTER 34
KIERA

I SIGHED, TURNING TO FACE HIM. "YOU DIDN'T NEED TO FOLLOW me, Aiden. I would've come back for you."

He stepped close enough for me to see him in the faint, silvery light. He carried something lumpy on his back. "I wanted to make sure you were all right."

I'm not.

I gestured around me. "I've never been in the woods before. I can see why you and Maz love it so much."

His smile gleamed. "The forests of Twaryn and Dagriel are different than here. But it does always feel a bit like coming home."

Crickets chirped and leaves rustled as we stood gazing at each other. These silences between us were always different, as well. This one had a warm familiarity that made me want to close my eyes and rest in it.

"Why did you rescue Garyth's family?" Aiden asked.

The warmth faded. I shrugged, trying to look nonchalant. "I was there, and Melaena couldn't do it."

"But you insisted on coming along."

I gritted my teeth. "Yes, I see that was unnecessary now. But I simply wanted to ensure they reached safety."

"You are *never* unnecessary."

My heart galloped like that damn horse at the vehemence in his voice, the heat in his nearness.

"Why do you continue to risk yourself for others? Why do you insist on staying in danger?" he whispered.

"Perhaps for the same reason you do," I breathed.

The truth tasted sweet on my tongue, like fresh rain. I might have helped Aiden escape prison so I could get in his good graces, but saving Ruru and helping Garyth's family flee the city were born of a desire to help, not harm.

A desire Aiden praised me for while Renwell punished me.

I swallowed hard. "Should we check the other inns? See if a room opened up?"

He shook his head. "I asked the bartender, and he said it was likely no one would be leaving this late." He slung his pack to the ground. "But he did lend me a tent and a bedroll."

A tent. *A* bedroll. Did he expect us to share?

"I've never spent the night in a tent," I said, my voice uneven.

He smiled up at me as he unpacked. "It's fairly easy. If you know what you're doing. Unless . . . you don't feel safe?"

There seemed to be another question hiding underneath his words. We were truly alone out here, but he wasn't worried about that. He was worried about the danger I might feel between us.

But, despite everything that awaited us back in Aquinon, being with him outside the city was where I felt safest of all.

"This is the only place I want to be right now," I whispered. "With you."

"You stole the very thought from my mind, little thief."

A silence stretched between us again, but this one was like the rope in his hands—taut, rough, burning against the skin.

Thunder rolled above us in the night sky, which was mostly hidden by the canopy of trees.

"I should raise the tent before it rains," he murmured, gazing up at me from his knees.

The look on his face—raw, unrestrained hunger—tied my tongue in knots. It was how he'd looked at me during the heist. And on the Temple roof. Like his control was hanging by a thread.

Mine was fraying faster than my heartbeat.

"I—I have to . . . er . . ." I gestured wildly in the direction of *The Twisted Tail* and bolted from the clearing. I used their lavatory with shaking hands and tried to calm myself down.

But I couldn't. I *wanted* him to look at me at like that. I *wanted* him to steal my control.

I wanted *him*.

By the time I returned, Aiden had the tent up and ready with a thick blanket rolled into it. The white canvas tent was hardly tall enough for me to stand up in, let alone Aiden, and wide enough for two people to lie side by side *very* close together.

My cheeks warmed as I looked up at him.

He brushed his knuckles over my cheek and sighed. "Get some sleep, Kiera. I'll keep watch outside."

"We can share it," I blurted out. "The tent, I mean. You need sleep too, Aiden."

He hesitated, the darkness making it difficult to decipher his expression. But there was no misunderstanding the warm growl in his voice. "Sleep is the last thing I need right now."

Delicate chills coated my skin. "Then I'll keep watch with you."

"Come with me a moment." His fingers twined with mine. "I want to show you something."

I allowed him to lead me away from the tent, stepping over winding roots and between bushes.

Thunder rippled once more, and the air grew warmer, but we walked on.

"Look," Aiden whispered. "Just there."

I glanced to where he pointed. A golden spark floated through some bushes, then died. But then another flared. And another and another.

I gasped. "Fireflies! I read about them in a book once."

"I found them after I set up the tent." Aiden's thumb stroked the back of my hand in that comforting way of his. But the touch felt too small for the spreading ache in my body.

"When I was young, I caught them in my hands," he continued. "I tried to put them in a jar, but Nikella told me to set them free. She said their light would die in captivity."

My heart trembled. I couldn't look away from the dance of light. But our fingers had started a dance of their own, stroking and pulling at each other. His callused finger scraped over the sensitive skin of my palm.

"You make me feel the same way," he said softly. "I'm never

sure if I should reach out and catch you. But that doesn't stop me from wanting to."

My breath stuck in my throat. Wave after wave of thunder rumbled overhead.

His hand cupped my jaw and gently turned my face to meet his. I was exquisitely powerless under those smoldering eyes.

"I crave your light, Kiera," he murmured, "yet I would hunt for you even when you're one with the shadows."

Fireflies wove around us, making this moment feel surreal. But fear still whispered in my mind.

"You don't know me, Aiden. Not truly."

He placed a hand above my pounding heart and guided my hand to feel his as it drummed steadily in his chest. "I know this. I trust this. Everything else is just choices we made in a world where our hearts didn't know each other."

"Aiden . . ." I rasped, pressing myself against him.

He saw me as the woman who risked her life to save others, as he did. He saw the woman I desperately wanted to be, but couldn't be all the time.

Tonight, I wanted more than that. I wanted to be his.

I closed my eyes, feeling the storm of our heartbeats as I felt the storm gather strength around us.

"I feel as though I'm back on the roof of the Temple," I admitted in a ragged whisper. "Arms outstretched, floating on the wind, coming back to you." Lightning flared, and I opened my eyes.

Aiden pressed his forehead against mine as the first raindrop fell. "Then let me catch you, Kiera."

I curled my hand around his neck. "You already did."

I kissed him in a burst of lightning and thunder. He kissed me back in a torrent of sweet rain.

My whole body sang with relief, then tightened with need as his lips clung to mine, capturing, savoring, keeping.

His hand trailed from my heart to my breast—where it lingered for a breath-shattering moment—then found a home on my hip.

He pulled me flush against him with a groan that dove straight through my core. His other hand wrapped itself in my braid and tugged my head backward.

I gasped, and he deepened the kiss, his tongue searching my mouth, his thumb skimming my exposed throat.

Gods, I wanted to drown in this feeling, in this kiss. I wanted it to last forever. It was like we'd never stopped. Like our last kiss had just been hovering in the air between us, waiting for us to find it again. To finish it.

We broke apart, panting. Rain dripped from his hair and jaw.

"No interruptions this time," I said.

A dark chuckle rumbled from his chest, sending a shiver down my spine. "The gods themselves couldn't keep me from you."

He grabbed my hand, and we sprinted through the rain back to the tent. The air had cooled, and the fireflies had disappeared, leaving a blanket of darkness slashed here and there by blades of lightning.

We dove into the tent. I wriggled to the back while Aiden tied the flaps shut. I tried to keep my mucky boots off the blanket.

"Allow me," Aiden murmured.

He knelt and gently pulled off each of my boots, raking off my stockings with them.

"You did this for me once before," I whispered, untying my cloak and tossing it aside.

I could hear the smile in his voice. "I remember. So beautiful, I thought. So proud. So dangerous."

Heat fluttered in my belly.

Two thumps told me he'd cast aside his boots as well. "It's your turn," he said.

My mind blanked as he drew us into a kneeling position in front of each other. "Wh-what?"

His breath warm on my face, he slowly unbuckled my knife brace and slipped it off. He took it and his knives and dumped them in a corner. "Tell me what you were thinking in the bathhouse. When I undressed and sat down behind you."

Every inch of my skin burned, banishing the cold.

I bit my lip and caught the hem of his thin shirt, peeling it over his head. "I thought about how god-like you looked. How much I wanted to touch you. How easy it would be to lift myself up to you with my hands on your thighs."

I pressed my hands into his taut stomach, then trailed them over his rain-slicked chest.

He groaned, his body shuddering. "I could see it in your eyes. The desire. You have no idea how tempted I was to give in."

"Show me," I whispered.

His warm, rough hands slipped under my shirt and started to lift it. When he hesitated, I raised my arms above my head. He tented the wet material on his fingers, dragging his hands along every inch of my skin on his way up.

His hands cupped my breasts, caressing my hardened nipples through the cloth that bound them. I gasped, my head falling back.

Aiden swore and ripped the shirt from me. "I wanted to wrap your naked body around mine." He flicked the hook on my breast band and tore the cloth away. My hands quickly covered my breasts. "I wanted to lick the water from your skin and fill my mouth with your taste."

He kissed my lips hard and fast, bending me backward over the muscled arm he braced against my lower back. His hand fisted in my braid again—something he seemed to like—and tugged on it as he drew his mouth down my jaw, throat, and chest. Sometimes, it was a soft kiss. Others, he slid his tongue along my damp skin. When he reached my breasts, he nudged my hands with his nose, kissing my fingertips as they fell away.

Then he sucked my nipple into his mouth and swirled his tongue over it.

Lightning flashed over the tent and behind my eyes as I arched back with a strangled whimper.

His deep growl of satisfaction echoed in my very blood.

Fucking Four, *this* was what he'd wanted to do weeks ago? Had I known, I might've flung myself out of that water and climbed onto his lap, bathhouse rules be damned.

He held me upright as he kissed one breast, then the other. Heat pulsed from his ravenous mouth to a blazing orb between my legs. I whimpered again when he pressed his hard, thick length to that exact spot.

He pulled away, drawing me upright. Even in the flickering darkness, I could see the raging desire in his eyes.

My aching breasts heaved against his bare chest with every breath. "Why did you stop?"

"I need to taste *all* of you, Kiera." His lips stole a kiss from mine. "If you'll let me."

My heart thundered louder than the storm. "Yes. Please."

He smiled against my mouth. "Gods damn it, those are beautiful words coming from you."

I growled and crushed my lips against his, slipping my tongue between his teeth, showing him I could take what I wanted too.

A chuckle rumbled in his chest as he kissed me back just as savagely, laying me down on the bedroll. I nipped his lower lip, and *that* cut his laughter short. Groaning, he devoured my mouth like a starving man.

All the while, his hands stripped me of my pants and undershorts until I was completely naked beneath him.

He tore himself away from me, kneeling between my legs as his gaze dragged over my body.

"Fucking Four," he breathed. "You will always be the most beautiful thing I've ever seen."

Something deep in my heart shimmered with joy.

"Now," he said, lifting one of my legs over his shoulder. "May I please . . ." He pressed his lips to the inside of my ankle. " . . . *please* . . ." The side of my knee. " . . . soak my tongue in your taste?"

My breath hissed through my teeth as my thighs clenched. "Aiden!"

"Yes, my little thief?"

Desire ripped through me like a hurricane. "Do anything you gods-damned want to! Just do it *now*."

"Mmm," he purred. "I like those words even better."

I opened my mouth to yell at him, plead with him, command him. But then his mouth sank onto my throbbing center. A moan trailed from my throat.

Gods, his mouth was so warm, his tongue so sure and strong as he tasted me.

I shuddered beneath him, but his hands held me steady, gripping my hips and lifting them.

"Aiden," I gasped, my voice thready with need.

He sucked hard, and I cried out, bucking against his mouth. He steadied me. But then his tongue pierced the neediest spot.

Pleasure stabbed through my body. "Yes," I panted. "M-more."

He growled, sounding only too happy to oblige. His tongue attacked me over and over, and I welcomed each thrust. He was wreaking havoc over my world. Ripples of fire enveloped me until my whole body burst in a shower of sparks.

I must have cried out again—perhaps many times—because he covered my mouth with his, wet and warm.

"Sweeter than honey, just like I thought," he murmured.

His favorite. I let out a choked laugh and kissed him.

I'd never felt so wild with desire for someone before. I'd never felt this raw happiness that made me feel vulnerable and powerful in equal turns. I'd also never been so desperate to make someone feel the same way.

"I need you, Aiden," I said between kisses, reaching for his pants and freeing the heavy length within. "Let me make you fall apart. I want—"

"Gods damn it, Kiera," he grunted as he hastily kicked off

402 • LEAH MARA

his pants and undershorts. "The only place I'm falling apart is inside you."

I groaned my approval, wrapping my legs around his waist. He stilled for a moment, his eyes darting to mine with a question.

"I take the tonic," I whispered. "Melaena had some."

His face smoothed, and he bent down to give me a long, lingering kiss. The kind that restoked the fire building inside me once more.

I slowly reached between us and gripped his hand where it fisted his cock. Then I guided it inside me. We both groaned as he pushed all the way in.

Holy Four, *this* would be what destroyed me.

He rocked into my body, lighting it up like the storm outside. Then he began kissing me again. Even if my soul were to pass a thousand Ages, I would never forget the way Aiden kissed me.

My hips rose to meet his fluid movements, and he groaned into my mouth. He abandoned my lips to suck on my neck and bite my earlobe. His greedy hands cupped my breasts and pinched my nipples.

I gasped and twisted my body hard.

His eyes widened as I reversed our positions. But then his lips curled with satisfaction. I pinned his wrists by his head.

"Don't touch me until I tell you to," I whispered in his ear, flicking my tongue against it. "It's my turn."

Goosebumps swept over his skin, and I sat back, grinning in triumph. But my grin faded to something else as I swirled my hips over him. His eyes were hooded with desire. Every muscle in his body was rigid. His fingers curled into fists as if to force himself not to touch me.

I braced myself on his abdomen, enjoying the languid pleasure I wrought between us.

"Gods, yes, Kiera," he groaned. "Dance on me, beautiful."

I nearly lost myself.

"What did you think?" I scraped my nails over his skin. "When you saw me dancing that night?"

He hissed, thrusting up into me. I saw stars.

"I thought"—he thrust again—"of all the treasure I was there to steal that night . . ." And again. "I wanted to steal you instead."

He drove upward once more, and this time, I shattered over him. I cried his name to the sky. I fell back over him, barely catching myself on his shoulders.

"Release me, Kiera," he murmured in my ear. "Command me to touch you."

I nodded, everything in my body feeling soft and warm. "I'm yours, Aiden."

He uttered a fierce cry and swept me up in his arms. We rolled together, and he leaned over me, his beautiful face desperate with desire.

"Say it again," he ordered, his hips flexing faster and faster.

Pleasure ricocheted through me, stealing my breath, my thoughts.

"Please," he begged, even as his body showed no mercy to mine. I relished in the wildness, the power, the *need*. "Please say it again."

I tangled my fingers in his hair, yanking him closer to me.

"I'm yours, Aiden." I gave him a scorching kiss before he ripped away.

"Mine," he growled. "Mine."

The possession in that word, the immediate truth of it, hit me just as he struck a spot deep inside me that sent me flying off the edge into a world of golden light.

Aiden's body shuddered, and his voice shattered over my name, like a wave over sharp rocks.

Then his arms were around me, catching me and guiding me back to him.

Our breaths gasped together. I held him to me, loving his sweaty skin against mine.

He gave me a gentle kiss on my forehead. "And I . . . am all yours. For as long as you wish to keep me, little thief."

CHAPTER 35
KIERA

My CHEST WARMED EVEN AS MY EYES PRICKLED.

Gods, how I wanted to keep him. I wanted everything with him.

Every word of kindness and praise, every look of understanding, every kiss that took my breath away. Everything he did seemed to crack open my heart and fill it with him.

Somehow, I'd always known he would be my undoing.

But right now, I didn't care.

Aiden took a corner of the blanket and cleaned both of us. Then he laid on his side and pulled my body snug against his.

I tucked my face into his shoulder and closed my eyes, breathing him in. I'd never felt such peace.

His fingers traced gentle circles on my skin as the rain pattered on the tent. I let him explore my body, even rolling over for him when he asked.

I tensed when he pressed a kiss between my shoulder blades, on the bed of scars there.

"I owe you for that kiss in the bathhouse," he murmured. "I told you I take back what is mine."

His fingers swept down my spine, eliciting a shiver from me.

I turned back over and prodded the scar on his shoulder, remembering the falcon inked there. I wanted to see it again. "You embraced my scars. I wanted to do the same for you."

His face hardened for a moment, as if an unwelcome memory had passed through his mind. He grasped my fingers and kissed the scars on my knuckles. "Such beautiful, dangerous hands." Then he dipped his head and kissed the thin scar on my chest.

I tunneled my fingers through his hair and lifted his face. "Where will you go?"

I almost wished I hadn't asked, but this might be the only time to ask it.

His brows drew down as he studied my face in the dim light. "You mean, after?"

I nodded, a lump already forming in my throat.

"I honestly don't know," he admitted. "For all my planning, I've never thought much about what comes after. At least not for myself."

He shifted so that he was lying on his side, propped on one elbow. But our fingers played together on my stomach as if we couldn't help touching each other.

"Maz will go home to Dagriel," he continued. "Ruru and Melaena want to stay in the city and pursue a better life under Everett's rule. Nikella will wander the world as she always does."

"But what about you?" I asked again. "Will you go back to Twaryn? Be a healer, perhaps?" I added with a small smile.

His throat bobbed, his eyes darting to mine, then away. "I haven't thought of where I'd go or what I'd do. But rather . . . who I want to be with."

My heart pounded. I licked my lips. "And?"

"What is your plan?" he asked abruptly. "For after?"

"I'm not sure either," I said carefully before giving him the safest answer. "Melaena offered to let me stay on at *The Silk Dancer*."

Aiden rolled onto his back, but his hand never left mine. "I see. I suppose you would be safe there. Especially if Everett rids Rellmira of Weylin's allies."

Worry tightened my belly. Everett was sweet and gentle, in love with his books. The idea of him ousting people like Renwell and Dracles from their positions didn't sound like him. But if he was to be king, he had to.

"Would you be happy there?" Aiden asked, interrupting my thoughts.

I will never know. "I suppose. The dancers are nice. I could earn good money. I like to dance. And Melaena is a kind friend."

Aiden said nothing, just stared at the tent roof.

"But," I said slowly, "I've always wanted to explore a life outside of Aquinon. Before you found me here in the woods, I was contemplating running away through them." I smiled to let him know I was jesting in part.

He smiled back at me. "I would've run away with you." He brushed a strand of hair from my cheek. "More and more of late, I can't seem to run in any direction that does not lead to you."

My heart twirled even as my mind cautioned the impossibility of such a thing. I couldn't leave my brother if he really did become king. And if he didn't, if I thwarted Aiden's plans for assassination, then I would still be chained to Father's side for the sake of my siblings.

That was *if* Father let me live when he found out his godsdamned gold was gone.

There was no way out for me. Even if I desperately wished that were true.

Either Aiden would leave the city defeated—or, gods forbid, dead—or he would be the man who killed my father.

But then another option occurred to me.

"Why don't you want to be king?" I asked. "Why don't you tell people like Garyth who you really are?"

Aiden's jaw tightened. "I'm not fit to be king. The things I've done . . . the lives I've destroyed. No one would want to put a crown on my head if they knew."

I frowned. He'd killed a few Shadow-Wolves and stolen from the High Treasurer. He ran a smuggling business and flouted the law. But I'd seen nothing that measured close to the number of my father's crimes.

"Why?" I whispered

When he didn't answer, I pushed closer to him, wrapping my arms around him and laying my cheek over his heartbeat. "I haven't run from any of your other scars, Aiden. Tell me this one."

He sighed, a long, slow breath I felt empty from his chest.

"I fought in Pravara, during the rebellion," he said in a distant voice.

I continued to breathe steadily and forced my muscles to stay relaxed. But my heart twisted with bitterness.

"I was young and wanted to help the people there who were clearly suffering under the weight of Weylin's taxes and unfair treatment. Parents could barely afford to feed their children with Weylin taking most of their crops and earnings for himself." He swallowed hard. "The farmers started fighting back, refusing to give up their harvests and chasing tax collectors out of town. The conflict escalated on each side, with the Pravarans begging the People's Council to fight for them via the law. But . . . well . . . I'm sure you know how that went."

I certainly did.

All this time, I had been on one side of that rebellion while Aiden had been on the other. Except I'd done little but stand by while the world as I knew it dissolved into chaos.

"I was so angry," Aiden whispered. "Which made me impulsive. I started teaching them to fight like Nikella had taught me. I hunted down weapons along with other like-minded rebels. We were going to make a true battle of it. But then Dracles came."

Pain shook his voice. "He descended on us with over five thousand soldiers, armed and trained. Five thousand against a few thousand farmers—most of whom had never even held a sword. It was a massacre. And I—" His voice broke, and he swallowed again. "I was held for questioning, then thrown in a prison wagon bound for Calimber. Too young and healthy to waste," he finished in a scathing tone.

I was sure there were more details he was leaving out, but

now I understood. Why he didn't want to involve more people than he had to. Why he'd been imprisoned in the mine. And further still, why he hated Father.

His report of the end of the rebellion confirmed what I'd heard. Father had left nothing to chance, spilling every drop of rebel blood he could find. Yet, the most dangerous rebel of all had escaped his fate.

A notion that yielded only gratitude in my traitorous heart.

Aiden lifted my gaze with a finger under my chin. "I owe it to my kingdom, to my people, to my soul to see Rellmira restored. That is why I must do what I've planned. And in a week, it will all be over and decided, one way or another."

My mind stilled. *A week, one way or another.* Gods, that was so soon. Sooner than Father's ultimatum.

Aiden continued, "But for the first time, I have hope. Hope that my heart might not be too scarred for a certain beautiful thief to consider stealing the rest of the pieces she hasn't already taken."

My eyes burned and blurred, and I let out a choked laugh. "It's not really stealing if you're handing that thief the key."

"I suppose not," Aiden said with a smile that warmed my soul. "But she was always good at stealing those, too."

I melded my lips to his, trying to banish every fear and loss I felt at his words, at the idea of having to let him go in seven days. *One way or another.*

He kissed me back like he would never have enough. Like we had more than today, more than a week. Our limbs tangled together and remained that way until we finally fell asleep at dawn.

I never answered him because I couldn't. My heart whispered words that I didn't dare release.

Because we were doomed. We always had been.

We slept for several hours until the heat of midday turned the tent stifling. With soft touches and stolen looks, we dressed and packed up the tent. Twice, I caught him humming a soothing tune deep in his throat. The sound made me smile.

We ate breakfast at *The Twisted Tail* and returned the bartender's tent and bedroll. Aiden paid him extra to get it laundered.

All too soon, we were back on our stolen, well-rested horse, headed for Aquinon with a stream of other travelers.

Aiden walked part of the way so he could show me how to sit properly and use my knees to guide the horse. He said it would be easier with a saddle, but he hadn't had the time to grab one.

I frowned at the shimmering green fields rolling toward the distant sea. "That stuff that Nikella threw on the ground and set on fire. What was it?"

Aiden took a moment to answer. He'd grown more and more reticent as we neared Aquinon. "Something of her own invention. She needed to test it."

"I'm guessing her test was successful," I said, remembering the wall of flame that seemed to rise from nothing.

"We'll see," Aiden said evasively.

I'd already tried to ask him about Nikella and Renwell at breakfast, but he'd quickly shaken off the question, saying it was her business. I doubted she would answer my questions either. And Renwell was one of the last people in Rellmira I wanted to talk to at the moment.

412 • LEAH MARA

We plodded along in silence until we reached the enormous city gate. We'd hidden our knives in a farmer's wagon ahead of us, stuffed in the hay beneath a half-dozen sheep's hooves.

But that wasn't why my heart pounded with fear, screaming at me to run as we passed under the shadow of the gate.

I felt like I was willingly stepping back into a cage, as unprepared for slaughter as the sheep in front of me.

Guards roughly checked each person for weapons and demanded their business. I frowned when I saw Gregor was among them. As much as I didn't want someone to come to harm for helping us, I'd assumed Renwell would've taken everyone for questioning, punishing those who were to blame for our escape.

But other than a few mild burns and scrapes, Gregor looked fine.

Aiden also pulled up short when he saw him. Gregor waved him over. I slid from the horse's back—catching myself this time—and walked the horse to him.

"Where are the other horses?" Gregor demanded in a low voice, his beady eyes flicking to me.

"On their way back," Aiden said smoothly. "Like I said, I'll pay you extra for the inconvenience."

Gregor sneered. "Inconvenience, yeah. Your companion sets fire to the street, and you steal three horses. That's more than an *inconvenience*. I want double," he hissed.

Aiden stiffened. "I'll give you what I can, but you're getting your horses back, Gregor, and the fire was mostly harmless." He leaned closer to the sweaty man, his face rigid with warning. "Don't forget you have just as much to lose as I do if there's talk."

Gregor paled, his eyes skipping to me once more. "Fine, whatever. Move along then." He seized the reins from my hand and hurried away.

Aiden scowled after him.

"Pleasant man," I muttered.

Aiden shook his head. "He has a right to be worried. He's lucky he didn't face a fiercer punishment."

We hurried after the sheep wagon and thrust our hands in the hay to retrieve our weapons. No one paid much attention to us, but I still couldn't shake the feeling that something was wrong. It wasn't like Renwell to leave someone unpunished. Coming back to the city felt too easy.

We'd barely finished re-arming ourselves when Ruru barreled up to us, his eyes wide and his hair sticking up on all ends.

"Have you seen Maz?" were the first words out of his mouth.

Dread pummeled my insides.

"No, what happened?" Aiden asked sharply, pulling both of us off to the side. "Where is he?"

Ruru's face screwed up in anguish. "I don't know! We were practicing at the Temple last night. He said he was going for a drink at *The Weary Traveler*, so I went home. But he wasn't there when I woke up, and it didn't look like he'd slept on his cot. Since none of you were home either, I thought maybe he was with you somewhere. I just checked the taverns, and no one's seen him." He glanced around. "Where's Nikella?"

Aiden growled with frustration. "She'll be back. Did you check the Temple?"

Ruru brightened. "No. Maybe he went back for more training?"

My stomach sank like a stone to the ocean floor. He wouldn't be there either. "Yes, go to the Temple, Ruru," I said roughly. "Aiden, you should meet with Melaena. Tell her what happened." I gave him a pointed look. "And see if Maz might have stopped by to visit one of the dancers. I'll search the taverns and inns again."

Ruru took off without another word. But Aiden hesitated, his green eyes searching my face. "Are you all right? Do you want me to stay with you, and we'll search together?"

I shook my head, forcing a smile. "I'll be fine. The sooner we find him, the sooner we can force him to buy us all some Sunshine for making us worry."

Aiden nodded. He clasped my hand once before he, too, disappeared.

I took a deep breath, my fingers already trembling, then raced toward *The Crescent Moon*.

Please, please, don't be there. Holy Four, let me be wrong. Let there be no mark on the wall.

I skid to a halt in the dirty alley, my panicky gaze searching for his mark. But there was only our old one. Nothing new. No sign that Renwell was calling for me.

I heaved a sigh of relief—

Just as a bag descended over my head, and something hit me hard from behind.

The world went black.

CHAPTER 36
KIERA

PAIN RICOCHETED IN MY SKULL AS I SLOWLY OPENED MY EYES.

Black spots swam over my vision. I tried to focus.

Golden hair. A familiar face.

"Maz," I croaked. "Maz!"

I reached for him, but something held me fast. I groaned, trying to collect my bearings.

I was face down on a long table. Ropes strapped my legs and shoulders to it. I was cold and damp, but clothed. Maz was bare from the waist up, his tattoos on full display.

My eyes rolled, searching the dimly lit room we were in. A cave. Shelves of jars full of murky liquid and floating *things*. A small barrel of fireseeds. Racks of weapons. A familiar whip braided with sharp chunks of glittering sunstone.

Just like his old lair in the palace dungeon.

No. Gods, no.

I whimpered, struggling against the ropes. I stretched my fingers toward Maz's limp ones.

"Wake up, Maz! Please!" A tear dripped down my nose.

"He can't hear you."

I gasped and wrenched my head as far as it would go, peering at the voice near the foot of the table.

Korvin.

He stood with his hands behind his back, watching me with a small smile on his face. His oily black hair hung in strings around his face. Those cold black eyes held no mercy, no emotion other than cruel delight. He, too, was shirtless, sweat dripping from his blood-streaked, muscular torso.

My body started to shake, and his smile grew.

"Don't worry, princess," he said, gesturing to the blood on his skin. "It's not yours. Or his." He nodded to Maz. "Not yet, anyway."

I cowered, wordless, helpless, as he sauntered between the tables that held me and Maz. Korvin passed me, stinking of carnage, and fondled the whip that had torn my back years ago.

"I've learned a lot since I last saw you," he murmured. "So many interesting things I want to try out."

My mind was blank with fear, a stark white canvas, while my heart pumped frantically. More tears slipped silently down my cheeks.

Korvin let the whip's strands fall back, the sunstone chips clinking together. "I've been waiting years to see . . ."

He approached me again, and I thrashed, desperate to get away.

"Hush now," he said, his eyes glittering like the sunstone. "You can't escape."

I pressed my face onto the table and closed my eyes, a

scream building in my chest. His sticky hands scraped over my skin, pulling my shirt collar down, exposing my scarred back.

"Ah, beautiful," he murmured, as if admiring a well-threaded tapestry. "My whip leaves such a unique pattern."

His fingers dug into my scars—the ones he'd lashed into my skin—and I cried out.

"Enough, Korvin!" Renwell's voice rang out.

Korvin jerked his hand away.

Renwell strode into sight, his features livid. "I forbade you from touching her." He glared down at me. "She's *mine*."

Korvin bared his teeth in a skull's grin. He leaned down to whisper in my ear. "Have fun, princess. I know I will."

Horror crashed into me. "What do you mean?" I rasped, my voice like claws against my throat. I glanced at my mentor. "Renwell?"

He slashed my ropes with his sunstone knife. "You're not learning from your own scars, Kiera. Perhaps you'll learn from someone else's."

My heart shattered with terror. "No. No!"

Korvin approached Maz with a thin, curved knife—one I'd seen used in butcher shops. For flaying fish and skinning hides. "I hear these Dags care a great deal for their inked markings," he murmured.

"No!" I screamed. "Stop!"

I tried to hurl myself off the table, but Renwell caught me. I beat him with my fists and kicked him in the shins.

"Gods damn you, Renwell! Don't fucking do it!" I struggled to throw him off me, but he held fast, his fingers like shackles on my arms. Korvin set the knife to Maz's skin, right over the peak of his beloved mountain tattoo—his home—and began to carve.

Maz woke with a shout.

"NO!" I clawed at Renwell's face as he dragged me away. "Let me go! I'll kill you! I'll kill both of you gods-damned lunatics!" My hands sought my knives, but they weren't there.

Maz's shouts turned to screams, and I started to sob. Renwell flung me across the hall and into another room. He slammed the door shut, breathing harshly. A scratch bled beneath his eye.

My eyes darted to the knife in Renwell's belt.

"Try for it," he whispered, stepping closer to me. "I would love—"

I lunged forward, but he spun away and seized my throat, crushing it. I gasped and clawed at his hand as I had at *The Crescent Moon*.

He sneered at me. "Did you really think—"

I made myself go limp, the full weight of my body dropping like a stone. Renwell swore, his grip weakening for a moment.

I twisted his arm and jammed my thumbs into the nerves at his wrist and elbow. He grunted in pain. I tore his hand off me and leapt for the knife once more.

He roared and drove his knee into my stomach. All the air gusted from my chest. He crouched and swept my legs out from under me. His boot heel was on my throat before I could catch a single breath.

In all our training sessions, he'd never shown me how to fight like *that*.

I stared up at the single, flickering brazier hanging from the ceiling, the fight bleeding out of me. Humiliation and despair poured into me like salt on gaping wounds. Maz's screams echoed faintly through the door.

Maz. Gods, why Maz? Why did I have to fail him, too?

Renwell must've seen the defeat in my eyes because he removed his boot. I scraped myself off the floor and huddled against the back wall.

"Why are you doing this?" I whispered.

"I have to free you of your weaknesses somehow," Renwell said. "Even if I have to cut them out."

I wrapped my arms around my shivering body.

He could let Korvin torture Maz for hours. I had no weapons. I would be hard-pressed to fight both him and Korvin. Even if I managed it, we must be in the Den. Dozens of Shadow-Wolves awaited us outside these rooms.

"You care for this Maz, don't you?" Renwell stalked closer to me. "As much as you do for your beloved Aiden?" He spat the name as if he hated even saying it.

I froze.

He swiped the blood from his cheek with a mirthless laugh. "I questioned Asher's servants. They told me about the enormous, golden-haired man they hadn't seen before, acting as a servant." He brought his nose within an inch of mine, breathing heavily on my face. "They also told me of a golden dancer kissing a guard they'd never seen before near the vault. A guard who sounded a lot like my prisoner."

Gods, he knew.

I opened my mouth to deny it, but nothing came out.

"Was it a simple seduction, Kiera?" Renwell whispered, his eyes burning into mine. "Like what you did to that idiot, Asher? Or was it something more?"

I swallowed, unnerved at the feverish rage in his eyes. "I did what I had to. What do you want from me?"

"I want the gods-damned truth. And it seems the only way I'm going to get it is by taking someone you care about and using him to make you talk." He backed away from me, pacing in front of the door. "Which was my original plan for Lord Garyth until *you* helped his family escape."

His words kindled my own anger. "You were going to use an innocent woman and a *little girl* to force Garyth to talk?"

"I told you everyone has a monster locked away inside of them—whether that's a murderer, a coward . . ." He sneered at me. "A *traitor*. All I ever have to do is find the right key." He smiled a little to himself. "Except for Korvin. His monster never had a cage."

Neither does yours, it seems.

"They're gone, Renwell," I said harshly. "I don't know where."

"Just as well. Garyth doesn't need to know that. For all that mumbling coward knows, we have them in a room next to his."

He was still alive then. But for how long?

Save my father if you can, Isabel's voice echoed in my mind.

I wish I could. But I can't even save myself. Or Maz.

"You got what you wanted," I whispered. "Now let me and Maz go."

Renwell laughed again, the sharp sound bouncing off the rock walls. "I haven't gotten what I wanted. Not by half. But I will."

I threw my arms wide. "What else do you want? The gold?"

"I don't care about the gods-damned gold. I want to know how your lover plans to kill your father." A slow, wicked smile curved through Renwell's dark beard. "Surely you know that one by now."

I inhaled sharply. He couldn't possibly know what had transpired between me and Aiden last night. But what else could I tell him? How much *should* I tell him?

I felt like I was falling down the cliff road, crashing against rocks, unable to slow myself down. How many others would fall with me?

"He doesn't tell me everything," I admitted hoarsely. "All I know is I'm to set fire to three buildings in the Old Quarter as a distraction for your dogs. In seven days' time."

Renwell's eyes gleamed. "Finally, something useful. You're the bait. He's the blade." He crossed his arms over his chest. "And how does my sweet little sister fit into this plan? Did she mention me?"

"No," I spat. *But Aiden said you shot her with an arrow before shooting his mother.* "I didn't even know you *had* a sister."

"I didn't either. That is, I didn't know she was still alive," he added, his voice distant. "Dear little Nik. The survivor."

My chest tightened. Did he know what had happened to her? Where those scars came from?

"I've told you everything I know," I said. "Now let me and Maz go."

Renwell's attention snapped back to me, and his arms fell to his sides. "No. You've broken both of my rules. You helped my quarry escape, using resources I'm certain you've kept hidden from me."

The tunnel.

"You also seem to know surprisingly little about this plan," he continued. "Are you lying to me, or are you simply a poor seductress?"

His serpentine stare made my insides crawl. His words threatened to poison my beautiful memory of being with Aiden, but I refused to let them.

"I'm not lying," I said, pouring every ounce of truth I felt into my expression. Like we were back to playing a game of Death and Four in his study, and I was trying to bluff my way to victory. But in this game, defeat most likely meant death.

"I have difficulty believing you're a poor seductress, Kiera," he whispered.

My skin grew cold and clammy, but I lifted my chin. "Believe what you will. Not every man gives up his secrets with a mere kiss."

Renwell's dark eyes dropped to my mouth. "Only the weakest men. And Aiden is not weak. Something we have in common, I suppose." He shook his head. "No. If I let you go back to him, it will be for one purpose only."

He pulled Mother's sunstone knife from his boot and unsheathed it.

I flinched. After our meeting at *The Crescent Moon*, I hated to see it in his possession.

He pointed the knife at me. "Kill Aiden, then come back to me."

CHAPTER 37
KIERA

MY WHOLE BODY REBELLED AT THE THOUGHT. "No."

"No?" Renwell's voice deepened, as dark and heavy as the bottom of the sea. "You dare defy me again?"

"I'm not an assassin."

"Yet you would let Aiden murder your father?"

"*No*, even though my father hasn't extended the same courtesy to *me*," I snarled.

Renwell's grip tightened on my knife. "I would never let him execute you."

"Let him?" I gave a shriek of laughter. "He is the king, Renwell. He can do whatever he pleases. But I will *not* be a murderer like he is."

"Oh, but you are. You just threatened to kill both me and Korvin." His eyes narrowed, and he tilted his head to the side. "And you murdered my Wolf."

I stilled, remembering the Wolf with my knife in his throat. "That was different. He . . . he would've killed me."

"And Aiden wouldn't if he knew who you truly were? The daughter of his worst enemy? I'm assuming he's told you his reasons for wanting your father dead."

The ground seemed to tilt beneath my feet. Aiden wouldn't kill me. But the secrets and lies had grown so great between us . . .

"He wants to put Everett on the throne," I said, grasping at straws. "Which is something I want as well. I could convince him to merely imprison Father and let Everett have the crown. You would support my brother, wouldn't you?"

Renwell's eyes narrowed. "Are you trying to force me to speak treason?"

"It's a simple question," I replied. Something deep in my gut told me his answer was important. "Everett will inherit under whatever circumstance. Will you serve him as you do my father?"

"I will serve whoever sits on the throne." Renwell smirked, running the knife edge over his pale finger. "But that means you must be an *excellent* seductress if you think you can bend your rebel assassin to your will. Do you think he cares for you, Kiera?"

I swallowed hard. We were treading into dangerous waters. One wrong word, and he would drag me beneath the current.

A bead of blood appeared on Renwell's finger. He sucked it clean, but it bubbled back up. "Aiden hasn't trusted you with his entire plan. He hid the gold from you. He's *used* you to get what he wants. What will he do with you when you're worthless to him?"

I will never be worthless to him. He wants me to be with him. The feelings between us aren't a lie.

But he doesn't know who you are. What you've done.

Triumph flared in Renwell's eyes as he watched the doubt cloud mine. "Kill him before he has a chance to kill you." He tilted the knife handle toward me. "You can't protect your family or your kingdom if you're dead. Remember who you're doing this for."

Mother, with this very knife stabbed in her chest. Everett, who will wear the crown better than our father. Delysia, who will finally gain the freedom to love and be happy.

Is Aiden worth more to me than them?

I grasped the knife hilt. Warmth from Renwell's touch bled into my numb fingers.

"You have to release Maz with me," I said, tearing my gaze from the haunting black knife. "It's the only way I can return." *The only way we can escape.*

"Done." Renwell brushed his still-bleeding finger over my cheek, painting me with his blood. "You always did have more wit and will than the rest of your family. We will do extraordinary things together, Kiera."

Something twitched in my chest at the blunt praise, at the thought of getting what I'd wanted for years—his job. But I ignored it. I didn't seize his words and hold them close—as if they were a safety net that he'd finally deigned to toss me as I drowned in a stormy sea of loneliness.

I might have before all of this. Before he put me in a prison cell with Aiden.

But now, it wasn't enough. Now, his words were more like a heavy net he cast about me, letting it drag me to a watery Abyss. Where I was utterly alone.

I seized the sheath from Renwell's grip, shoving the knife into it before stowing it in my boot.

He opened the door and gestured me through it. Didn't want to give his back to me, I supposed.

I hurried back into the dreadfully silent torture chamber. My heart collapsed at the sight of Korvin standing over Maz's body. Blood soaked every inch of Maz's body and hair, making him unrecognizable. Bits of skin and flesh littered the floor at Korvin's boots.

"Get away from him!" I shrieked.

Korvin whipped his head around, knife raised.

I stumbled forward, reaching for my mother's knife, but Renwell grabbed me and jerked me back.

"Release him, Korvin," he said sharply. "We're putting them both in a wagon."

Korvin scowled, gripping his knife tighter. "You're giving him back? But I just started! You made me wait for *hours*—"

"Keep talking and I'll take away the other one as well," Renwell said in a deadly quiet voice.

Korvin roared and threw his knife to the ground. My whole body flinched.

Renwell lifted my knife brace with all my knives from a hook and shoved it in my hands with a warning look. Then he gave a piercing whistle, and three Wolves rushed into the room. "Put these two in a wagon and dump them in the Old Quarter. *Discreetly.*"

Two Wolves approached Maz while a third stalked toward me. I stared numbly at his grotesque Wolf mask, letting him snatch my arm and drag me from the room. I glanced back to make sure they were bringing Maz as well.

Holy Four, don't take his soul yet. Please, please.

The Wolves brought us through the tunnels and tossed us into a wagon waiting in their training yard. They threw a heavy blanket over our bodies. Maz's bloodied, torn skin stuck to my clothing. I checked his pulse with shaking fingers. Weak but there.

Forgive me, Maz. Please don't leave me. Not you too.

I clung to his slippery fingers and buried my sobs deep in my chest.

The ride was brutal. I felt every stone we rolled over as if it were a mountain. When the wagon tilted as we climbed the cliff road, I tried to steady Maz's body, to keep him from pitching against the wagon. But he was heavy. So, so heavy.

After an eternity, we rattled to a stop. The blanket flew off, revealing a darkening sky above an empty alleyway. How long had I been gone? Was Aiden looking for me?

The Wolves yanked me out of the wagon, and I barely caught myself from falling. My knife brace fell to the ground.

"Be careful with him," I rasped, trying to catch Maz as they hauled him out of the wagon like a dead animal.

They ignored me, and I buckled under Maz's weight. They were gone by the time I rolled Maz off me. I buckled my knives to my waist and stumbled around until I figured out where we were. Not far from our apartment.

But I couldn't carry him alone.

I ran to the nearest doors and pounded on them. The few people that answered took one look at my bloodied appearance and slammed the door in my face before I could speak a word.

"Gods damn it!" I screamed at the sky.

But it wasn't their fault. Not really. Just like the woman and her brother. People were afraid. And they had every right to be.

I huddled near Maz, searching for his pulse again. Still there, but gods, I was running out of time. I could try to find Aiden. But he might still be with Melaena. I couldn't leave Maz for that long.

I smoothed Maz's blood-soaked hair away from his slack face. "I'm so sorry," I whispered. Then I carefully hooked my hands in his armpits—where the skin was untouched—and began to heave.

We'd made it ten feet when I heard footsteps pounding toward us. I cradled Maz to the dusty ground and whipped out two of my knives.

"Kiera!"

"Aiden," I choked out, sheathing my knives.

Aiden sprinted toward me, his eyes wide with fear. "What happened? Are you hurt?" He seized my arms, searching for wounds. Then his gaze fell to Maz, and he jerked backward. "Maz?"

I wanted to crumple in his arms and finally release my anguish, but that wouldn't help Maz.

"I—I found him like this. I tried to get him to our rooms. The blood is all his."

Aiden knelt next to him, expertly surveying the damage Korvin had done. "No one followed you?"

I shook my head.

"He must've been tortured and dumped here as a warning —like Asher," he muttered. "Stay with me, brother," he added to Maz. Then he crouched and slid Maz's bloody bulk onto his shoulders.

Maz moaned and twitched.

"Hurry," Aiden said, his face contorted. "This will hurt him. Get his cot ready."

I flew ahead, my boots barely touching the ground. I raced up the steps to our rooms and ripped the blankets off Maz's cot. I poured all the water we had into a basin and collected clean towels and Aiden's medicine kit.

Aiden stumbled into the room, his breathing harsh. "Help me," he gritted out.

Together, we eased Maz onto his stomach on his cot. Aiden tugged off his cloak and washed his hands.

"I don't have enough medicine to stop the bleeding," he said in a rough, strident tone I'd never heard. His eyes never left Maz's back. "Go to Sophie and ask her if she has any silvertree powder left."

"What about the clawberry paste? Can't you—"

"I don't have enough, and it won't work on raw flesh. *Go.*"

I fled.

The next hour was something from one of my nightmares.

Sophie didn't have any more of the powder. But a woman who'd recently suffered an amputated leg had some. I sprinted across the quarter to find the woman and demand her powder. She gave up the half-full tin with wide eyes.

Night fell on my way back. The unmistakable shadows of Wolves lurked down the alleys, so I heaved myself onto the rooftops and kept running. Running, jumping, flying.

My previous theory had been right. Fear mattered little

when I would do anything to reach Maz with the medicine that might save his life.

My body burned and shook with exhaustion by the time I burst back into the apartment. Nikella jumped to her feet, spear in hand, then relaxed when she saw me. She must've just gotten back.

Ruru knelt by Maz's head, holding his hand, while Aiden sponged blood away from Maz's back and spread a thin jelly on his skin.

I shoved past Nikella and thrust the tin of silver powder toward him. "All I could find."

"It will be enough," Aiden said, quickly shaking the powder over Maz's back.

It has to be.

Maz shivered and groaned. Wisps of steam rose from his skin as the powder seemed to crawl into his wounds and harden like a shell, turning iron-gray with his blood.

"What do we do now?" Ruru asked, his cheeks stained with dirt and tears.

Aiden sighed, sitting back. "We wait."

We sat silently around Maz for hours while his body trembled, and he occasionally cried out. At some point, sleep came for me, and I woke in my dark room on my cot—my bloodied shirt gone with a blanket pulled up to my chin.

My heart tripped. *Mother's knife.* But my pants and boots hadn't been touched, the knife hilt digging into my ankle.

Ruru's soft breathing soothed my racing heart. Until I heard something else.

I crawled to the door and pressed my ear against it.

Someone was singing in a deep, beautifully rich voice. That voice reached into my chest and snared my heart.

Aiden.

I released a painful sigh. The melody was slow and mournful, the words gut-wrenching. A song for a fallen warrior. A prayer for his life. A plea to see the light once more, to feel the touch of a loved one again. A promise to never leave a soul alone.

"Brother?"

I smothered a gasp. Maz! He spoke! I reached for the door handle, then hesitated.

"I'm here, Maz," Aiden said.

Maz coughed a bit, then groaned. "Are they . . . are they all gone? My stories." His voice broke, and my heart broke with it. "Tell me the truth."

A heavy silence filled the room.

"Everything on your shoulders is gone," Aiden said softly. "But the rest are intact."

"Gods," Maz croaked. "Gods, I have lost my honor. Again. My family—"

"Will be proud of your sacrifice," Aiden snarled. "Those tattoos were just ink on skin. The stories they represent, the *strength* they bind, is etched into your very soul, Mazkull. No blade can destroy that."

Maz began to weep, a sound that tore something deep inside me. I finally released the tears I'd been holding back. Silently, wretchedly alone in the dark.

Until Aiden sang once more.

CHAPTER 38
AIDEN

Dawn filled the room with crimson light.

My eyes felt filled with sand every time I blinked, but I couldn't sleep. I couldn't leave Maz alone as he suffered through the night. My singing had soothed him somewhat when he woke for a few brief moments. My voice had been rough and out of practice, but strangely, the song had brought me a small measure of peace as well.

Perhaps because I'd been tempted to sing for the first time in a long time earlier that day. But such simple happiness never lasted.

I'd had to carry both Ruru and Kiera to bed as they'd fallen asleep at his side. I'd taken Kiera's stained shirt off her, trying not to think about how different things were the last time I'd removed her clothes merely one night before.

I'd attempted to tug off her boots, but she'd whimpered and held onto them. Perhaps fear still pumped through her body. I'd seen some warriors fall asleep fully clothed and armed between skirmishes, unwilling to be caught off guard.

That same fear had flooded my body like lightning when I saw her dragging Maz. She'd been drenched with blood, her face pale as death. I'd been searching the alleys for hours when I couldn't find her among the taverns. I'd started to think that both she and Maz were lost to me.

My business with Melaena had been short. I'd told her we'd got Garyth's family out safely, and she told me that Renwell had burst in with his Wolves. He'd searched every room but found nothing before seeming to realize his quarry must be headed for the city gate.

She'd stashed the papers that Helene had given her, and I told her to keep them. She would have to be one of Everett's best allies and closest resources once his father was dead.

Then I'd asked her about Maz, and she said he'd never shown up there either.

Gods, if I hadn't stumbled on Kiera and Maz when I did . . . If Kiera hadn't found enough silvertree powder . . . If I hadn't paid Skelly a year's wages to find some in the secret markets of Eloren . . .

I stared at the hard gray shell over Maz's shoulders. The powder had cauterized his wounds and would protect his raw skin until it began to scab. Then I would have to dampen it to get it to dissolve. But it could take days, and we only had a week left here.

The door opened, and Nikella slipped inside with her walking stick. She never went anywhere without it or the spear it usually carried.

"How is he?" she whispered, nodding to Maz.

"The same," I said, scraping my palms over the stubble on my cheeks and jaw. "He woke for a few moments last night. He was coherent enough to understand what happened."

Nikella sat next to me on my cot, which I'd dragged next to Maz's. "I imagine he didn't take it well."

"No." I remembered his anguished face when I'd told him of the damage. Korvin's knife had cut away something much deeper than skin. "But he'll rally. He always does."

Nikella rested her hand on my shoulder, the most affection she usually showed. "We should discuss your plan."

"It hasn't changed."

"Perhaps it should."

I grunted, raking my hands through my hair. "The loss of Maz as a fighter and leader is great, yes. But we can still carry on."

Nikella pinned me with her usual stare. "You've also lost Garyth and Asher. Renwell is suspicious of Melaena and seems to be drawing lines between all of us, using your heist. I've moved out of the Temple for Librius's sake, but how long before he discovers where we are and what we're doing?"

"I've been playing this game with him for years, Nikella, and he still hasn't caught me."

Her hand fell away from me. "I played games with him for much longer than you have. You can't out-manipulate him."

"Then I'll kill him too," I snarled. "He deserves it for this. For everything else."

Nikella silently looked at me, unperturbed that I'd just threatened to kill her brother.

"I can't stop now," I said, a needle of desperation piercing my anger. "We're so close. I thought I'd never have this chance again, but I do. And nothing will stop me from taking it."

"Is it worth your life? His?" She nodded to Maz. Then at the door to the next room. "Theirs?"

My heart wrenched, trying to block the fear that battered it. "I won't lose them. I can keep them safe."

We sat in silence, letting the frailty of my promise tremble in the morning light.

I could lose them. I'd lost many before. But my courage couldn't bear that truth just now.

Don't mourn what you haven't yet lost.

That was what Maz had told me when it was Kiera's unconscious body I was staring down at.

But they were still here. They were still alive, and I would keep them that way. By killing Weylin—and Renwell, if I stumbled across the rat.

"Get some sleep," Nikella finally said. "I'll watch him."

I didn't argue with her. She folded her cloak on the floor for a cushion while I pushed my cot away from Maz's and collapsed onto it.

Sleep overwhelmed me, blessedly empty darkness.

When I woke, sweaty in the afternoon light, Nikella looked as though she hadn't moved a muscle. But Kiera and Ruru were awake, eating cheese and fruit with some bread. Kiera clutched a brown bottle of some liquid in her lap.

Her eyes met mine immediately, and some of the tension melted from my body. I knew that brief, blazing happiness I'd found with her in that tent in the woods wouldn't last. But, gods damn it, I wanted to find it again.

Soon.

Despite the sleep she must've finally gotten, her face was still pale and drawn. A frown pinched my lips, and she looked away.

Perhaps she wasn't so eager to revisit our time in the woods.

The tension seeped back into my muscles, and I rose wearily from my cot. I checked Maz's back, pleased that no blood had leaked through, and the silvertree casing hadn't cracked. Someone had already replaced the dirty water and towels from last night.

I was about to leave for a wash myself when Maz groaned and shifted. I flew back to his side. "Don't move too much, Maz."

"Fucking Four," he mumbled into his pillow. "It itches like a thousand mosquito bites."

A grin strained my tired face. "Glad to hear it, brother. Means it's working. Can you drink? Eat? You need to get your strength back up."

Maz grunted, which I took to mean yes.

Kiera and Ruru rushed over with the remnants of their lunch. They fed him bits of it while Nikella quietly excused herself to ask Sophie for more.

Kiera flashed the bottle she'd been holding at him. "Sunshine, Maz," she said in a brittle voice. "You said mead could cure anything, right?"

He huffed a laugh, then grimaced in pain. "I sure did, lovely. Gods, I love you."

I stiffened, but she smiled, tipping the bottle to his lips.

Ruru fed him a chunk of bread, and Maz smiled at him. "I love you too, Ruru."

Then he looked past them to me, his eyes warming with gratitude. "And you, brother."

A lump swelled in my throat. "Look at you, not even drunk yet, and proclaiming love for everyone in the room."

"Nearly dying makes a man think. Tell Nikella I love her too when she gets back. No, wait, don't. I want to see her face when I say it."

I shook my head with a chuckle. Fierce hope blistered a hole in my chest. If he was back to talking like his usual self, that was a good sign there might not be lasting damage. But I also knew that he joked to hide his pain. And judging by the creases near his eyes, he was in a lot of it.

I poured him a cup of water and nudged it into Kiera's other hand. "Give him some of this, too."

She gazed up at me, a storm of emotions brewing in those lovely eyes. Our fingers brushed together, and she bit her lip before quickly bringing the cup to Maz. A little water sloshed over the rim.

He looked between the two of us, a mischievous look erasing some of the pain there. "I will also need a story later," he said pointedly. "The other half of the cure, you know."

I rolled my eyes at him as he slurped his water.

But the exasperation and joy at his consciousness drained away as the harsher realities settled back in. I needed to ask him what happened. Later, when we were alone. I let Kiera and Ruru have their moments of happiness with him.

After I'd sent them off to Sophie to help her with the laundry and to take baths themselves, I sat next to Maz. Nikella had gone back to the Temple to check on Librius, leaving just the two of us.

Some of his pain had eased with food and water—and Kiera's Sunshine—but he was starting to fade once more.

"You love her, don't you," he said between labored breaths. "Kiera. I saw it on your face when I told her."

My fists clenched. "That's not what we need to talk about."

"I disagree."

"Of course you do."

He groaned. "Just admit it, you stubborn ass."

"It's not important right now."

"Oh, it matters *much* more than you think it does."

I glared at him.

"Do you?" he prodded.

My heart pounded faster and faster, as if trying to outrun the truth. But it couldn't. *I* couldn't. It filled every inch of my skin, every drop of my blood, every breath in my body.

"Yes," I said quietly. "I do."

Maz gave me a sad smile. "Yes. You do. I need you to hold onto that—hold onto *her*—for the battle to come. I need someone you love watching your back since I won't be there to do it. Someone who loves you, too."

I swallowed against the sharp knot in my throat. "Nikella will be watching my back."

"You need Kiera too," Maz insisted. "I feel it"—his fingers tapped his side near his stomach—"in here."

I chuckled dryly. "And your gut's never been wrong."

"Never." He smirked. "Except maybe about Lorel. I think she really did know that Bella was in my tent when she set it on fire."

I laughed with my whole chest, and Maz joined me in a wheezing way.

"I appreciate your concern, brother," I said, "but we need to talk about what happened. Tell me everything."

Maz grimaced and closed his eyes. "There's not much to tell. I went for a drink at *The Weary Traveler*, but got jumped from behind before I reached it. I woke up strapped to a table with that bloody crow of a man, *Renwell*, standing over me."

My jaw flexed. If I ever got a hold of that gods-damned murderer . . .

"He asked me where the gold was. Somehow, he knew it was me at the heist."

"One of the servants must've talked."

"I told him I knew nothing and that perhaps he could find it up his own ass—"

"Maz," I groaned.

"What? He just smiled at me like he knew something I didn't. Then he asked about Nikella. I don't know how he found out about her, but I told him demons from the Abyss didn't have sisters."

I pinched the bridge of my nose. "Fucking Four, Maz, is that when Korvin started slicing you?"

Maz grew solemn. "No. That came later. He must've drugged me because the next thing I knew, that maniac was carving away my life. I thought I heard a woman screaming. But I didn't see anyone else."

I grimaced. Renwell might have more prisoners in his Den. Garyth was probably there, if he was still alive.

Maz groaned. I rose and squeezed a drop of dreamdew from one of his darts into his water cup. I tipped the cup into his mouth, making him drink the whole thing.

"Since you sent away my lovely, you'll have to tell me the

story of what I missed," he said, slurring, his eyelids already drooping.

I told him of our escape with Garyth's family. He was snoring before I even spoke of *The Twisted Tail.*

"Dream well, Maz," I whispered.

I sat back and waited for the others to return. The truth he'd gotten me to admit swirled around me like a restless wind.

As much as Maz wished to protect me, I still couldn't let Kiera in on the rest of my plan. I couldn't put her in worse danger by dragging her back to the palace to face the man she was running from. And I didn't want her to try to convince me otherwise if she knew how I felt about her.

That I did love her. That she'd stolen bits of my shattered heart since the moment she freed me from my chains.

So, I would ready my weapons. I would put Maz on the ship when it arrived.

And I would rid Rellmira of its greatest threat before I found Kiera again and begged her to take the rest of my heart in exchange for hers.

CHAPTER 39
KIERA

TOMORROW.

Everything ended tomorrow. For better or for worse. Even though I wasn't sure if there was a "better" for me.

The last six days had passed in a haze. Most of it waiting by Maz's side—wishing him to wake up, telling him silly stories when he did, feeding him when he was hungry. All while trying not to let my guilt eat me alive from the inside.

Aiden eventually dissolved the clay shell from Maz's back, leaving a mess of raw skin that was already scabbing and turning pink rather than red. But his tattoos were gone. Aiden had heavily wrapped him in bandages, but Maz didn't speak a word that day.

Occasionally, Ruru sat with us, passing on gossip and sticky bread and telling Maz about his training. He cajoled me into running the rooftops with him a few times, but my heart wasn't in it. My heart was under the knife in my boot.

Mother's knife seemed to grow heavier and sharper the closer we came to the end of Aiden's plan.

We hadn't spoken much since the night he found me with Maz. We both seemed to be avoiding each other. I knew my reasons, but what were his?

He didn't seem to suspect me or my story of "finding" Maz in the alley. He didn't seem angry with me. Every so often, I caught him looking at me with a strange look on his face. As if his gaze was the only way he could reach me because there was something insurmountable between us. Something that he planned to remove.

But he didn't know I'd been tasked to remove *him*—a crime I already knew I couldn't commit. But no choice was so simple anymore. What would happen to him if I didn't obey Renwell? What would Renwell and my father do to everyone I'd grown to care about when I didn't assassinate their enemy?

Aiden might be their enemy, but with every day that passed, it became clear he was *not* Rellmira's enemy.

Yet, ever since Renwell released us, I'd been waiting for another repercussion of some kind, especially since I hadn't acted on his last order. But none came. And the silence was suffocating.

Which was why I'd come to see Melaena one last time. She didn't know it was goodbye, but from the somber mood in the sitting room, she could feel it as I did.

"Did you get the food baskets I sent for all of you?" she asked, spinning a silver bracelet around and around her slender wrist.

"Yes," I said, trying to smile for her benefit. "I think Maz appreciated the love notes from the dancers the most. But we all loved the food, especially the cinnamon ham."

"I wish I could've done more," she whispered, her beautiful eyes filling with tears. "I wanted to come visit, but . . . but I think Renwell is still watching me."

My smile died. No words of comfort came because it was likely true, and there was nothing I could do about it. A few of the dancers had left after Renwell's invasion of the club. Shows had been cancelled. Melaena had been skittish since the moment I'd shown up.

Melaena buried her face into her hands. "Gods, Kiera. It feels like it did before. During the rebellion. The hunts. The executions. The waiting, the gods-damned waiting, to see where—*who*—Weylin will strike next."

"I've always hated waiting."

"Yes, I suppose you would have a lot of experience with that. Being a personal guard and all."

I nearly laughed, taking a sip of the red wine she'd offered me. "Yes. That."

Her eyes narrowed. "You would've had a different angle of that dark time, though. What was it like in the palace during the rebellion?"

I slowly swirled the crimson liquid in the crystal glass. Maz's blood splashed over my memory, and I set the glass down. "Much like what you experienced, I'm guessing. Servants disappeared overnight. No one wanted to speak or look each other in the eye anymore. Fear so thick you could ball it up and toss it back and forth."

My eyes caught on the tapestry covering the tunnel, the

one Renwell probably guessed was here now. Yet he hadn't come looking for it.

A question had stuck in my mind since the night I'd helped Helene and Isabel escape. And now that this whole charade was almost over, what did I have to lose by asking it?

"The tunnel," I began, the words thick in my throat. "You said your family used it to help rebel supporters flee Aquinon seven years ago."

Melaena nodded.

I took a deep breath. "Why didn't the Mendacis family use it? You must've known them."

She blinked, her expression vacillating between confusion, shock, then sad understanding. "It was you, wasn't it?" she asked softly. "The girl Julian was secretly seeing."

Hearing his name struck me like a fist to my chest. I didn't confirm, averting my eyes to stare at the tapestry.

"He never told anyone your name, only that he was in love with a girl and didn't want to leave her behind."

Yet I always seem to be the one left behind. My face crumpled with pain, despite my best efforts.

Melaena slid over to my couch and pulled my head to rest on her shoulder as she rubbed my arms. "No wonder he didn't want to tell us who you were. A royal servant and the son of a rebel." She shook her head, her long beaded earrings brushing over my cheek.

No. A princess and a traitor. That's how Father put it before ordering the Mendacis family execution.

"My father tried many times to convince his father to leave," Melaena said, her voice shaky. "But Julian's father wouldn't listen. Insisted it was his gods-given duty to stand up to the crown for the people's sake. He asked us to take his family—his wife, Julian, and the two girls. But . . . they refused. Renwell rounded them up two days later."

"I know the rest," I said quickly, not wanting to relive it.

Melaena's throat bobbed. "Julian was my friend. A year younger than me, but we learned from the same Teachers, went to the same parties, knew the same people."

A worm of jealousy burrowed into my gut. She had more time with him. She hadn't had to hide her friendship with him. I'd met Julian at one of the few open gatherings we'd had at the palace before Father closed it off to everyone but his most trusted officials and nobles.

But Julian had loved me. He'd wanted to stay for me. He'd wanted to stand up to Father the way his father did.

The last time we spoke, I'd told him he was a fool, that he should run. He refused.

But now, perhaps, I was the fool. Caring for Aiden and the others the way I did. My love for Julian was the one of the reasons he was killed. I didn't want to do the same to Aiden or anyone else.

I leaned away from Melaena. "I need to stop Aiden," I whispered. "Tell me how to do it."

Her mouth dropped open, a tear still trickling down her cheek. "What do you mean, Kiera? Why would you want to stop him?"

I growled with impatience, shooting to my feet and pacing the room. "I don't want to stop Everett becoming king. I want to keep Aiden from getting killed." I aimed a heavy glance at her. "Like Julian."

Her face cleared, and she gave me a sympathetic smile. "Because you love him."

I twitched away from the word. I wasn't sure what I felt. There were too many knives—too many lies and secrets—embedded in my feelings.

She sighed. "I don't think you *can* stop him. Aiden . . . well, you've seen him, heard him. He'd give his life for the sake of Rellmira."

"That's exactly what I'm trying to keep from happening!"

She threw up her hands. "And I'm saying he has no fear for his life at this point. The number of setbacks he's overcome, everything at stake, the vengeance that's been haunting him for years . . . He won't stop. Maybe not even for you."

I froze. *Not for his life. Not even if I asked.*

But what about everyone else's lives?

Renwell knew what day Aiden planned to attack, thanks to me. He could set up any number of precautions. If Aiden knew his plan was at risk, would he stop it? Retreat to fight another day?

Dread punched me low in the stomach. The only way to convince Aiden his plan was in jeopardy was to tell him what I'd done. Who I was.

And pray that he wouldn't kill me like Renwell thought he would.

Heart in my throat, I drew Melaena up and hugged her fiercely, her familiar scent reminding me of the joy I'd found at her club, of Mother's words, of Delysia's room.

Of things I'd lost.

"Thank you," I said tightly, "for the home I never knew I

needed and the friendship I always wanted. I hope I'm worthy of it after tomorrow."

"Kiera—" Brow wrinkled, Melaena tried to keep hold of me, but I shook her off.

"Keep the club closed tomorrow. Don't go anywhere until one of us comes for you."

Fear brightened Melaena's eyes. "Kiera, don't do anything reckless."

I stabbed the button for the tunnel with my finger and gave her a sad smile over my shoulder. "No, I'm about to do something right." I shut the door between us and ran.

By the time I reached the apartment, it was a mess of activity. A wagon waited outside, attached to a pair of horses. The pyrist, Floren, sat on the driver's seat.

The warmth fled my body. "You!" I gasped. My gaze flew to the open door of the apartment. "Gods, no. Maz, is he . . . Are you—"

Floren shook his head, his sweaty scalp gleaming in the dying light. "I'm here to pick up a live one for the harbor. For passage on a ship, not for burial," he clarified.

A ship? I raced inside.

Nikella and Aiden were transporting Maz from his cot to a stretcher. Ruru sat at the table, holding Maz's axe and whistler, sniffling quietly.

"Where are you taking him?" I demanded.

"Ship," Aiden grunted, settling Maz on the stretcher.

Maz faced me with a hopeful smile. His beard has grown longer, and his eyes had gotten back a bit of their sparkle. "I'm going home, lovely."

"Home? To Dagriel?"

"Yes. I won't be going back as a triumphant warrior, but at least I'll be home. With my family."

I grabbed his hand and squeezed it. "Don't be ridiculous. You're every inch the triumphant warrior. Think of all the stories you'll regale the women of Dagriel with."

He chuckled.

Nikella and Aiden carried him out of the apartment and laid him in the wagon. Ruru and I followed.

Ruru nestled his axe next to him and moved to add his whistler, but Maz stopped him. "Keep it, little brother. Then bring it back to me one day when you're a warrior, too."

Ruru clutched it to his chest as if it were Maz's first-born. "I will, Maz. I won't let you down."

"Impossible." Maz's gaze shifted to me from his awkward position. "A moment, Kiera?"

The other three shuffled a few feet away to give us some privacy.

"What is it?" I asked, tears already gathering like rain in a cloud.

"Protect him," he said simply. "Protect all of them. He needs you. *I* need you to take my place. Promise me."

"I'll try, Maz. I swear it."

Maz smiled peacefully. "Then say yes when he asks you to come with him after tomorrow. I want to see you again, Kiera."

Tears leaked from my eyes, and I told my last, most painful lie. "Y-you will. You'll show me all of Dagriel. I want to see everything—the snow, the mountains, and those strange animals you tell stories about."

"And the people," Maz added.

"Especially the people."

He winked at me, and I managed to smile through my tears before I backed away.

Nikella climbed up next to Floren, who snapped the reins and rode away with Maz. Ruru headed back inside, his head hanging low. I wiped my cheeks dry as Aiden stepped closer to me, his hand brushing mine.

"You're not going with him?" I asked, not brave enough to look into his eyes.

"I'll see him soon."

"Because you'll be getting on the ship too?"

He didn't answer. Instead, he hooked my chin with his finger and turned my face until my gaze landed on his.

"My fate is not yet decided, little thief. But tonight is all ours, if we wish it."

My heart turned to stone. I couldn't be with him like this. I had to talk to him before I lost myself to the temptation that reached for me behind his intense eyes.

Gods, how easy it would be to run away. To hide in this new, vibrant, intoxicating *thing* between us. But I had to stop running away and hiding. I had to face my demons.

"Can we talk?" I asked. "Once Ruru is asleep?"

Aiden's brows lowered, but he nodded. He released me, and we joined Ruru in the apartment. Ruru had grabbed some potato soup from Sophie, and for dessert, we ate leftover chocolate-covered raspberries from Melaena.

I could barely eat, my nerves twisted into such tight knots I wanted to vomit.

My courage flagged every time I met Aiden's warm green eyes. But then I remembered my promise to Maz. I remembered Melaena saying he wouldn't stop for himself.

This is the only way. You have to tell the truth.

All too soon, Ruru rose and reverently placed Maz's whistler on a shelf by the door. Then he traipsed off to bed.

"Maz passed on his love of weaponry, I think," Aiden said, shaking his head with a small smile.

I nodded, drumming my fingers on the table and glancing out into the night. Gods damn it, I'd almost rather face down a pack of Wolves than the truth.

Aiden laid his hand over my dancing fingers. "What is it, Kiera? You can tell me anything."

My eyes darted to Maz's empty cot, then to the door behind which Ruru slept.

Do it. Make him understand your intention was good. That you simply wanted to protect your family. And now you want to protect your new one as well.

I met Aiden's steady, earnest, caring gaze and broke.

"Don't attack tomorrow night," I whispered.

He stiffened. "What are you talking about? Why not?"

Gods, I couldn't breathe. "J-just don't. It's not safe. He knows. Renwell knows you're attacking tomorrow."

Aiden leapt from his chair, letting it fall with a crash. I rose as well, stumbling back toward the door. In case I needed to flee.

"What in the deep, dark, wandering hell do you mean, Kiera?" he rasped.

My whole body shook. I slowly reached into my boot. "I'm not who I said I was," I whispered, the words scratching past my tightened throat. I withdrew Mother's knife from its sheath in my boot. "I was sent to—"

He seized my wrist in a grip so hard I cried out. All the blood had drained from his face, horror flooding his eyes.

"Where did you get that knife?" he hissed.

"What?" I twisted in his grasp, but he didn't budge, his gaze fastened to the gold-hilted sunstone knife. "I'm trying to tell you. Why are you—"

"*Tell me where, Kiera!*" he roared.

I gasped. "It's my mother's."

He flung my wrist away from him as if I'd stabbed him. He staggered backward, looking me up and down as if he'd never seen me before. "Your—your mother."

I stood there, trembling, confused. Until it hit me. The only possible way he could recognize this knife. The knife Mother had carried on her only when she went to visit the Temple. As she did the night she was murdered.

My world shattered.

"*You,*" I gasped. "*You* killed my mother."

Aiden flinched, then his face steeled with rage. "And you're Weylin's gods-damned daughter! A spy sent to kill me!"

"*You murdered my mother, you bastard!*"

I lunged at him with the knife just as the door exploded open behind me. I started to pivot just as Aiden roared, "Nikella! NO!"

Pain stabbed through my neck.

I staggered, my vision blurring.

My fingers reached toward the pain. Feathers. A dart. Gods, which one?

I fell to my knees. Mother's knife fell with me.

Mother. Murdered by the man I thought I . . .

Someone cradled me to the ground as consciousness fled my mind as if it were a sinking ship. I fell to the darkest depths.

May the gods bring my soul to yours, Mother. I can't lose you again.

CHAPTER 40
KIERA

No one waited for me on the other side of the Abyss.

Only demons wearing the faces of my failures ready to drag me into the Longest Night.

CHAPTER 41

AIDEN

"FUCKING FOUR, NIKELLA," I SNARLED, PLUCKING THE GREEN-feathered dart from Kiera's neck. "You could've killed her."

"Don't be a fool," Nikella said coldly. She put the empty whistler back on its shelf. "I saw Ruru load it with a sleeping dart when Maz was telling him how to clean it earlier." Her eyes narrowed. "You let your heart rule your head too much, Aiden."

Words I'd heard from her throughout most of my years.

Ruru burst out of his room, holding one of the little knives Kiera had given him. When he saw her limp on the floor and the dart in my hand, his eyes widened. "What did you do?" he cried, rushing forward.

I caught him around the chest. "Easy, Ruru. You don't understand what's going on."

"Do you, Aiden?" Nikella shook her head.

I stared at Kiera—was that even her name? The princesses

were named Emilia and Delysia. The knife drew my eyes like a crack in a mirror.

Memories assaulted me, and I squeezed my eyes shut, trying to fight them off. I couldn't succumb to them now.

You killed my mother.

Gods, it couldn't be true. But how else would she have Brielle's knife? *When* had Kiera gotten it? I'd never seen her with it before, and I would've noticed by now.

So many questions.

This didn't feel real.

Nikella pulled a rope coil from the wall. "Bind her first. Then we talk."

I almost stopped her, my first instinct to protect Kiera dying under the weight of her lies.

Why? Why did you lie to me? Why did you betray me?

The pain hit me all at once, and I shoved away from her as Nikella bound her wrists and legs.

Ruru watched with an open mouth, until he spotted the knife too and reached for it.

I kicked it away. "Don't touch it!" I snapped.

He stared at me.

I sighed, rubbing my hands over my numb face. "Have you ever seen that knife before?"

"Only her throwing knives," he said, nodding to where Nikella was unbuckling Kiera's knife brace.

Nikella dragged the unconscious Kiera into her room. She came back out with the rest of Ruru's knives and shut the door. She handed the knives to Ruru. "Keep these close."

"Gods damn it," I muttered. "Why did you put her to sleep,

Nikella? Now I can't ask her any of the thousand questions I have."

Nikella sat in the chair Kiera had vacated moments ago. "I heard you two yelling from the bottom of the stairs. I heard what she said." She leveled me with an eerily calm look. "She was going to kill you, Aiden."

"No," I said, righting my chair and sitting in it. Ruru retreated to a far corner of the room and sat, watching us. "She was angry and in shock. I had no idea . . ."

"Who she was?" Nikella bit out.

I glared at her. "I told you how we met, the story she gave me. That must've been a lie as well."

"Was she sent by Renwell?"

My heart was falling, crashing, breaking all over again. This was what happened when I trusted. She'd stabbed me in the back as surely as *her* father had stabbed mine.

"I don't know," I whispered, staring at my hands. Murderous hands. "Probably. She said Renwell knew I was attacking tomorrow night. She told me not to."

"She must've informed him," Nikella said grimly. "My gods-damned brother and his manipulations."

How had Kiera, a *princess*, become entangled with that monster?

You forget you're a monster, too.

I'm not.

I'm not.

Nikella steepled her fingers and stared at me over them. "What did she know about your plan, Aiden? What could she have told him?"

It struck me then how much trust I'd given her so quickly.

Telling her my secrets about Pravara and the mine. Telling her about my past. She must've picked up a few tricks of manipulation from her master.

"Gods," I breathed. "She really was eavesdropping that day."

"What day?"

I shook my head. "It doesn't matter. She knows my past. She knows my identity. As for the plan . . . she only knew her part. And yours," I said, nodding to Ruru.

Ruru rubbed his only thumb over his knife, his face wrinkled with confusion and exhaustion. "But I haven't run into any trouble on my routes. Everything is still set up and ready to go. Why would she train as hard as she did to protect me if she was planning to betray us? Why would she save me from the Wolves?"

"To earn our trust," I said bitterly. "A gamble that clearly paid off."

Ruru scrambled to his feet. "But she admitted what she'd done, didn't she? Warned you about tomorrow? Why would she do that if she didn't . . . if she didn't care?"

My heart broke a little more at the crestfallen look on Ruru's face. And gods, what would Maz think? I'd never wished so hard in all my life for Maz to have been right.

But he'd been wrong about Kiera.

We all had.

"That's not what matters now," Nikella told Ruru before she looked back at me. "Did she know about the Den? The warriors? The other bombs?"

I shook my head. "I didn't tell her. I didn't want her to try to come along." Or maybe, deep down, I still hadn't trusted her.

"But she could've told him about Librius and the Temple," Nikella said. "She knows about Maz's ship."

"You've been to the Temple. Librius is safe. And she would never hurt Maz."

"You don't know that."

I slammed my fists on the table, making Ruru jump. "Gods damn it, Nikella! I know I made a mistake trusting her. I know she's the enemy, but all I care about is killing my *true* enemy. And I am not letting a little traitor get in my way."

Nikella's eyes darkened. The shadows from the lamp made her scar look deeper than ever. "You could be leading us into a trap."

"Renwell doesn't know everything. He *can't* unless either of you, Maz, Librius, or Melaena also betrayed me."

Ruru laid his hand on my arm, his brown eyes sincere but still fearful. "Never, Aiden. I swear on my family's souls."

Nikella simply stared at me. The tiniest wisp of pity flickered in her eyes. She knew how deeply this betrayal cut. She knew everything I'd been through over the years. She knew I trusted her.

But gods, I needed to unleash the agony stabbing its way through my body. It was devouring every bit of light I had left.

I shoved back in my chair and stood up. My hands shook, and I curled them into fists. "Keep her asleep. Don't let her out." I jabbed my finger at Ruru. "Don't go near her. I don't want her exploiting you."

"Where are you going?" Nikella asked, her fingers curling around her staff.

"To see how deeply I was betrayed," I growled. "Stay here."

Then I fled. I ran faster than I ever had, desperate to get

away from her and her lying mouth. Her beautiful, lying mouth. *Gods.*

Climbing to the rooftops, I pushed myself harder, not caring for the pain that blossomed every time I landed roughly.

I raced for the Temple, memories rising from their graves, unwilling to stay buried. But this time, they shimmered against newer, livelier memories. Of Kiera. Of our time on the roof.

I checked on Librius. Safe and well. I didn't tell him why I asked.

Then I pushed on to Melaena's, my lungs burning, excising the demons that writhed beneath my skin.

I charged into her room as I had the night I'd been searching for Kiera. The night of the heist. Gods, had she told Renwell about that too? But then why had he let us go through with it?

Too many questions. Too many knots to unravel.

Melaena shrieked when I barged into her room, and guilt pinched me when I remembered her fear over the last intrusion she experienced.

But I was nearly feverish with desperation.

I demanded to know if she'd ever told Kiera about my plan, the little Melaena knew about it. And she said no.

"What's going on, Aiden?" she gasped, clutching her dressing robe around her. "I thought she was trying to save your life. She loves you!"

"No, she doesn't!" I roared. I shoved my hands through my wild hair. "It was a lie. It was all a lie. She betrayed me."

I rushed out the door with Melaena calling my name. I

hurried back through the tunnel, hardly noticing the crushing fear I usually felt in dark, cramped spaces.

On a whim, I quickly inventoried all the items in the warehouse—the ones Kiera had been so interested in—but they all seemed to be there.

"What was your game, little thief?" I muttered, slamming the door and locking it behind me. "And did you win?"

I ran down the street leading to the main road, turned a corner, and barreled into two Shadow-Wolves. That *thing* that had been snapping and snarling in my chest, pushing against the bars of its cage since Kiera had leapt at me with her mother's knife, suddenly broke free.

I whipped out my knives and slashed at the Wolves. They ducked and evaded, unsheathing their own knives. That damned black sunstone.

I roared again, with rage, with heartbreak, and attacked again and again. They kicked me, adding more pain on the outside to equal the inside.

I stabbed one in the chest, but the other kicked the back of my knee. I fell. But I blocked his downward strike and slammed my knife into his gut. I shoved his body off my blade. I didn't even stop to see if they lived or died. I simply moved on, covered in blood and bruises.

Limping my way down the cliff road, I spied *Mynastra's Wings* still in the harbor. That was a good sign. I got close enough to the ship to ensure all was well before turning around. I couldn't face Maz. Not like this. Not with Kiera's betrayal. It would cut deeper than Korvin's knife had.

I froze, placing a bloody hand on a wall to steady myself. Gods, had she known about that too? Was that her fault?

No, she'd been devastated by what happened. Or was it guilt?

Fucking Four, I was going mad.

I stumbled to the Docks room I rented. The first one I'd brought her to after our escape. I collapsed into one of the hammocks, closing my eyes, reliving every moment with her. Searching for more lies. Had she felt anything for me? Or was I simply a mark?

My doubts chased me into my dreams.

When I woke, at least a few answers had revealed themselves. I rose, washed myself, and sent a note to Nikella via messenger.

It was near noon by the time she showed up. She entered the room with her staff. "Aiden."

"Nikella." I swallowed hard. "Did she wake?"

Nikella gave a curt nod. "I gave her food and water like you said but kept her tied up. I gave her more dreamdew before I left. I gave the whistler and the knives to Ruru and made him fetch these for you."

She slung a pack off her back and pulled out my twin swords, the ones I usually kept in the underground training room of the Temple. She had smuggled them in a few years ago, but I never used them outside the Temple because they were too hard to hide.

But I wasn't hiding tonight.

I rested the long, slightly curved swords in their black leather sheaths next to the crates of bombs Librius and Nikella had made.

"Are you sure about this, Aiden?"

"Yes. She didn't know enough about my plan to destroy it. I checked everything and everyone last night. We're secure."

"What will you do with her?"

My jaw tightened. "I'll go back for her when it's over. I'll set her loose to return to her brother when he wears the crown."

Nikella pursed her lips. "You won't just be killing Weylin anymore, Aiden. You'll be killing her father. Right after she found out you killed her mother."

My vision hollowed out to a memory—of wide, panicked blue eyes. Long, golden hair. Lips forming a desperate plea.

Please, Aiden.

I jerked my head with a growl, shaking the image away. "I don't have a choice."

"Strong minds know there's always a choice."

"Weylin needs to die for what he's done. Even if that means she loses both her parents as I have. I will ask forgiveness for the first death. But not the second."

Nikella studied me for a long moment in the same way she'd studied me when I fell or skinned my knee as a child. Or when I insisted on helping lead a rebellion of farmers in Pravara. Or when I finally crawled out of that gods-forsaken mine and into the light.

Or when I told her I'd killed the queen of Rellmira.

She was looking to see how deeply I was wounded. Not just on the outside, but the inside as well. She wanted to see how the pain had changed me.

When I was little, I used to think she could see my soul with one look. She always seemed able to read my mind, why not my soul too? Later, I learned it was just her way of surviving. And helping others to as well.

At last, she spoke. "So be it. Shall we load the ship?"

I nodded but hesitated while picking up a box. "Did she . . . say anything to you?"

"Not a word."

I ground my teeth together. "Don't say anything to Maz. Or anyone else on the ship. Understood?"

"Yes."

We silently carried the crates of explosives and our hidden weapons on board *Mynastra's Wings*. The docks were fairly quiet with only a few ships in the harbor. All seemed quiet and normal on deck but below—

Belowdecks housed almost fifty Dag warriors and twenty sailors polishing weapons and armor.

Readying for battle.

CHAPTER 42

AIDEN

NIGHT HAD FALLEN. AND WITH IT, A SILENCE SO COMPLETE, I looked forward to destroying it.

I crouched in the shadows of Skelly's dark ship and kept my eyes fastened on the cliff road gate.

Waiting, waiting, waiting . . .

A faint explosion echoed down to me, and I tensed. A moment later, the gate slammed shut.

Yes! I breathed a sigh of relief. The piles of gold I'd paid the guards had worked. I'd hated giving more to them than the seventy warriors waiting beneath my feet. But revenge burned stronger than greed.

I ducked my head in the hatch. "It's time."

The bone-rattlers who had decided to join our fight climbed out first. They'd strapped wide swords next to their strings of bones, which they'd tied up to keep silent. They wore scarves over their long hair and smudged soot around their eyes.

Skelly gave me a nod from the ship's helm. He'd keep a lookout for us and make sure our escape vessel was ready for departure.

The Dags emerged next, led by Nikella, stripped of her cloak and staff. Her black hair was braided like the Dags, and she'd foregone face paint except for a strip of black around her eyes. She carried her double-headed spear in one scarred fist and some of our bombs in a pack slung across her back.

The rest of our bombs were scattered among the Dag warriors.

They wore full armor, with dented metal strapped to their chests, shins, and arms. Their long, braided hair was threaded with metal and leather, and their entire faces were painted in blue, black, and red. They carried axes, swords, and a few bows with arrows. One of Maz's sisters carried a pair of scythes.

All were from Maz's Yargoth clan. All looked grim and determined. Especially his three sisters, who wore murderous expressions under their war paint.

They wanted revenge for their brother.

I slipped my father's ring from my pocket onto my finger. Nikella had brought it with her earlier. I wanted a part of him with me tonight.

I ran down the gangplank dressed in all black with no cloak, my twin swords strapped to my back and my two daggers sheathed in my belt. I also carried two pouches with Librius's explosives. I'd refused any face paint. I wanted Weylin to know exactly who was here to kill him.

Everyone followed me quickly and quietly to the Den.

The bone-rattlers scurried forward and threw their grapple

hooks over the large black doors. They climbed over. A shout went up.

Unease rippled through the waiting warriors. I unsheathed my swords. Gods, it felt good to hold them again.

A moment later, the gate was unbarred and shoved open.

We swept inside, weapons raised. A handful of Shadow-Wolves sprinted toward us with sunstone spears and knives. My heart pounded at the first clash, the first shriek of metal disintegrating.

But I'd prepared my warriors.

As I tangled with one of the Wolves, two of the archers climbed up the guard station and shot down at the Wolves. Three of them fell instantly, and the one I fought swung wildly, leaving himself open for my sword through his heart. He fell with a choking gasp.

The yard fell silent. Only the perpetual crash of the waterfall disturbed the quiet.

The skirmish had only taken moments. Five dead Wolves. No casualties on our side. I ripped the mask off the one I'd killed. A boy, hardly a few years older than Ruru.

My stomach clenched, and I glanced at Nikella, her face grim and her spear wet with blood.

"Bar the gate and set a watch!" I called out, my voice sounding too loud.

A few of the Dags with bombs scrambled to obey me, knowing their part was to wait for any Wolves fleeing back to their Den. They had to keep the way clear once I was done.

"That was too easy," Nikella murmured. "It's a tr—"

"Don't," I hissed. Then louder, "Fan out. Search every cave

in groups. Make sure there are no surprises. Take the sunstone weapons if you want."

We moved forward steadily, carefully, and plunged into the caves. When I had infiltrated here before getting caught and thrown in a cell, I'd been careful to map out as many of the tunnels as I could in my mind. That way I could sketch them out for everyone later.

I'd never told Kiera that was why I was really here. That . . . and the secret passage.

Small groups broke off to investigate each branch of the tunnel. No shouts, no alarms.

Surely this wasn't all.

Nikella took the prison tunnel toward the sea cave exit with Maz's sisters and a few sailors. I hurried toward Renwell's office door and tried it.

Locked.

I had something for that—but after I checked the last tunnel. It ended in a murky cave, lit by a single torch. The air was thick with the coppery smell of blood and oiled metal. Two tables with ropes took up most of the room. Dozens of weapons and shelves decorated the rough walls.

Korvin's chamber. This must be where he tortured Maz.

Bile rose in my throat, and I gripped my swords harder. If that evil maniac was here . . .

I swept through the room quickly, finding no one. But two doors opened off the main room. The first room was empty. The second—

"Garyth." I choked on my shock and the putrid smell of rotting flesh and human waste.

A feeble moan answered me from the body tied to a wide

468 · LEAH MARA

table. I almost didn't recognize him from the few times I'd spied on him at Melaena's club from the secret balcony.

One of his legs was missing below the knee, tied with a tourniquet so tight only a few drops of blood trickled into the shallow puddle on the floor. His fingernails had been ripped off, and both his arms were bent at terrible angles. A pile of engorged black leeches wriggled over the many shallow cuts on his chest and stomach.

"Fucking Four," I breathed. The man had been here for *days*, suffering like this.

I snatched the little bloodsuckers off his skin while he groaned, his eyes finally opening.

"You came," he murmured.

I frowned. "Do you know who I am?"

"He said you would come."

Was he delirious? "Who said that—Renwell? Korvin?"

Garyth's bloodshot eyes finally focused on me. Confusion filled them. "Are you a dream? A lost soul come to haunt me?"

"No." I cut the ropes binding him, but he didn't move. "I'm Aiden, and—"

"Aiden?" Garyth's eyes shone with tears. "At last. Where is my family? Are they here? Does he have them?"

I shook my head vehemently. "No. He never did. They're safe. Waiting for you."

Tears trickled from his eyes to the bloody floor. "My sweet girls. I pray they don't join me for a long, long time." He refocused on me. "Thank you. I can die at peace now."

"We can get you out of here," I said, even as I gazed at his many injuries, my heart falling. "We have a ship and medicine—"

He slowly shook his head. "No, Aiden. I've only held on this long for my family. And now that they're safe . . ."

A shout resonated from somewhere in the caves. *Gods damn it.*

"Forgive my cowardice," Garyth whispered. "I told him everything I knew. I thought they had my family."

"There's nothing to forgive," I said sharply, edging toward the door and peering out of it.

Garyth continued to mumble. ". . . blinded by Weylin's promises . . . didn't know he murdered . . . too late . . ."

Another shout and the clash of weapons echoed toward me.

"Kill me, Aiden."

I froze. His voice had become clear as glass. Clear as the nightmare that had haunted me for years.

Wide blue eyes pled with me. No, they were Garyth's gray ones.

"Please."

Please, Aiden.

"I can't," I whispered raggedly, my swords slipping in my sweaty grip. "Don't ask this of me."

Garyth groaned. "It would be a mercy."

Mercy, please.

"Shut up," I snarled. Black spots danced over my vision.

Boots pounded up to the room, and Nikella flew inside, her cheek and her spear bloodied.

"Ambush!" she gasped. "I thought you were—" Her eyes fell to Garyth, and understanding flashed through her eyes.

She approached him steadily. "Do you wish for the gods to find your soul now?"

"Yes," Garyth breathed.

"Then we will release it together," Nikella said and plunged a short knife into his chest.

My own numb heart winced. Garyth breathed his last.

Nikella wiped her knife and stowed it. Then she placed her hand on my shoulder until I met her gaze. "Keep fighting, Aiden. Fight for the souls still left."

I nodded, again and again, until my head cleared. I squeezed some of the spattersap from the pouch at my waist onto Garyth's body and laid the torch against it. Flames poured over his twisted flesh.

"May the gods find your soul," I murmured.

Then Nikella and I raced back to the battle.

"A few dozen Wolves were hiding in a deep cave," Nikella panted. "But they weren't expecting our numbers."

Chaos reigned in the main tunnel. Wolves clad in their usual black fought with my warriors. These Wolves were bigger, stronger, and faster than the ones in the yard. *These* were the true killers.

One of them grabbed Maz's sister, Yarina, by her hair. Nikella threw her spear straight through his torso. She leapt forward, whipping her spear from his body while Yarina lopped off his head with her scythe.

A Wolf cut down a sailor and spun for another. I plunged into the melee and sank both my swords into his stomach. He smashed his metal mask against my face, eliciting stars. But I roared, yanking out my swords and crossing them over his neck. One jerk, and his head rolled to the ground.

Fiery pain seared across my forearm as another Wolf sliced

me. I swung hard at him, but he blocked my strike with a strange black gauntlet. My sword shattered.

Fucking Four! Sunstone!

The shriek and shatter of more metal told me others were finding the same sunstone on other Wolves.

The Wolf struck again and again. I blocked and slashed where I could, but this fight wouldn't last long if all our weapons were destroyed.

"Bombs!" I yelled.

My Wolf faltered for a moment, enough for me to kick him backward. I doused him with spattersap and grabbed a torch.

Dags tossed their powder bombs while others shot them with fiery arrows. They exploded, showering the confused Wolves with bursts of flame.

I held the torch to the boot of my fallen Wolf. Fire engulfed him. He rose, screaming, as I tossed more spattersap in his path and on any Wolf I ran past. He flailed blindly through the tunnel, sparking a wildfire among his comrades.

Blood-chilling howls tore from their throats as half the Wolves caught fire and the other half were slaughtered as they tried to flee.

Nikella impaled a snarling Wolf on her spear while a huge Dag—one of Maz's cousins—threw another into two of his burning brethren.

Smoke and the smell of charred flesh made my eyes water. Coughing echoed in the tunnel. We hadn't counted on the battle being underground, but rather in open air beyond the gate.

"Push them out!" I shouted.

Locking into step side by side with their weapons out, the

Dags and sailors started herding the remaining Wolves toward the training yard.

I stayed behind with the bodies. Covering my mouth and nose with my shirt, I walked among them. Thirteen dead Dags. Ten dead sailors. Twenty dead Wolves.

Gods, I hadn't expected such losses. There might be more by night's end. Wounds and infections would take their toll as well.

Nikella coughed next to me, staring down at a Dag woman, her throat slashed. "Renwell must have guessed our entry point. He had those Wolves lying in wait."

"Then he probably thinks we aren't still alive. I need to get that door open."

Nikella stared at me incredulously. "He'll be waiting for you on the other side. You know that."

"He won't be expecting Librius's final work of art," I said, patting another pouch at my hip. "Take care of the bodies. I'll let you know when I'm through." I turned and sprinted back to Renwell's office before she could argue.

I carefully fed spattersap—a highly flammable plant sap filled with fireseeds—into the door lock.

"Please, Holy Four, let this work," I prayed.

I took up a bow and arrow and lit the arrow tip on fire. Holding my breath, I aimed and released.

CHAPTER 43
KIERA

AN HOUR EARLIER . . .

Explosions startled me awake. Darkness met my eyes. My skin burned, and I couldn't move.

For one, terrifying moment I thought I was back in Korvin's torture chamber. Then the truth seeped through my soul like bitter tea.

Aiden had killed my mother. He'd taken the knife she brought with her for protection and used it to murder her before fleeing.

The nightmares I'd suffered. The grief I'd endured. The life I'd lost.

All because of him.

My body curled in on itself, straining against the ropes that bound it.

How could I have been so blind, so foolish? How could I have let my guard down? Renwell was right—I didn't really know who he was. I thought Aiden had trusted me by showing me bits of his painful past when, really, he'd been hiding the worst secret of all.

Did he truly hate my father so much that he had to kill my mother? My sweet, gentle, innocent mother? The woman who could barely bring herself to pluck the weeds from her garden because she felt everything deserved life.

Tears dripped from my eyes as if bleeding from my agonized heart.

Another explosion thundered over the building. Ruru.

I struggled to sit up. Fucking Four, was it time? Had it started? Gods damn it, he was out there alone. Would Renwell send his Wolves after him?

Groaning, I tried to wriggle out of my ropes, silently counting the seconds.

. . . *seventy-eight, seventy-nine . . . where are all my gods-damned knives? Eighty-two, eight-three . . .*

Boom! The third explosion made the floor tremble.

If that didn't get the Wolves' attention, nothing would.

Please don't linger, Ruru. Run far, far away.

Growling in frustration, I rolled from my cot onto the floor and shimmied toward the door. Sweat snaked down my spine as I heaved to a sitting position, then hobbled to my feet.

Whoever tied me had done so with my hands behind my back, so I had to turn then hop several times to push the door handle down.

When the door finally opened, I fell through it on my ass.

Flopping around like a fish out of water, I quickly maneuvered to my knees to survey the room.

Everything was gone. Maz's whistler, Nikella's staff, all the knives—including my mother's.

"Gods damn it!" I shouted at the ceiling.

Nikella had given me a bit of bread and water when I'd woken for a few minutes earlier in the day. But no utensils, and Ruru's cot had been as empty, as if he were never coming back.

I squeezed my eyes shut. Nikella hadn't said a word when she fed me, then drugged me once more. And I hadn't had the strength to question her. She was the one who shot me, after all. Perhaps she'd known it was the sleeping dart. Perhaps not.

But if she was feeding me, that must mean they wanted to keep me alive. For what purpose, only the gods knew. I was no good to anyone now.

There were only two people left in the world who might still need me and care for me. Everett and Delysia. And if Aiden was currently attacking the palace, I needed to get to them. I needed to make sure they didn't land in the crossfire between Aiden's murderous vengeance and Father's retaliation.

Bending backward, I tried to reach the knots around my legs. Thanks to Melaena's training, I was more flexible than I'd ever been, but not *that* flexible.

I kicked over a chair and kept kicking it until a leg broke off. I squirmed next to it, trying to saw the ropes on the jagged stump. Splinters bit into my palms, but I kept working. Maybe it was my imagination, but a few strands of the rope seemed to fray.

The door suddenly opened, and I froze.

Ruru slipped inside, shutting the door behind him. He dropped all his weapons and a small bag that jingled.

"Ruru," I whispered, fairly certain he could see me bathed in the moonlight.

"Who are you?" he demanded, stepping into the light.

He looked unscathed, thank the gods. But the anger and betrayal written on his young face were sharper than the splinters in my skin.

"I was born Princess Emilia Torvaine," I whispered, watching the hurt deepen in his eyes. "I go by Kiera because that's what my mother wanted to call me."

He shifted his weight on his feet, looking away from me at the mention of my mother.

My heart sank. "Did you know her? Do you know what Aiden did?"

He shook his head. "I knew something happened that night, but he never spoke about it. I also know she was a kind lady. She gave out gold coins to orphans who showed up at the Temple. Orphans like me," he mumbled, kicking his bare foot over the wooden floor.

Grief swelled in my throat. "She was very kind, yes. I have two siblings, you know. An older brother—just like your brother, Daire—and a younger sister."

"Prince Everett and Princess Delysia," he said flatly.

"Yes. They're in danger. I need to go help them."

He crossed his arms over his thin chest. "I'm not supposed to let you go."

"Please, Ruru. I know I lied to you and betrayed you. But please believe me when I say I did everything in my power to protect you. To keep you out of harm's way."

"But you were telling *Renwell* all our secrets," he spat out.

"I didn't tell him everything. Only what I had to. Just enough to keep him satisfied. I didn't tell him about you. I told him *I* was meant to set off those bombs so that he wouldn't try too hard to capture the perpetrators."

"Well, I suppose you succeeded in that."

I frowned. "What do you mean?"

Ruru threw his arms wide. "No Wolves showed up to my fires. I even waited a little longer than I was supposed to, but no one came. Some of the guards at the city prison raised an alarm. But still no Wolves."

I bowed my head. I thought he would at least send a few, enough to lend credence to my cover. Had he cut ties with me when I didn't assassinate Aiden? Or had he been unable to send anyone? Where *was* Aiden?

"Something's wrong," I said, staring up at Ruru. I put every ounce of fervor I possessed into my expression and my words. "You *need* to let me loose so I can find out. I'm the only who can get into the palace. I can make sure everyone is all right." *Right before I throw Aiden in prison for murdering my mother.*

Ruru hesitated, uncertainty loosening his features. "I'm not supposed to go looking for them under any circumstances. I'm supposed to leave the city by way of the city gate. Or, in the worst need, on Skelly's ship."

"You can still do that," I said softly. "Take all your weapons and money—take *my* money—and leave. Get somewhere safe. Just . . . untie me first."

Ruru sighed, rocking back on his heels. Then he pulled one of the knives I'd given him from his belt. He knelt in front of me and cut through my ropes.

Blood rushed back to my fingers and toes. The sting of many cuts from the wood worsened. But I threw my arms around Ruru's shoulders.

"You're the very best of friends, Ruru," I said, squeezing him hard and inhaling his familiar scent of dirt, sweat, and sticky bread.

He gave me a brief hug and backed away. "I wish you had been a better one."

My heart jerked as if he'd stabbed it. "I hope one day I can be," I whispered.

"Here." He brought me my knife brace—loaded with my knives—my sack of gold, and Mother's knife.

My eyebrows arched. "Were you going to run away with these? Or did you always plan to set me free?" I slipped the knife into my boot without looking at it.

Ruru's dark eyes were solemn as an owl's. "I owe you my life, Kiera. I don't think you saved me to thicken a lie. I think you saved me because that's who you are. You protect people." He shrugged. "Sometimes you just protect the wrong people."

I stilled, my sore fingers halfway through buckling on my knife brace.

The wrong people. He thought my father, Renwell, Korvin, and their allies were the wrong people. And on most counts, he was right.

I finished buckling my brace. "I wanted to tell Aid—everyone the truth. That's what I meant to do last night. I wanted to protect all of you."

"I know," he said, holding my bag of gold out to me. "In case you need to run, too."

I shook my head. "Keep it. There is no escape for me anymore."

Ruru's fingers curved around the gold, and he shoved it in his pocket. "What are you going to do?"

"I'm going to protect the right people," I said grimly. *Everett and Delysia.* "And enforce justice if I can. Will you be all right?"

He gave me a faint version of his usual smile. "I always am. Good luck, Kiera."

"And you, Ruru." I clasped his shoulder, then hurried into the empty night.

I wore no cloak, no mask. I carried nothing but my knives.

I ran through the alleys, which were indeed empty, up to the Noble Quarter gate. Two guards paced beneath the torchlight. Wrapping my arms around my waist to cover my knives, I hurried up to it.

"Melaena at *The Silk Dancer*," I said breathlessly.

"No one gets through," the tall guard said

"You've seen me a dozen times! Melaena's expecting me!"

He leaned closer, pressing his nose between the bars of the gate, and surveyed me. "*No one* gets through."

"What's all the gods-damned noise about?" the other guard demanded. "We heard explosions."

"I don't know," I said impatiently. "But I need to see Melaena *immediately.*"

"Are you deaf or just stupid? We have orders to not let a single person through this gate."

I kicked the gate, making the guard jerk backward, but then I stilled. "You haven't let anyone else through this gate all night?"

"No." The tall guard sneered, hefting his spear. "So, why would we let *you* in?"

I whirled and ran back into the shadows. Father must've ordered them to keep the gate shut. Had Renwell warned him of a possible attack? There would be more guards if that were the case.

How was Aiden planning to get into the palace, then?

Moments slipped by like a waterfall, too fast for my liking, as I picked the lock on the warehouse and dove into the tunnel. I whisked through the dark, silent club, quiet as a cat, and snuck into the back alley.

I'd almost reached the bridge when my steps slowed. I didn't have Renwell's Death token with me. And if the guards at the gate wouldn't let me through . . .

But it didn't matter what their orders were. Everett and Delysia could be in danger on the other side of the bridge, so I was getting across one way or another.

My hands clasped my knife hilts, and I strode into the light.

The two guards snapped to attention, lifting their spears as they eyed me suspiciously.

"Let me pass," I said, my chin held high.

They both laughed. "No," said one. "Get gone before we make you."

"I am Princess Emilia Torvaine, and you *will* let me pass," I commanded, my voice carrying over the thunderous waterfall.

They froze. A flicker of uncertainty rose in their eyes.

"You're bluffing," one spat. "The princesses never leave the palace. Especially not looking like a street urchin."

I stepped further into the light, angling my face for them to catch any trace of Father's features that lingered in mine.

"Would you care to wager your lives on that?" I said in the deadly soft voice Renwell liked to use.

One of them paled while the other turned bright red with anger. "You dare threaten us?"

Gods damn it, I didn't have time for this. I ripped two knives from my brace. "I'll do much more than that if you don't let me pass." I flipped the knives over, catching them by their tips. "Last chance."

The pale one nudged the other. "Let her through."

Snarling under his breath, the angry one finally stepped aside, and I stalked past them. I didn't stow my knives until I was halfway across the bridge.

The water pounded below me as the moon and stars shone above. Yet it reminded me of being on the Temple roof at sunset . . . with Aiden.

I had no idea what awaited me in the palace. But if I fell tonight, I was taking him with me.

CHAPTER 44

AIDEN

Boom!

The lock on the door exploded into a smoking black hole, and the door shivered and rocked on its hinges.

One door down. One to go.

I slung the bow around my shoulders and slid an arrow into my pocket.

Carrying a torch, I stepped into Renwell's office, tracking blood and mud on his dark rug. All it held was a desk, a chair, and a candelabra with blackened stubs. No paintings, no ornaments. I stuck the torch in a bracket.

Nikella appeared in the doorway. "The rest of the Wolves are dead. No sign of more from beyond the gate yet." She eyed the fractured door. "I see the sap worked."

"Very well," I said, striding to the door laid into the opposite wall. Renwell hadn't even bothered to hide it. Probably assumed no one would ever make it this far. "You could search his desk." I gestured behind me.

She shook her head. "He wouldn't keep anything useful there. Especially if he knew we might be infiltrating. I'll stand guard outside the door." She laid her hand across her heart. "May the gods go with you, Aiden."

"And may they bring me back," I said with a grim smile.

She turned and closed the battered door as far as it would go.

I tried the other door's handle, but it was locked. I filled the keyhole with sap once more and lit another arrow. I backed away as far as I could, making sure Nikella kept the other door shut. Then I fired again and faced the wall as a second explosion shook the room. Bits of dust and rock rained over my head.

Gods damn it, Librius, I hope your last bomb doesn't bring down the whole Den.

I hurried over to the door, which swung open to reveal a crumbling set of stairs that twisted up and out of sight.

Yes! Just like she said it would be.

I tossed the bow aside and ensured I still had my remaining sword, daggers, and two pouches. No going back now. I grabbed the torch and started climbing the steps.

The tunnel was narrow, barely wide enough for one person. Cobwebs littered the walls, and the air smelled like it hadn't stirred since the Age of Gods.

A faint rumble hummed through the tunnel as I climbed. The waterfall? The tunnel supposedly cut through the cliffside from the Den to the palace.

Perhaps Renwell was waiting at the end. Or did he think we'd perished in his ambush?

Either way, I had to hurry.

484 • LEAH MARA

Thoughts of Kiera invaded my mind as I climbed faster. Had she woken? What did she think of me now? And why, *why*, did she betray us?

My jaw hardened. First, I needed to steal back the crown. Then I would find Kiera and demand answers. In exchange for a few of my own.

At long last, I reached a wooden door with rusted hinges. Carefully setting the torch down, I slowly unspooled Librius's latest creation—a string painstakingly dipped and dried in spattersap. I lined the doorway with it, sticking the string to the frame with chunks of clay infused with the mico powder from the powder bombs. I left the clean end of the string dangling near the doorknob, just as Librius instructed me.

Abandoning the torch, I pressed my lips to my father's ring, then unsheathed my sword. I twisted the doorknob. It stuck a bit, but gave way.

The door creaked open, pushing a tapestry out with it. Dozens of lit candles made the wide, circular room glow. The royal bedchamber.

But the bed was empty.

A man wearing the gold-and-sunstone crown and royal colors of Rellmira paced the marble floor. Weylin.

I stepped into the light just as Weylin noticed me. He whipped out the sword at his side.

"Gods damn Renwell," he breathed, a smile curling through his dark gray beard. "He's always right."

I didn't speak. I couldn't. Finally coming face to face with the man responsible for so much death and suffering stole the warmth from my blood. Was this how Kiera felt when she realized what I'd done?

"Before I have you slaughtered where you stand, boy, tell me where my gold is," Weylin commanded.

I threw my head back and laughed. "What gold? There is no gold." I stepped closer, my fingers tightening around my sword hilt, vengeance pumping through my veins. "Is that why you killed my father? For his gold?"

Weylin spat on the floor, his face turning purple with fury. "I don't know who your gods-damned father is, boy. But I'm going to smear your blood all over this city for stealing my gold."

I edged closer and closer to him. "Oh, but you did know my father, Weylin. You knew him well enough to understand the only way to kill him was to stab him in the back like the coward you still are. Then you ordered your dog to kill my mother. She died because of you. But not before she gave birth to your downfall." I halted a sword-length away from him, my fists trembling with rage. "Me."

All the blood drained from Weylin's face, turning it ashen. "Falcryn. It can't be." He stumbled back a step, and I followed.

I held up my hand bearing my father's ring, the light glinting off the gold. "I am Aiden Falcryn, and I will make you pay for your crimes, *usurper*."

Weylin bellowed and slashed at me. I smoothly evaded and drove my heel into his ribs. He staggered back but kept his footing.

"You have no rights here," he seethed. "You have no right to assassinate your king! *I am your king!*"

Red clouded my vision. "I have every right!" I roared, raising my sword and slicing downward to that gods-damned crown, but he dodged and scrambled away.

I stalked after him. "What right did you have to murder my family and steal their throne? What right did you have to butcher innocent Pravarans who dared to raise their voices under your oppression? What right did you have to torture and starve your own people to service your greed in that gods-damned prison mine?" I swung again, my sword whistling through the air an inch from his nose.

He snarled and stabbed at me. But I knocked his sword away. Then I attacked him with a flurry of blows that drove him against the wall. With one final swing, I hit the sword out of his hand, and it clattered to the marble floor, out of reach.

I dug the tip of my sword into the base of his sweaty throat. Blood welled. I stared at it, the first drops of my victory.

This was it. The moment I could finally end it all. Save Rellmira the pain of having this murderer as a king.

My breath seared my throat, and I nearly shook with the fire in my blood.

But then I looked into his eyes. Kiera's eyes. My heart twitched.

You'll be killing her father. Right after she found out you killed her mother.

My sword point wavered.

"Don't, Aiden!"

Both our heads jerked up to see Kiera dashing through the room. Pain slammed into my side, and I grunted, looking down. Weylin had stuck a small knife beneath my ribs. Blood oozed through my shirt. I staggered back.

Kiera leapt in front of her father, her wide eyes bouncing from the knife in my side to my face. I grunted and jerked it out, then tossed it onto Weylin's bed. Gods-damned coward.

The knife was too small to do much damage, but it stung like a dozen nettles.

"What are you doing here, Kiera?" I rasped, pressing my free hand over the wound.

She seemed to gather her fury once more, those treacherously beautiful lips twisting in anguish. "Keeping you from killing the rest of my family," she spat.

Weylin straightened behind her, his smug smile slipping back onto his face. "You're finally proving your loyalty, daughter."

I ignored him, as did Kiera. I slowly started to circle around her, but she turned as well, blocking me from Weylin. "You don't know the whole story."

"What's there to know? You killed my mother with this very knife," she snarled, waving the hated black blade at me.

"*I killed her because she asked me to!*" I roared, the truth finally clawing out of my chest like a savage beast that had been kept too long in captivity.

Kiera's face whitened. "Enough, Aiden! No lie can save you now."

"Lies have saved you plenty," I growled, nodding to where her father was creeping toward his bedroom door. "After all, you learned from the best."

Kiera's eyes filled with angry tears. "Nothing you say can justify her murder. Nothing."

"Want to bet, princess?" I hissed. "I killed Brielle to save her from being executed by *him!*" I jabbed my sword in Weylin's direction, and they both froze.

Weylin recovered first. "Lies! Don't listen to—"

"How do you think I knew about this secret passage

between the Den and the royal bedchamber?" I demanded. "A passage only the king and queen and their High Enforcer know about. She *told* me about it!"

Kiera shook her head, stepping back to look between me and Weylin. "That—that can't be true."

Weylin said nothing, but his fingers curled into white-knuckled fists.

I sneered at him. "Brielle was trying to smuggle me into the palace any way she could because she didn't want to have to kill you herself. Because she knew exactly what kind of monster you are. And she had decided to take that crown from you for herself."

The veins in Weylin's face and neck thickened, and he bared his teeth. "That bitch should've died on the executioner stand like the gods-damned traitor she was!"

Kiera gasped. "You ... you ..."

"Shut up!" Weylin snarled at her. Then he glared at me. "I discovered your little plan with my stupid wife. I stopped it then, and I'll stop it now. Renwell!" he shouted.

Renwell sauntered into the room with a dozen Shadow-Wolves who lined the walls opposite me and Kiera.

I gripped my sword and kept my back to the tunnel door. I couldn't kill my way to Weylin. I'd lost my vengeance the moment I'd seen her eyes in his. My hand was slick with blood from my knife wound, but I wasn't going to die in this gods-damned room.

"Renwell," Kiera breathed, not seeming to care where I was. "Did you know? About my mother?"

Weylin released a cruel laugh. "Idiot girl. He's the one who told me Brielle had been sneaking off to meet someone. We don't suffer traitors, do we, Renwell?"

But Renwell didn't answer. He merely looked at Kiera with something almost like regret. Or anger. The knife slipped from Kiera's hand to clang against the floor.

"Speaking of which," Weylin continued, smirking at her, "do your duty and kill the traitor behind you. Even though you didn't find my gold, you can at least kill the man who stole it."

"She won't kill him," Renwell said, his voice slithering through the room. "She's had days to do so under my orders." His dark eyes found me, hatred pouring from his gaze. "I fear she's come to care for the rebel assassin."

Gods, if he were just a little closer, I'd rush forward and slit his throat like one of his sadistic Wolves.

Weylin's face hardened. "Then she has failed me for the last time." He nodded to Renwell. "Kill the traitorous whore."

Renwell unsheathed a long sunstone sword. Kiera stumbled back, and I leapt for her.

But then Renwell whipped his sword through Weylin's neck, severing his head from his shoulders.

CHAPTER 45

KIERA

I DIDN'T SCREAM.

I didn't scream as Renwell beheaded my father with one slice. I didn't scream as my father's body crumpled to the floor. Or when his head rolled to Renwell's boots.

All the air had left my body. The room. The world. The candlelight whitened around my vision, Renwell a dark shadow in the center like the slitted pupil of a snake's eye.

I fell to my knees. My heart thrashed against my chest.

Dead. Father is dead. Dead like Mother. Dead because he wanted her to be. Now he's dead because of Renwell . . . Renwell . . .

"Why?" I choked out.

"I told you I would never let him execute you," Renwell said softly.

He'd killed my father—his king—to save me?

Aiden shifted behind me, and I felt a sliver of worry for the wound leaking blood down his side. But that feeling was drowned out by a horrible reality. Everyone in this room had blood on their hands now. Nothing but blood. Father now lay in a sticky bed of it.

He was gone. His soul released. But no one uttered the prayer. Even I couldn't form the words.

I stiffened. Gods, how would Everett and Delysia react? I hadn't had time to check on them, hearing the commotion from Father's room. I needed to find them.

Rising to my feet, I stepped forward shakily. "Let me pass, Renwell. I need to tell Everett and Delysia what happened. I need to make sure they're all right."

He didn't answer me. Instead, he lowered his sunstone sword—a wicked weapon I'd never seen before—and threaded it through the crown that lay in a pool of my father's blood.

A grin spread over his harsh features. He eased the stained crown off the sword and placed it on his head.

"What are you doing, Renwell?" I demanded, my voice punctured with disbelief.

He continued to smile at me and jerked his chin. A Wolf slinked to his side. "Secure the prince and princess and the rest of the palace. No one leaves."

His words snapped something inside me, severed as quickly as Father's neck. He had betrayed me, too. "Gods damn you to the deep, dark, wandering hell," I snarled, flicking one of my knives at his throat.

His sword whipped in front of his face, shattering my knife like glass. I flung the next three so quickly, they whirred like hummingbirds. He slashed each one, but not fast enough to avoid the shards slicing across his face.

I roared in frustration and seized Mother's knife from the

floor.

"Cease!" Renwell thundered. "Or I will send my Wolves to cut the throats of your brother and sister."

I froze, trembling. "You can't do that."

"I can and I will." He tapped his sword on the marble floor. "I've been planning this for a long time, Kiera. There's very little I won't do."

My mind couldn't fathom the meaning behind his words. He'd never said anything about wishing to be king. He'd rarely said a word against my father.

No one fails me twice.

Those had been Father's words to Asher. Yet, we all thought Renwell had failed when he hadn't been able to save Mother. But he hadn't truly failed. He'd been acting on Father's orders all along.

"You *did* see me that night, didn't you?" Aiden's rough voice made me turn. But he wasn't looking at me. He was staring at Renwell, contempt written into his sweaty, soot-streaked face. "When Brielle died."

"I did," Renwell said. "And I see you found the present I left for you in Asher's vault."

Aiden clenched his bloody fist, his father's gold ring flashing in the candlelight. "You wanted to see if I'd pick it up."

"I guessed who you were after the glimpse I caught of you fleeing Brielle and when I captured you in the Den. That brand from the mine covered by a falcon tattoo was too coincidental. I found your father's ring when I was emptying Asher's vault ahead of your little heist—a way to further prove my theory. Then, of course, I saw you with my sister, and that confirmed it."

His words hit me like a hailstorm. "You *knew*?" I choked out. "You *knew* he killed my mother. That he'd been a prisoner. That he might be the true heir. *And you put me in a cell with him?*"

I could feel Aiden's stare burning into my cheek, but I stayed focused on Renwell. On his calm, steady gaze.

"Yes," he said simply.

"You lied to me," I said hoarsely. "All this time. You were using me."

"I kept secrets. And I used them to unlock certain doors when necessary."

I barked out a bitter laugh. "Like Asher's vault? Is that why you let my heist happen? So you could steal a bit for yourself?"

Renwell smirked. "Oh, I all but emptied his vault, leaving just enough for you."

That was why Father had been so angry, why he'd killed Asher and threatened me.

Because of Renwell.

"That gold was quite useful paying for the additional Wolves I needed," Renwell continued. "The ones that should be attacking the Den right about now."

Aiden stiffened. "We already slaughtered the Wolves you hid in your caves."

Renwell chuckled softly. "Fool. Those were just my way of making you work harder to get here. And to make you think you'd won the night." He sheathed his glittering shadow of a sword. He nodded to his Wolves. "Take her. Kill the other."

My heart cried out, and I looked wildly at Aiden. His eyes darted from Renwell to me, his sword raised, as he made a quick decision.

He lunged for me, wrapping his arm around me and pinning my arms to my body. His sword grazed my neck. "Not another step," he hissed at the advancing Wolves.

Something flickered over Renwell's face that I'd never seen before—fear. I felt the same flicker in my chest as the cold steel licked my skin.

"Halt!" Renwell shouted. The Wolves stilled as one.

Aiden slowly dragged me toward the old door I'd seen hanging open when I burst into Father's room.

"Don't go with him, Kiera," Renwell said, his cold voice filtering through my fear. "Don't make the same mistake your mother did." I flinched. "Use your mother's knife. Kill him. He's wounded. Do it. *Do it!*"

I shuddered. The knife was trapped next to Aiden's leg. I could jab my elbow into his wounded side and thrust the blade into his thigh, like he did to that Wolf when we escaped the Den.

Then I could bury it in his heart like he did to Mother.

So much death. And I still hadn't protected my brother and sister.

"Everett, Delysia," I whispered brokenly.

"You can't save them now," Aiden breathed in my ear. "He'll use them against you. Make you his puppet."

I shivered. But would he kill them if I were gone?

Renwell's eyes sharpened, and he sneered. "Ah, you've fallen for my little spy as well, Falcryn. You won't kill her."

"No, I won't." Aiden shoved me behind him. "I just needed to get her to the door." He flung some sort of liquid from a pouch that splattered in an arc at the Wolves' boots.

Eyes widening with recognition, Renwell hurled himself

backward as Aiden seized one of the burning candles and threw it on the liquid. Flames roared from the floor to the ceiling, tongues of fire dancing over the shrieking Wolves.

"Go!" Aiden shouted, pushing me down toward some stairs that trailed into darkness.

He sheathed his sword and slammed the door shut. Then he grabbed a smoldering torch from the ground and lit an odd string.

But still I hesitated.

Everett . . . Delysia . . .

"We can't stay, Kiera," Aiden snarled, capturing my arm and dragging me down the stairs.

Something fizzled and spat behind us, and a bitter smell filled my nose. Then . . . *BOOM!*

"Fucking Four!" Aiden shouted, throwing his body over mine as the tunnel shook us like the only two coins in a purse.

Rocks crashed and crumbled down the stairs, bouncing off our ankles.

"Run!"

This time, I obeyed, skidding down the stairs as more rocks tumbled around us. "Did you have to blow up the whole godsdamned tunnel?" I yelled over my shoulder.

"Librius must have made it too strong," Aiden grunted. "It was simply supposed to block the entrance."

"Yes, by destroying the tunnel!" I tripped, and Aiden yanked me upright before I could fall. I jerked out of his grasp.

We raced down the trembling stairs and burst into a room, coughing on the dust cloud that chased us.

"Let's go," Aiden commanded, striding for the door.

"No."

He spun around. "Yes."

I pointed Mother's knife at him, even though it seemed like a dull threat now. "I'm not going anywhere with you. I won't leave my brother and sister."

"And what is your plan, then?" His words echoed from the night we met.

"I'll stay here. I'll find a way to get them out." Maybe Melaena would help me. If she didn't hate me. If Renwell didn't find me first.

Aiden slowly stalked toward me, crowding against my limp blade and backing me against a wall. He anchored both his palms by my head, smelling of battle. His green eyes burned through me to my soul.

"D-don't," I whispered.

"Don't what?"

For a moment, everything else burned away as we panted against each other's lips. Flames of a familiar feeling singed my blood. We stood in a scorched ring of everything we'd destroyed together—my family, his vengeance, our kingdom.

Yet, that traitorous feeling had not perished. The embers remained stubbornly alive beneath the ashes of our secrets, waiting for a breath of hope.

"I will never forgive you," I said.

The spark in his eyes vanished. "Fight me, hate me, princess. But I refuse to let you die."

My lips curled into a snarl, and I pressed the tip of my knife harder into his chest.

He gave me a bitter smile. "Go ahead. It's harder than it looks."

Mother . . . what do I do?

"I will go with you for now," I said through clenched teeth. "But I *will* come back for my brother and sister."

He was silent for a moment, looking between my eyes. "I'm glad at least *they* have earned your loyalty."

My cheeks burned as he backed away. He led the way out of what must have been Renwell's office. Unease trickled between my shoulder blades at the empty tunnels of the Den. Would I never truly escape this gods-damned hole?

"Nikella should've been here," Aiden murmured and picked up the pace.

We ran through the Den, breaking into a sprint when the sounds of fighting reached us.

War raged through the training yard. Shadow-Wolves poured through the open gate while strange warriors covered in paint and blood tried to cut them off at the chokepoint.

Nikella led the charge, her black hair flying, slinging her spear like a bolt of lightning. The warriors—Dags from the look of them—roared and tore through the oncoming shadows. A few bone-rattlers were stealing sunstone weapons from the racks and tossing them to empty-handed warriors.

I snatched as many sunstone knives as I could while Aiden hefted a sunstone-headed spear. With one hard look at each other, we leapt into the fray, battling our way to Nikella.

Bodies shoved against me from all sides. Something sliced across my arm, and I frantically stabbed at anyone wearing a mask or black cloth.

"Nikella!" Aiden shouted, cutting down a Wolf who had felled a Dag. "Bombs?"

She impaled a Wolf. "None!"

Aiden swore.

A fist crashed into my jaw, and I fell. My vision rippled and blurred as pain ricocheted through my body. Boots trampled me. My hands were empty. Defenseless. I'd never trained to fight in such chaos.

I crawled out of the bloody tangle. Gods, we were never going to escape. Renwell had won. He would slaughter every man and woman in here and drag me back to the palace, anyway. Hand me over to Korvin for my disobedience.

My mind stilled. *Korvin.*

I flew back through the tunnels, my ribs and jaw aching from the many blows. The acrid smell of burnt flesh sent my stomach hurtling toward my throat. I clamped my hand over my mouth and kept running, trying to ignore the twisted black lumps that littered the way to Korvin's torture chamber.

Chunks of the rock walls and ceiling had crashed to the floor—probably from all the explosions. But the barrel of fire-seeds I'd remembered seeing before was still intact amid the rubble. I grabbed it and charged back to the battle.

I breathed a sigh of relief to see Aiden and Nikella still fighting, but our forces were dwindling.

I skirted the twisted mass of bodies and climbed one of the guard lookouts by the gate, plucking a torch as I went. I stepped out onto the gate post, teetering on one boot. None of the Wolves shoving their way in looked up.

Holy Four, forgive me.

I flung the fireseeds over the Wolves, and after one thudding heartbeat, hurled the torch into their midst.

Flames rushed toward my face, and I threw myself backward, crashing onto the wooden platform. Panicked shouts rose. Over them all, I heard Aiden's roar.

"Push through! For Maz! For Rellmira!"

More shouts punched the air alongside the sputtering flames.

I hauled myself to my feet just as Aiden fought his way through the gate, a pack of bloodthirsty Dags at his back.

His gaze darted up to me. "Move, Kiera!"

I scrambled to join them, dancing around piles of blazing fireseeds and Wolf bodies. We stampeded toward the Docks with a dozen Wolves on our heels.

A plank was already waiting for us on *Mynastra's Wings*. A red-haired man on the ship waved and shouted. A handful of sailors on deck shot harpoons at the Wolves as we boarded. My legs nearly gave way on the rickety plank, but a Dag woman practically threw me onto the deck.

The red-haired man shouted down the hatch. "Row for your gods-damned lives!"

The ship started to coast from its berth. A few sailors quickly pulled up the gangplank before it fell into the water, leaving a group of seething Shadow-Wolves on the dock. As one, they threw back their heads and uttered a shrieking howl.

Chills erupted on my skin. Were they calling for reinforcements? Or their master?

Above me, white sails puffed and snapped with a gust of wind.

"Thank fucking Myn!" the red-haired man bellowed, striding back to the large wheel.

"Thank fucking Myn!" the sailors chorused back, shaking their strings of bones.

I stood rooted to the deck as groaning warriors collapsed around me. He wasn't here. *He wasn't here.*

A hand closed over my shoulder, and I whirled around. *Aiden.* Blood, sweat, and soot covered every inch of his skin, but he was alive.

"You saved us back there," he said. "Thank you."

I didn't do it for you, I wanted to say.

The red-haired man—probably the captain, Skelly—called for Aiden, then pointed to the stone wall that curved around the harbor to the guard towers. "Friend of yours?" he shouted.

A rider swathed in black astride a black horse galloped along the narrow path atop the wall.

My body quivered with dread. *Renwell.*

Aiden swore and hurried to Skelly. "Can you reach open water before he reaches the guard tower?"

"Bloody watch me. Spread her wings!" he shouted.

Sailors scrambled up the rope ladders that hung from the mast. In moments, they released two more sails that stretched out from the ship like wide white wings. The ship sailed faster, dipping higher and lower. My stomach rolled with it.

Renwell nearly kept even with us, beating his horse with the reins.

My heart pounded like the waves against the ship's hull. Closer, closer to the tower. The huge watchfire burned like the sun in a sea of darkness.

Aiden walked among the exhausted warriors. "Get below deck. Don't let them see you. We don't want to fight if we don't have to."

They slowly disappeared down the hatch, leaving trails of blood behind them.

"You too," Aiden murmured next to me as we both watched Renwell nearing the tower.

"He's coming for me," I whispered.

"He can't have you."

Nikella joined us at the railing, staring at her brother as he leapt from his horse and sprinted up the tower steps just as we sailed past.

I breathed a sigh of relief, then choked when Renwell stepped to the edge of the tower. With a bow and arrow. He aimed at Aiden, but Nikella quickly shoved him out of the way.

Renwell roared with fury and swung the arrow toward me. We locked eyes across the water. He fired, and my body jolted. His arrow struck the railing in front of me.

And somehow, I knew. I knew he'd missed on purpose.

Thank the gods for your *little weaknesses, Renwell. I'll make sure they're your downfall.*

Let the war begin.

BONUS SCENE

Scan the code to join my newsletter and receive a **bonus spicy scene in Aiden's POV** (the tent scene in Chapter 34).

You won't want to miss being in Aiden's head during that scene—trust me ;)

READ MORE

FROM LEAH MARA

If you would like to read more of my books, please scan the code below:

ACKNOWLEDGMENTS

Thank you so much for reading *Keys to the Crown*! I hope you loved reading it as much as I loved writing it.

This story has been living in my head (in bits and pieces) for seventeen years, so the sheer relief, anxiety, and joy of releasing this book has been astronomical.

First and foremost, I need to thank my amazing husband. I can't even imagine what this book would look like without his constant support. He's my brainstorming partner, my alpha reader, and my #1 fan. He even designed those super-cool sunstone knives for the section breaks!

Also, to the sweetest little boy in the whole world: I love you!

I want to thank my family for being so kind and supportive ever since I said I wanted to be an author. And to Eddie and Crispin—your snuggles make me so happy.

Thank you to all my editors for this book: Melissa, Jennifer, and Sarah. The three of of you really helped make this story shine!

Jamie, it's amazing that you've read two different versions of this story over several years. Thank you for all your thoughtful notes!

Thank you to Bianca for the gorgeous covers.

Last, but definitely not least, thank you to all the readers on BookTok and Bookstagram who have read an ARC, shared, and supported this book. You all are the best!

ABOUT THE AUTHOR

Leah Mara loves to write stories where the romances are just as epic as the unique worlds they're set in.

She discovered the magic of reading at a young age, and once she learned she could create that magic with writing, she never looked back.

Leah also enjoys road trips, games of any kind, binge-watching TV shows, staying up way too late, and spending time with her family at home in Minnesota.

Made in the USA
Monee, IL
19 August 2025

23779523R00308